MARION COUNTY PUBLIC LIBRARY
321 MONROE STREET
FAIRMONT, WV 26554

IN VITAM MORTEM

EST
1637

JAN 1 3 2017

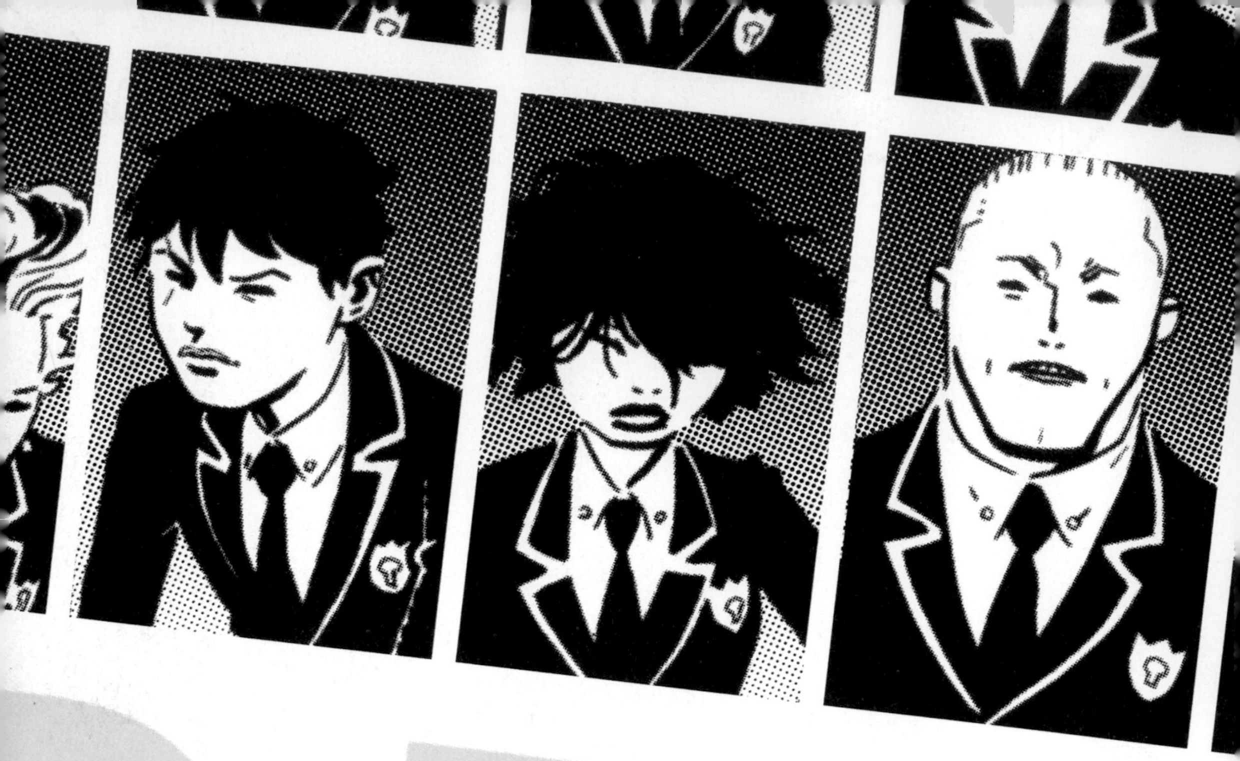

RICK REMENDER
writer

WES CRAIG
artist

co-creators

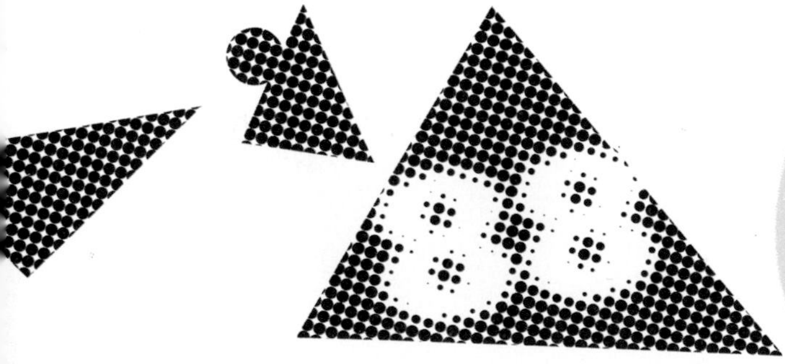

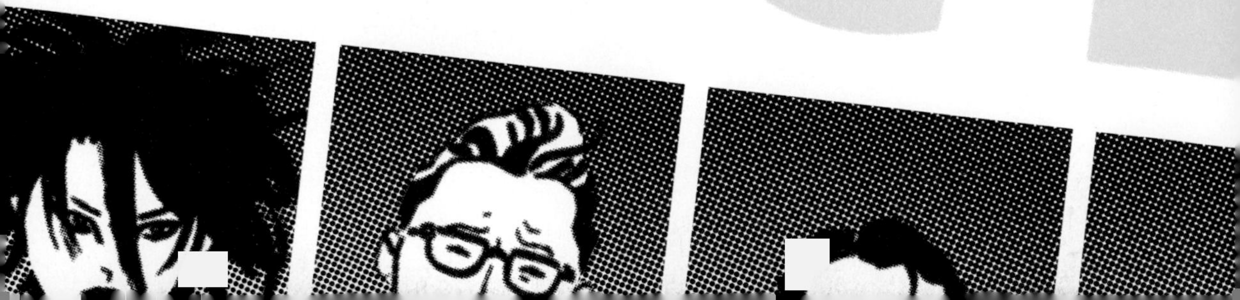

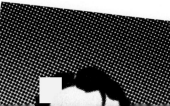

JORDAN BOYD
colorist

RUS WOOTON
letterer • logo design

SEBASTIAN GIRNER
editor

IN VITAM MORTEM

IMAGE COMICS, INC.

Robert Kirkman • Chief Operating Officer
Erik Larsen • Chief Financial Officer
Todd McFarlane • President
Marc Silvestri • Chief Executive Officer
Jim Valentino • Vice-President
Eric Stephenson • Publisher
Corey Murphy • Director of Sales
Jeff Boison • Director of Publishing Planning & Book Trade Sales
Jeremy Sullivan • Director of Digital Sales
Kat Salazar • Director of PR & Marketing
Branwyn Bigglestone • Senior Accounts Manager
Sarah Mello • Accounts Manager
Drew Gill • Art Director
Jonathan Chan • Production Manager
Meredith Wallace • Print Manager
Briah Skelly • Publicist
Sasha Head • Sales & Marketing Production Designer
Randy Okamura • Digital Production Designer
David Brothers • Branding Manager
Olivia Ngai • Content Manager
Addison Duke • Production Artist
Vincent Kukua • Production Artist
Tricia Ramos • Production Artist
Jeff Stang • Direct Market Sales Representative
Emilio Bautista • Digital Sales Associate
Leanna Caunter • Accounting Assistant
Chloe Ramos-Peterson • Administrative Assistant

imagecomics.com

JEFF POWELL
collection design

DEADLY CLASS VOLUME 4: DIE FOR ME. First Printing. JULY 2016. Published by Image Comics, Inc. Office of publication: 2001 Center Street, 6th Floor, Berkeley, CA 94704. Copyright © 2016 Rick Remender and Wes Craig. All rights reserved. Originally published in single magazine form as DEADLY CLASS #17-21. DEADLY CLASS™ (including all prominent characters featured herein), its logo and all character likenesses are trademarks of Rick Remender and Wes Craig, unless otherwise noted. Image Comics® and its logos are registered trademarks of Image Comics, Inc. No part of this publication may be reproduced or transmitted, in any form or by any means (except for short excerpts for review purposes) without the express written permission of Image Comics, Inc. All names, characters, events and locales in this publication are entirely fictional. Any resemblance to actual persons (living or dead), events or places, without satiric intent, is coincidental. **PRINTED IN THE U.S.A.** For information regarding the CPSIA on this printed material call: 203-595-3636 and provide reference # RICH – 694660. For international rights inquiries, contact: foreignlicensing@imagecomics.com. ISBN 978-1-63215-718-8

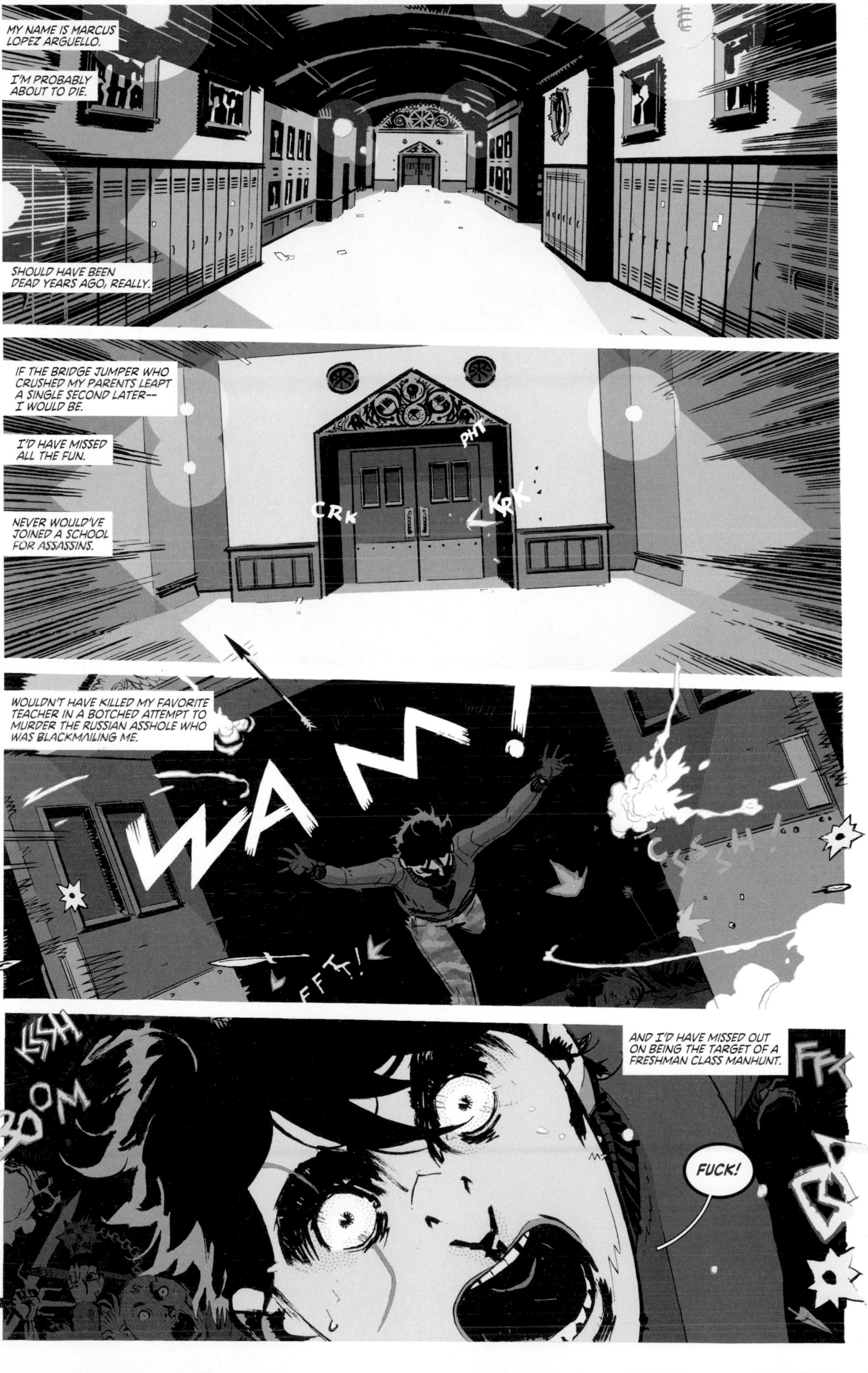
MY NAME IS MARCUS LOPEZ ARGUELLO.
I'M PROBABLY ABOUT TO DIE.
SHOULD HAVE BEEN DEAD YEARS AGO, REALLY.
IF THE BRIDGE JUMPER WHO CRUSHED MY PARENTS LEAPT A SINGLE SECOND LATER-- I WOULD BE.
I'D HAVE MISSED ALL THE FUN.
NEVER WOULD'VE JOINED A SCHOOL FOR ASSASSINS.
PHT
CRK
KRK
WOULDN'T HAVE KILLED MY FAVORITE TEACHER IN A BOTCHED ATTEMPT TO MURDER THE RUSSIAN ASSHOLE WHO WAS BLACKMAILING ME.
WAM!
CSSSH!
FFT!
KSSH
BOOM
AND I'D HAVE MISSED OUT ON BEING THE TARGET OF A FRESHMAN CLASS MANHUNT.
FFT
FUCK!

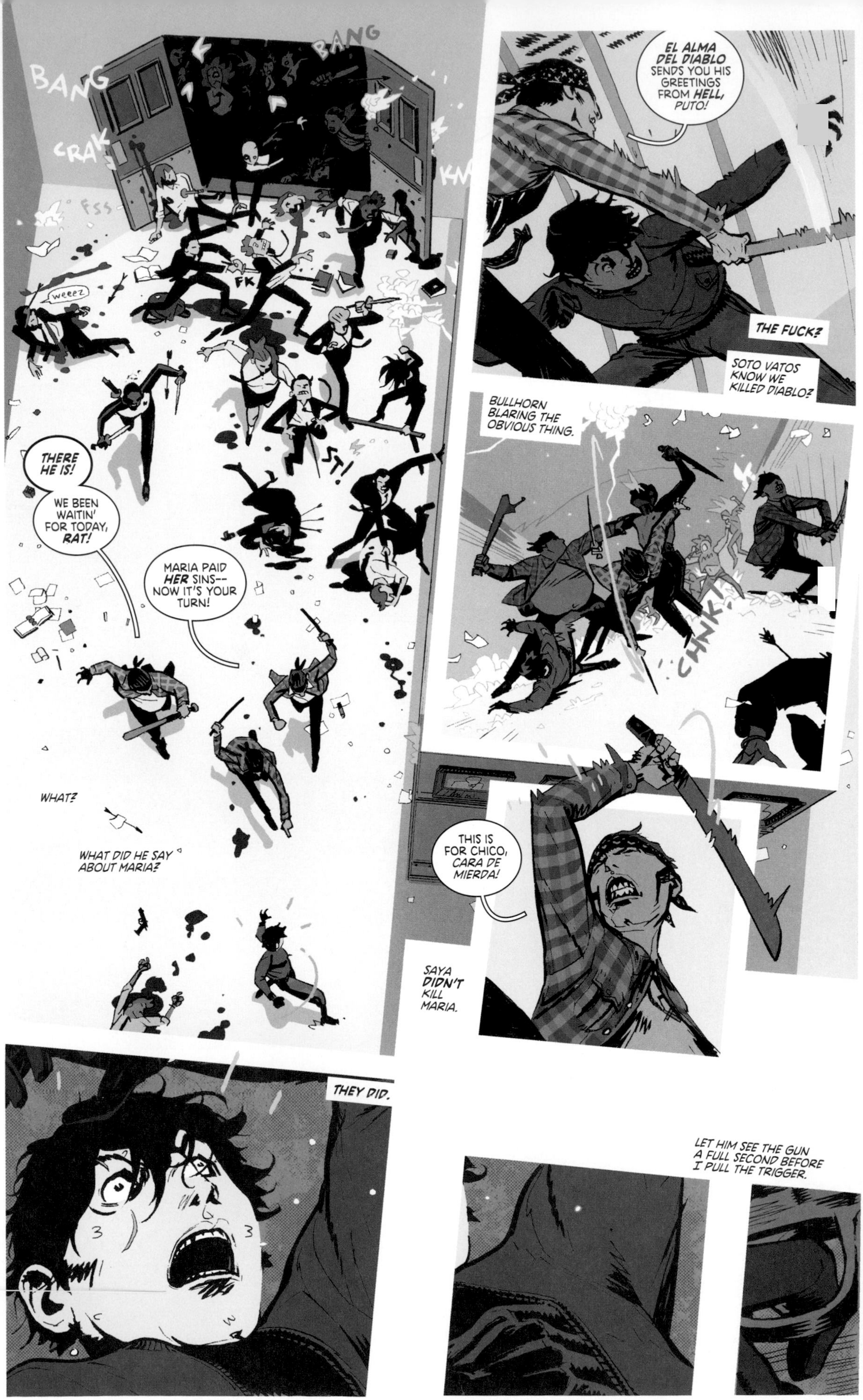
BANG
BANG
CRAK
FSS
weeez
FK
THERE HE IS!
WE BEEN WAITIN' FOR TODAY, RAT!
MARIA PAID HER SINS-- NOW IT'S YOUR TURN!
WHAT?
WHAT DID HE SAY ABOUT MARIA?
EL ALMA DEL DIABLO SENDS YOU HIS GREETINGS FROM HELL, PUTO!
THE FUCK?
SOTO VATOS KNOW WE KILLED DIABLO?
BULLHORN BLARING THE OBVIOUS THING.
CHNK!
THIS IS FOR CHICO, CARA DE MIERDA!
SAYA DIDN'T KILL MARIA.
THEY DID.
LET HIM SEE THE GUN A FULL SECOND BEFORE I PULL THE TRIGGER.

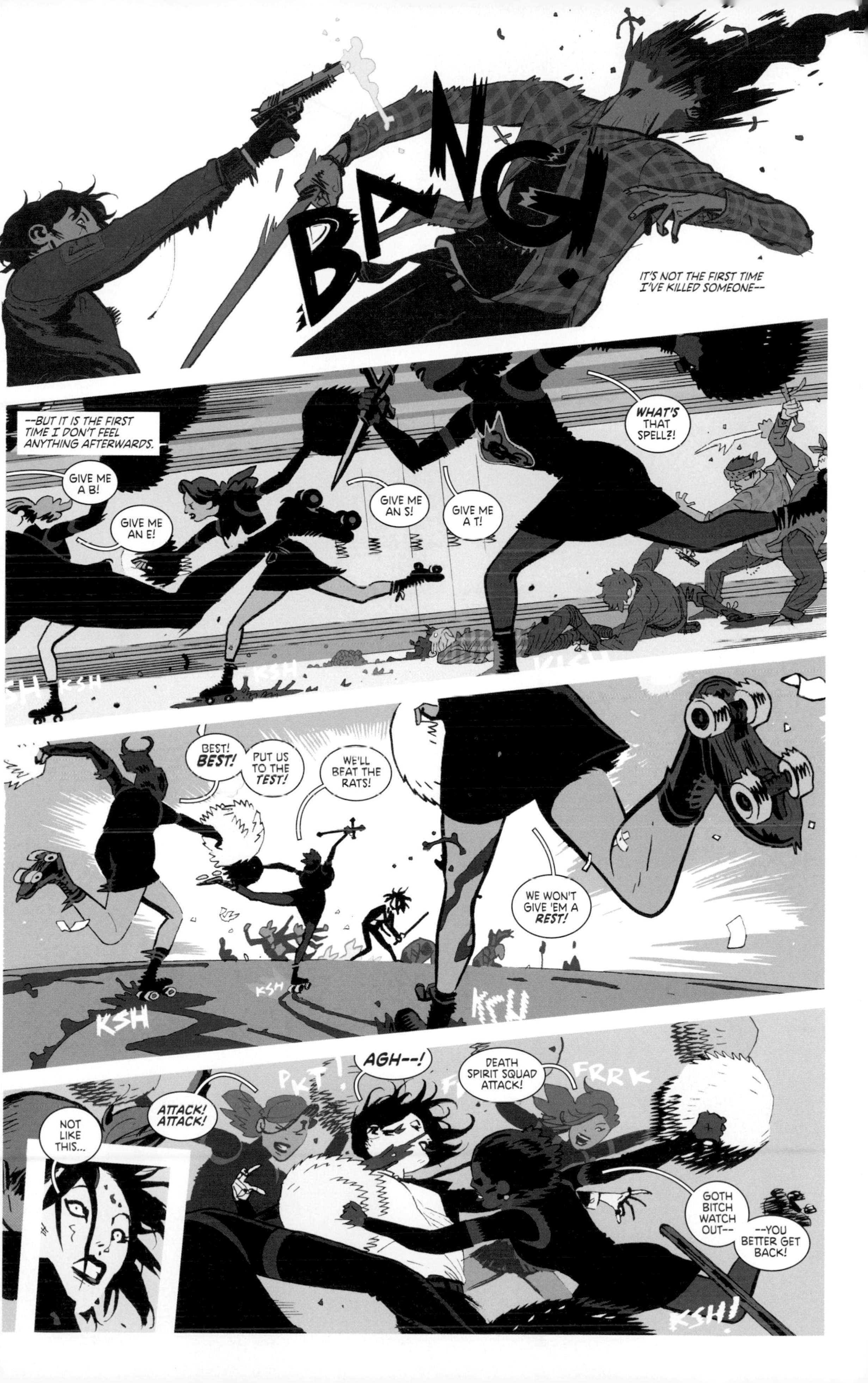

BANG!
IT'S NOT THE FIRST TIME I'VE KILLED SOMEONE--
--BUT IT IS THE FIRST TIME I DON'T FEEL ANYTHING AFTERWARDS.
GIVE ME A B!
GIVE ME AN E!
GIVE ME AN S!
GIVE ME A T!
WHAT'S THAT SPELL?!
KSH KSH
KSH
BEST! BEST!
PUT US TO THE TEST!
WE'LL BEAT THE RATS!
WE WON'T GIVE 'EM A REST!
KSH
KSH
NOT LIKE THIS...
ATTACK! ATTACK!
PKT!
AGH--!
DEATH SPIRIT SQUAD ATTACK!
FRRK
GOTH BITCH WATCH OUT--
--YOU BETTER GET BACK!
KSH!

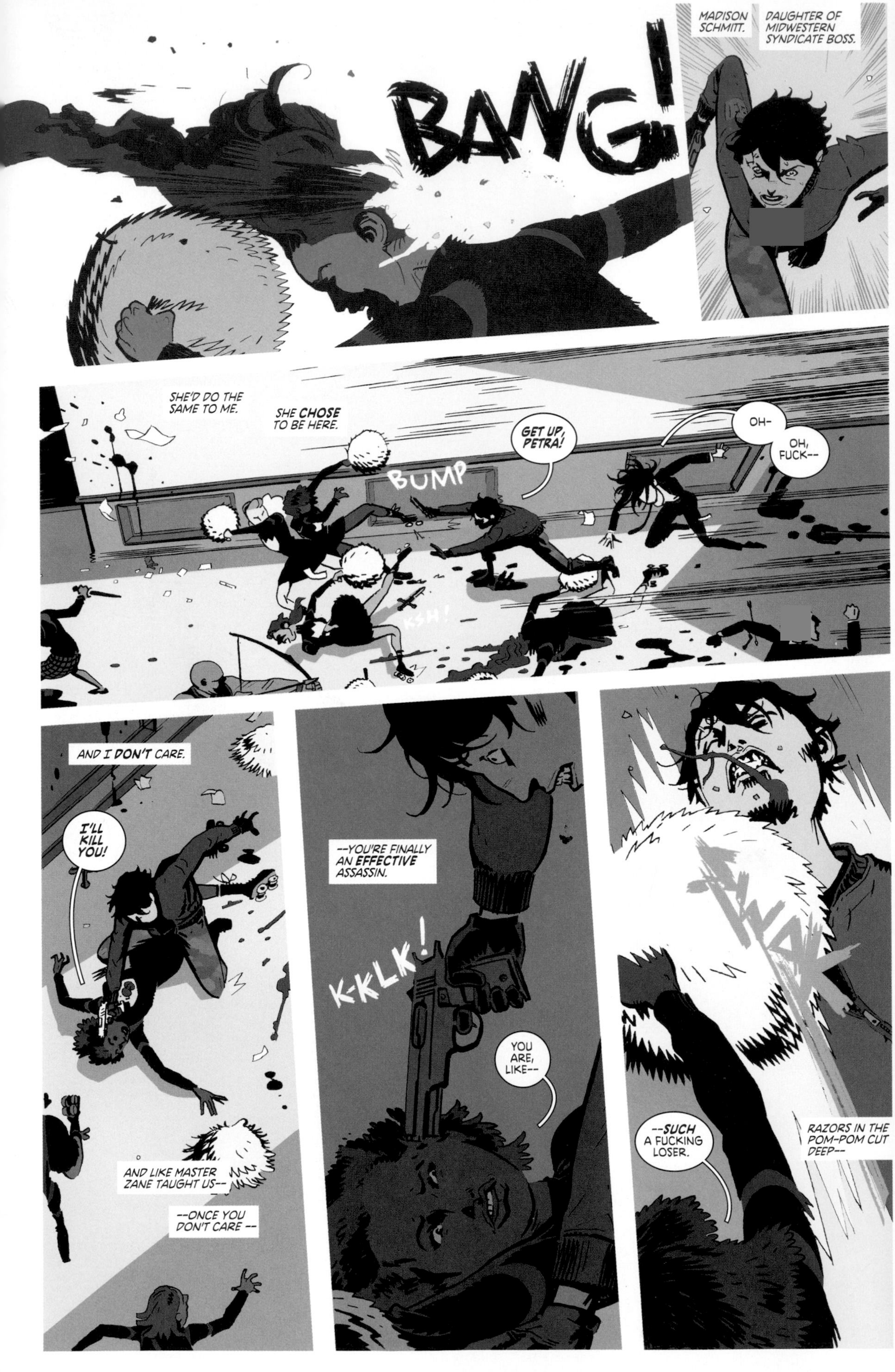
BANG!
MADISON SCHMITT.
DAUGHTER OF MIDWESTERN SYNDICATE BOSS.
SHE'D DO THE SAME TO ME.
SHE CHOSE TO BE HERE.
BUMP
GET UP, PETRA!
OH-
OH, FUCK--
KSH!
AND I DON'T CARE.
I'LL KILL YOU!
AND LIKE MASTER ZANE TAUGHT US--
--ONCE YOU DON'T CARE --
--YOU'RE FINALLY AN EFFECTIVE ASSASSIN.
K-KLK!
YOU ARE, LIKE--
--SUCH A FUCKING LOSER.
RAZORS IN THE POM-POM CUT DEEP--

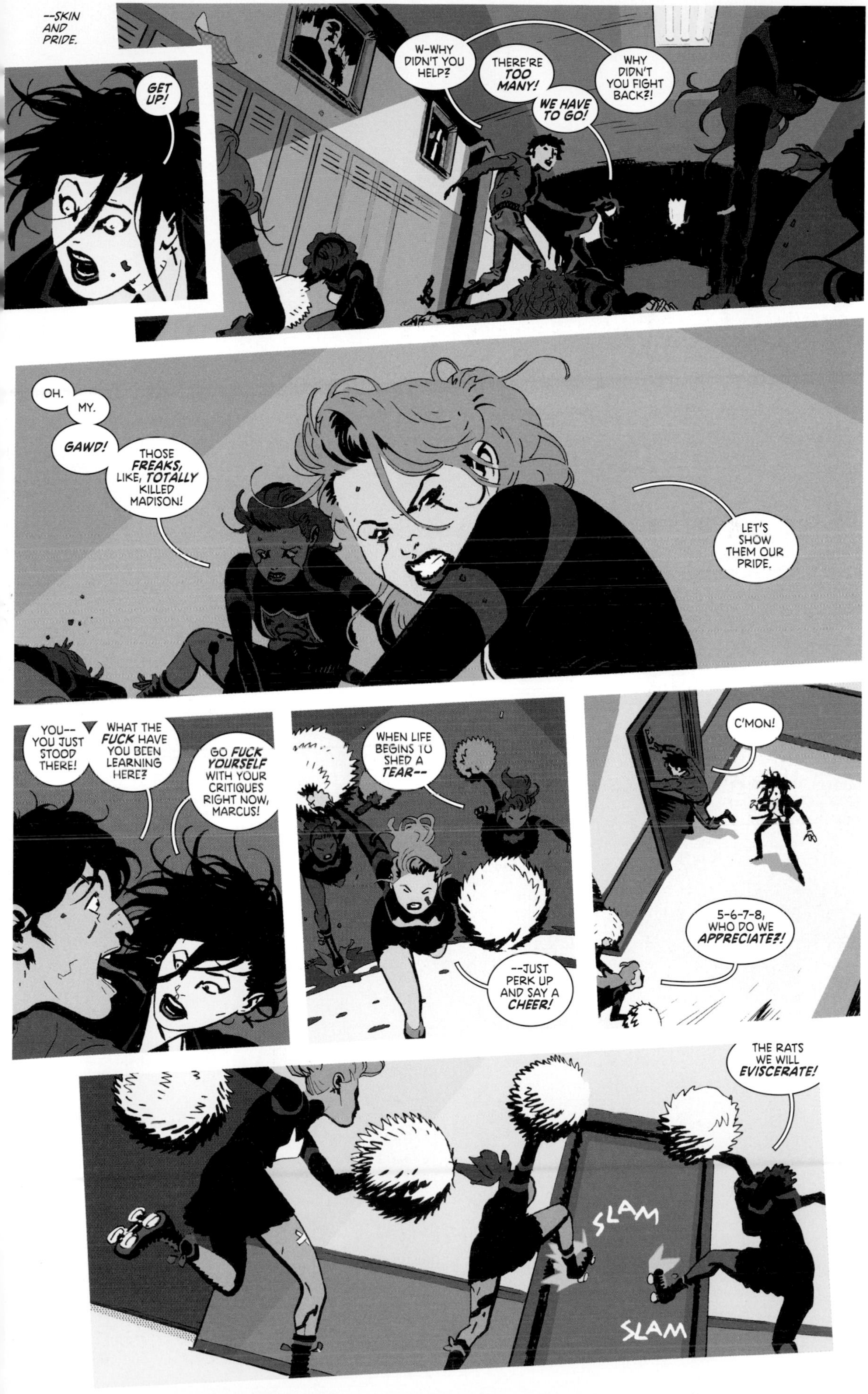
--SKIN AND PRIDE.
GET UP!
W-WHY DIDN'T YOU HELP?
THERE'RE TOO MANY!
WE HAVE TO GO!
WHY DIDN'T YOU FIGHT BACK?!
OH.
MY.
GAWD!
THOSE FREAKS, LIKE, TOTALLY KILLED MADISON!
LET'S SHOW THEM OUR PRIDE.
YOU-- YOU JUST STOOD THERE!
WHAT THE FUCK HAVE YOU BEEN LEARNING HERE?
GO FUCK YOURSELF WITH YOUR CRITIQUES RIGHT NOW, MARCUS!
WHEN LIFE BEGINS TO SHED A TEAR--
--JUST PERK UP AND SAY A CHEER!
C'MON!
5-6-7-8, WHO DO WE APPRECIATE?!
THE RATS WE WILL EVISCERATE!
SLAM
SLAM

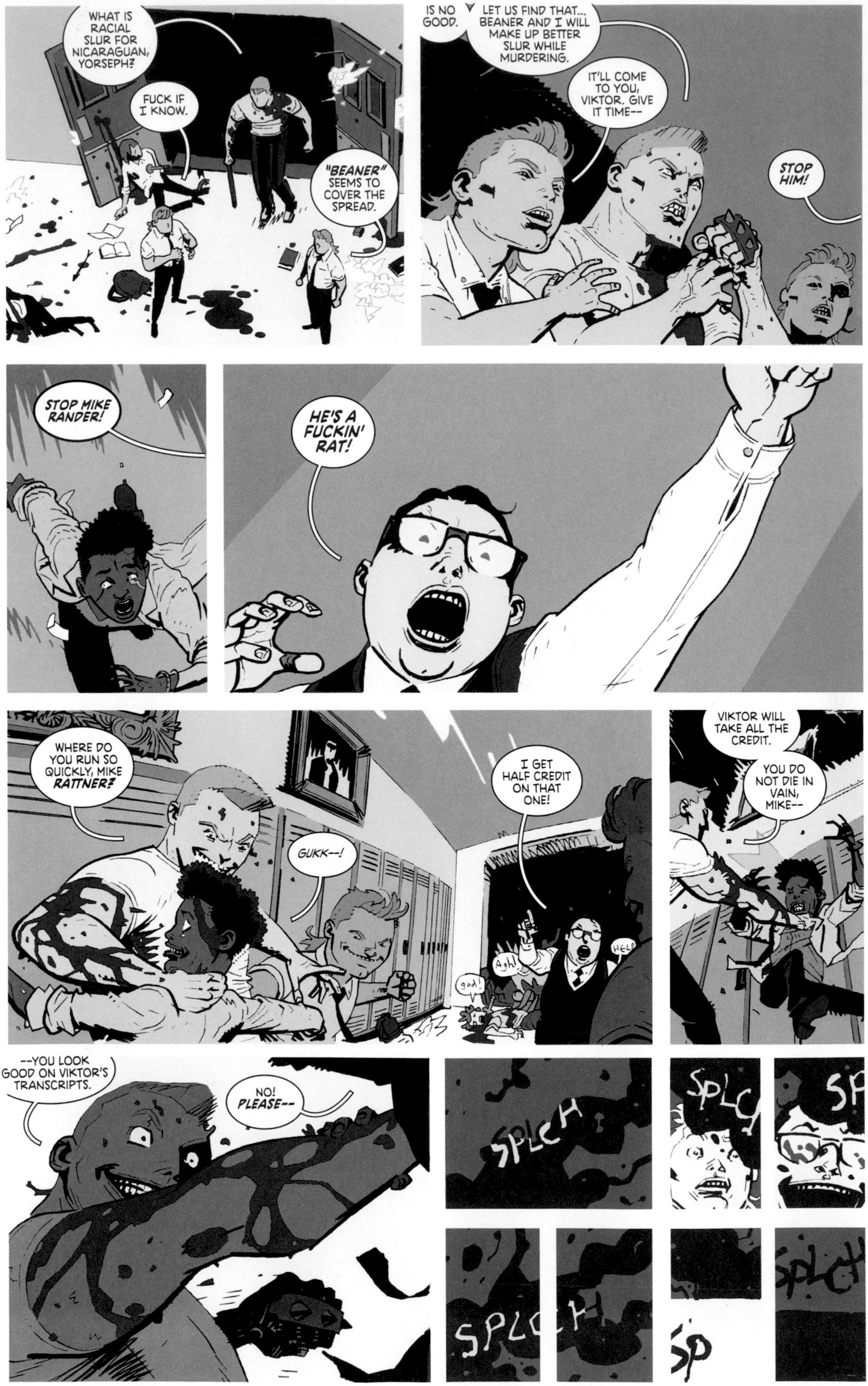
WHAT IS RACIAL SLUR FOR NICARAGUAN, YORSEPH?
FUCK IF I KNOW.
"BEANER" SEEMS TO COVER THE SPREAD.
IS NO GOOD.
LET US FIND THAT... BEANER AND I WILL MAKE UP BETTER SLUR WHILE MURDERING.
IT'LL COME TO YOU, VIKTOR. GIVE IT TIME--
STOP HIM!
STOP MIKE RANDER!
HE'S A FUCKIN' RAT!
WHERE DO YOU RUN SO QUICKLY, MIKE RATTNER?
GUKK--!
I GET HALF CREDIT ON THAT ONE!
Agh!
HELP
god!
VIKTOR WILL TAKE ALL THE CREDIT.
YOU DO NOT DIE IN VAIN, MIKE--
--YOU LOOK GOOD ON VIKTOR'S TRANSCRIPTS.
NO! PLEASE--
SPLCH
SPLCH
SP
SPLCH
SPLCH
SP

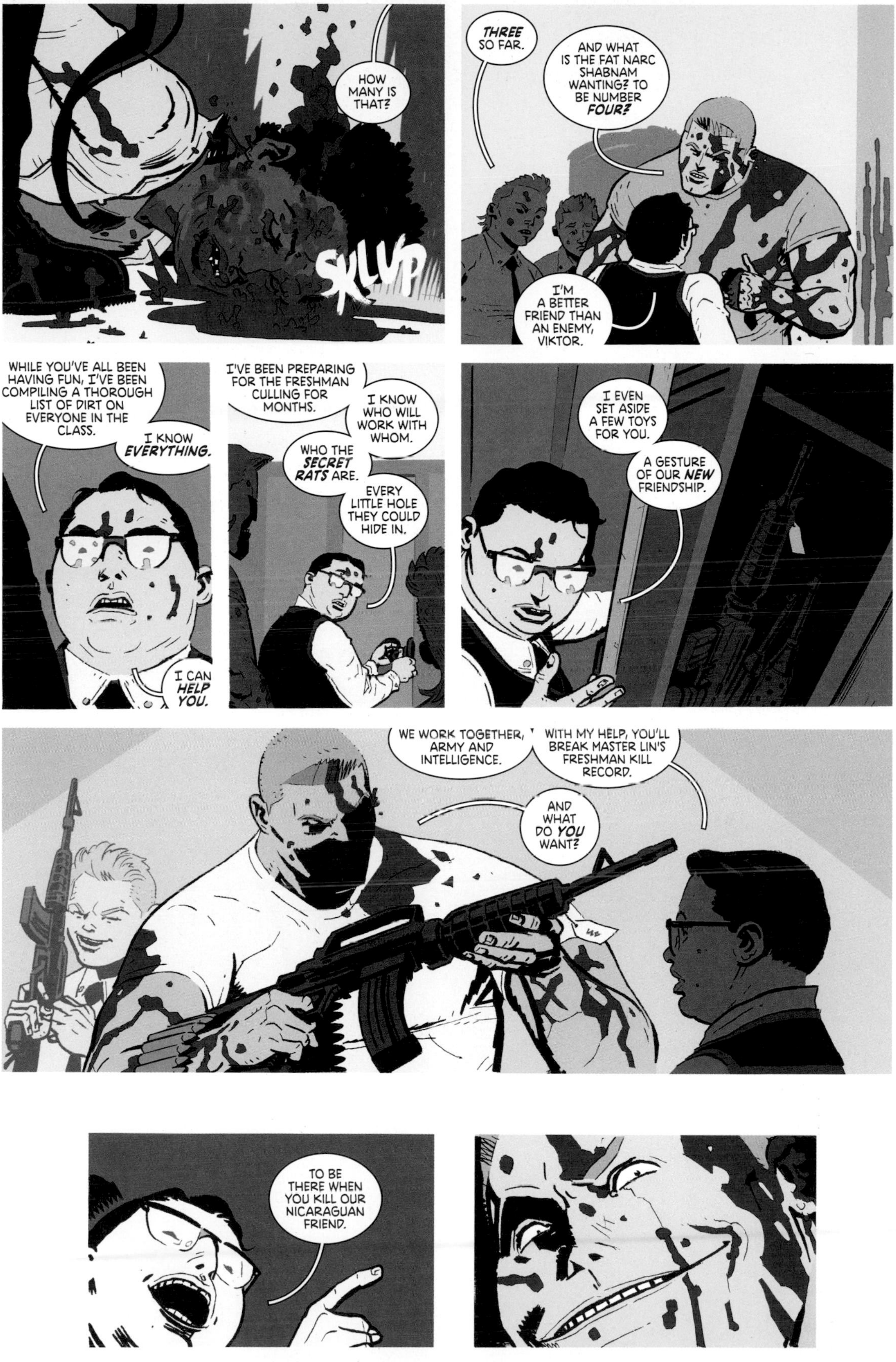
HOW MANY IS THAT?
SKLUP
THREE SO FAR.
AND WHAT IS THE FAT NARC SHABNAM WANTING? TO BE NUMBER FOUR?
I'M A BETTER FRIEND THAN AN ENEMY, VIKTOR.
WHILE YOU'VE ALL BEEN HAVING FUN, I'VE BEEN COMPILING A THOROUGH LIST OF DIRT ON EVERYONE IN THE CLASS.
I KNOW EVERYTHING.
I CAN HELP YOU.
I'VE BEEN PREPARING FOR THE FRESHMAN CULLING FOR MONTHS.
I KNOW WHO WILL WORK WITH WHOM.
WHO THE SECRET RATS ARE.
EVERY LITTLE HOLE THEY COULD HIDE IN.
I EVEN SET ASIDE A FEW TOYS FOR YOU.
A GESTURE OF OUR NEW FRIENDSHIP.
WE WORK TOGETHER, ARMY AND INTELLIGENCE.
WITH MY HELP, YOU'LL BREAK MASTER LIN'S FRESHMAN KILL RECORD.
AND WHAT DO YOU WANT?
TO BE THERE WHEN YOU KILL OUR NICARAGUAN FRIEND.

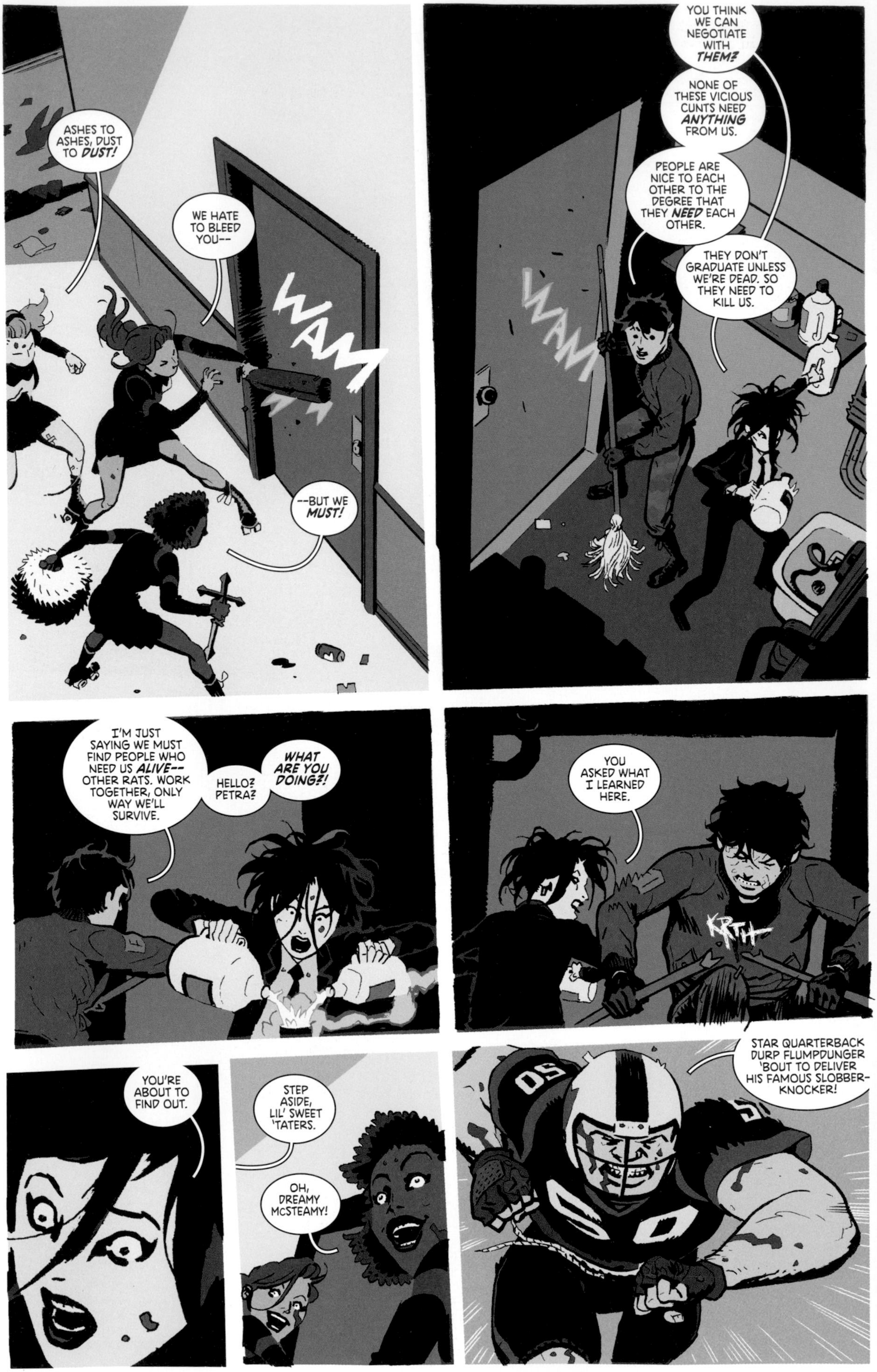
ASHES TO ASHES, DUST TO *DUST!*
WE HATE TO BLEED YOU--
WAM
--BUT WE *MUST!*
YOU THINK WE CAN NEGOTIATE WITH *THEM?*
NONE OF THESE VICIOUS CUNTS NEED *ANYTHING* FROM US.
PEOPLE ARE NICE TO EACH OTHER TO THE DEGREE THAT THEY *NEED* EACH OTHER.
THEY DON'T GRADUATE UNLESS WE'RE DEAD. SO THEY NEED TO KILL US.
WAM
I'M JUST SAYING WE MUST FIND PEOPLE WHO NEED US *ALIVE*-- OTHER RATS. WORK TOGETHER, ONLY WAY WE'LL SURVIVE.
HELLO? PETRA?
WHAT ARE YOU DOING?!
YOU ASKED WHAT I LEARNED HERE.
KRTH
YOU'RE ABOUT TO FIND OUT.
STEP ASIDE, LIL' SWEET 'TATERS.
OH, DREAMY McSTEAMY!
STAR QUARTERBACK DURP FLUMPDUNGER 'BOUT TO DELIVER HIS FAMOUS SLOBBER-KNOCKER!

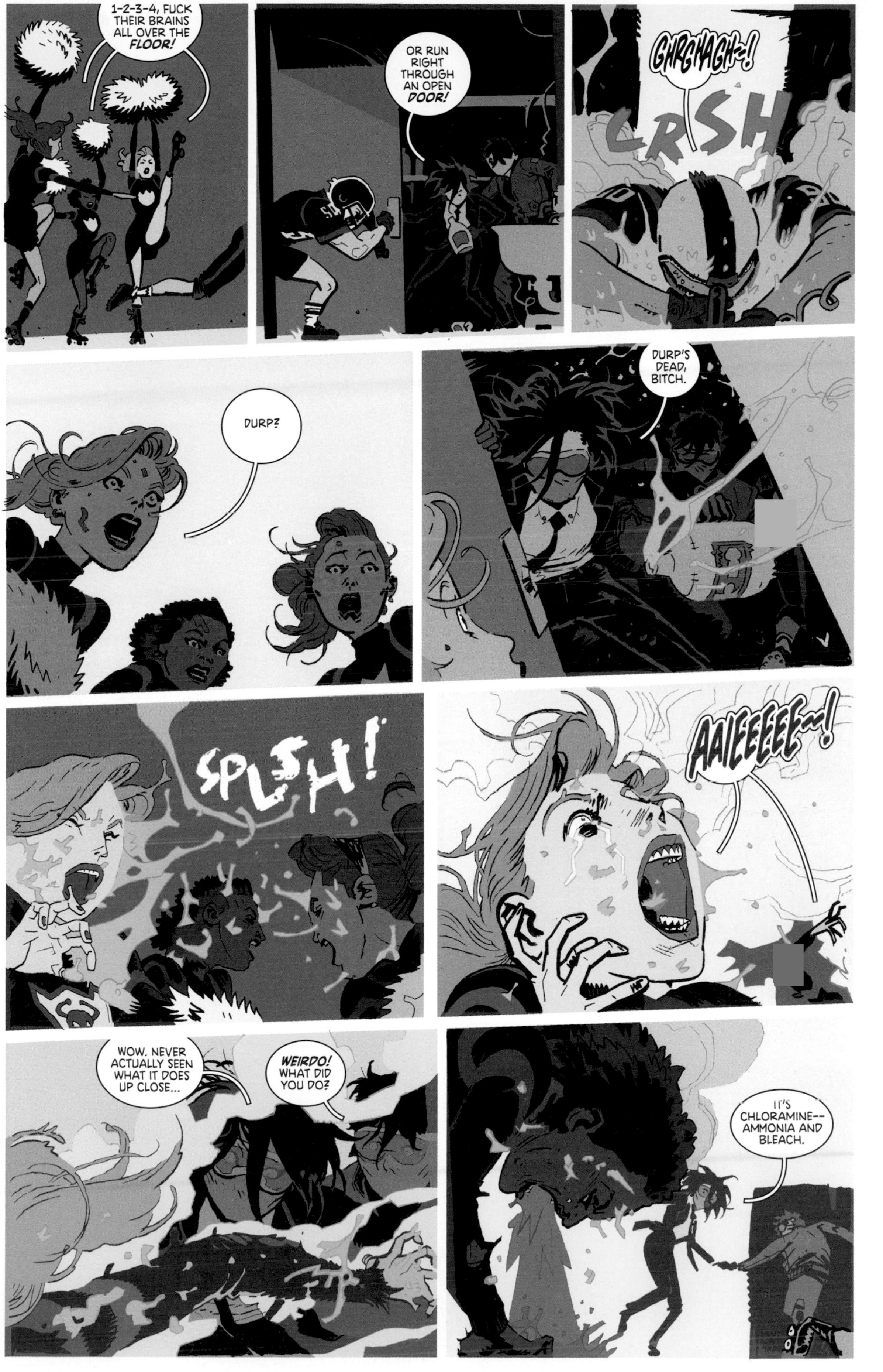
1-2-3-4, FUCK THEIR BRAINS ALL OVER THE FLOOR!
OR RUN RIGHT THROUGH AN OPEN DOOR!
GHRGHAGH--!
CRSH
DURP?
DURP'S DEAD, BITCH.
SPLSH!
AAIEEEEE--!
WOW. NEVER ACTUALLY SEEN WHAT IT DOES UP CLOSE...
WEIRDO! WHAT DID YOU DO?
IT'S CHLORAMINE-- AMMONIA AND BLEACH.

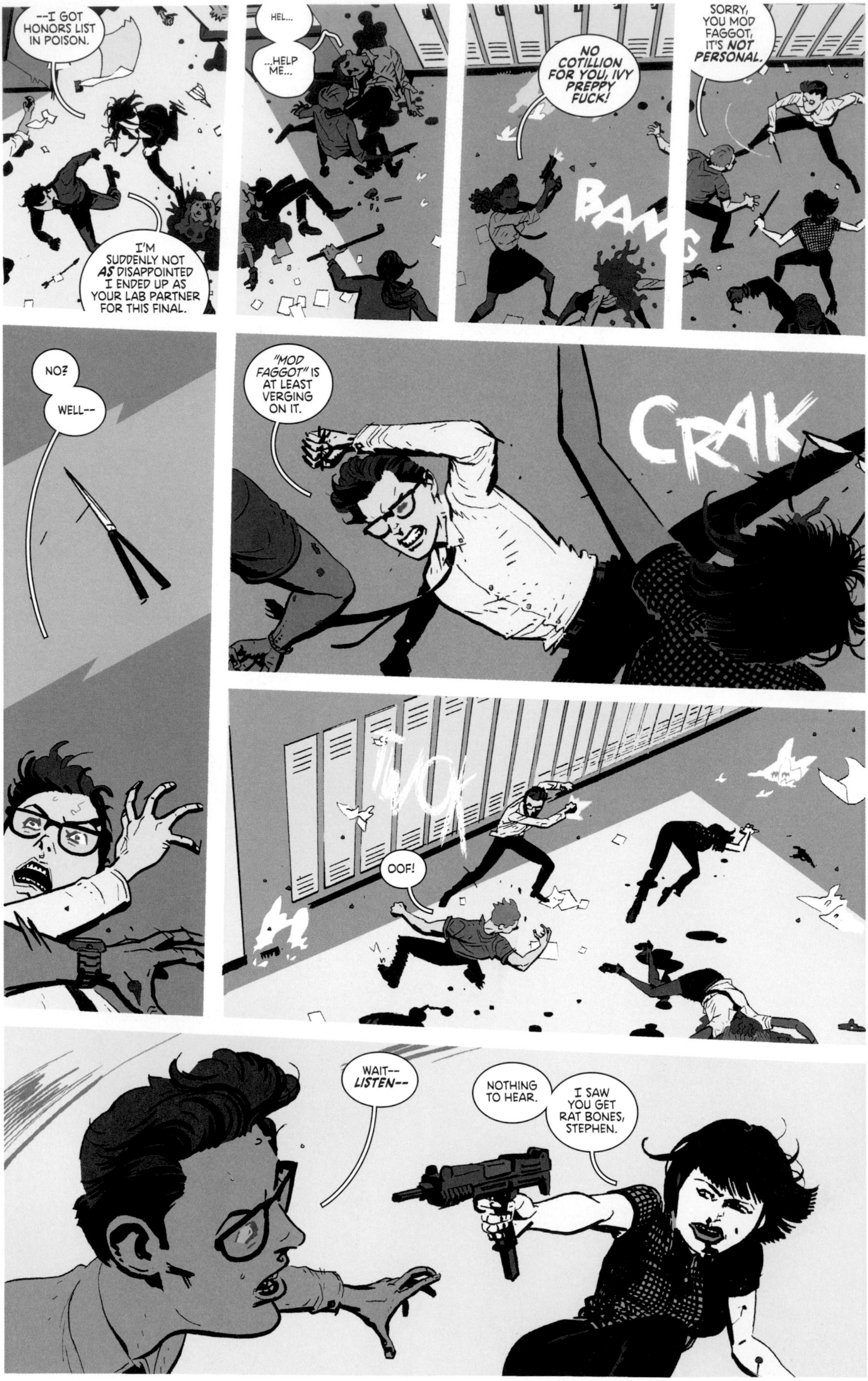
--I GOT HONORS LIST IN POISON.
I'M SUDDENLY NOT AS DISAPPOINTED I ENDED UP AS YOUR LAB PARTNER FOR THIS FINAL.
HEL...
...HELP ME...
NO COTILLION FOR YOU, IVY PREPPY FUCK!
BANG
SORRY, YOU MOD FAGGOT, IT'S NOT PERSONAL.
NO?
WELL--
"MOD FAGGOT" IS AT LEAST VERGING ON IT.
CRAK
THOK
OOF!
WAIT-- LISTEN--
NOTHING TO HEAR.
I SAW YOU GET RAT BONES, STEPHEN.

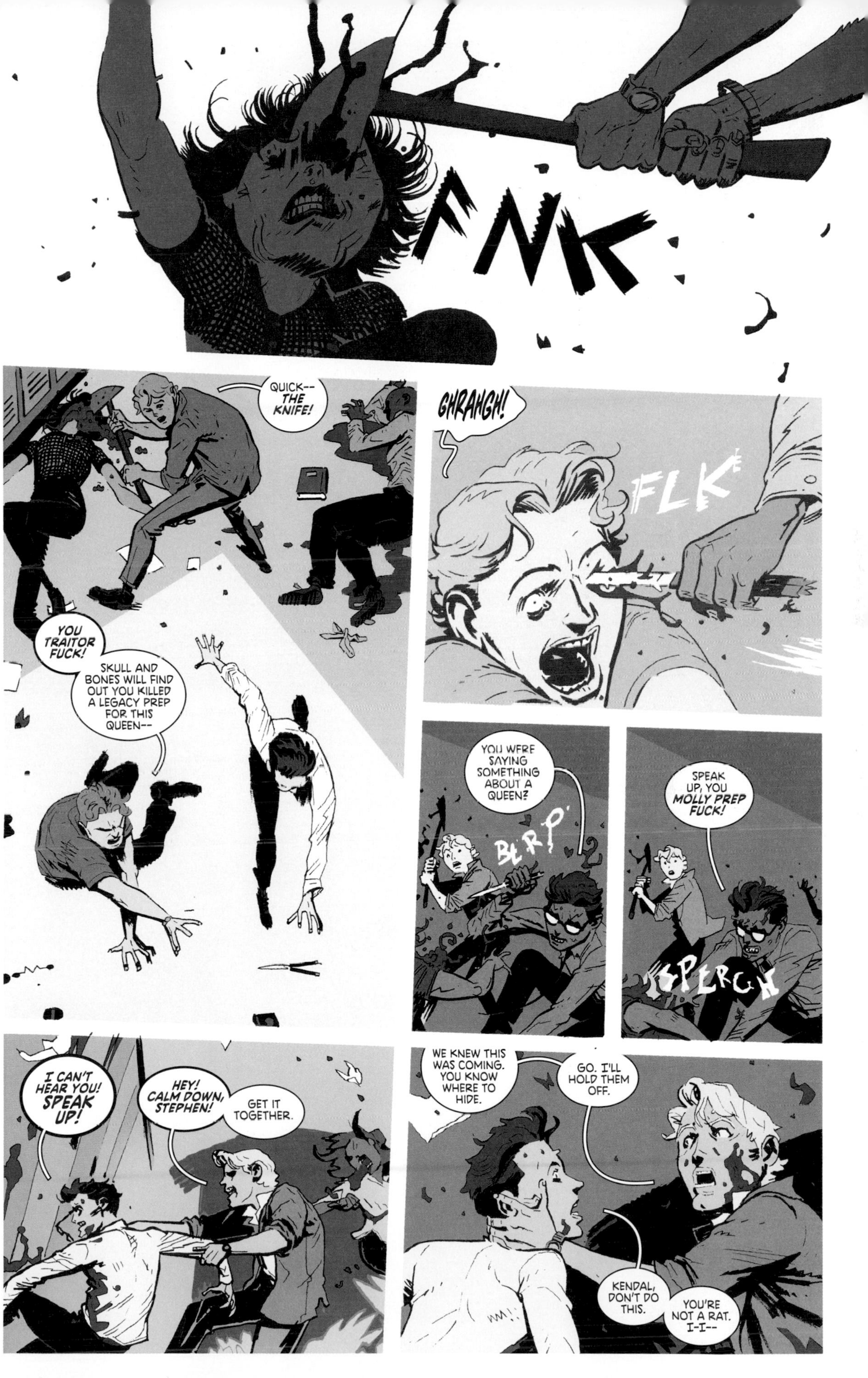
FNK
QUICK-- THE KNIFE!
YOU TRAITOR FUCK!
SKULL AND BONES WILL FIND OUT YOU KILLED A LEGACY PREP FOR THIS QUEEN--
GHRAHGH!
FLK
YOU WERE SAYING SOMETHING ABOUT A QUEEN?
BLRP
SPEAK UP, YOU MOLLY PREP FUCK!
SPLRCH
I CAN'T HEAR YOU! SPEAK UP!
HEY! CALM DOWN, STEPHEN!
GET IT TOGETHER.
WE KNEW THIS WAS COMING. YOU KNOW WHERE TO HIDE.
GO. I'LL HOLD THEM OFF.
KENDAL, DON'T DO THIS.
YOU'RE NOT A RAT. I-I--

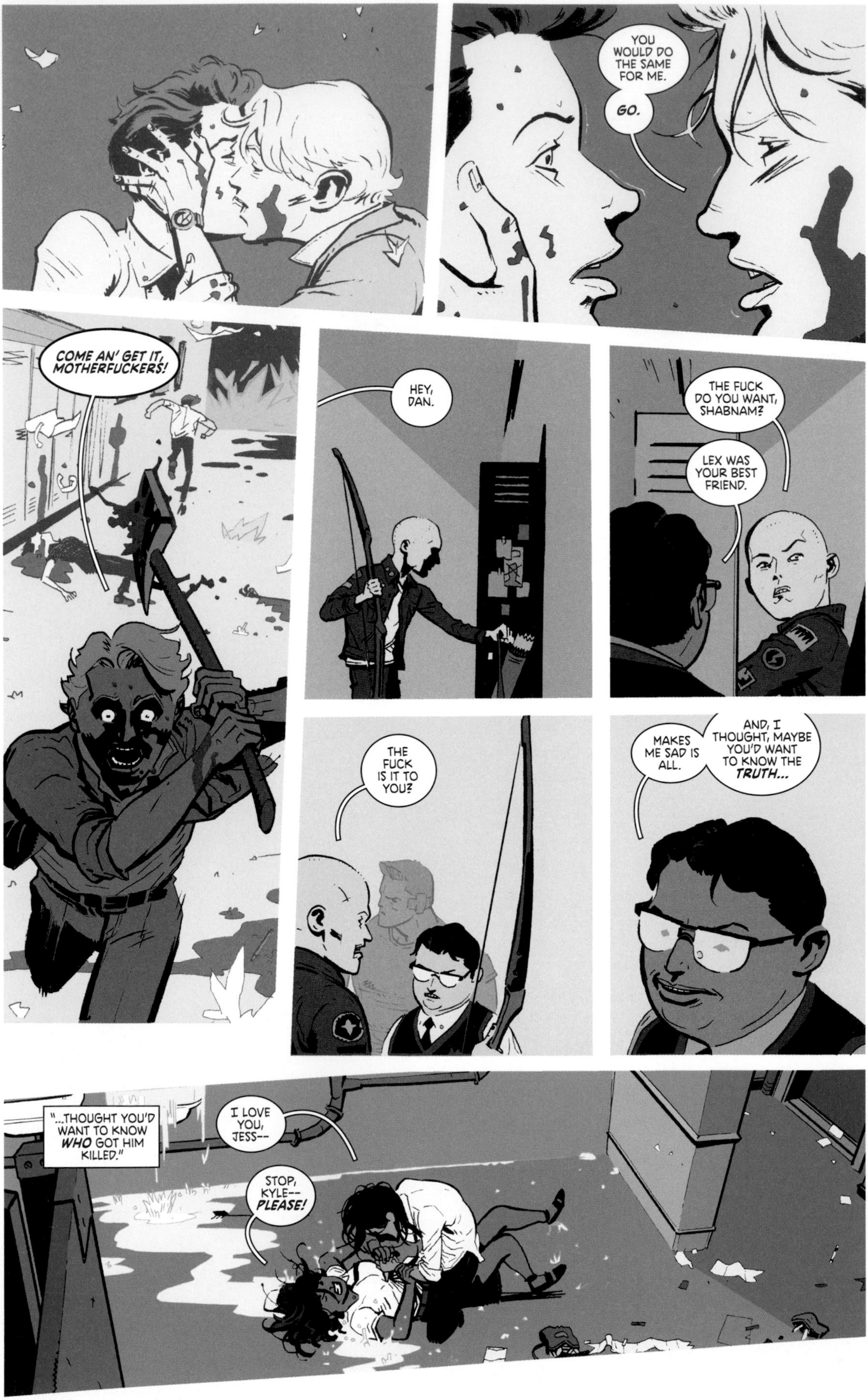
YOU WOULD DO THE SAME FOR ME.
GO.
COME AN' GET IT, MOTHERFUCKERS!
HEY, DAN.
THE FUCK DO YOU WANT, SHABNAM?
LEX WAS YOUR BEST FRIEND.
THE FUCK IS IT TO YOU?
MAKES ME SAD IS ALL.
AND, I THOUGHT, MAYBE YOU'D WANT TO KNOW THE TRUTH...
"...THOUGHT YOU'D WANT TO KNOW WHO GOT HIM KILLED."
I LOVE YOU, JESS--
STOP, KYLE-- PLEASE!

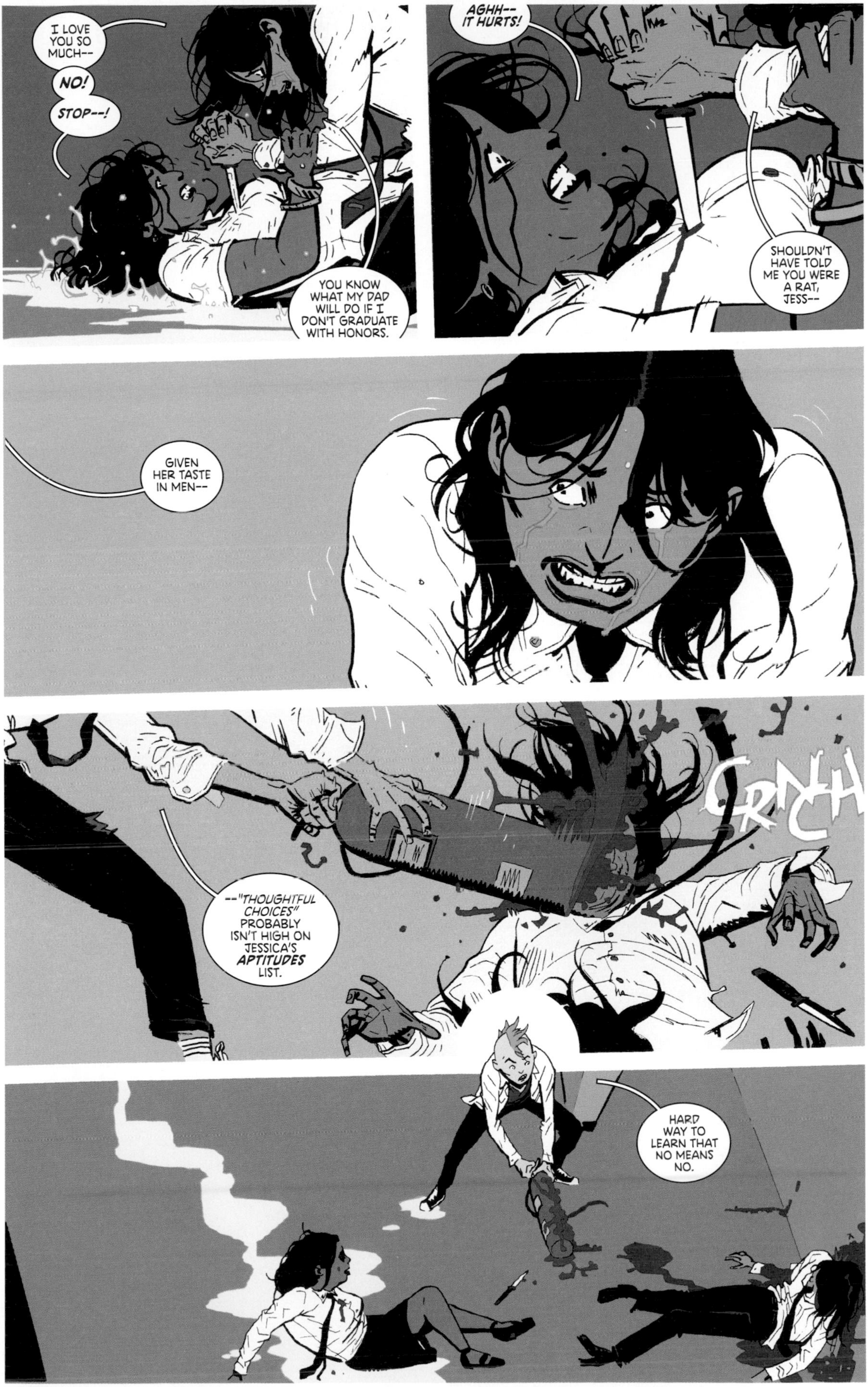
I LOVE YOU SO MUCH--
NO!
STOP--!
YOU KNOW WHAT MY DAD WILL DO IF I DON'T GRADUATE WITH HONORS.
AGHH-- IT HURTS!
SHOULDN'T HAVE TOLD ME YOU WERE A RAT, JESS--
GIVEN HER TASTE IN MEN--
CRNCH
--"THOUGHTFUL CHOICES" PROBABLY ISN'T HIGH ON JESSICA'S APTITUDES LIST.
HARD WAY TO LEARN THAT NO MEANS NO.

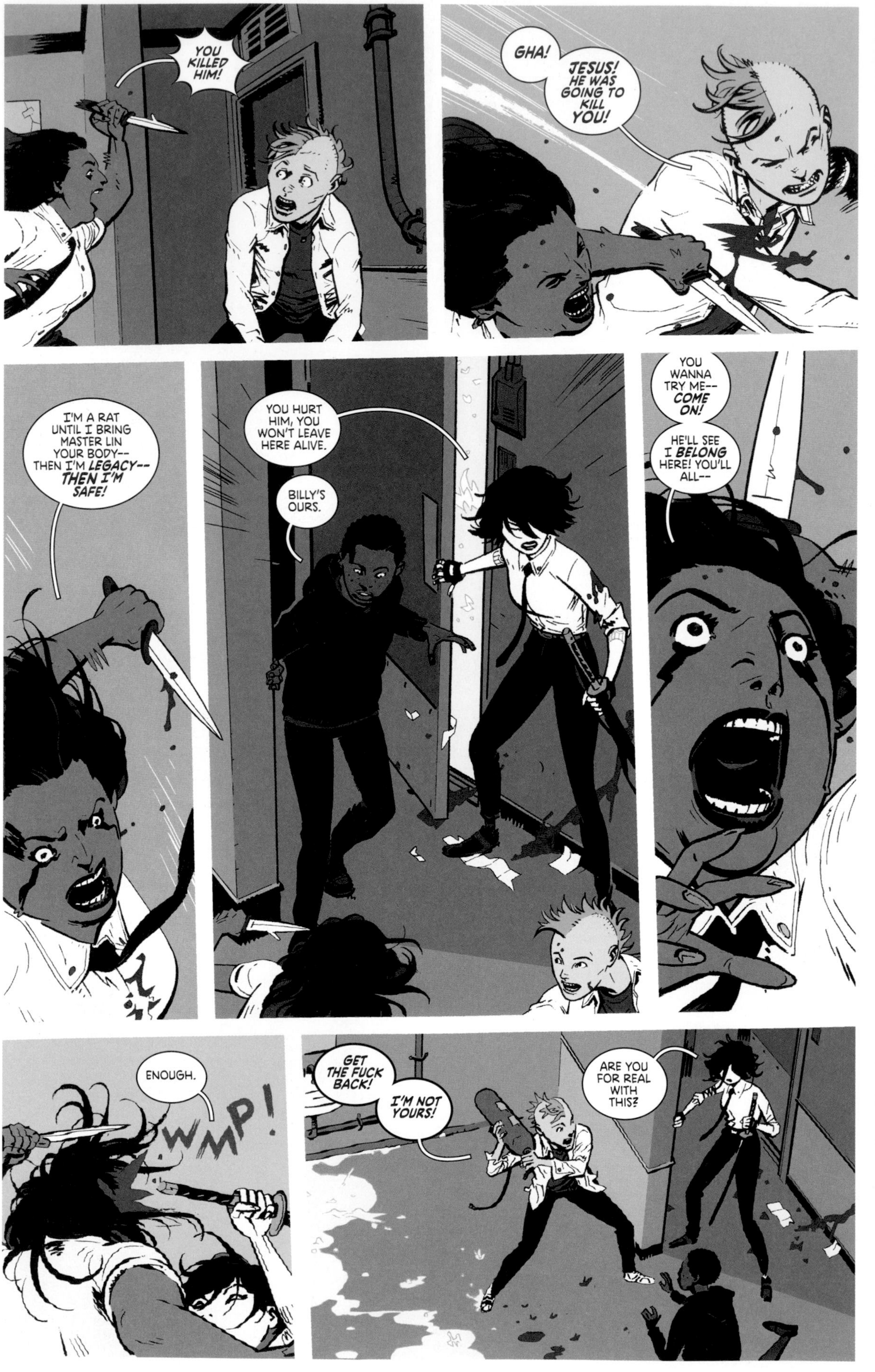
YOU KILLED HIM!
GHA!
JESUS! HE WAS GOING TO KILL YOU!
I'M A RAT UNTIL I BRING MASTER LIN YOUR BODY-- THEN I'M LEGACY-- THEN I'M SAFE!
YOU HURT HIM, YOU WON'T LEAVE HERE ALIVE.
BILLY'S OURS.
YOU WANNA TRY ME-- COME ON!
HE'LL SEE I BELONG HERE! YOU'LL ALL--
ENOUGH.
WMP!
GET THE FUCK BACK!
I'M NOT YOURS!
ARE YOU FOR REAL WITH THIS?

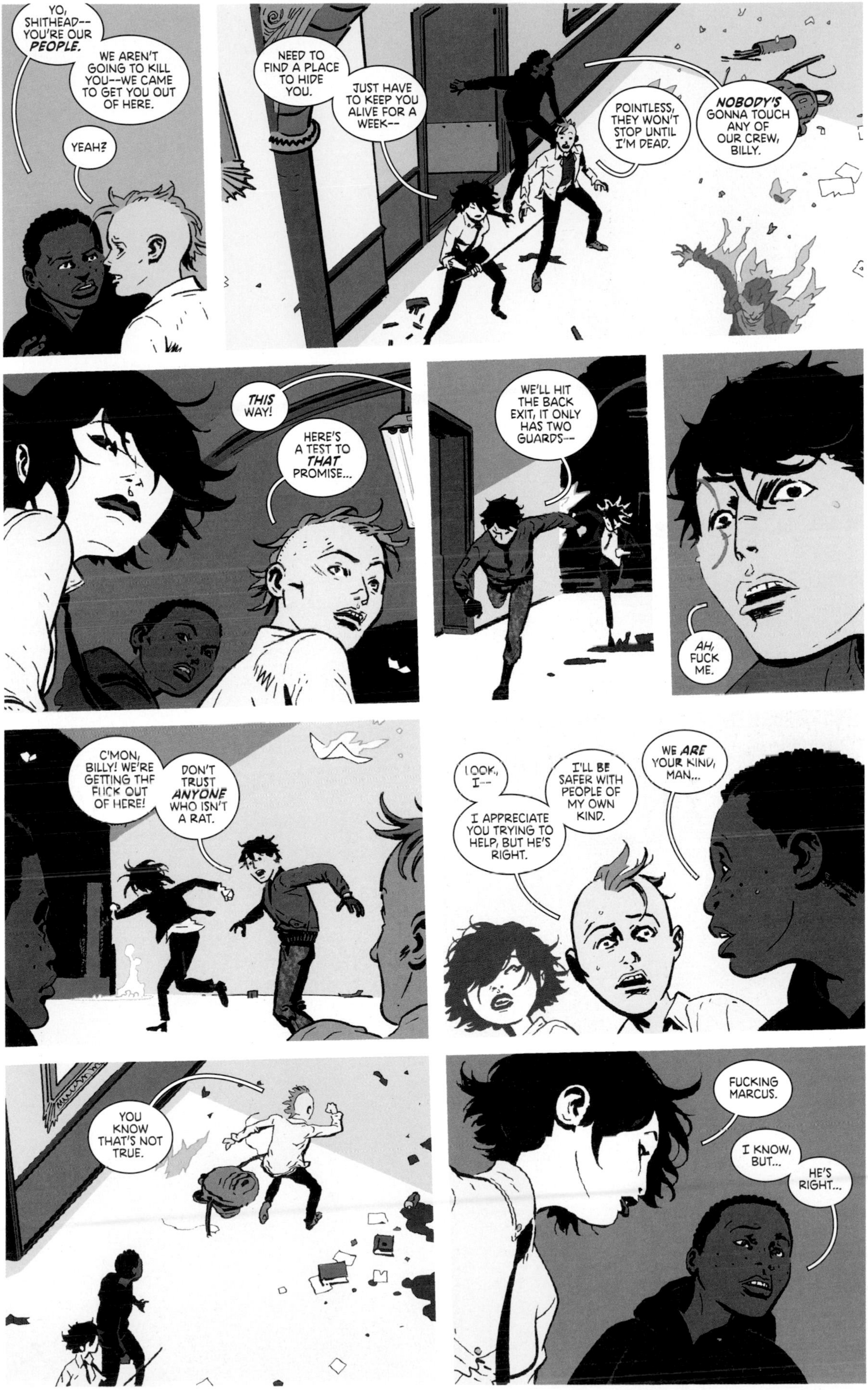
YO, SHITHEAD-- YOU'RE OUR PEOPLE.
WE AREN'T GOING TO KILL YOU--WE CAME TO GET YOU OUT OF HERE.
YEAH?
NEED TO FIND A PLACE TO HIDE YOU.
JUST HAVE TO KEEP YOU ALIVE FOR A WEEK--
POINTLESS, THEY WON'T STOP UNTIL I'M DEAD.
NOBODY'S GONNA TOUCH ANY OF OUR CREW, BILLY.
THIS WAY!
HERE'S A TEST TO THAT PROMISE...
WE'LL HIT THE BACK EXIT, IT ONLY HAS TWO GUARDS--
AH, FUCK ME.
C'MON, BILLY! WE'RE GETTING THE FUCK OUT OF HERE!
DON'T TRUST ANYONE WHO ISN'T A RAT.
LOOK, I--
I'LL BE SAFER WITH PEOPLE OF MY OWN KIND.
I APPRECIATE YOU TRYING TO HELP, BUT HE'S RIGHT.
WE ARE YOUR KIND, MAN...
YOU KNOW THAT'S NOT TRUE.
FUCKING MARCUS.
I KNOW, BUT...
HE'S RIGHT...

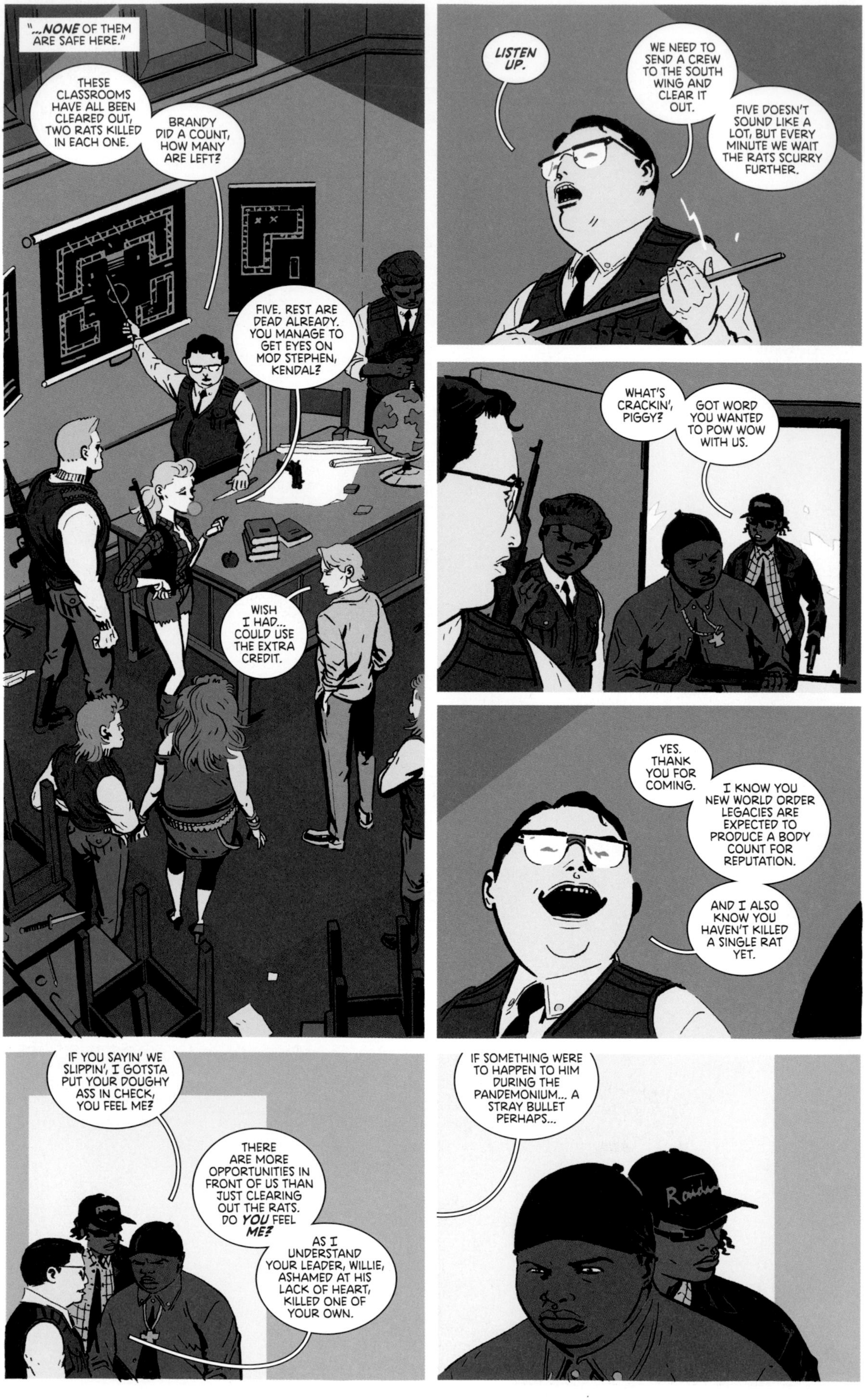
"...NONE OF THEM ARE SAFE HERE."
THESE CLASSROOMS HAVE ALL BEEN CLEARED OUT, TWO RATS KILLED IN EACH ONE.
BRANDY DID A COUNT, HOW MANY ARE LEFT?
FIVE. REST ARE DEAD ALREADY. YOU MANAGE TO GET EYES ON MOD STEPHEN, KENDAL?
WISH I HAD... COULD USE THE EXTRA CREDIT.
LISTEN UP.
WE NEED TO SEND A CREW TO THE SOUTH WING AND CLEAR IT OUT.
FIVE DOESN'T SOUND LIKE A LOT, BUT EVERY MINUTE WE WAIT THE RATS SCURRY FURTHER.
WHAT'S CRACKIN', PIGGY?
GOT WORD YOU WANTED TO POW WOW WITH US.
YES. THANK YOU FOR COMING.
I KNOW YOU NEW WORLD ORDER LEGACIES ARE EXPECTED TO PRODUCE A BODY COUNT FOR REPUTATION.
AND I ALSO KNOW YOU HAVEN'T KILLED A SINGLE RAT YET.
IF YOU SAYIN' WE SLIPPIN', I GOTSTA PUT YOUR DOUGHY ASS IN CHECK, YOU FEEL ME?
THERE ARE MORE OPPORTUNITIES IN FRONT OF US THAN JUST CLEARING OUT THE RATS. DO YOU FEEL ME?
AS I UNDERSTAND YOUR LEADER, WILLIE, ASHAMED AT HIS LACK OF HEART, KILLED ONE OF YOUR OWN.
IF SOMETHING WERE TO HAPPEN TO HIM DURING THE PANDEMONIUM... A STRAY BULLET PERHAPS...

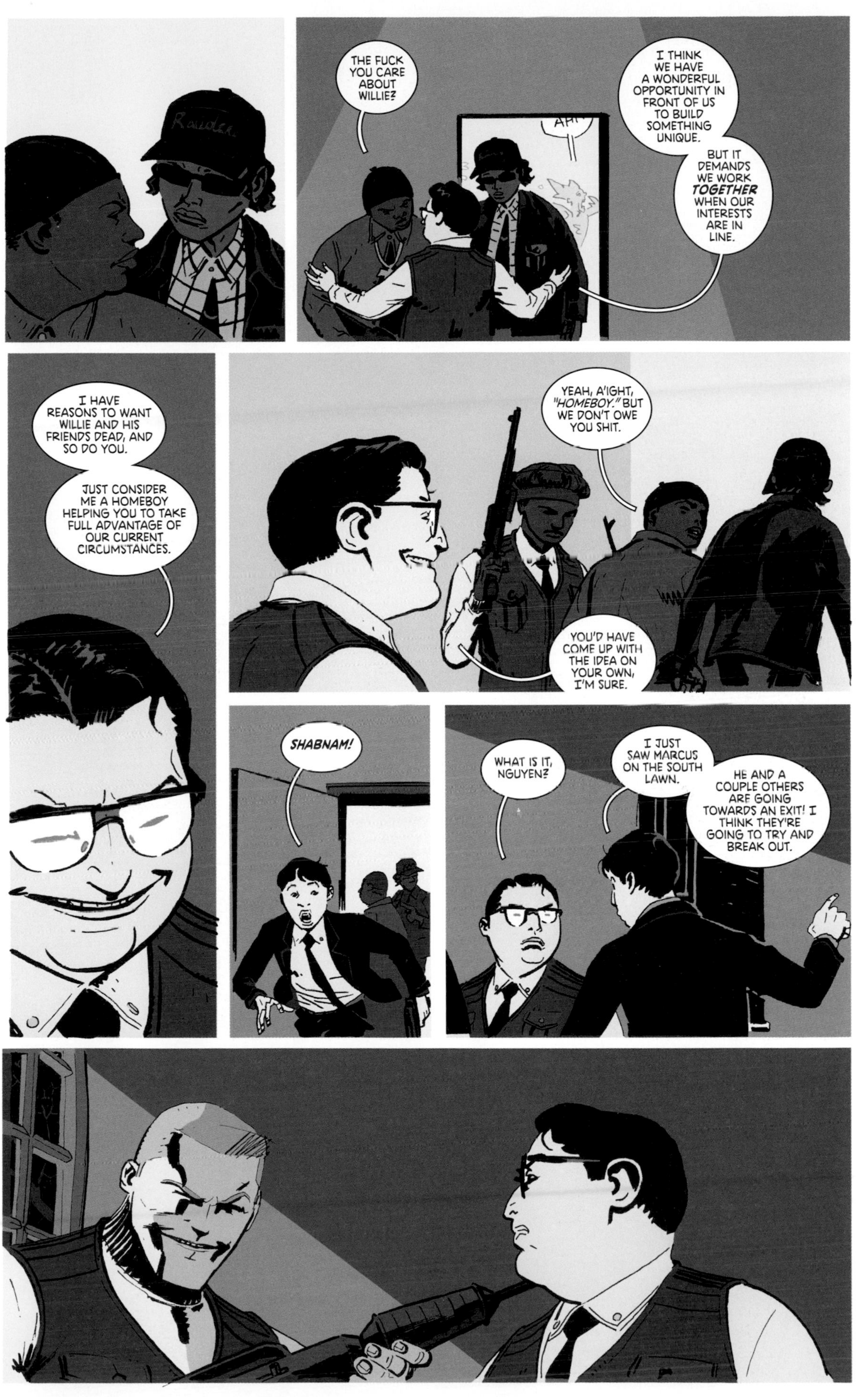
THE FUCK YOU CARE ABOUT WILLIE?
I THINK WE HAVE A WONDERFUL OPPORTUNITY IN FRONT OF US TO BUILD SOMETHING UNIQUE.
BUT IT DEMANDS WE WORK TOGETHER WHEN OUR INTERESTS ARE IN LINE.
I HAVE REASONS TO WANT WILLIE AND HIS FRIENDS DEAD, AND SO DO YOU.
JUST CONSIDER ME A HOMEBOY HELPING YOU TO TAKE FULL ADVANTAGE OF OUR CURRENT CIRCUMSTANCES.
YEAH, A'IGHT, "HOMEBOY." BUT WE DON'T OWE YOU SHIT.
YOU'D HAVE COME UP WITH THE IDEA ON YOUR OWN, I'M SURE.
SHABNAM!
WHAT IS IT, NGUYEN?
I JUST SAW MARCUS ON THE SOUTH LAWN.
HE AND A COUPLE OTHERS ARE GOING TOWARDS AN EXIT! I THINK THEY'RE GOING TO TRY AND BREAK OUT.

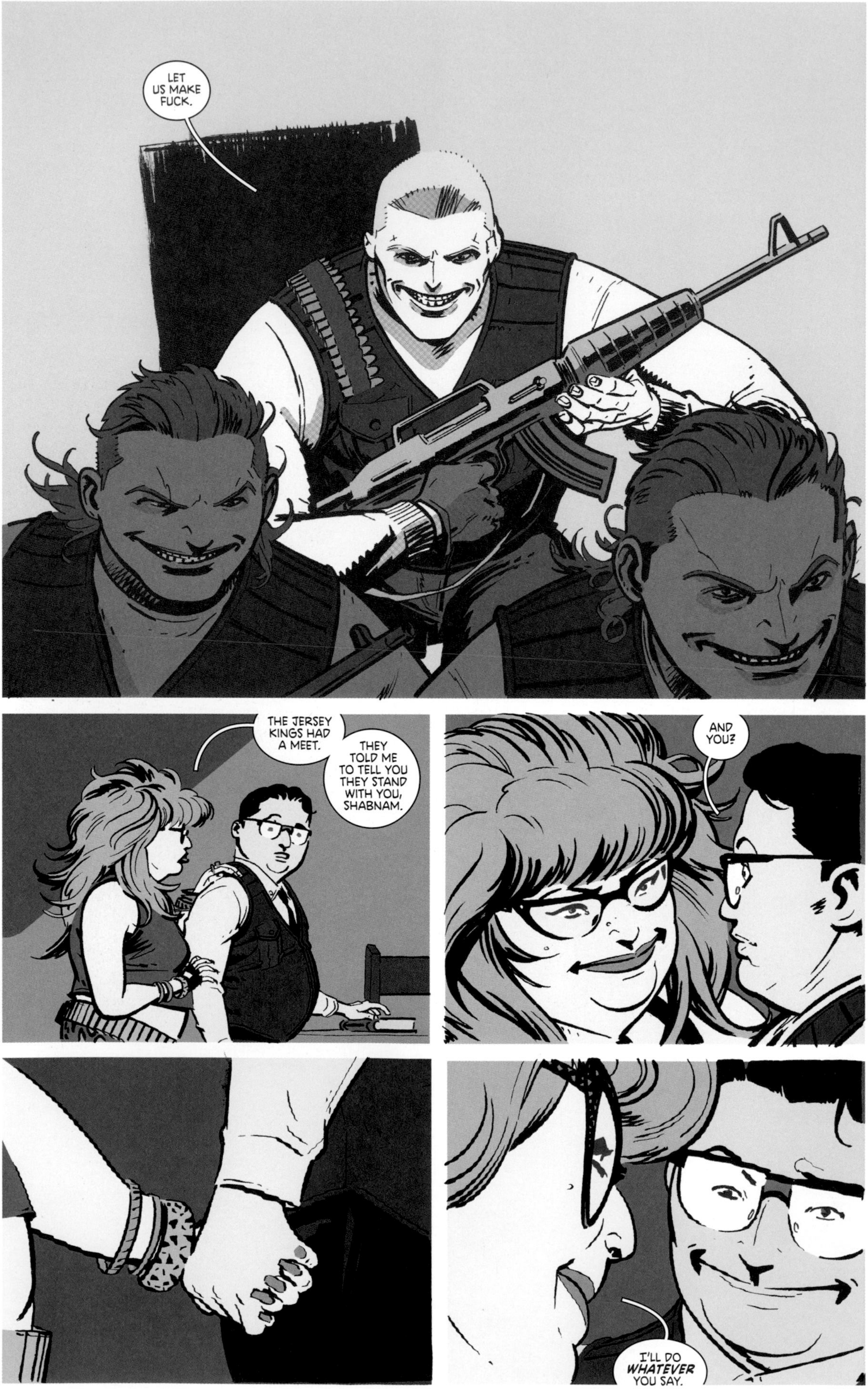
LET US MAKE FUCK.
THE JERSEY KINGS HAD A MEET.
THEY TOLD ME TO TELL YOU THEY STAND WITH YOU, SHABNAM.
AND YOU?
I'LL DO *WHATEVER* YOU SAY.

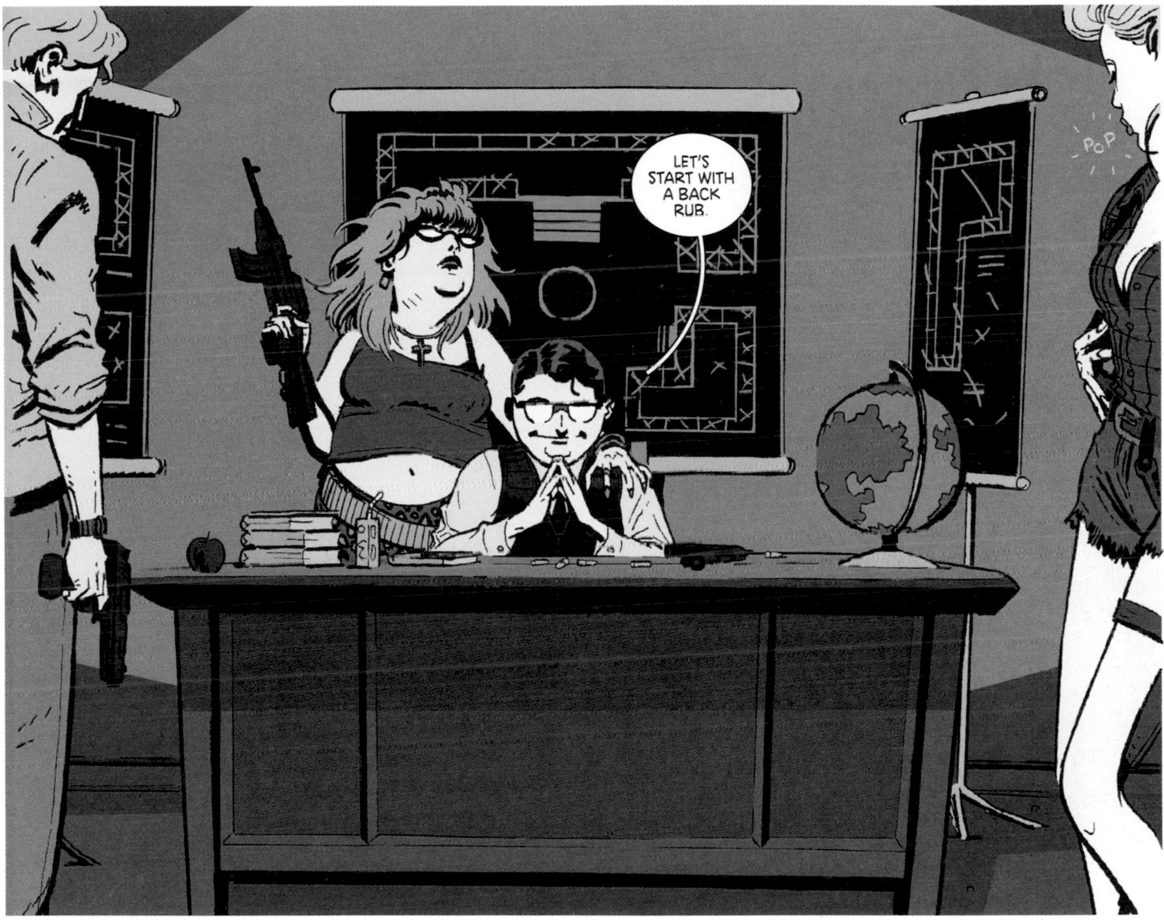
LET'S START WITH A BACK RUB.
POP

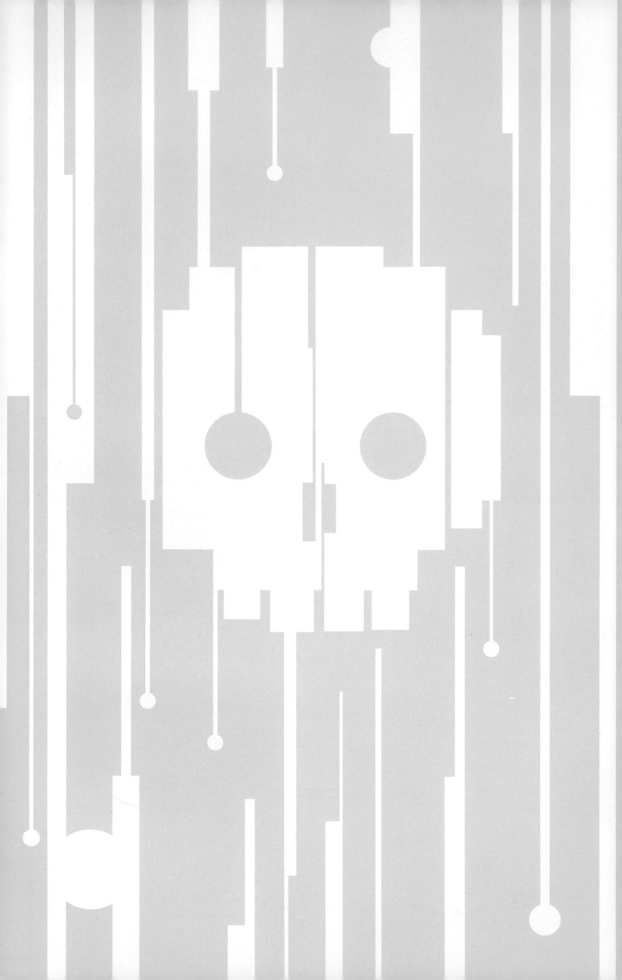

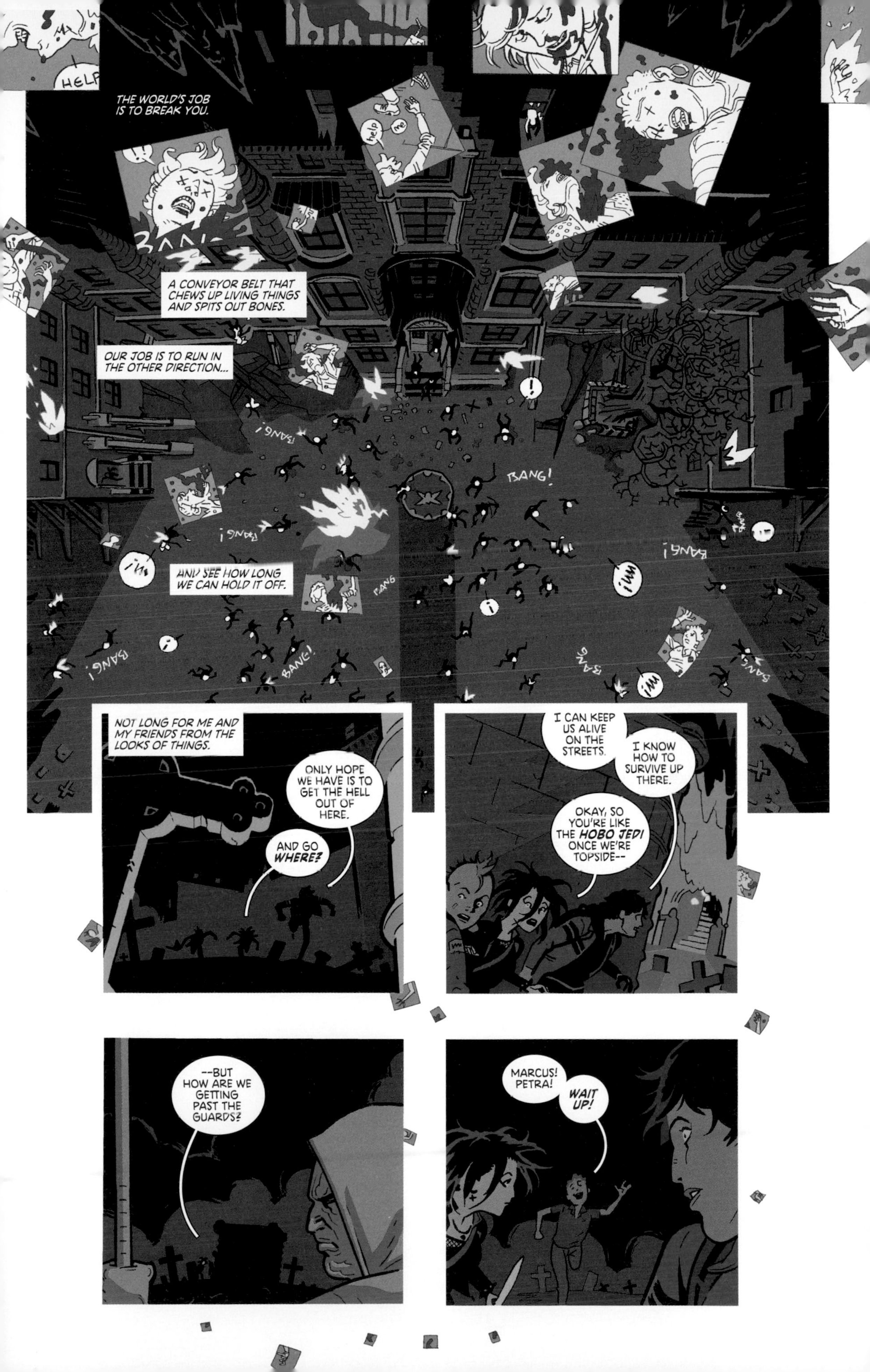
HELP
THE WORLD'S JOB IS TO BREAK YOU.
help me
A CONVEYOR BELT THAT CHEWS UP LIVING THINGS AND SPITS OUT BONES.
OUR JOB IS TO RUN IN THE OTHER DIRECTION...
BANG!
AND SEE HOW LONG WE CAN HOLD IT OFF.
BANG!
NOT LONG FOR ME AND MY FRIENDS FROM THE LOOKS OF THINGS.
ONLY HOPE WE HAVE IS TO GET THE HELL OUT OF HERE.
AND GO WHERE?
I CAN KEEP US ALIVE ON THE STREETS.
I KNOW HOW TO SURVIVE UP THERE.
OKAY, SO YOU'RE LIKE THE HOBO JEDI ONCE WE'RE TOPSIDE--
--BUT HOW ARE WE GETTING PAST THE GUARDS?
MARCUS! PETRA!
WAIT UP!

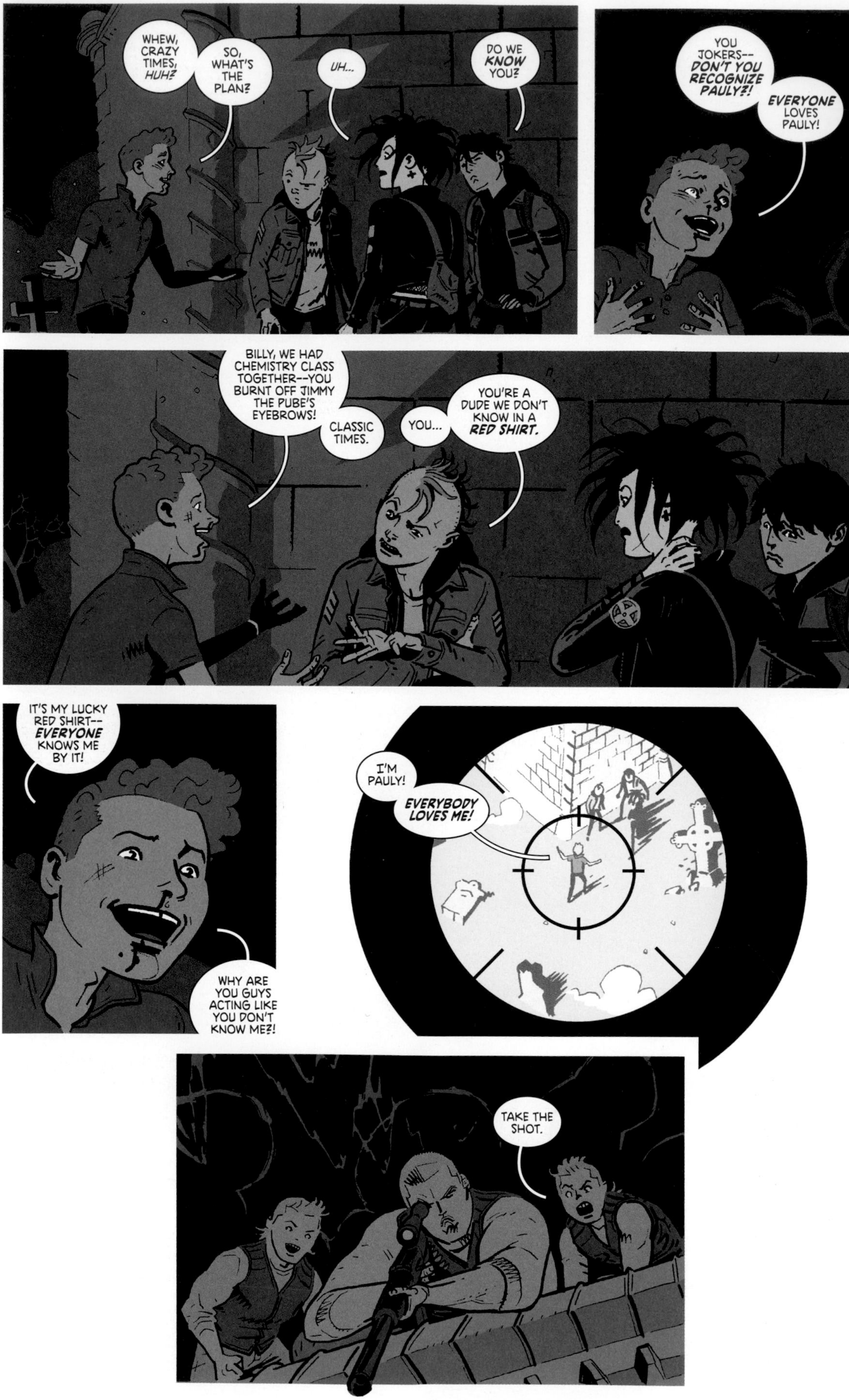
WHEW, CRAZY TIMES, HUH?
SO, WHAT'S THE PLAN?
UH...
DO WE KNOW YOU?
YOU JOKERS-- DON'T YOU RECOGNIZE PAULY?!
EVERYONE LOVES PAULY!
BILLY, WE HAD CHEMISTRY CLASS TOGETHER--YOU BURNT OFF JIMMY THE PUBE'S EYEBROWS!
CLASSIC TIMES.
YOU...
YOU'RE A DUDE WE DON'T KNOW IN A RED SHIRT.
IT'S MY LUCKY RED SHIRT-- EVERYONE KNOWS ME BY IT!
WHY ARE YOU GUYS ACTING LIKE YOU DON'T KNOW ME?!
I'M PAULY!
EVERYBODY LOVES ME!
TAKE THE SHOT.

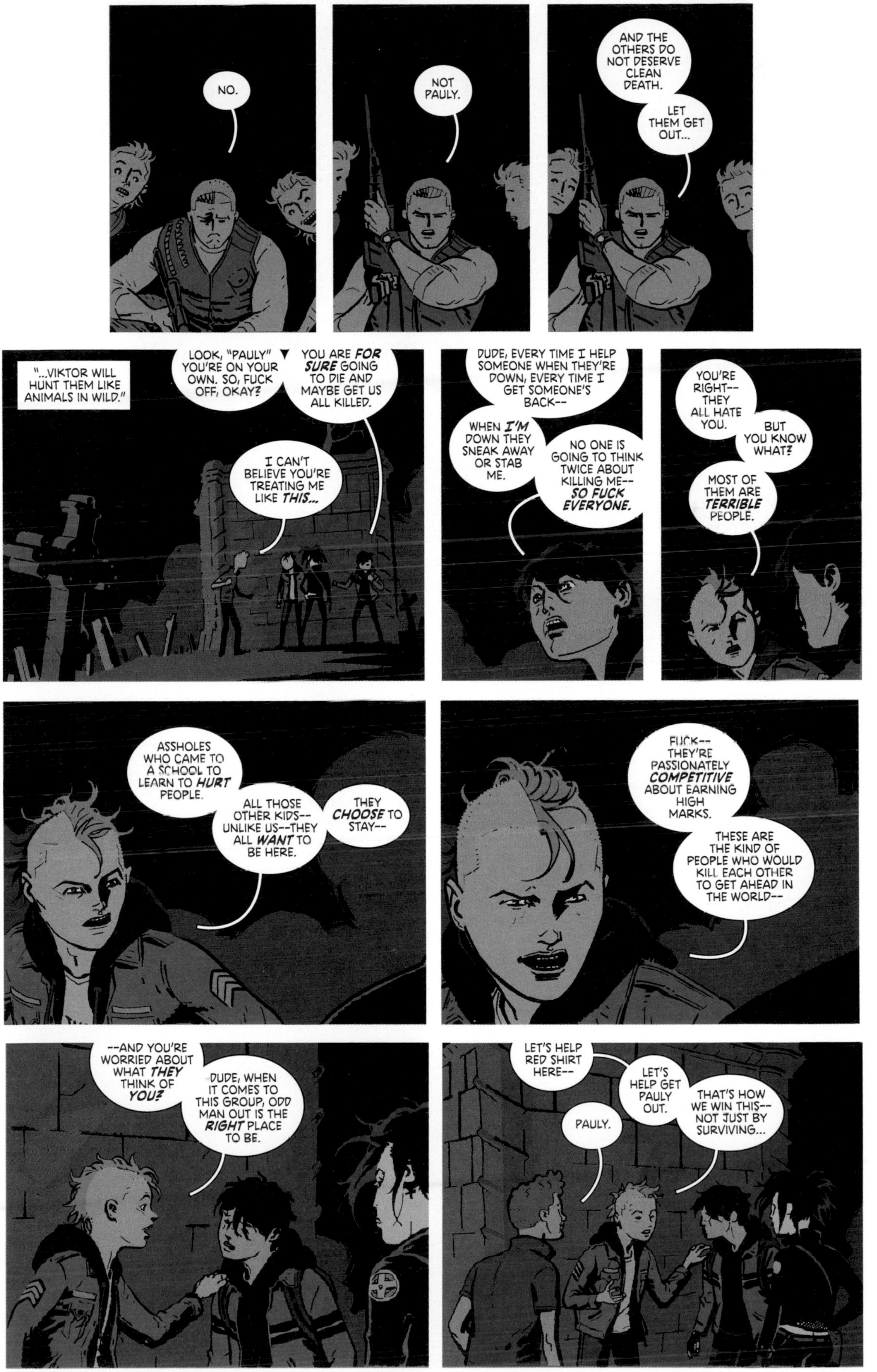
NO.
NOT PAULY.
AND THE OTHERS DO NOT DESERVE CLEAN DEATH.
LET THEM GET OUT...
"...VIKTOR WILL HUNT THEM LIKE ANIMALS IN WILD."
LOOK, "PAULY" YOU'RE ON YOUR OWN. SO, FUCK OFF, OKAY?
YOU ARE FOR SURE GOING TO DIE AND MAYBE GET US ALL KILLED.
I CAN'T BELIEVE YOU'RE TREATING ME LIKE THIS...
DUDE, EVERY TIME I HELP SOMEONE WHEN THEY'RE DOWN, EVERY TIME I GET SOMEONE'S BACK--
WHEN I'M DOWN THEY SNEAK AWAY OR STAB ME.
NO ONE IS GOING TO THINK TWICE ABOUT KILLING ME-- SO FUCK EVERYONE.
YOU'RE RIGHT-- THEY ALL HATE YOU.
BUT YOU KNOW WHAT?
MOST OF THEM ARE TERRIBLE PEOPLE.
ASSHOLES WHO CAME TO A SCHOOL TO LEARN TO HURT PEOPLE.
ALL THOSE OTHER KIDS-- UNLIKE US--THEY ALL WANT TO BE HERE.
THEY CHOOSE TO STAY--
FUCK-- THEY'RE PASSIONATELY COMPETITIVE ABOUT EARNING HIGH MARKS.
THESE ARE THE KIND OF PEOPLE WHO WOULD KILL EACH OTHER TO GET AHEAD IN THE WORLD--
--AND YOU'RE WORRIED ABOUT WHAT THEY THINK OF YOU?
DUDE, WHEN IT COMES TO THIS GROUP, ODD MAN OUT IS THE RIGHT PLACE TO BE.
LET'S HELP RED SHIRT HERE--
LET'S HELP GET PAULY OUT.
PAULY.
THAT'S HOW WE WIN THIS-- NOT JUST BY SURVIVING...

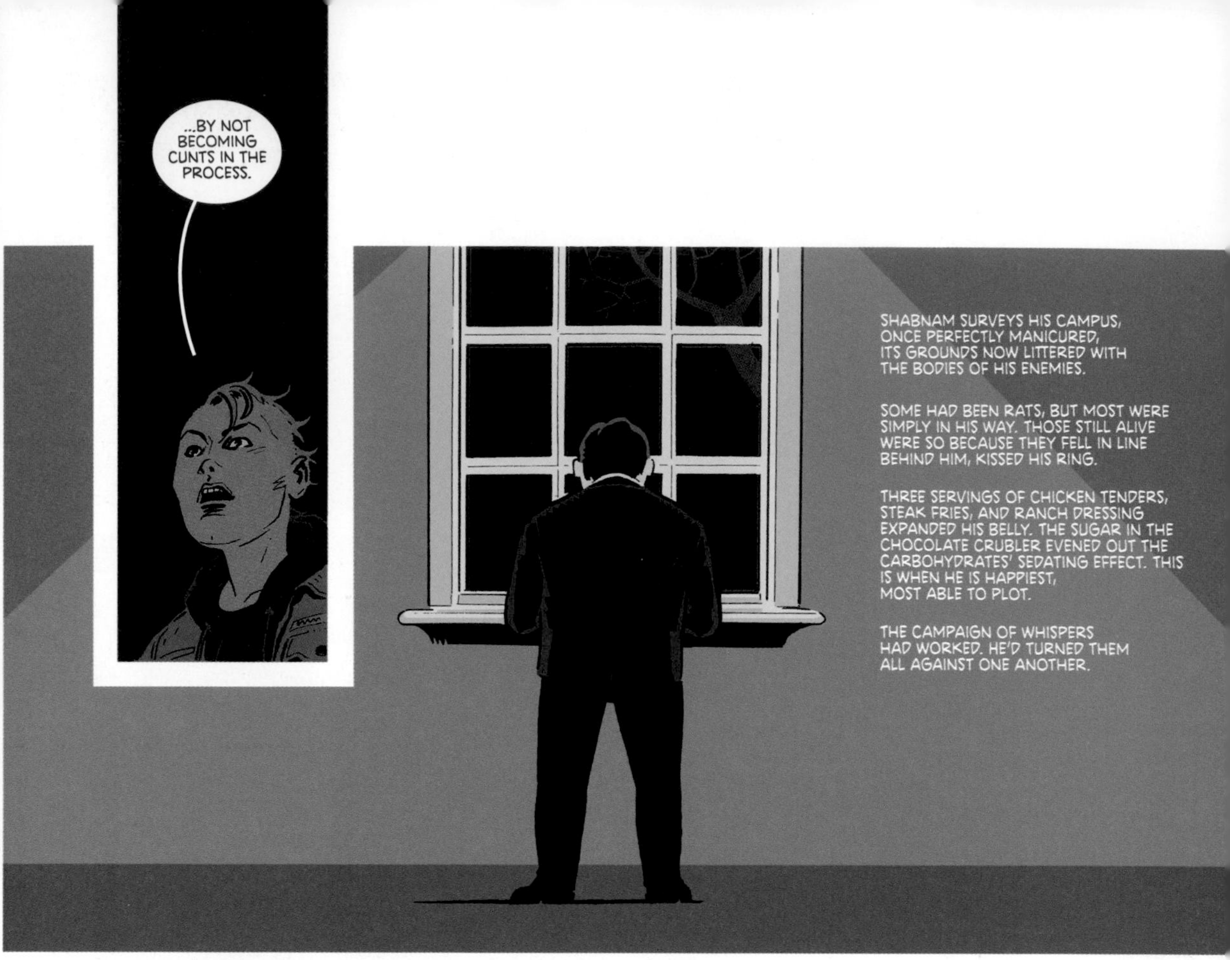
...BY NOT BECOMING CUNTS IN THE PROCESS.
SHABNAM SURVEYS HIS CAMPUS, ONCE PERFECTLY MANICURED, ITS GROUNDS NOW LITTERED WITH THE BODIES OF HIS ENEMIES.
SOME HAD BEEN RATS, BUT MOST WERE SIMPLY IN HIS WAY. THOSE STILL ALIVE WERE SO BECAUSE THEY FELL IN LINE BEHIND HIM, KISSED HIS RING.
THREE SERVINGS OF CHICKEN TENDERS, STEAK FRIES, AND RANCH DRESSING EXPANDED HIS BELLY. THE SUGAR IN THE CHOCOLATE CRUBLER EVENED OUT THE CARBOHYDRATES' SEDATING EFFECT. THIS IS WHEN HE IS HAPPIEST, MOST ABLE TO PLOT.
THE CAMPAIGN OF WHISPERS HAD WORKED. HE'D TURNED THEM ALL AGAINST ONE ANOTHER.

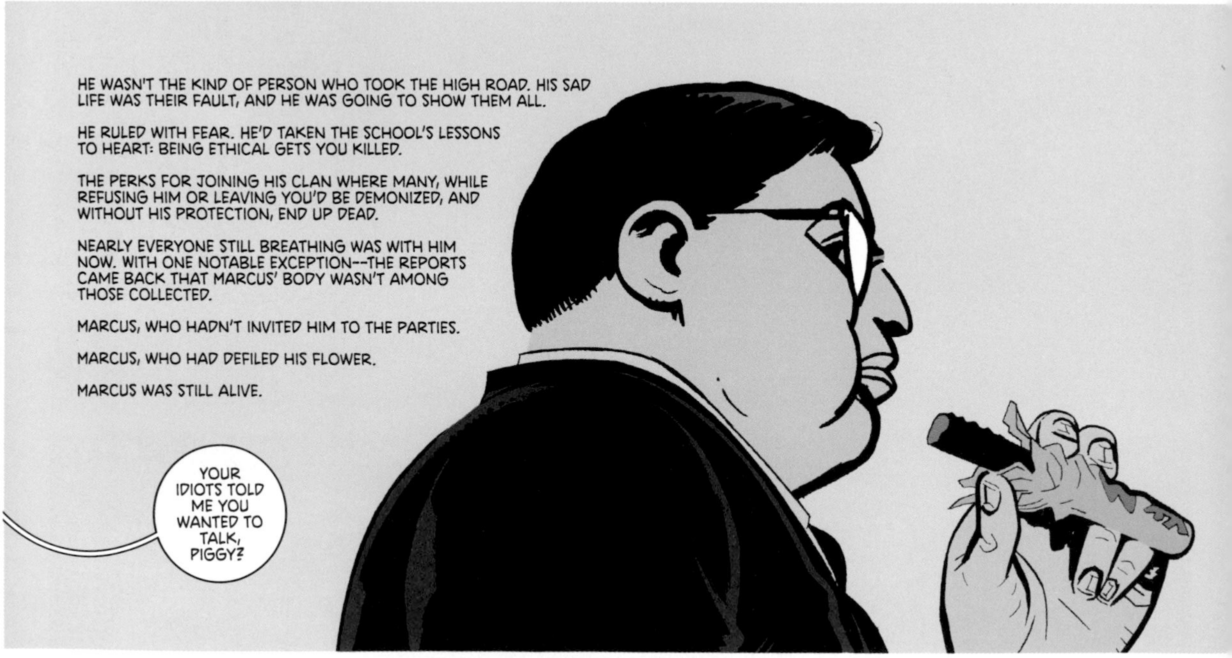
HE WASN'T THE KIND OF PERSON WHO TOOK THE HIGH ROAD. HIS SAD LIFE WAS THEIR FAULT, AND HE WAS GOING TO SHOW THEM ALL.
HE RULED WITH FEAR. HE'D TAKEN THE SCHOOL'S LESSONS TO HEART: BEING ETHICAL GETS YOU KILLED.
THE PERKS FOR JOINING HIS CLAN WHERE MANY, WHILE REFUSING HIM OR LEAVING YOU'D BE DEMONIZED, AND WITHOUT HIS PROTECTION, END UP DEAD.
NEARLY EVERYONE STILL BREATHING WAS WITH HIM NOW. WITH ONE NOTABLE EXCEPTION--THE REPORTS CAME BACK THAT MARCUS' BODY WASN'T AMONG THOSE COLLECTED.
MARCUS, WHO HADN'T INVITED HIM TO THE PARTIES.
MARCUS, WHO HAD DEFILED HIS FLOWER.
MARCUS WAS STILL ALIVE.
YOUR IDIOTS TOLD ME YOU WANTED TO TALK, PIGGY?

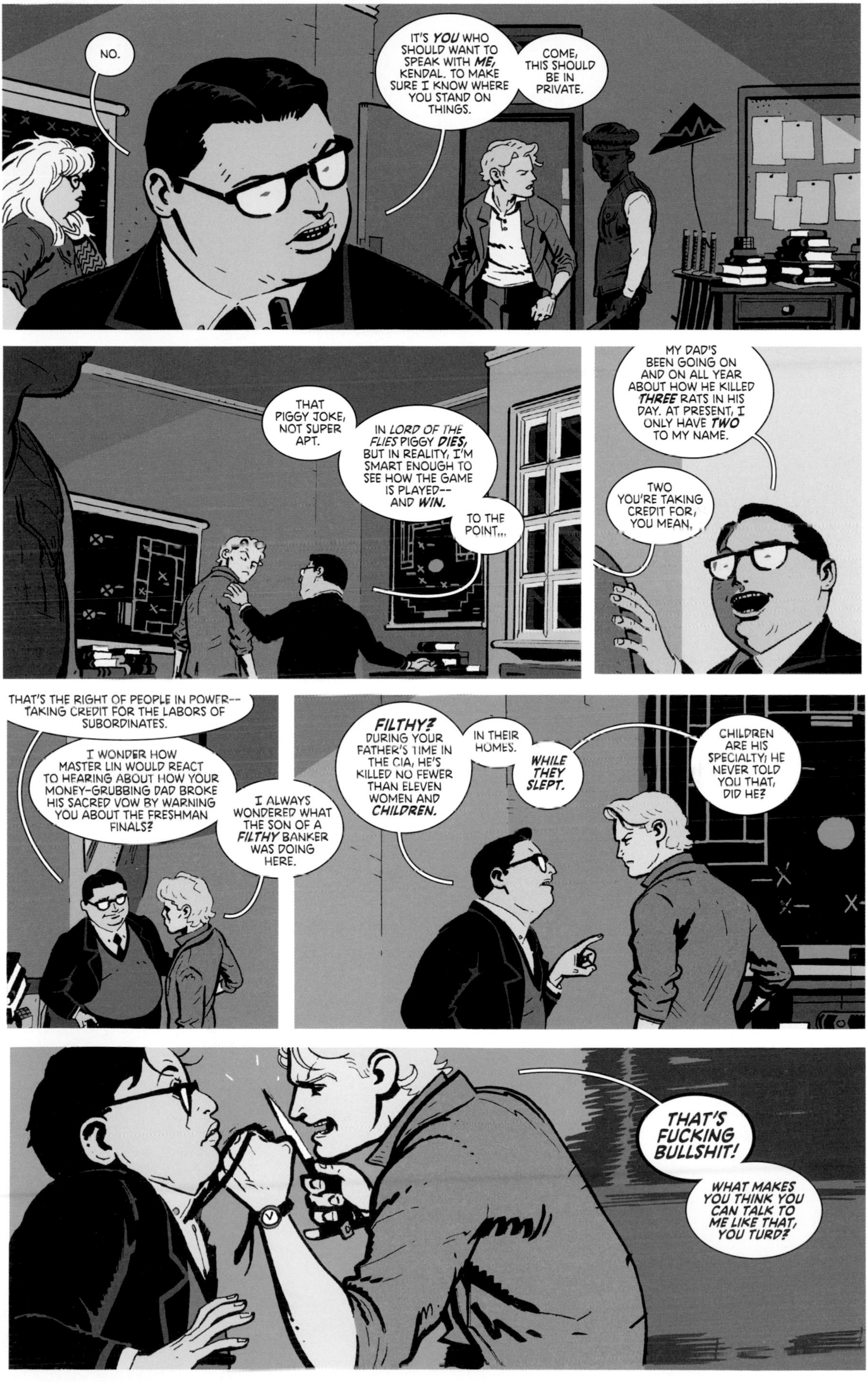
NO.
IT'S YOU WHO SHOULD WANT TO SPEAK WITH ME, KENDAL. TO MAKE SURE I KNOW WHERE YOU STAND ON THINGS.
COME, THIS SHOULD BE IN PRIVATE.
THAT PIGGY JOKE, NOT SUPER APT.
IN LORD OF THE FLIES PIGGY DIES, BUT IN REALITY, I'M SMART ENOUGH TO SEE HOW THE GAME IS PLAYED-- AND WIN.
TO THE POINT...
MY DAD'S BEEN GOING ON AND ON ALL YEAR ABOUT HOW HE KILLED THREE RATS IN HIS DAY. AT PRESENT, I ONLY HAVE TWO TO MY NAME.
TWO YOU'RE TAKING CREDIT FOR, YOU MEAN.
THAT'S THE RIGHT OF PEOPLE IN POWER-- TAKING CREDIT FOR THE LABORS OF SUBORDINATES.
I WONDER HOW MASTER LIN WOULD REACT TO HEARING ABOUT HOW YOUR MONEY-GRUBBING DAD BROKE HIS SACRED VOW BY WARNING YOU ABOUT THE FRESHMAN FINALS?
I ALWAYS WONDERED WHAT THE SON OF A FILTHY BANKER WAS DOING HERE.
FILTHY? DURING YOUR FATHER'S TIME IN THE CIA, HE'S KILLED NO FEWER THAN ELEVEN WOMEN AND CHILDREN.
IN THEIR HOMES.
WHILE THEY SLEPT.
CHILDREN ARE HIS SPECIALTY; HE NEVER TOLD YOU THAT, DID HE?
THAT'S FUCKING BULLSHIT!
WHAT MAKES YOU THINK YOU CAN TALK TO ME LIKE THAT, YOU TURD?

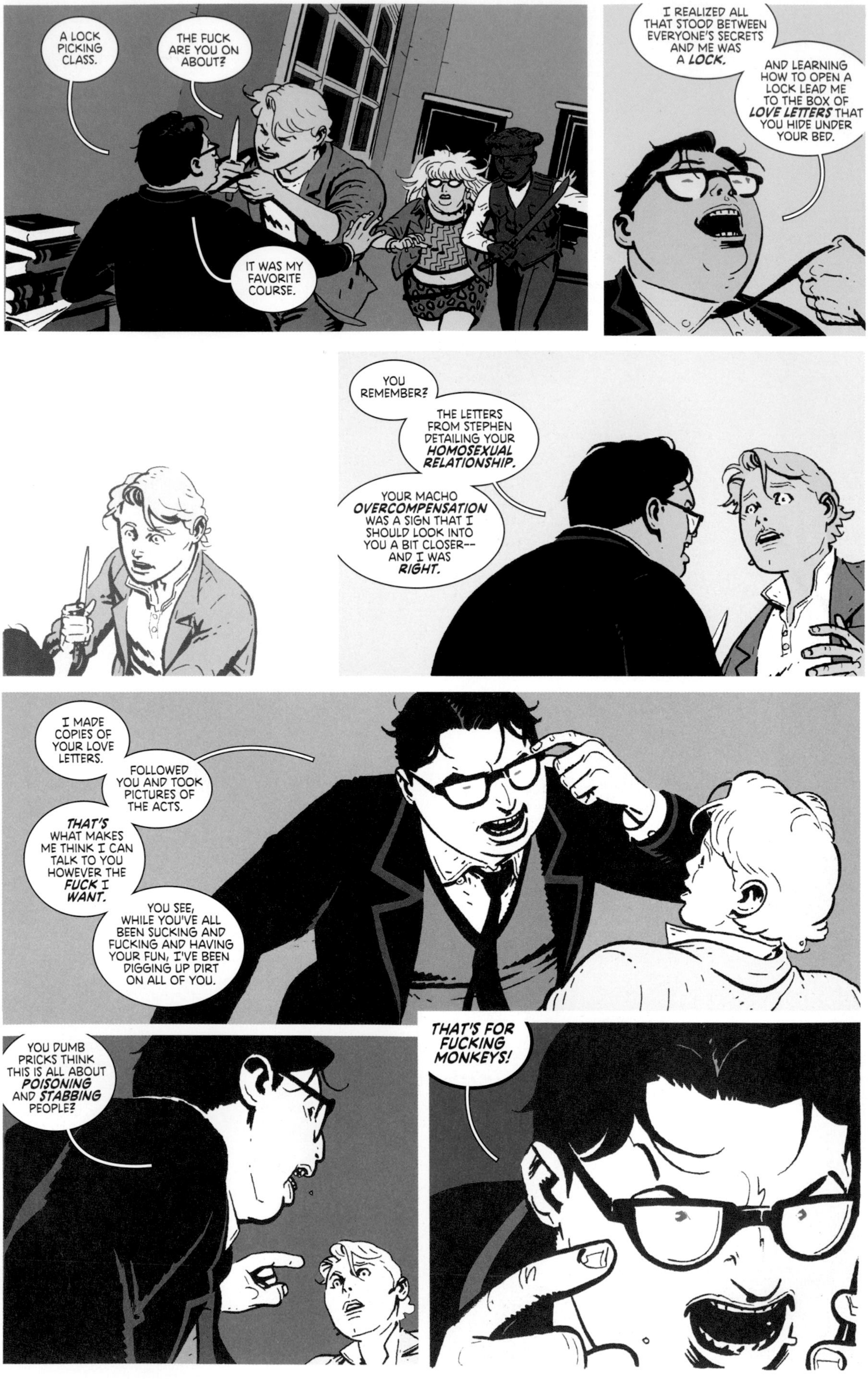
A LOCK PICKING CLASS.
THE FUCK ARE YOU ON ABOUT?
IT WAS MY FAVORITE COURSE.
I REALIZED ALL THAT STOOD BETWEEN EVERYONE'S SECRETS AND ME WAS A LOCK.
AND LEARNING HOW TO OPEN A LOCK LEAD ME TO THE BOX OF LOVE LETTERS THAT YOU HIDE UNDER YOUR BED.
YOU REMEMBER?
THE LETTERS FROM STEPHEN DETAILING YOUR HOMOSEXUAL RELATIONSHIP.
YOUR MACHO OVERCOMPENSATION WAS A SIGN THAT I SHOULD LOOK INTO YOU A BIT CLOSER-- AND I WAS RIGHT.
I MADE COPIES OF YOUR LOVE LETTERS.
FOLLOWED YOU AND TOOK PICTURES OF THE ACTS.
THAT'S WHAT MAKES ME THINK I CAN TALK TO YOU HOWEVER THE FUCK I WANT.
YOU SEE, WHILE YOU'VE ALL BEEN SUCKING AND FUCKING AND HAVING YOUR FUN, I'VE BEEN DIGGING UP DIRT ON ALL OF YOU.
YOU DUMB PRICKS THINK THIS IS ALL ABOUT POISONING AND STABBING PEOPLE?
THAT'S FOR FUCKING MONKEYS!

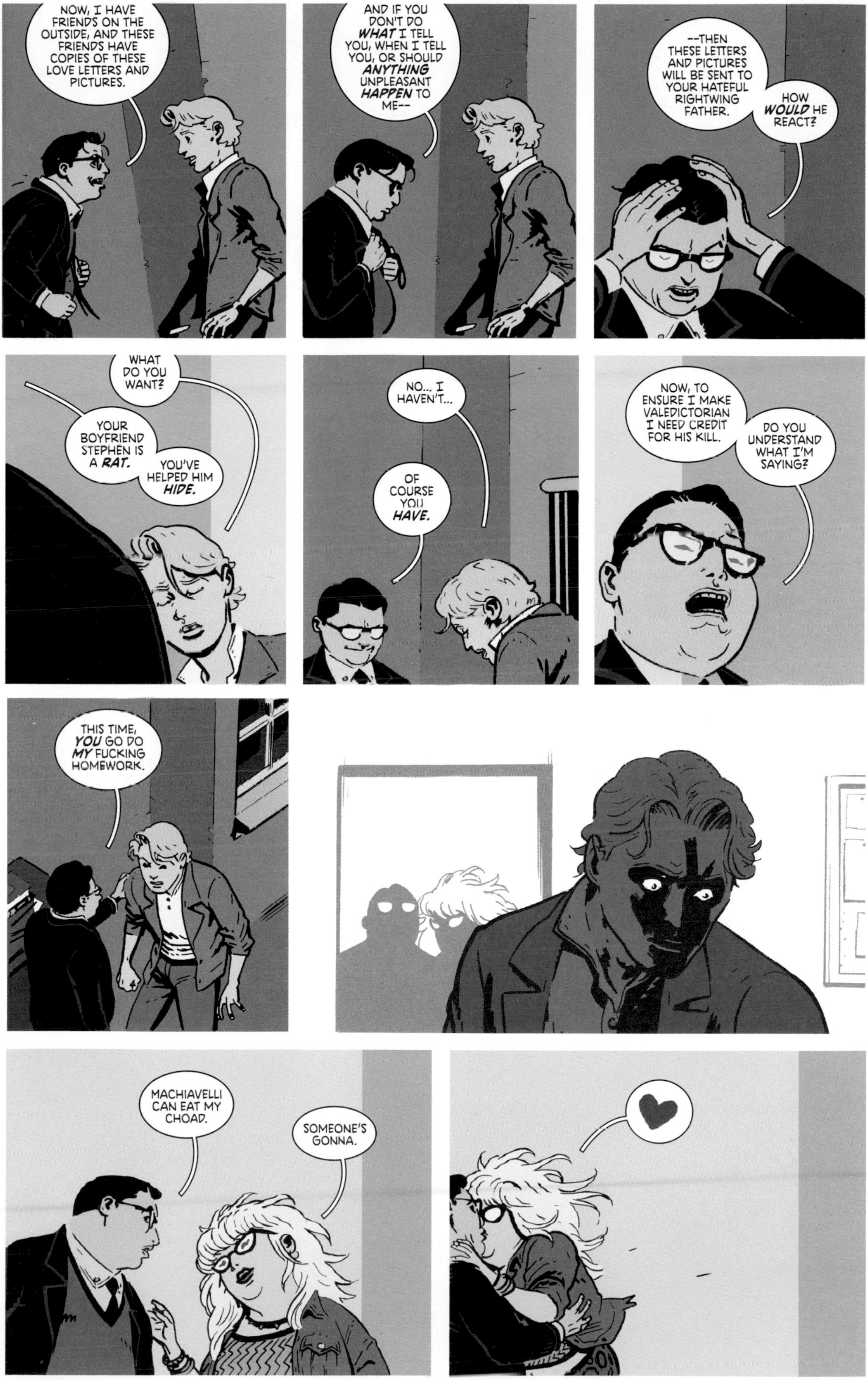
NOW, I HAVE FRIENDS ON THE OUTSIDE, AND THESE FRIENDS HAVE COPIES OF THESE LOVE LETTERS AND PICTURES.
AND IF YOU DON'T DO WHAT I TELL YOU, WHEN I TELL YOU, OR SHOULD ANYTHING UNPLEASANT HAPPEN TO ME--
--THEN THESE LETTERS AND PICTURES WILL BE SENT TO YOUR HATEFUL RIGHTWING FATHER.
HOW WOULD HE REACT?
WHAT DO YOU WANT?
YOUR BOYFRIEND STEPHEN IS A RAT.
YOU'VE HELPED HIM HIDE.
NO... I HAVEN'T...
OF COURSE YOU HAVE.
NOW, TO ENSURE I MAKE VALEDICTORIAN I NEED CREDIT FOR HIS KILL.
DO YOU UNDERSTAND WHAT I'M SAYING?
THIS TIME, YOU GO DO MY FUCKING HOMEWORK.
MACHIAVELLI CAN EAT MY CHOAD.
SOMEONE'S GONNA.

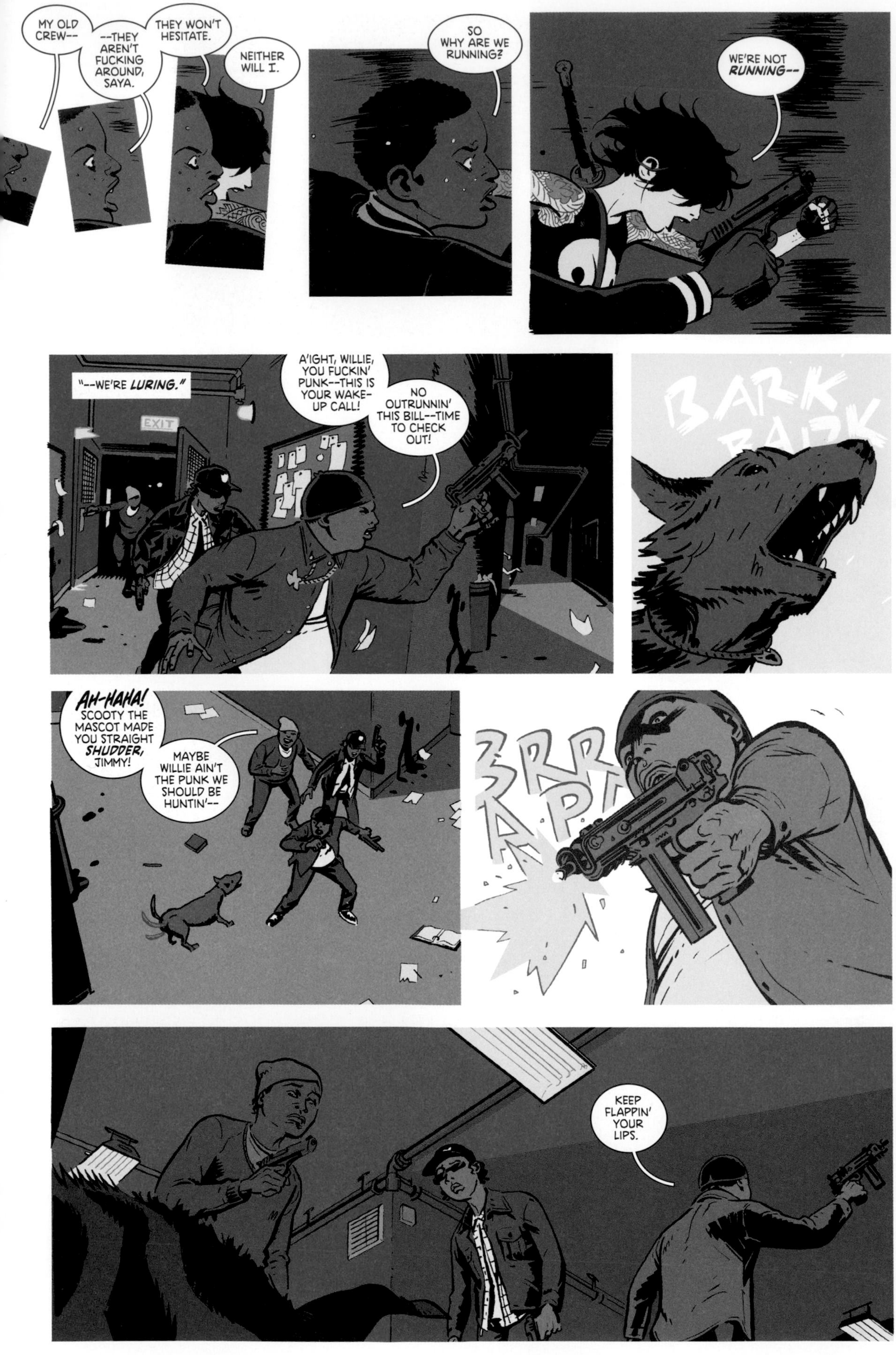
MY OLD CREW--
--THEY AREN'T FUCKING AROUND, SAYA.
THEY WON'T HESITATE.
NEITHER WILL I.
SO WHY ARE WE RUNNING?
WE'RE NOT RUNNING--
"--WE'RE LURING."
EXIT
A'IGHT, WILLIE, YOU FUCKIN' PUNK--THIS IS YOUR WAKE-UP CALL!
NO OUTRUNNIN' THIS BILL--TIME TO CHECK OUT!
BARK
AH-HAHA! SCOOTY THE MASCOT MADE YOU STRAIGHT SHUDDER, JIMMY!
MAYBE WILLIE AIN'T THE PUNK WE SHOULD BE HUNTIN'--
KEEP FLAPPIN' YOUR LIPS.

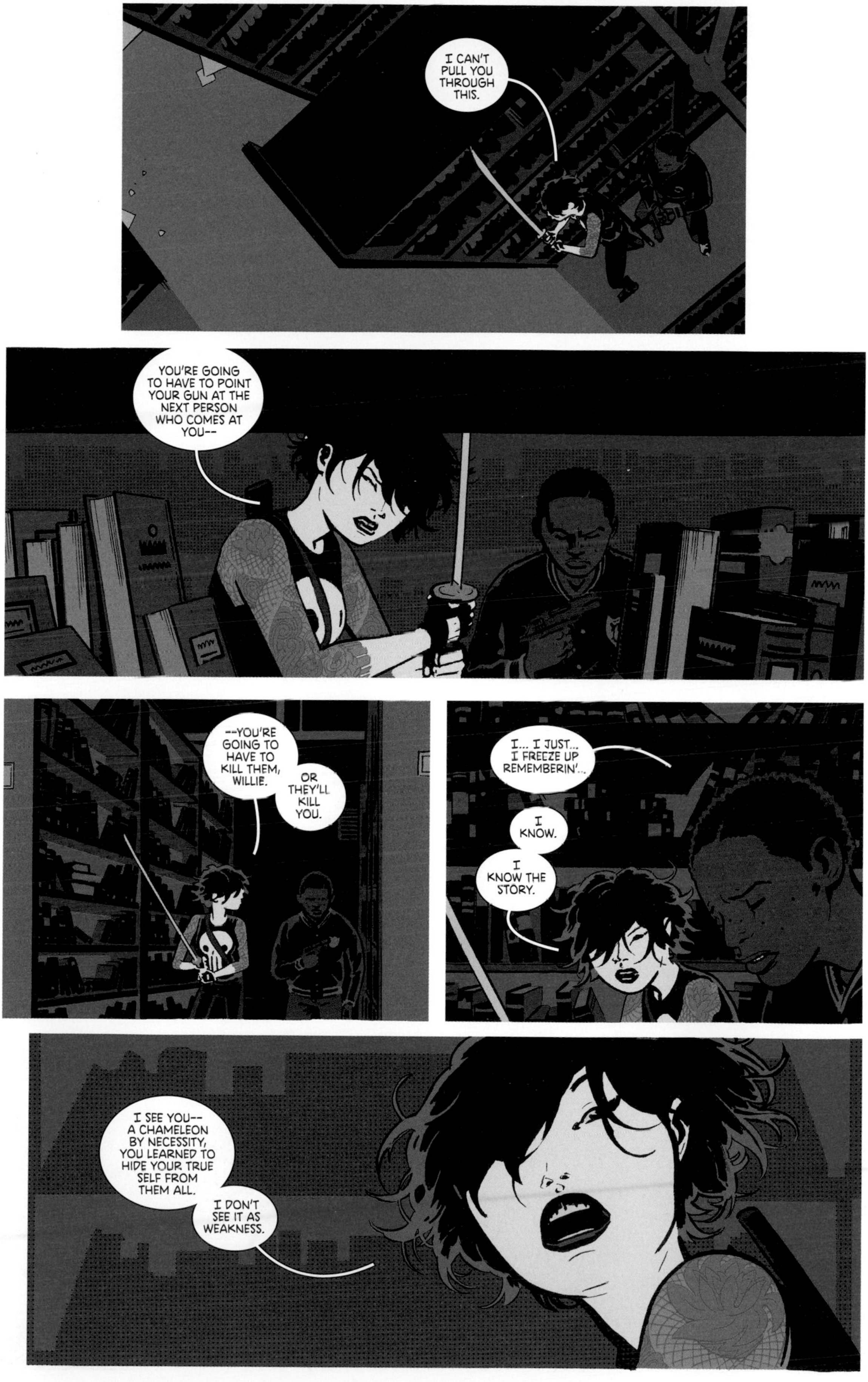
I CAN'T PULL YOU THROUGH THIS.
YOU'RE GOING TO HAVE TO POINT YOUR GUN AT THE NEXT PERSON WHO COMES AT YOU--
--YOU'RE GOING TO HAVE TO KILL THEM, WILLIE.
OR THEY'LL KILL YOU.
I... I JUST... I FREEZE UP REMEMBERIN'...
I KNOW.
I KNOW THE STORY.
I SEE YOU-- A CHAMELEON BY NECESSITY, YOU LEARNED TO HIDE YOUR TRUE SELF FROM THEM ALL.
I DON'T SEE IT AS WEAKNESS.

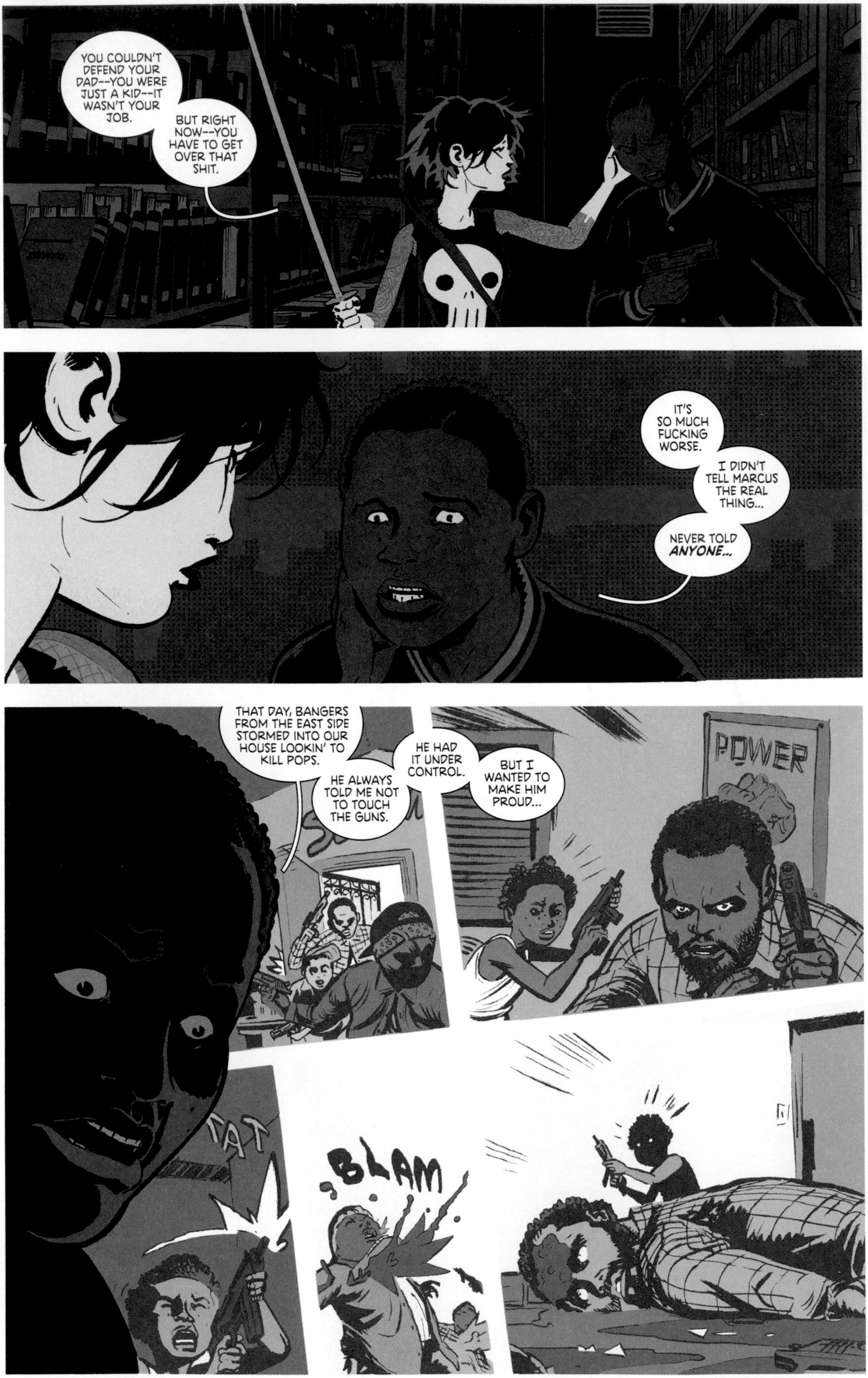

YOU COULDN'T DEFEND YOUR DAD--YOU WERE JUST A KID--IT WASN'T YOUR JOB.
BUT RIGHT NOW--YOU HAVE TO GET OVER THAT SHIT.
IT'S SO MUCH FUCKING WORSE.
I DIDN'T TELL MARCUS THE REAL THING...
NEVER TOLD *ANYONE...*
THAT DAY, BANGERS FROM THE EAST SIDE STORMED INTO OUR HOUSE LOOKIN' TO KILL POPS.
HE ALWAYS TOLD ME NOT TO TOUCH THE GUNS.
HE HAD IT UNDER CONTROL.
BUT I WANTED TO MAKE HIM PROUD...
POWER
TAT
BLAM

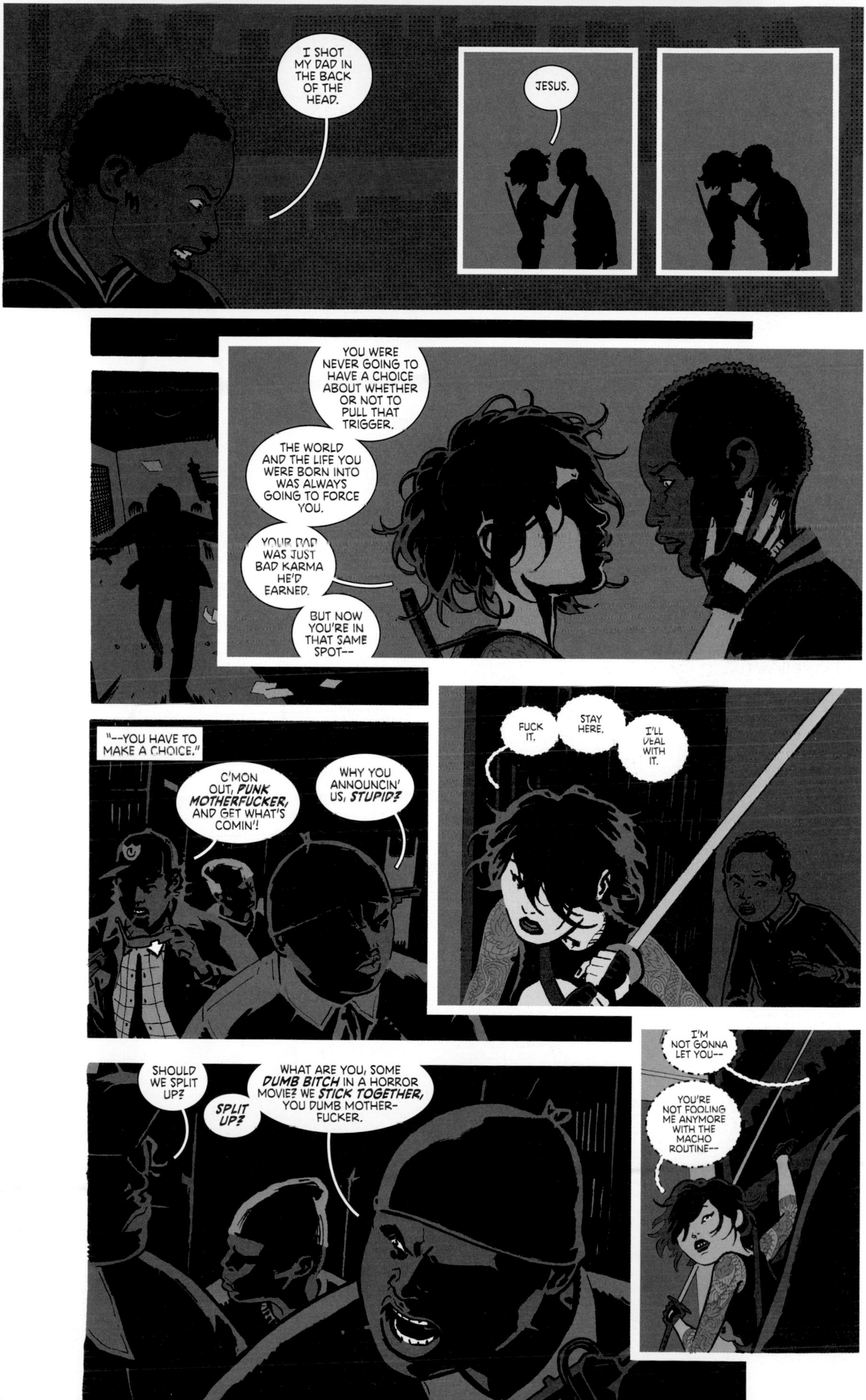
I SHOT MY DAD IN THE BACK OF THE HEAD.
JESUS.
YOU WERE NEVER GOING TO HAVE A CHOICE ABOUT WHETHER OR NOT TO PULL THAT TRIGGER.
THE WORLD AND THE LIFE YOU WERE BORN INTO WAS ALWAYS GOING TO FORCE YOU.
YOUR DAD WAS JUST BAD KARMA HE'D EARNED.
BUT NOW YOU'RE IN THAT SAME SPOT--
"--YOU HAVE TO MAKE A CHOICE."
C'MON OUT, PUNK MOTHERFUCKER, AND GET WHAT'S COMIN'!
WHY YOU ANNOUNCIN' US, STUPID?
FUCK IT.
STAY HERE.
I'LL DEAL WITH IT.
SHOULD WE SPLIT UP?
SPLIT UP?
WHAT ARE YOU, SOME DUMB BITCH IN A HORROR MOVIE? WE STICK TOGETHER, YOU DUMB MOTHER-FUCKER.
I'M NOT GONNA LET YOU--
YOU'RE NOT FOOLING ME ANYMORE WITH THE MACHO ROUTINE--

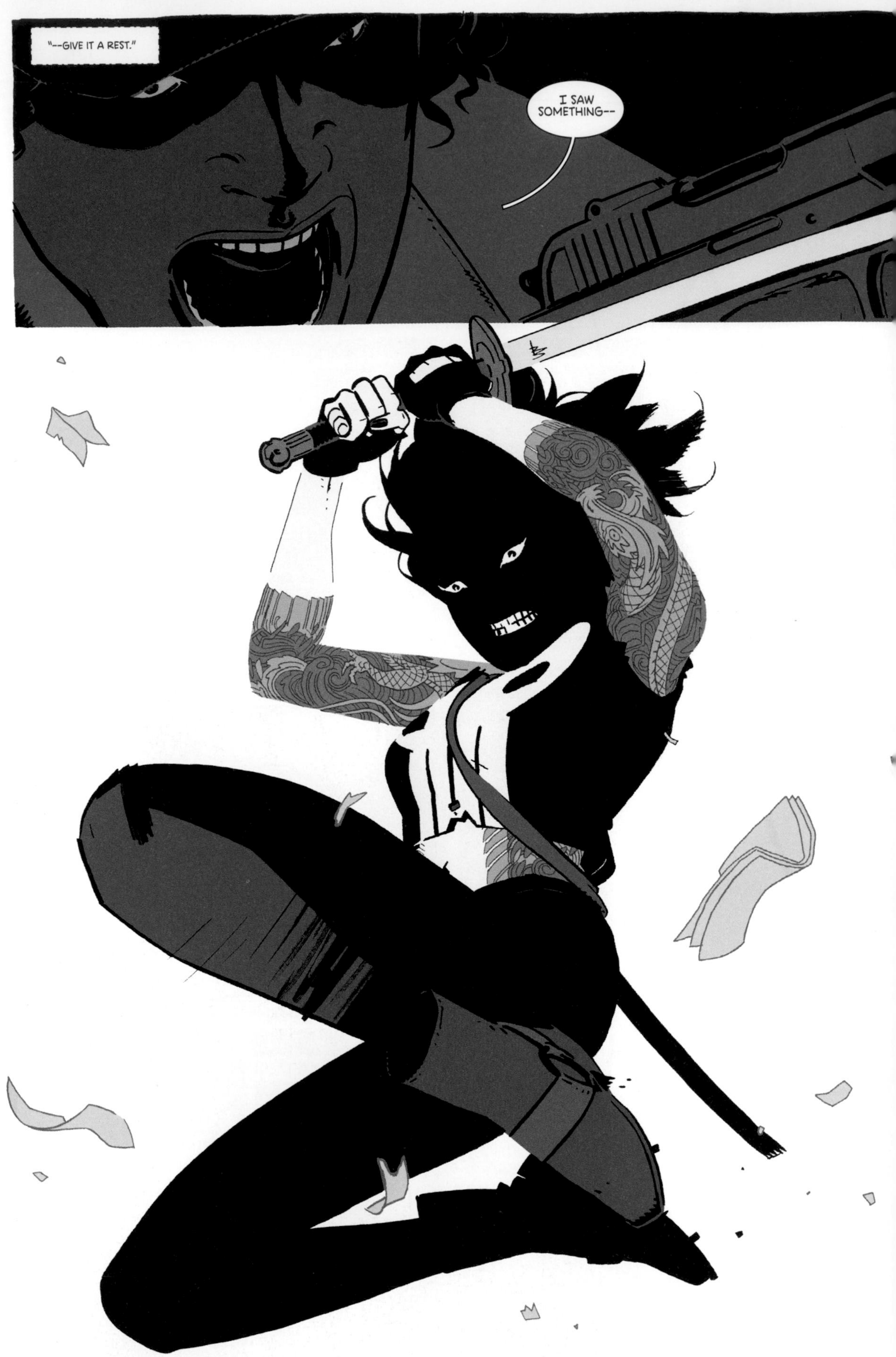
"--GIVE IT A REST."
I SAW SOMETHING--

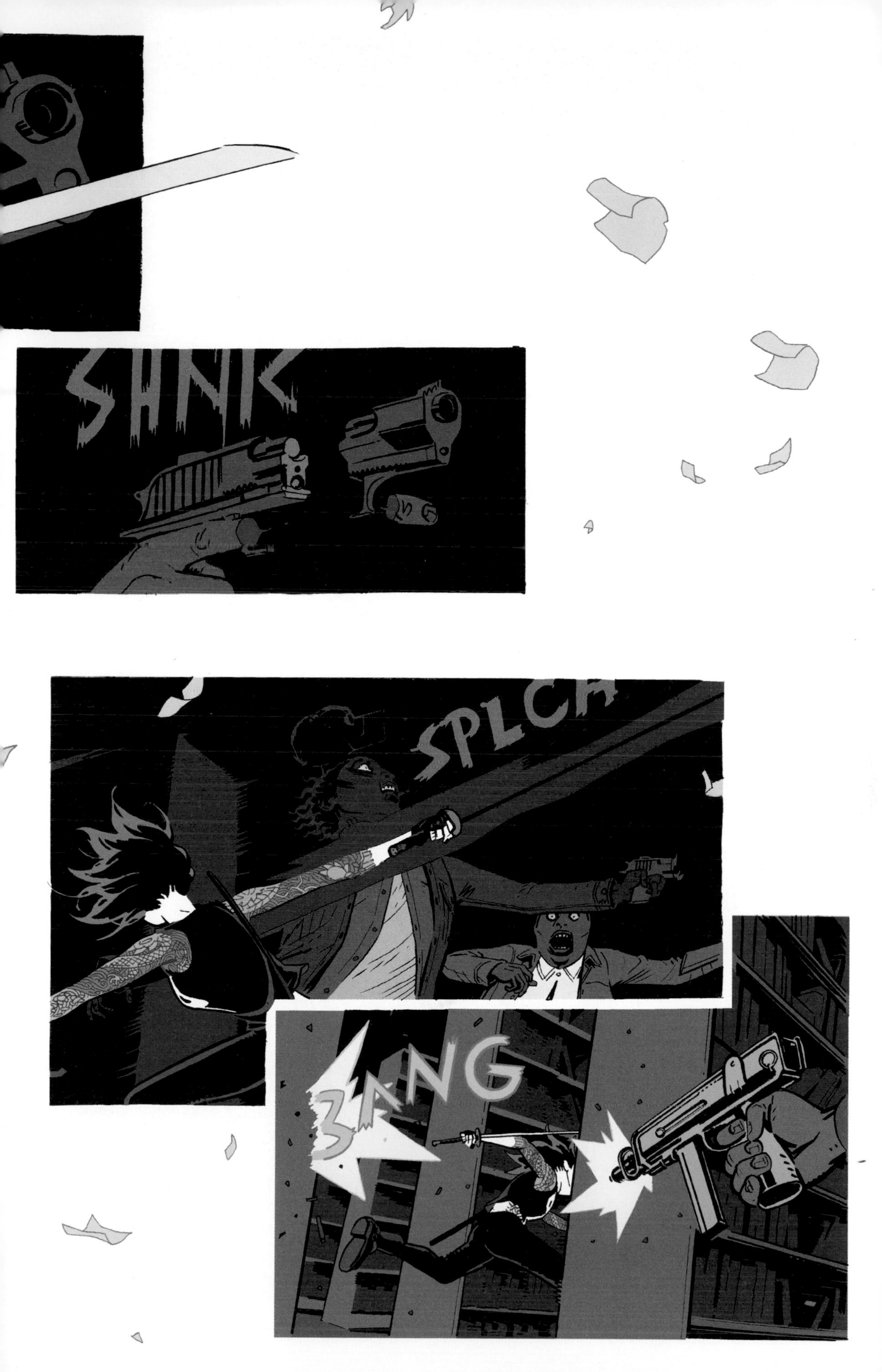
SHNK
SPLCH
BANG

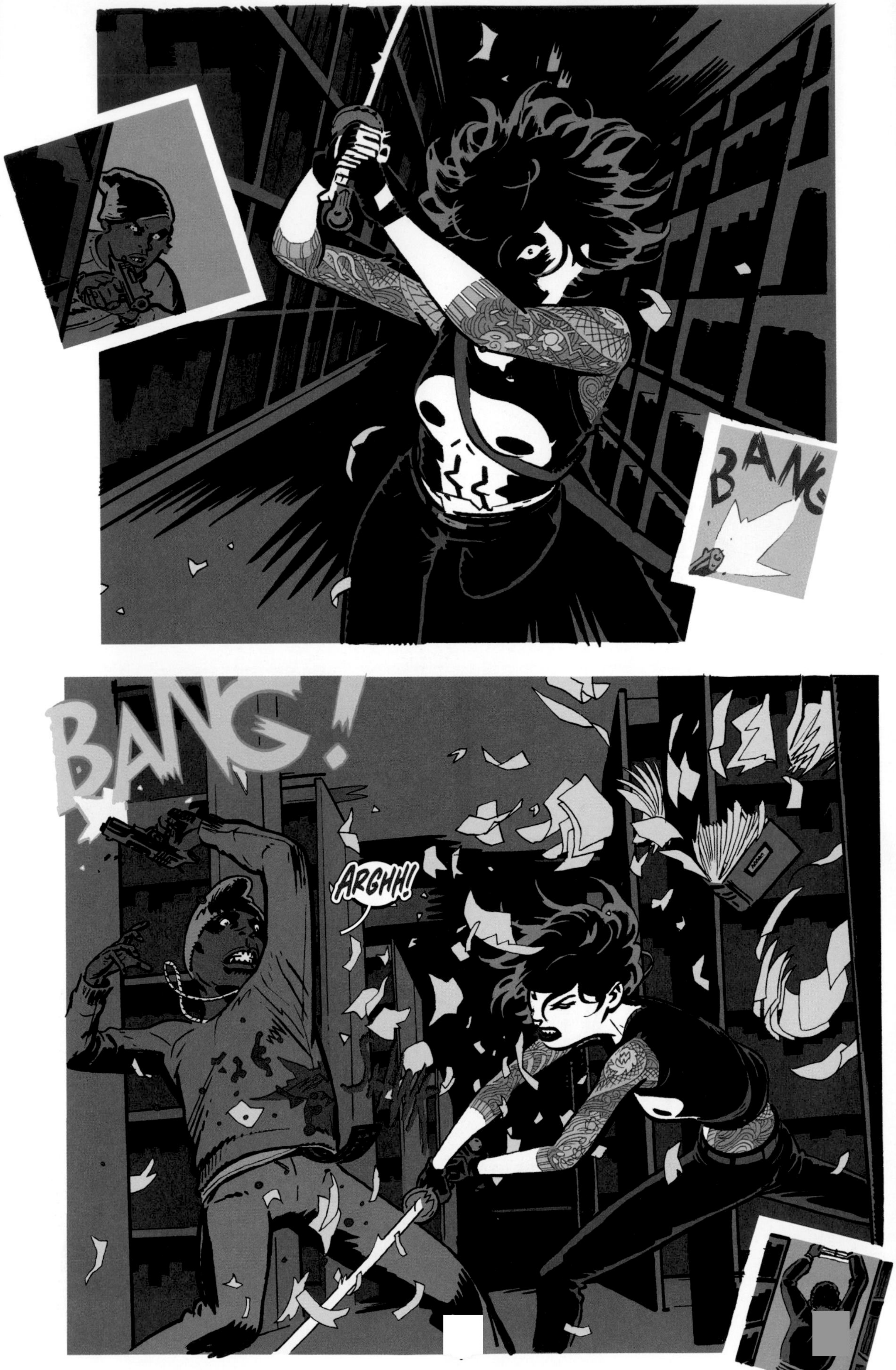
BANG
BANG!
ARGHH!

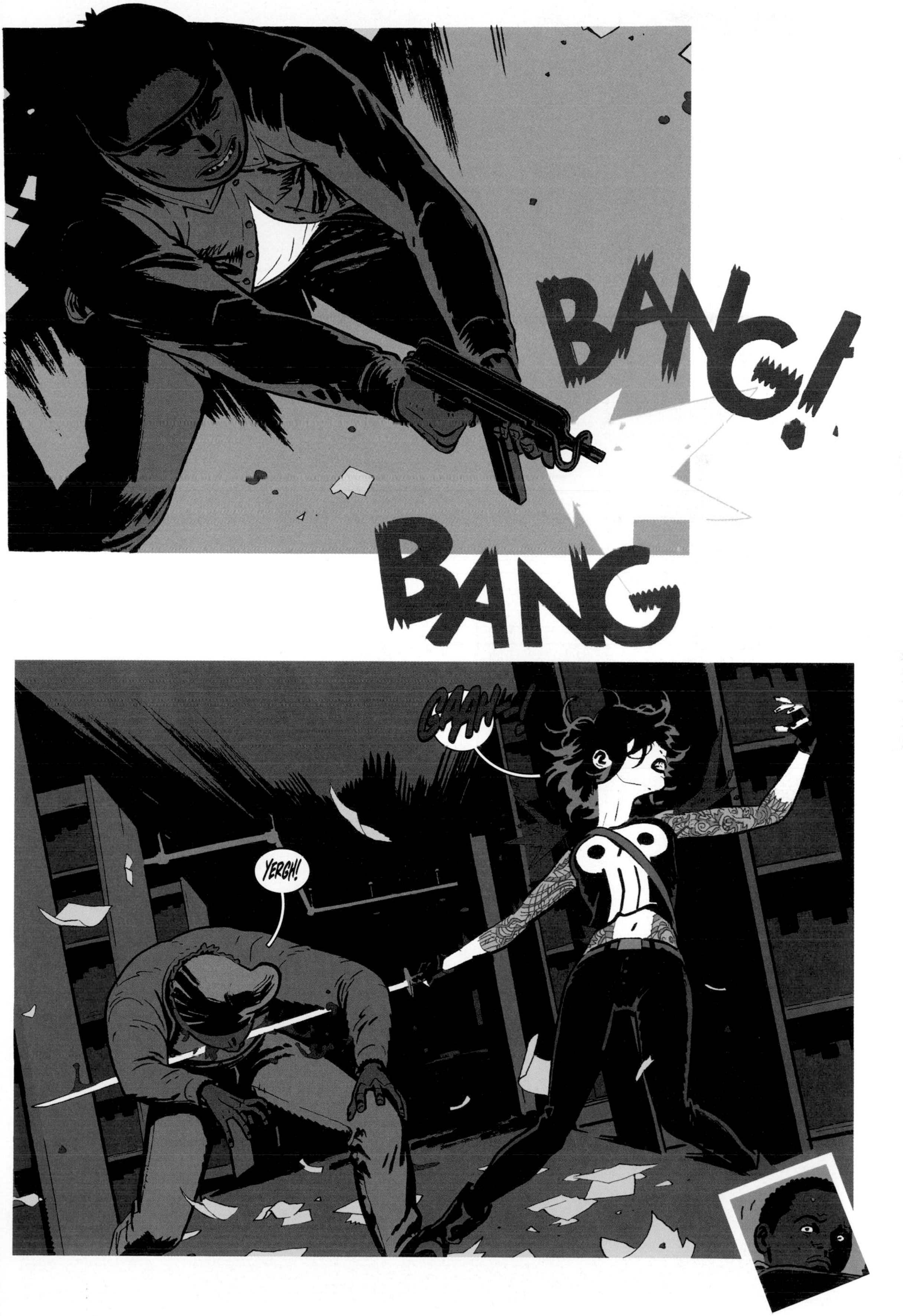
BANG!
BANG
GAAH—!
YERGH!

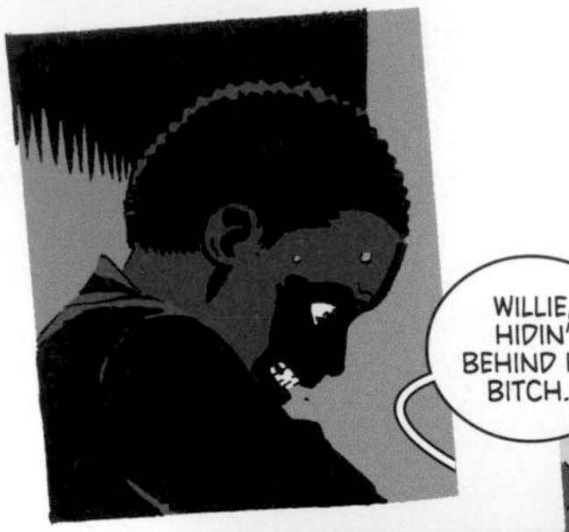
WILLIE, HIDIN' BEHIND HIS BITCH.
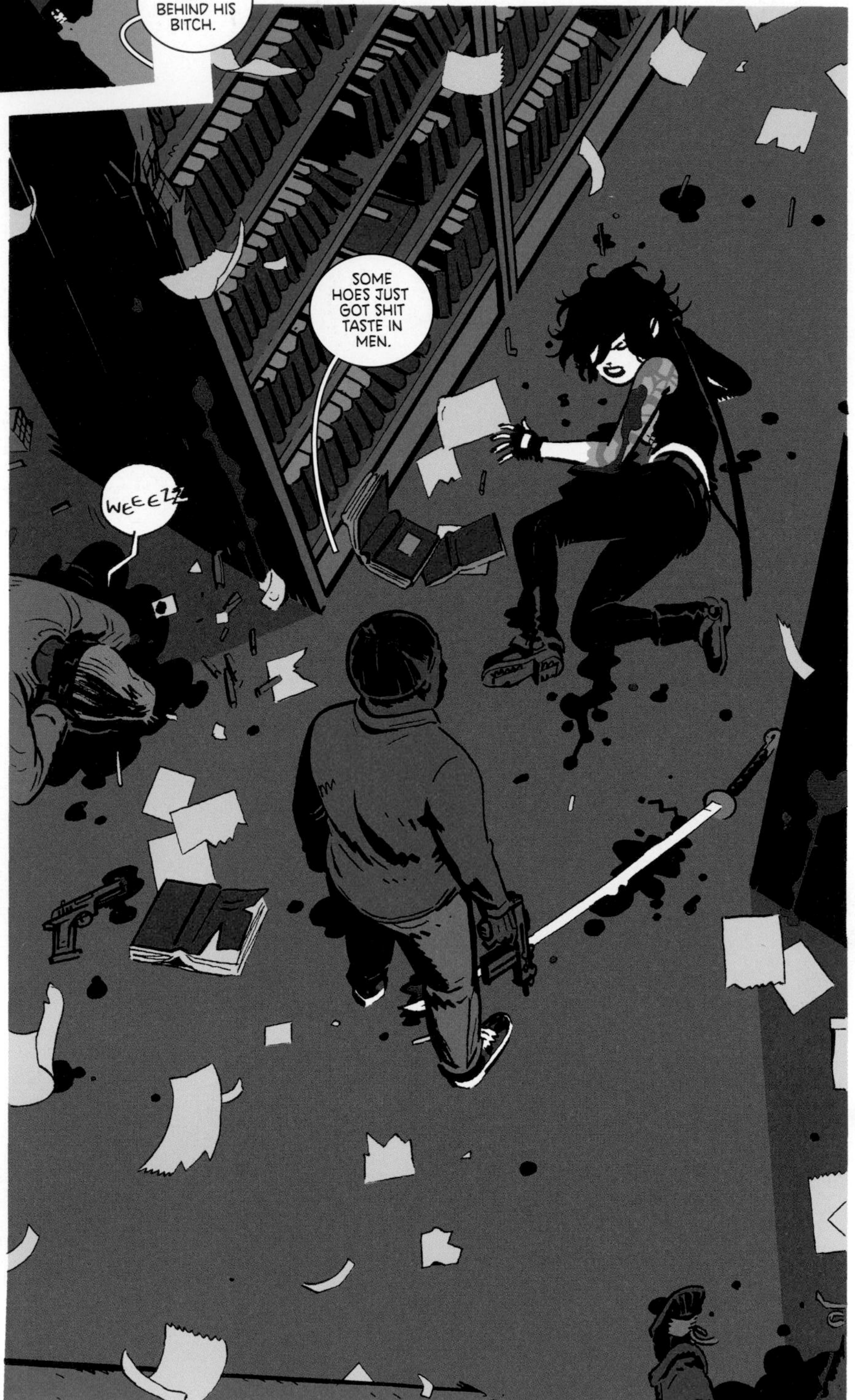
SOME HOES JUST GOT SHIT TASTE IN MEN.
WEEEZZ

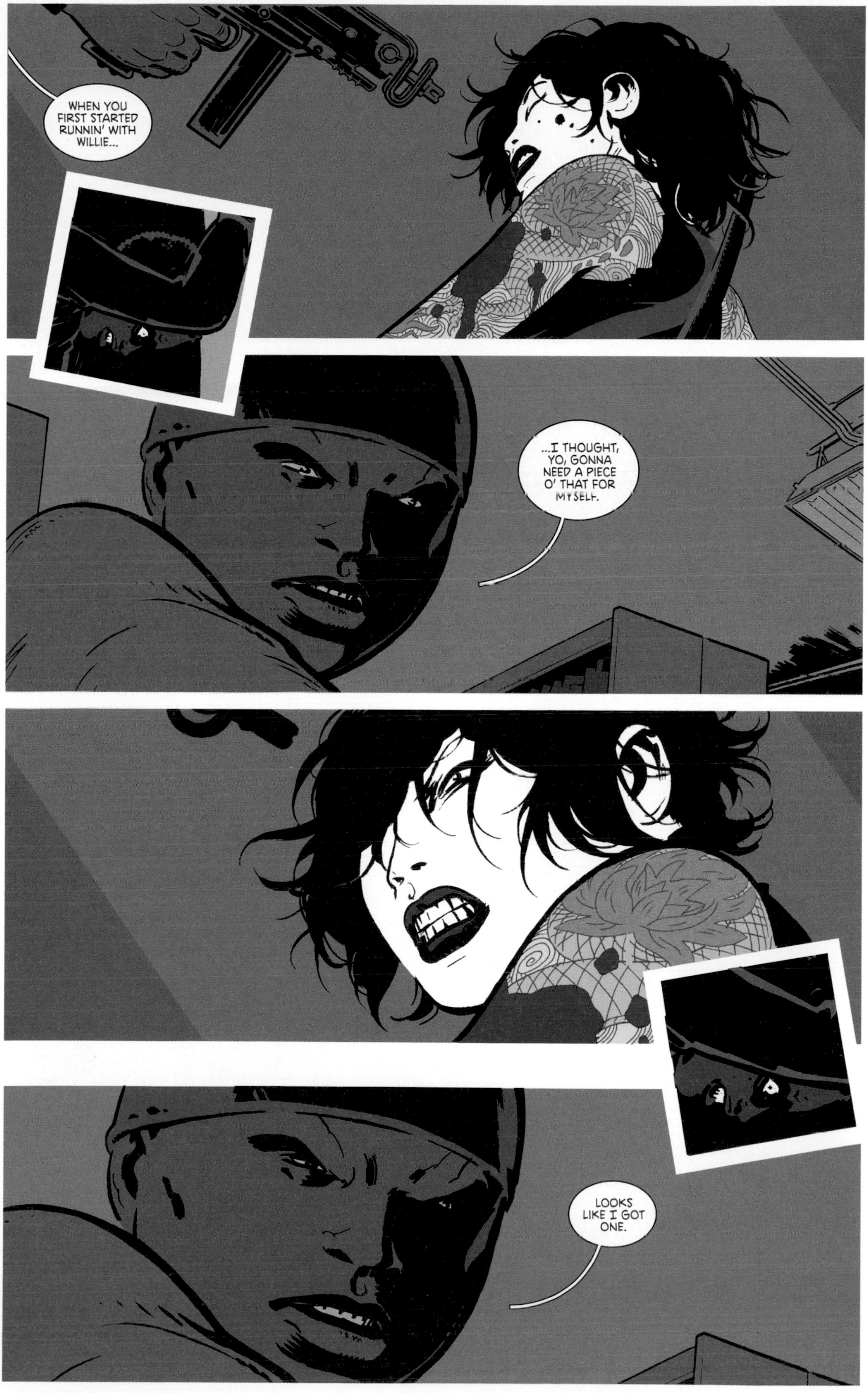
WHEN YOU FIRST STARTED RUNNIN' WITH WILLIE...
...I THOUGHT, YO, GONNA NEED A PIECE O' THAT FOR MYSELF.
LOOKS LIKE I GOT ONE.

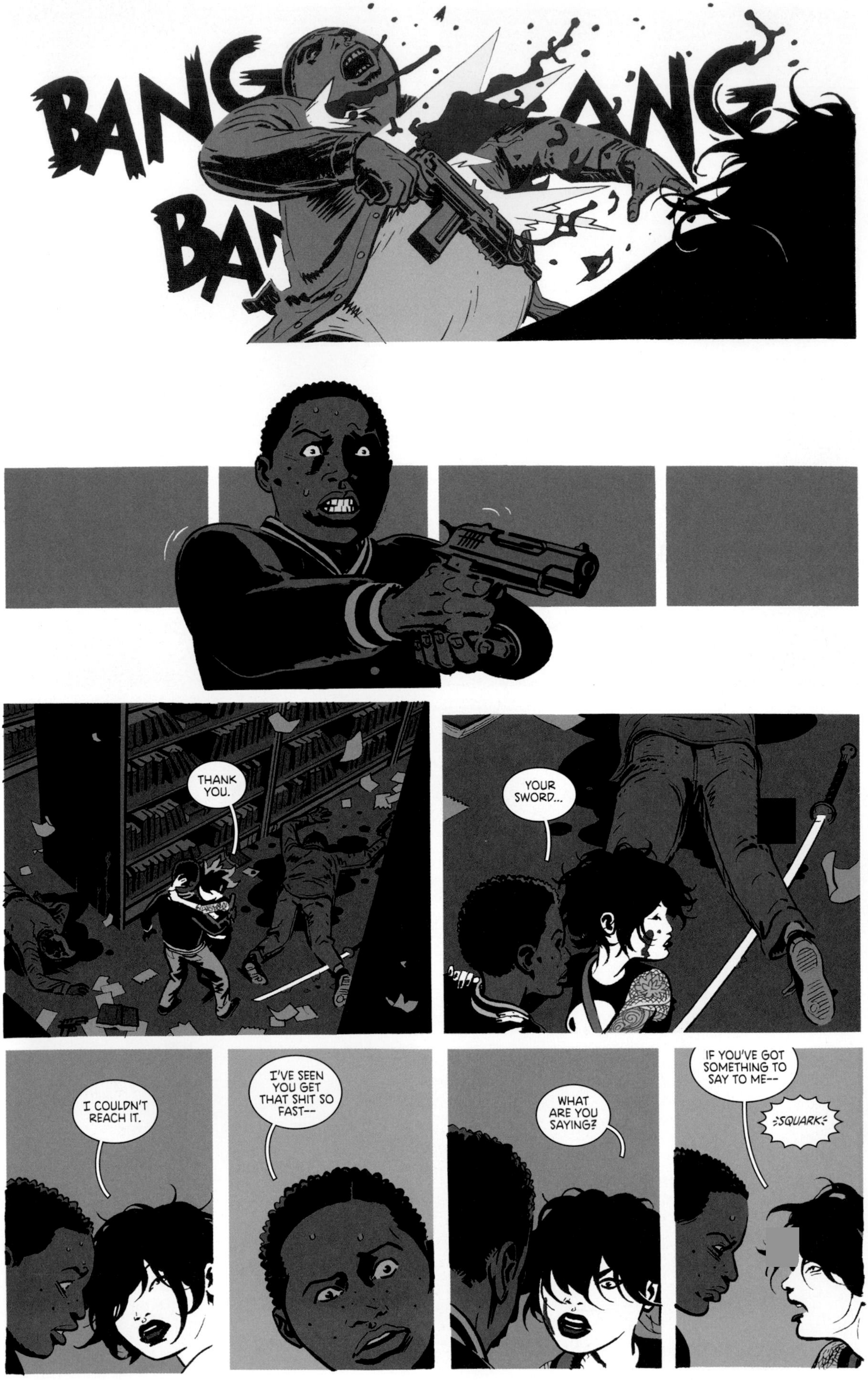
BANG
BANG
BA
THANK YOU.
YOUR SWORD...
I COULDN'T REACH IT.
I'VE SEEN YOU GET THAT SHIT SO FAST--
WHAT ARE YOU SAYING?
IF YOU'VE GOT SOMETHING TO SAY TO ME--
SQUARK

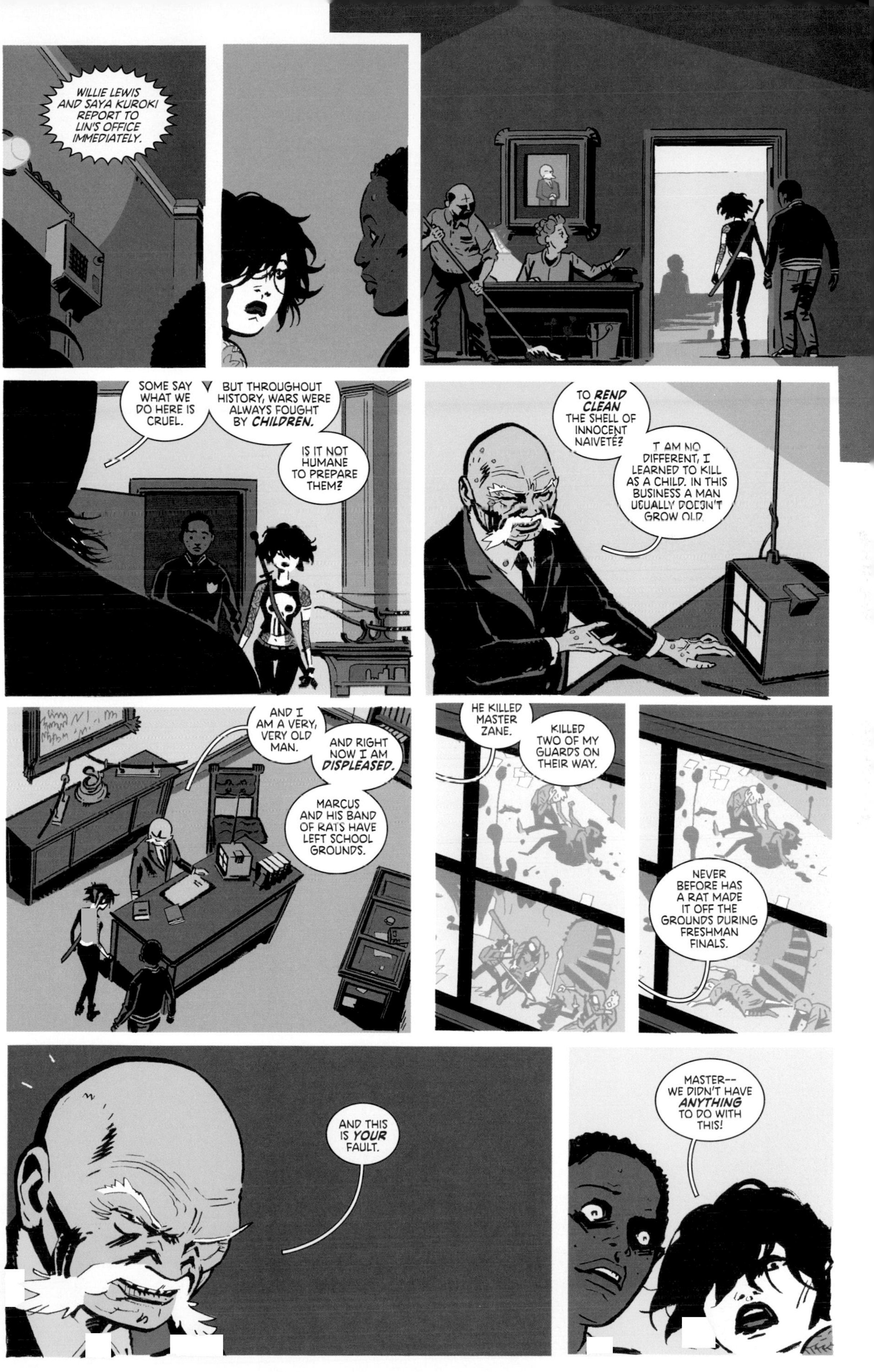
WILLIE LEWIS AND SAYA KUROKI REPORT TO LIN'S OFFICE IMMEDIATELY.
SOME SAY WHAT WE DO HERE IS CRUEL.
BUT THROUGHOUT HISTORY, WARS WERE ALWAYS FOUGHT BY CHILDREN.
IS IT NOT HUMANE TO PREPARE THEM?
TO REND CLEAN THE SHELL OF INNOCENT NAIVETÉ?
I AM NO DIFFERENT, I LEARNED TO KILL AS A CHILD. IN THIS BUSINESS A MAN USUALLY DOESN'T GROW OLD.
AND I AM A VERY, VERY OLD MAN.
AND RIGHT NOW I AM DISPLEASED.
MARCUS AND HIS BAND OF RATS HAVE LEFT SCHOOL GROUNDS.
HE KILLED MASTER ZANE.
KILLED TWO OF MY GUARDS ON THEIR WAY.
NEVER BEFORE HAS A RAT MADE IT OFF THE GROUNDS DURING FRESHMAN FINALS.
AND THIS IS YOUR FAULT.
MASTER-- WE DIDN'T HAVE ANYTHING TO DO WITH THIS!

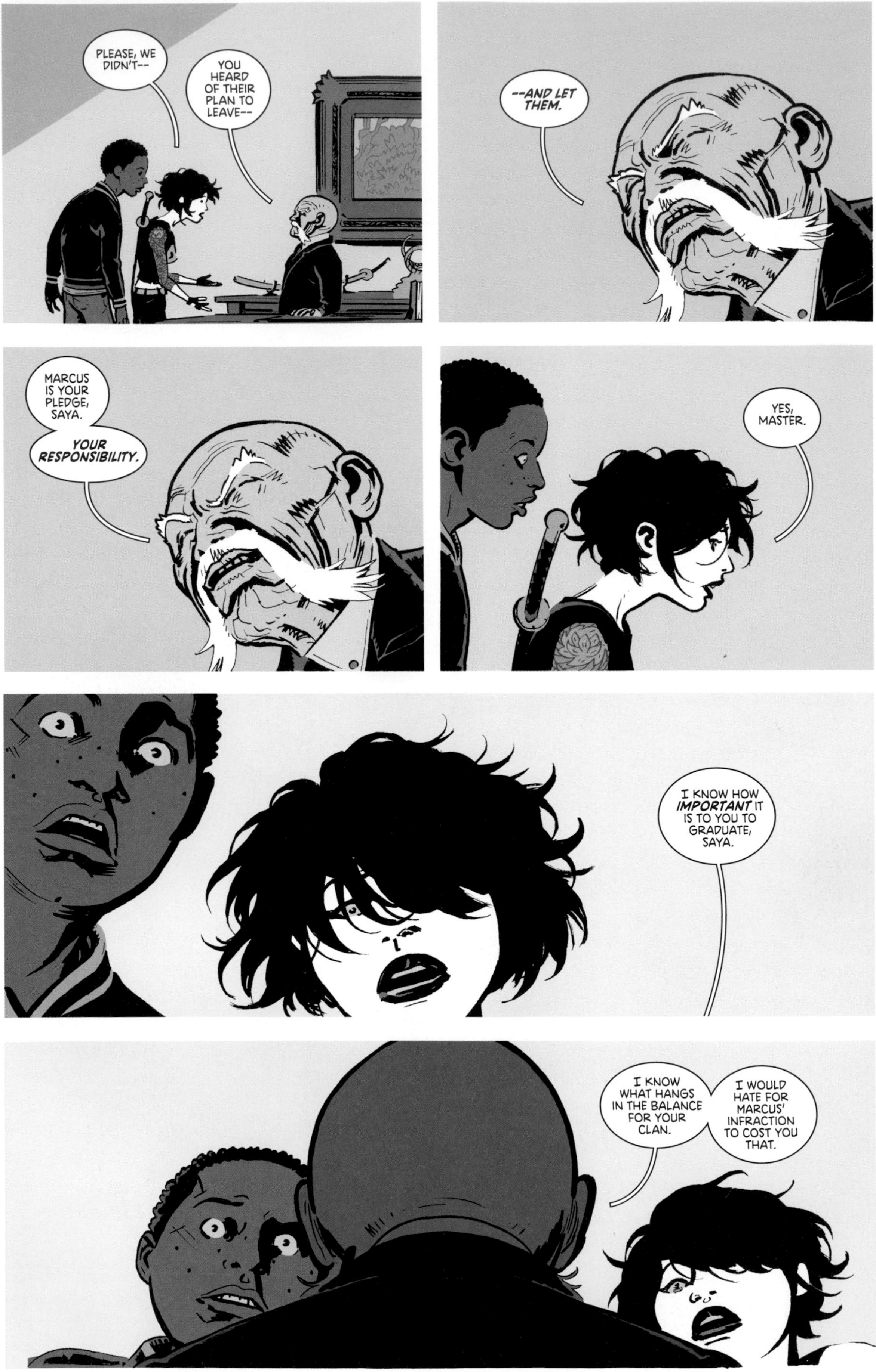
PLEASE, WE DIDN'T--
YOU HEARD OF THEIR PLAN TO LEAVE--
--AND LET THEM.
MARCUS IS YOUR PLEDGE, SAYA.
YOUR RESPONSIBILITY.
YES, MASTER.
I KNOW HOW IMPORTANT IT IS TO YOU TO GRADUATE, SAYA.
I KNOW WHAT HANGS IN THE BALANCE FOR YOUR CLAN.
I WOULD HATE FOR MARCUS' INFRACTION TO COST YOU THAT.

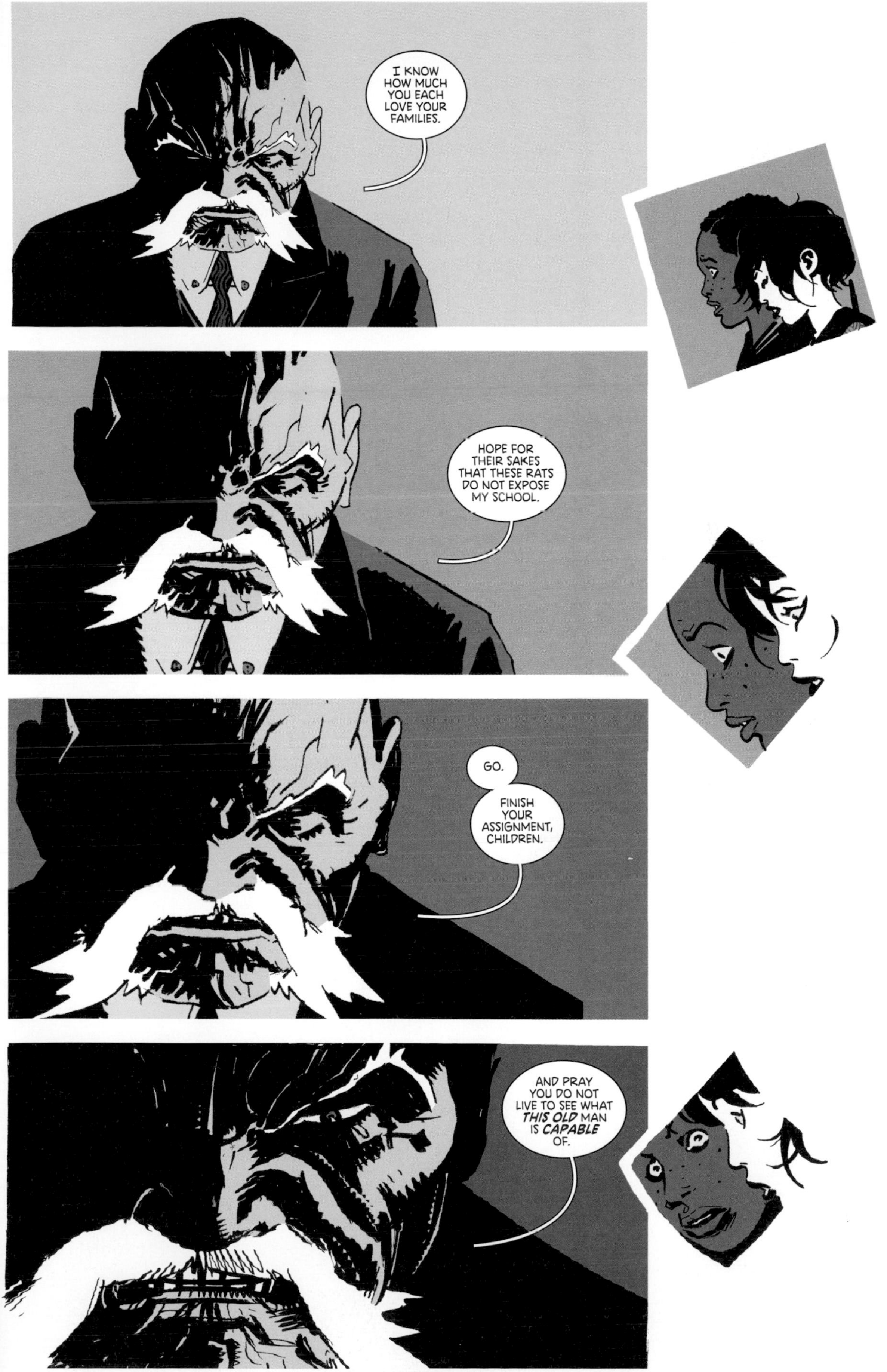
I KNOW HOW MUCH YOU EACH LOVE YOUR FAMILIES.
HOPE FOR THEIR SAKES THAT THESE RATS DO NOT EXPOSE MY SCHOOL.
GO.
FINISH YOUR ASSIGNMENT, CHILDREN.
AND PRAY YOU DO NOT LIVE TO SEE WHAT THIS OLD MAN IS CAPABLE OF.

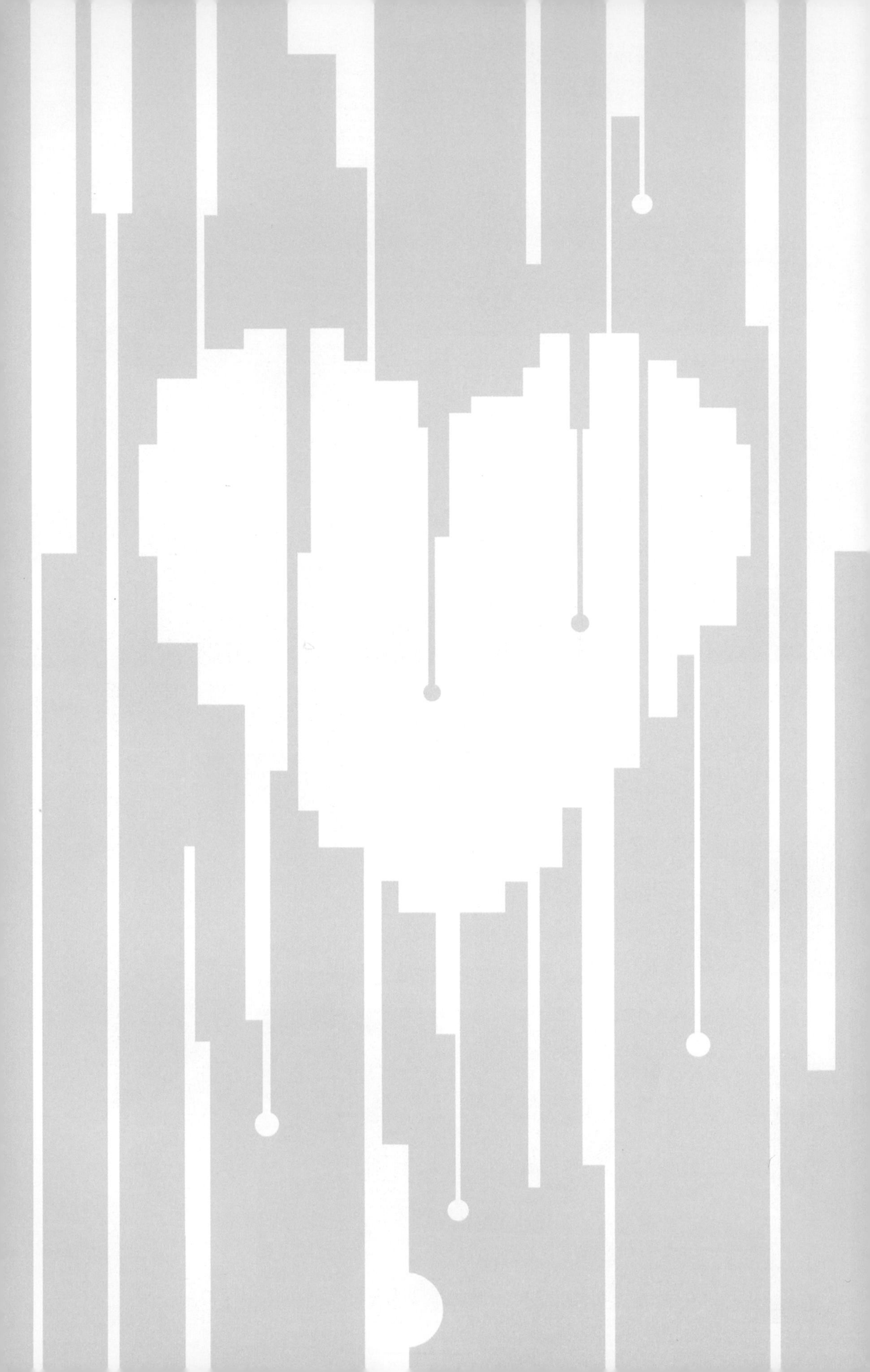

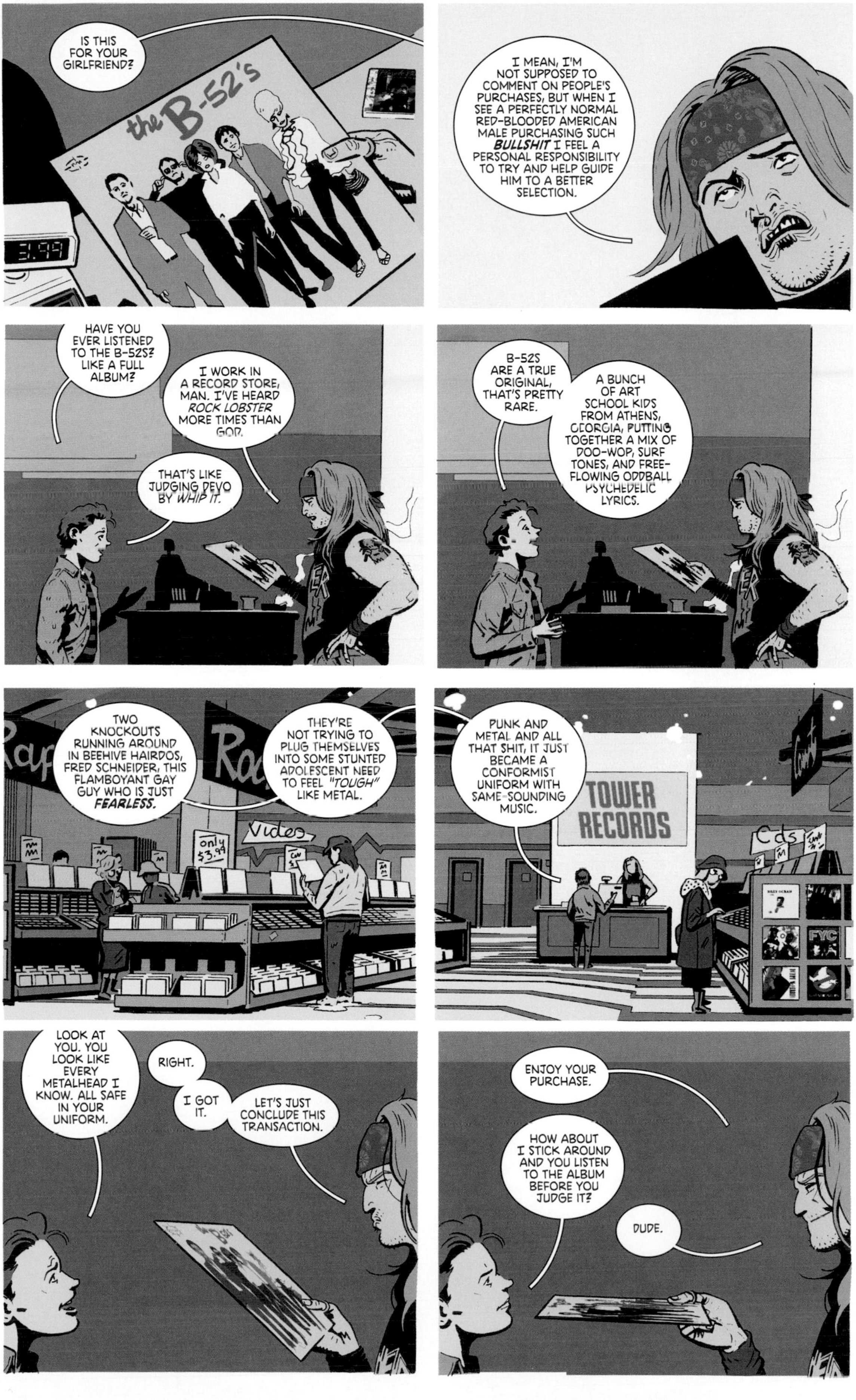
IS THIS FOR YOUR GIRLFRIEND?
the B-52's
3.99
I MEAN, I'M NOT SUPPOSED TO COMMENT ON PEOPLE'S PURCHASES, BUT WHEN I SEE A PERFECTLY NORMAL RED-BLOODED AMERICAN MALE PURCHASING SUCH **BULLSHIT** I FEEL A PERSONAL RESPONSIBILITY TO TRY AND HELP GUIDE HIM TO A BETTER SELECTION.
HAVE YOU EVER LISTENED TO THE B-52S? LIKE A FULL ALBUM?
I WORK IN A RECORD STORE, MAN. I'VE HEARD *ROCK LOBSTER* MORE TIMES THAN GOD.
THAT'S LIKE JUDGING DEVO BY *WHIP IT.*
B-52S ARE A TRUE ORIGINAL, THAT'S PRETTY RARE.
A BUNCH OF ART SCHOOL KIDS FROM ATHENS, GEORGIA, PUTTING TOGETHER A MIX OF DOO-WOP, SURF TONES, AND FREE-FLOWING ODDBALL PSYCHEDELIC LYRICS.
TWO KNOCKOUTS RUNNING AROUND IN BEEHIVE HAIRDOS, FRED SCHNEIDER, THIS FLAMBOYANT GAY GUY WHO IS JUST **FEARLESS.**
THEY'RE NOT TRYING TO PLUG THEMSELVES INTO SOME STUNTED ADOLESCENT NEED TO FEEL *"TOUGH"* LIKE METAL.
Rap
Rock
Video
only $3.99
PUNK AND METAL AND ALL THAT SHIT, IT JUST BECAME A CONFORMIST UNIFORM WITH SAME-SOUNDING MUSIC.
TOWER RECORDS
Cds
FYC
LOOK AT YOU. YOU LOOK LIKE EVERY METALHEAD I KNOW. ALL SAFE IN YOUR UNIFORM.
RIGHT.
I GOT IT.
LET'S JUST CONCLUDE THIS TRANSACTION.
ENJOY YOUR PURCHASE.
HOW ABOUT I STICK AROUND AND YOU LISTEN TO THE ALBUM BEFORE YOU JUDGE IT?
DUDE.

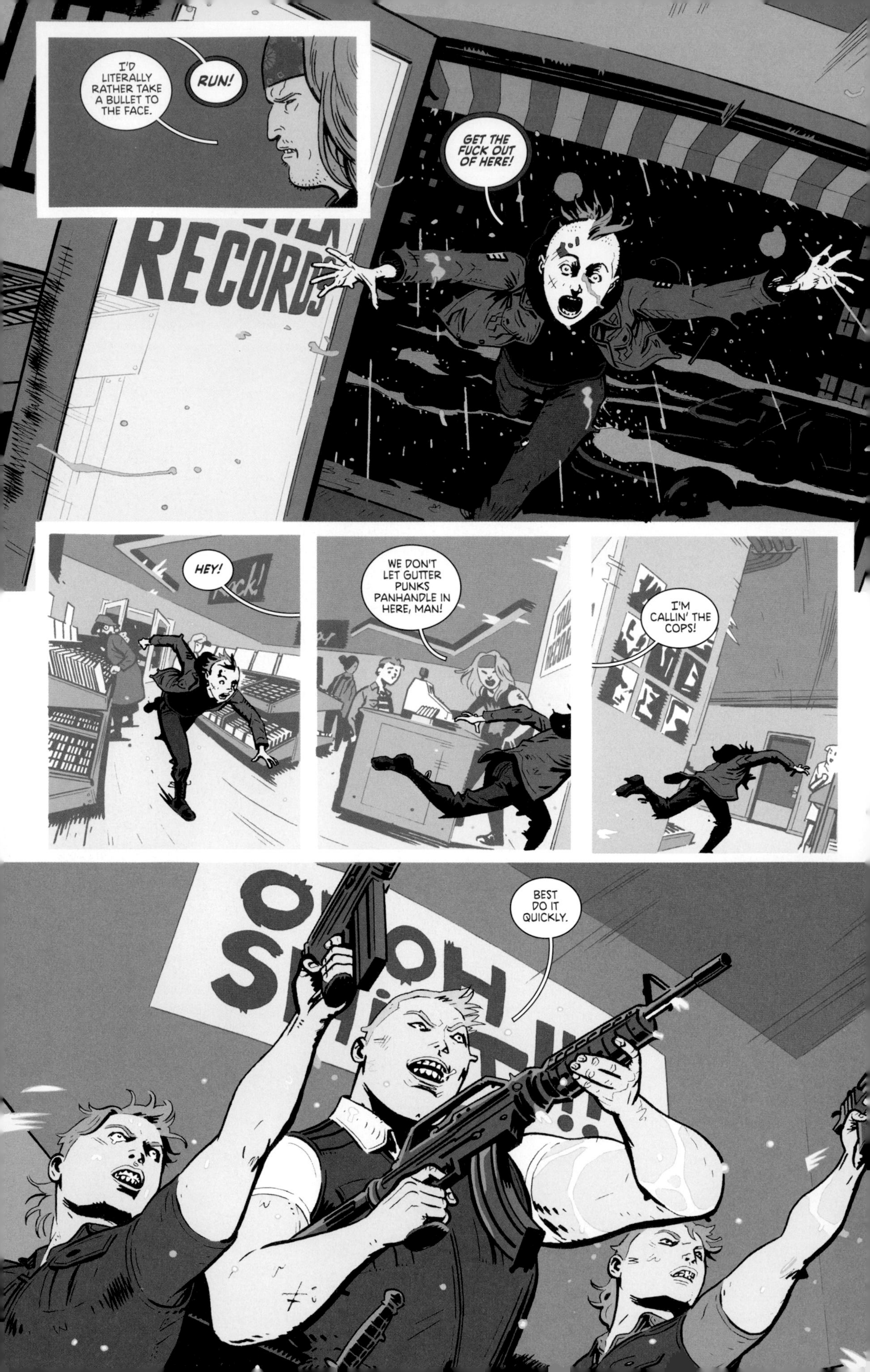
I'D LITERALLY RATHER TAKE A BULLET TO THE FACE.
RUN!
GET THE FUCK OUT OF HERE!
RECORDS
HEY!
WE DON'T LET GUTTER PUNKS PANHANDLE IN HERE, MAN!
I'M CALLIN' THE COPS!
BEST DO IT QUICKLY.

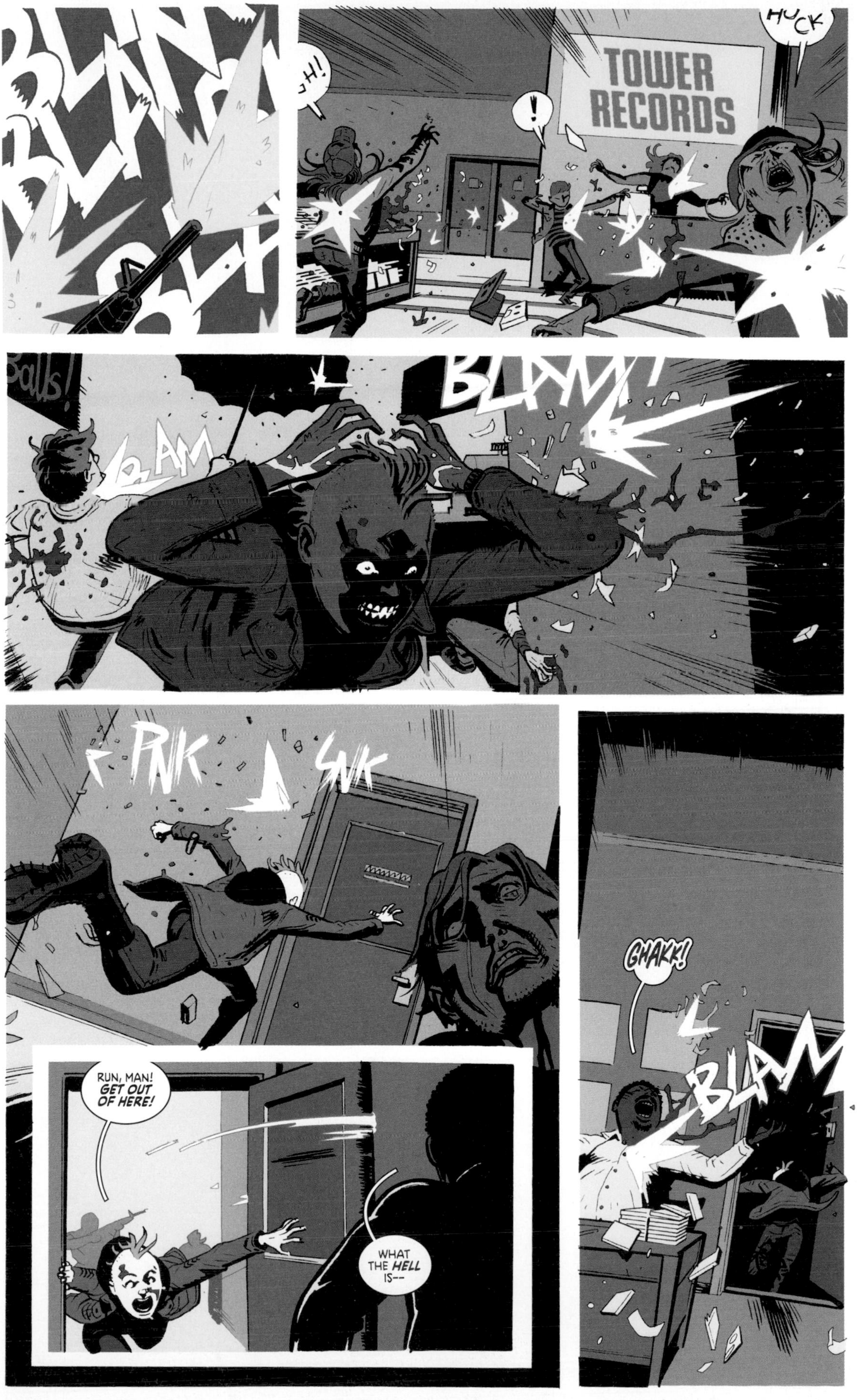

!
TOWER RECORDS
BAM
PNK
SNK
RUN, MAN! GET OUT OF HERE!
WHAT THE HELL IS--
GHAKK!

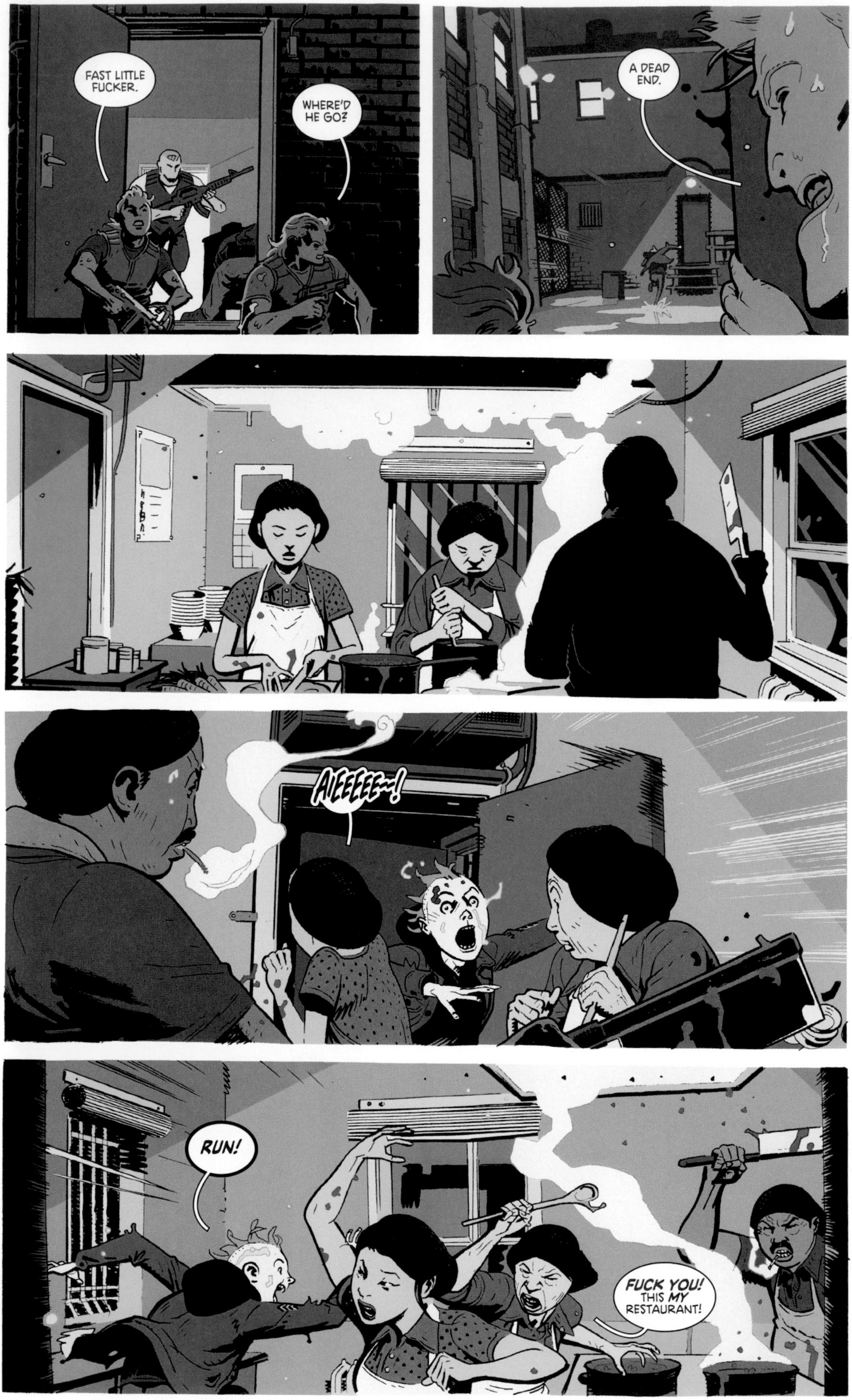
FAST LITTLE FUCKER.
WHERE'D HE GO?
A DEAD END.
AIEEEEE~!
RUN!
FUCK YOU! THIS MY RESTAURANT!

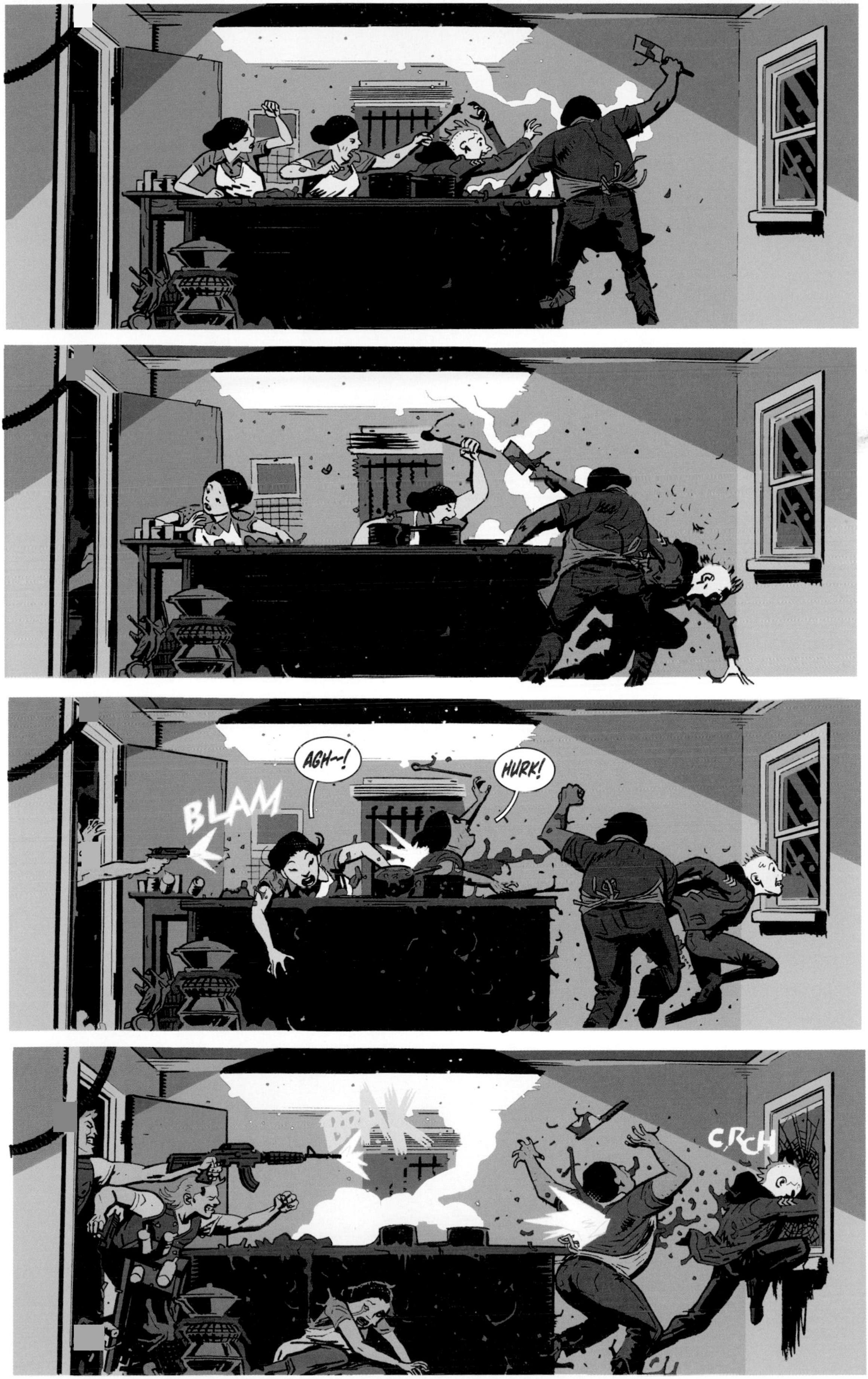
AGH~!
HURK!
BLAM
BRAK
C,RCH

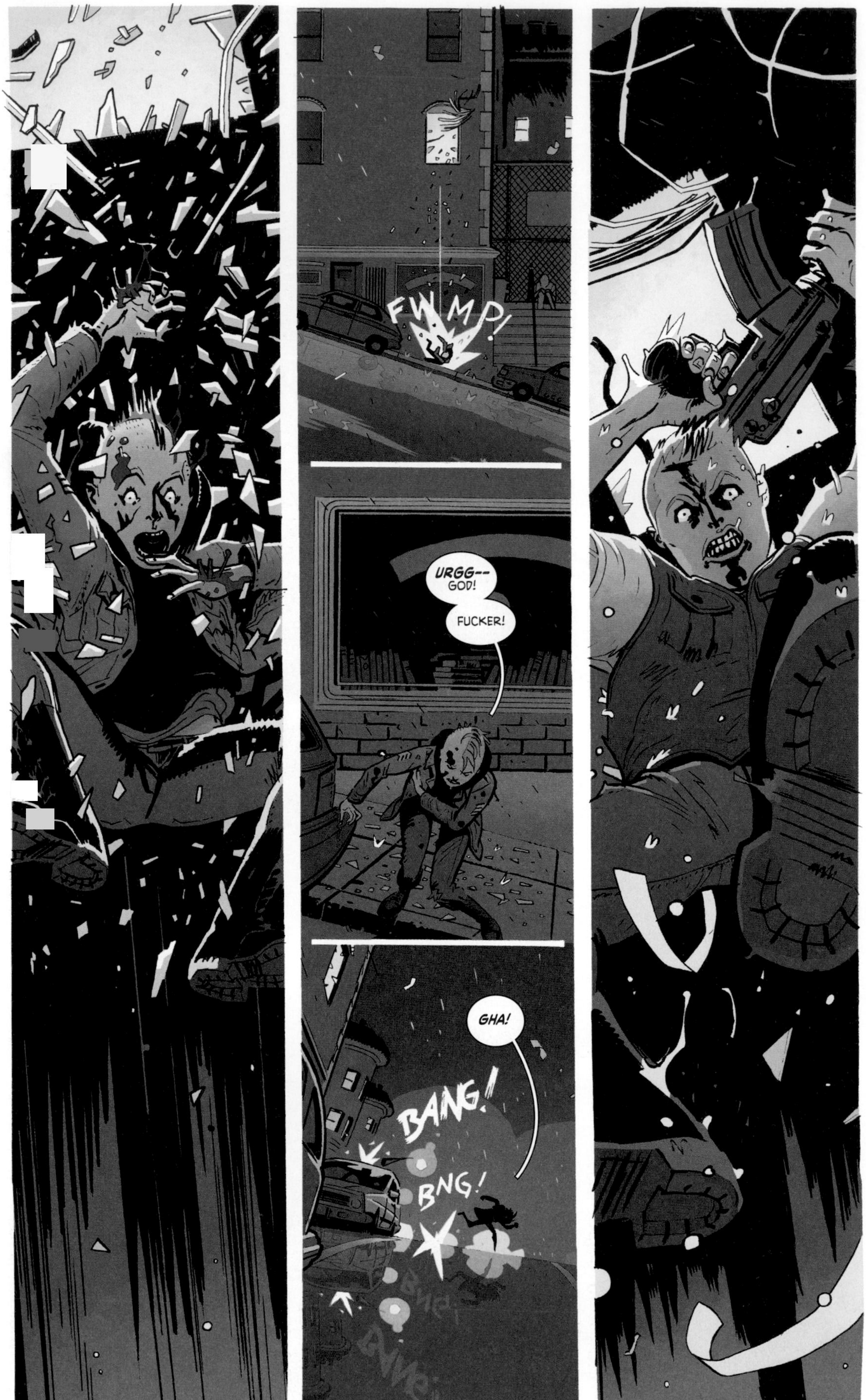
FWMP!
URGG-- GOD!
FUCKER!
GHA!
BANG!
BNG!

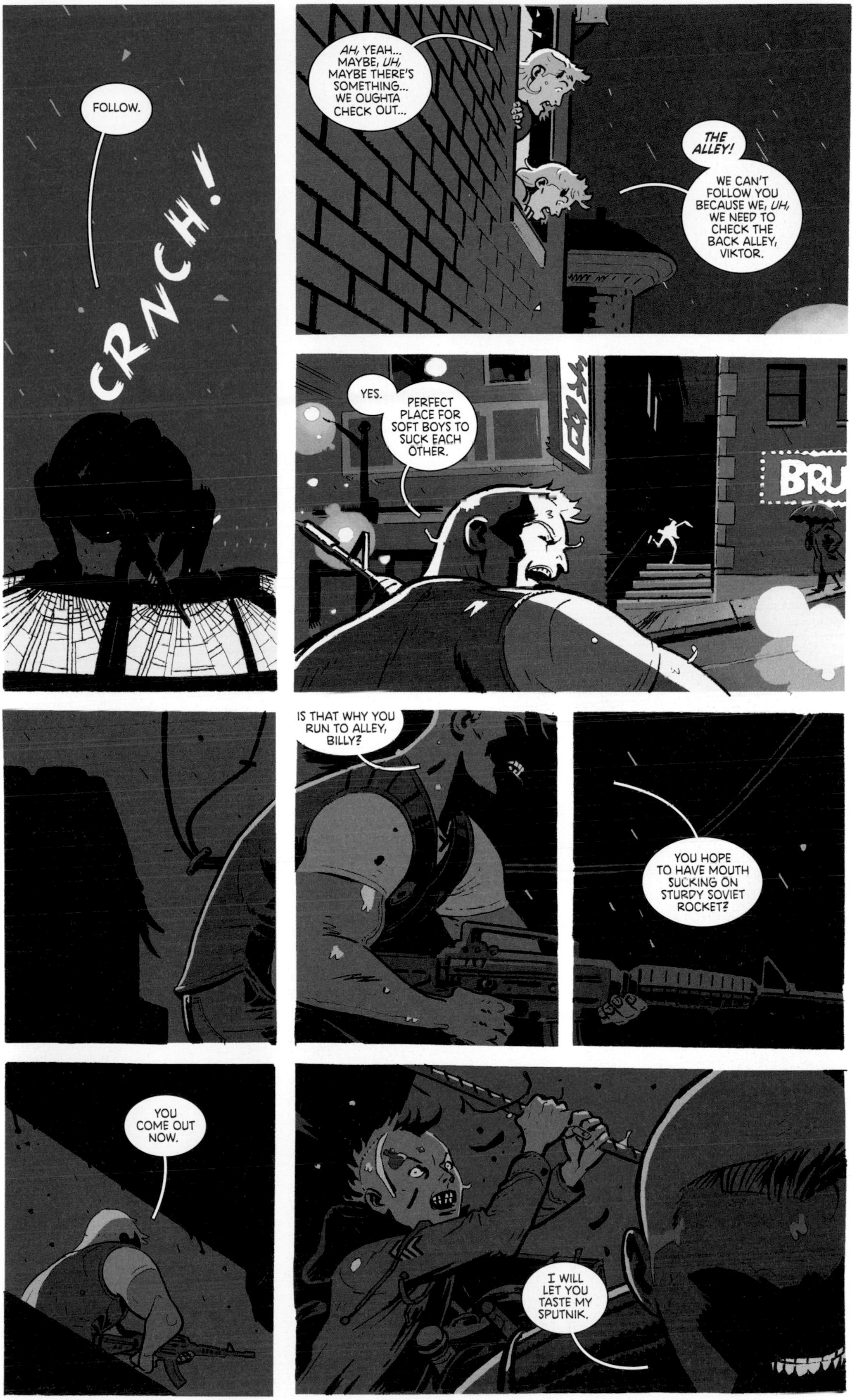
FOLLOW.
CRNCH!
AH, YEAH... MAYBE, UH, MAYBE THERE'S SOMETHING... WE OUGHTA CHECK OUT...
THE ALLEY!
WE CAN'T FOLLOW YOU BECAUSE WE, UH, WE NEED TO CHECK THE BACK ALLEY, VIKTOR.
YES.
PERFECT PLACE FOR SOFT BOYS TO SUCK EACH OTHER.
BRU
IS THAT WHY YOU RUN TO ALLEY, BILLY?
YOU HOPE TO HAVE MOUTH SUCKING ON STURDY SOVIET ROCKET?
YOU COME OUT NOW.
I WILL LET YOU TASTE MY SPUTNIK.

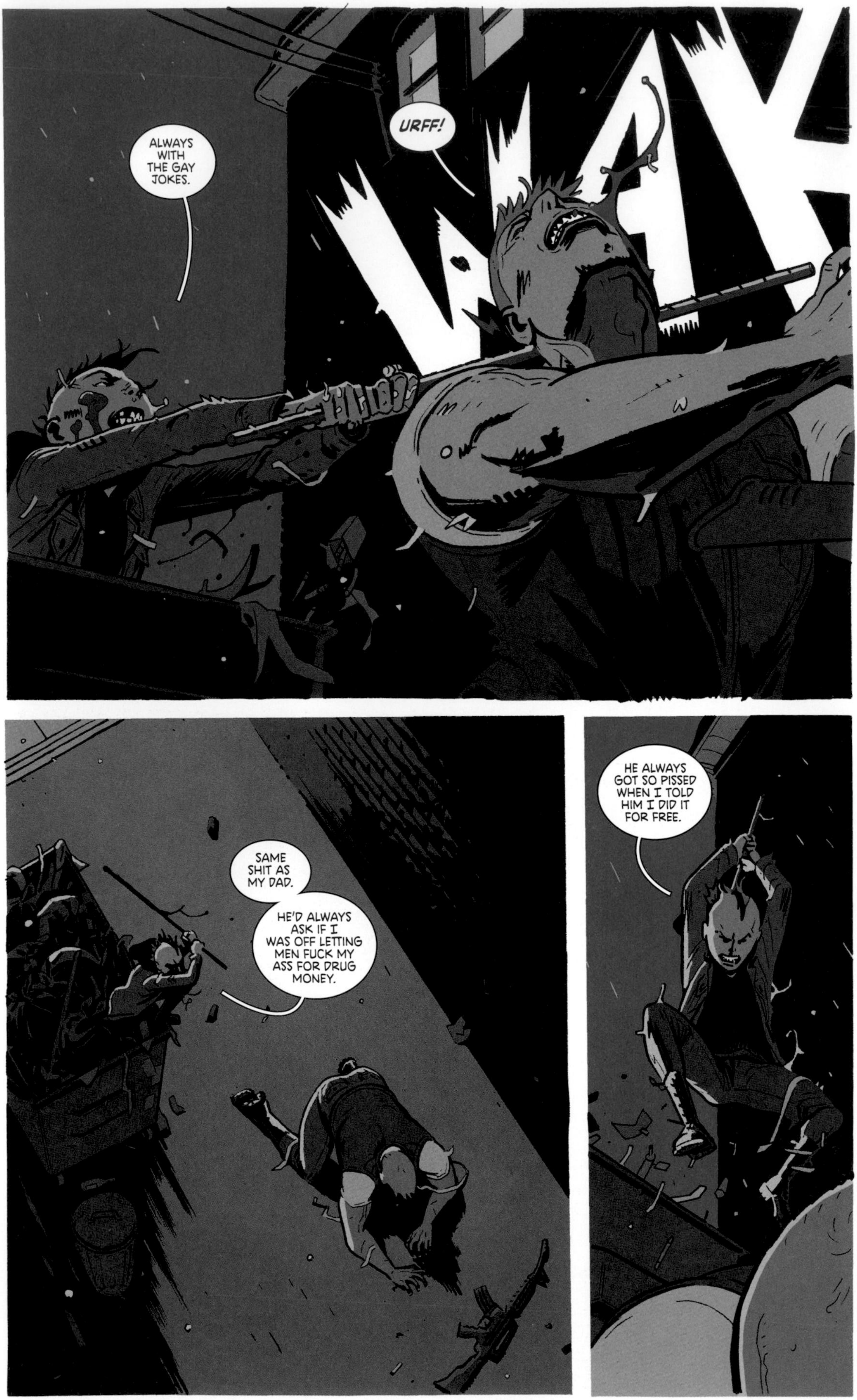
ALWAYS WITH THE GAY JOKES.
URFF!
SAME SHIT AS MY DAD.
HE'D ALWAYS ASK IF I WAS OFF LETTING MEN FUCK MY ASS FOR DRUG MONEY.
HE ALWAYS GOT SO PISSED WHEN I TOLD HIM I DID IT FOR FREE.

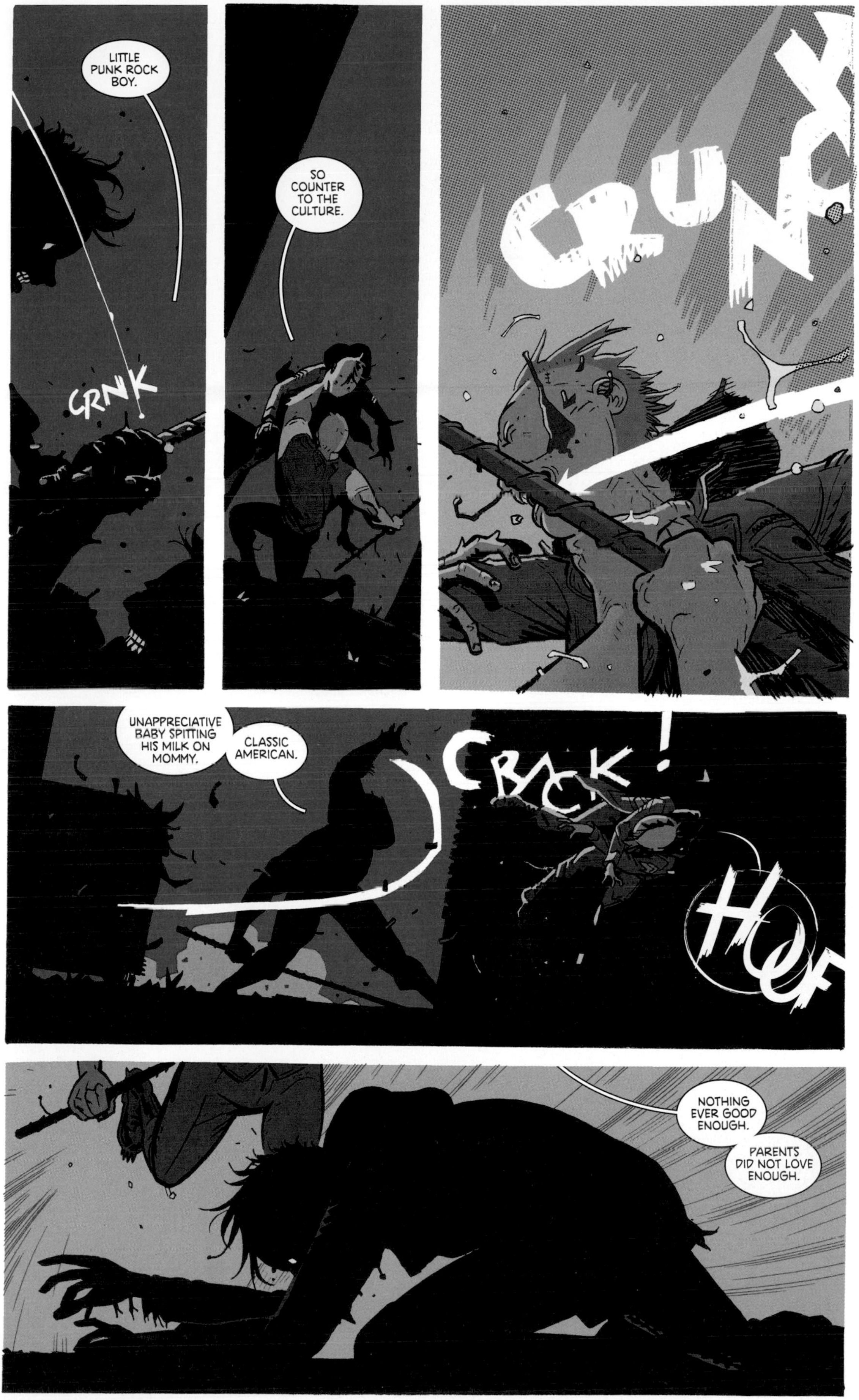
LITTLE PUNK ROCK BOY.
CRNK
SO COUNTER TO THE CULTURE.
CRUNX
UNAPPRECIATIVE BABY SPITTING HIS MILK ON MOMMY.
CLASSIC AMERICAN.
CRACK!
HOOF
NOTHING EVER GOOD ENOUGH.
PARENTS DID NOT LOVE ENOUGH.

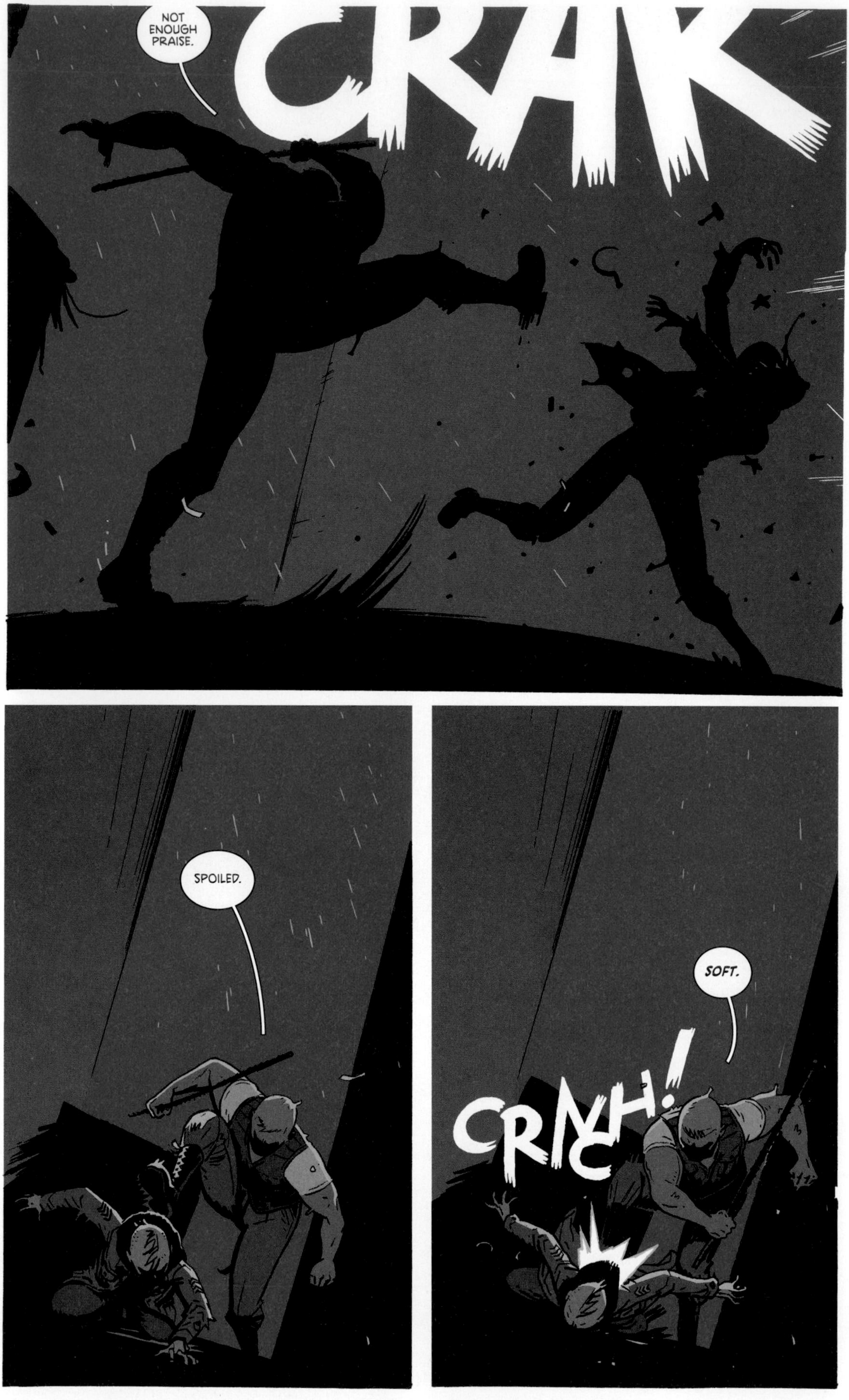
NOT ENOUGH PRAISE.
CRAK
SPOILED.
SOFT.
CRNCH!

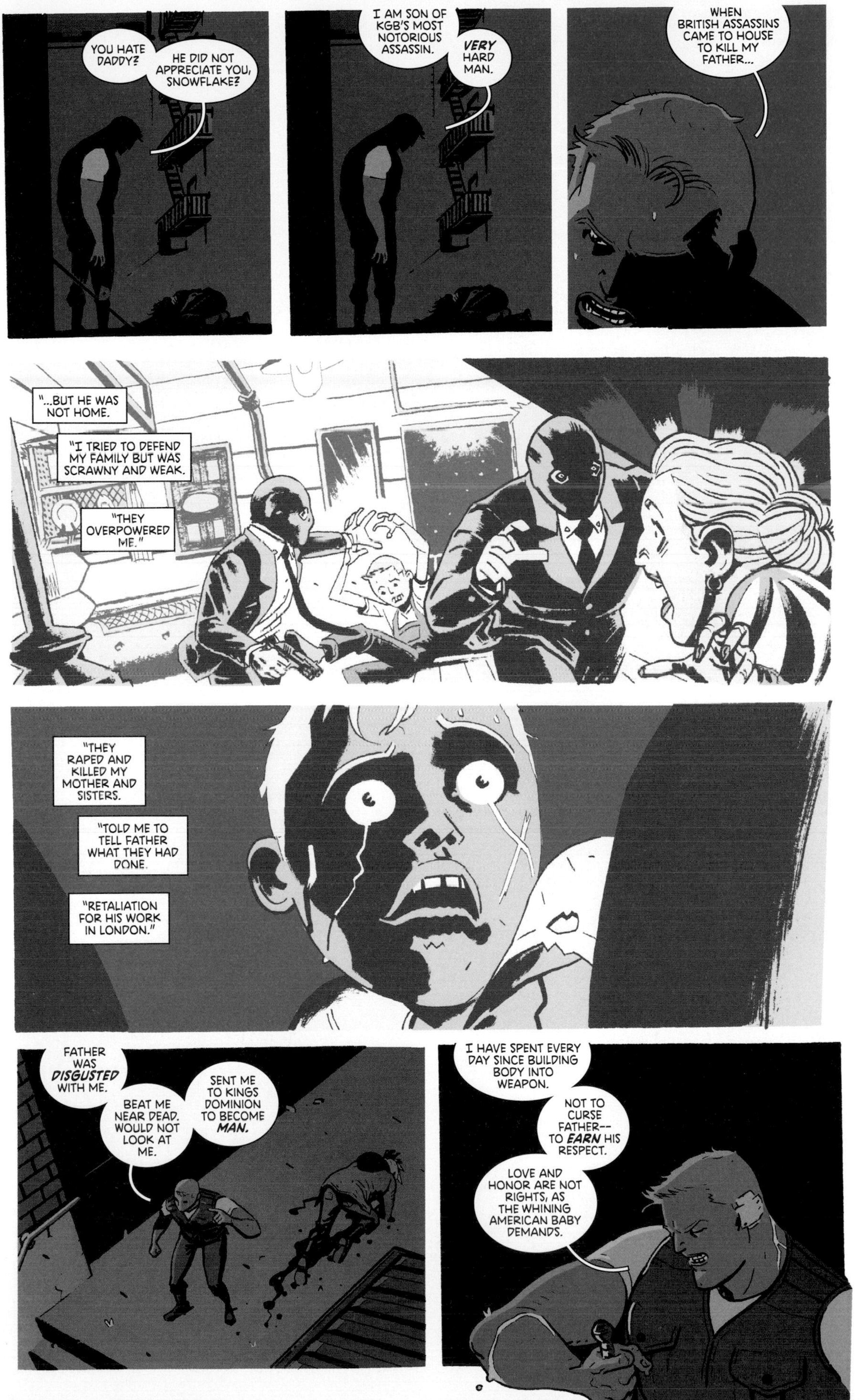
YOU HATE DADDY?
HE DID NOT APPRECIATE YOU, SNOWFLAKE?
I AM SON OF KGB'S MOST NOTORIOUS ASSASSIN.
VERY HARD MAN.
WHEN BRITISH ASSASSINS CAME TO HOUSE TO KILL MY FATHER...
"...BUT HE WAS NOT HOME.
"I TRIED TO DEFEND MY FAMILY BUT WAS SCRAWNY AND WEAK.
"THEY OVERPOWERED ME."
"THEY RAPED AND KILLED MY MOTHER AND SISTERS.
"TOLD ME TO TELL FATHER WHAT THEY HAD DONE.
"RETALIATION FOR HIS WORK IN LONDON."
FATHER WAS DISGUSTED WITH ME.
BEAT ME NEAR DEAD. WOULD NOT LOOK AT ME.
SENT ME TO KINGS DOMINION TO BECOME MAN.
I HAVE SPENT EVERY DAY SINCE BUILDING BODY INTO WEAPON.
NOT TO CURSE FATHER-- TO EARN HIS RESPECT.
LOVE AND HONOR ARE NOT RIGHTS, AS THE WHINING AMERICAN BABY DEMANDS.

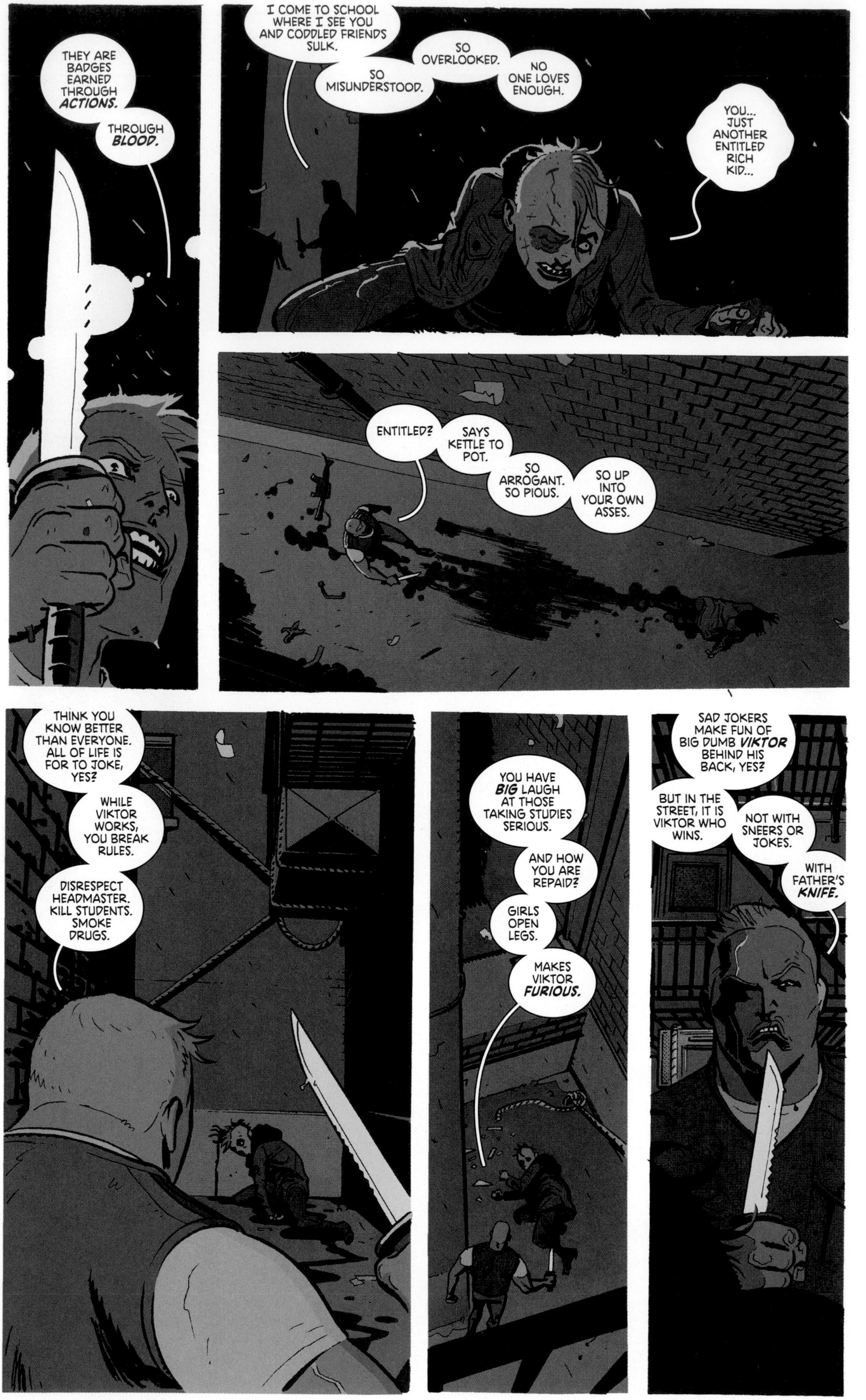
THEY ARE BADGES EARNED THROUGH ACTIONS.
THROUGH BLOOD.
I COME TO SCHOOL WHERE I SEE YOU AND CODDLED FRIENDS SULK.
SO MISUNDERSTOOD.
SO OVERLOOKED.
NO ONE LOVES ENOUGH.
YOU... JUST ANOTHER ENTITLED RICH KID...
ENTITLED?
SAYS KETTLE TO POT.
SO ARROGANT. SO PIOUS.
SO UP INTO YOUR OWN ASSES.
THINK YOU KNOW BETTER THAN EVERYONE. ALL OF LIFE IS FOR TO JOKE, YES?
WHILE VIKTOR WORKS, YOU BREAK RULES.
DISRESPECT HEADMASTER. KILL STUDENTS. SMOKE DRUGS.
YOU HAVE BIG LAUGH AT THOSE TAKING STUDIES SERIOUS.
AND HOW YOU ARE REPAID?
GIRLS OPEN LEGS.
MAKES VIKTOR FURIOUS.
SAD JOKERS MAKE FUN OF BIG DUMB VIKTOR BEHIND HIS BACK, YES?
BUT IN THE STREET, IT IS VIKTOR WHO WINS.
NOT WITH SNEERS OR JOKES.
WITH FATHER'S KNIFE.

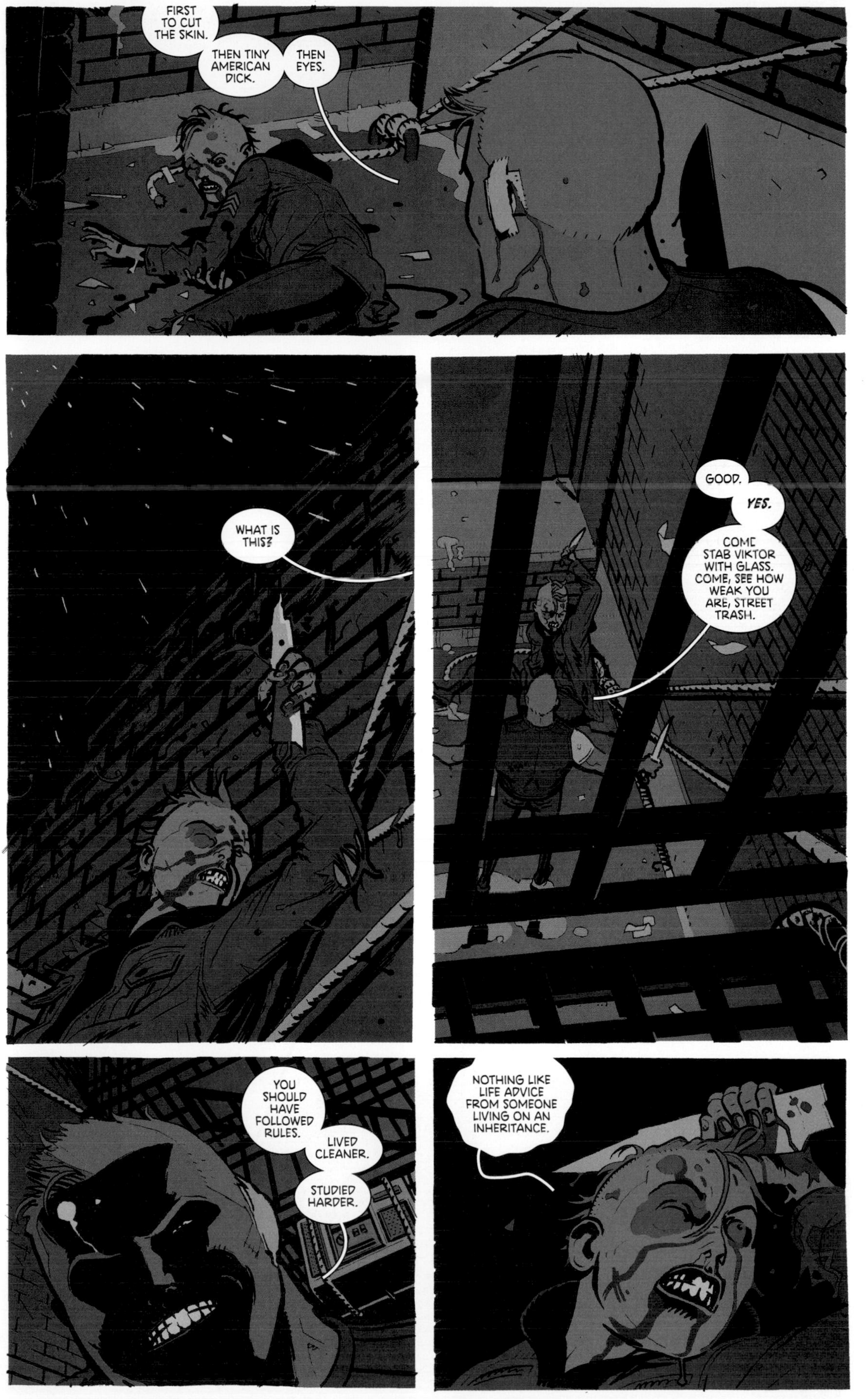
FIRST TO CUT THE SKIN.
THEN TINY AMERICAN DICK.
THEN EYES.
WHAT IS THIS?
GOOD.
YES.
COME STAB VIKTOR WITH GLASS. COME, SEE HOW WEAK YOU ARE, STREET TRASH.
YOU SHOULD HAVE FOLLOWED RULES.
LIVED CLEANER.
STUDIED HARDER.
NOTHING LIKE LIFE ADVICE FROM SOMEONE LIVING ON AN INHERITANCE.

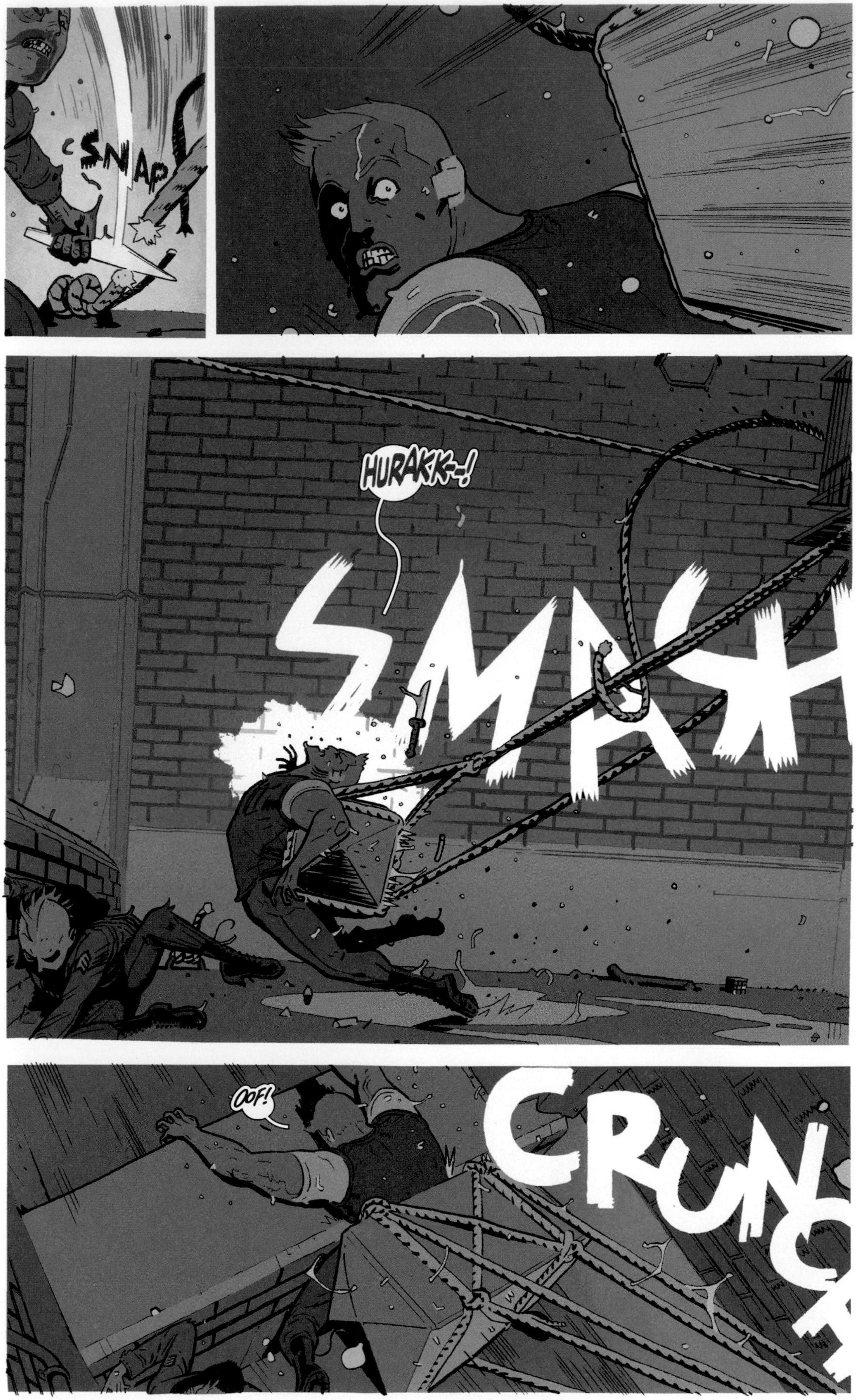
SNAP
HURAKK--!
SMASH
OOF!
CRUNCH

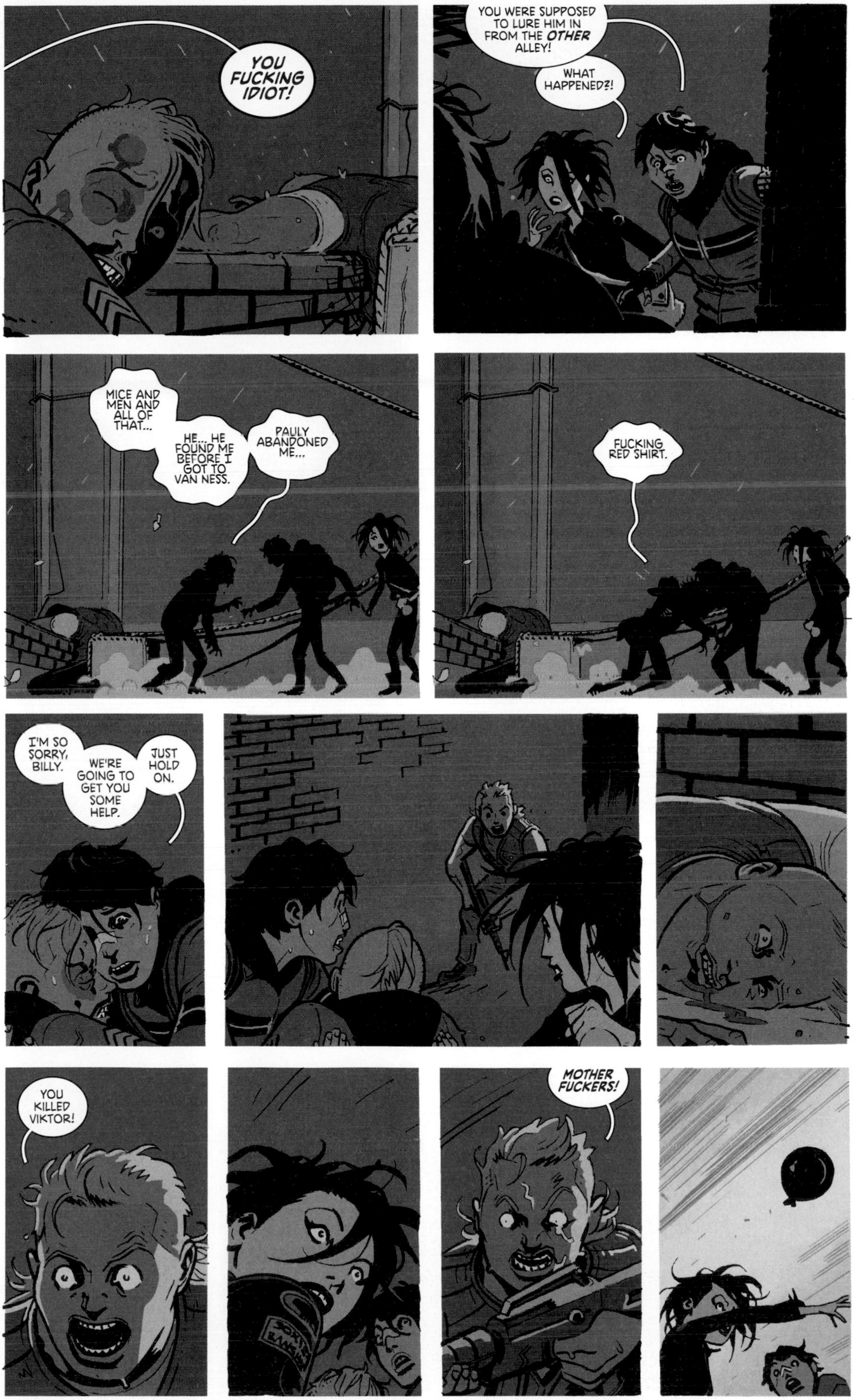
YOU FUCKING IDIOT!
YOU WERE SUPPOSED TO LURE HIM IN FROM THE *OTHER* ALLEY!
WHAT HAPPENED?!
MICE AND MEN AND ALL OF THAT...
HE... HE FOUND ME BEFORE I GOT TO VAN NESS.
PAULY ABANDONED ME...
FUCKING RED SHIRT.
I'M SO SORRY, BILLY.
WE'RE GOING TO GET YOU SOME HELP.
JUST HOLD ON.
YOU KILLED VIKTOR!
MOTHER FUCKERS!

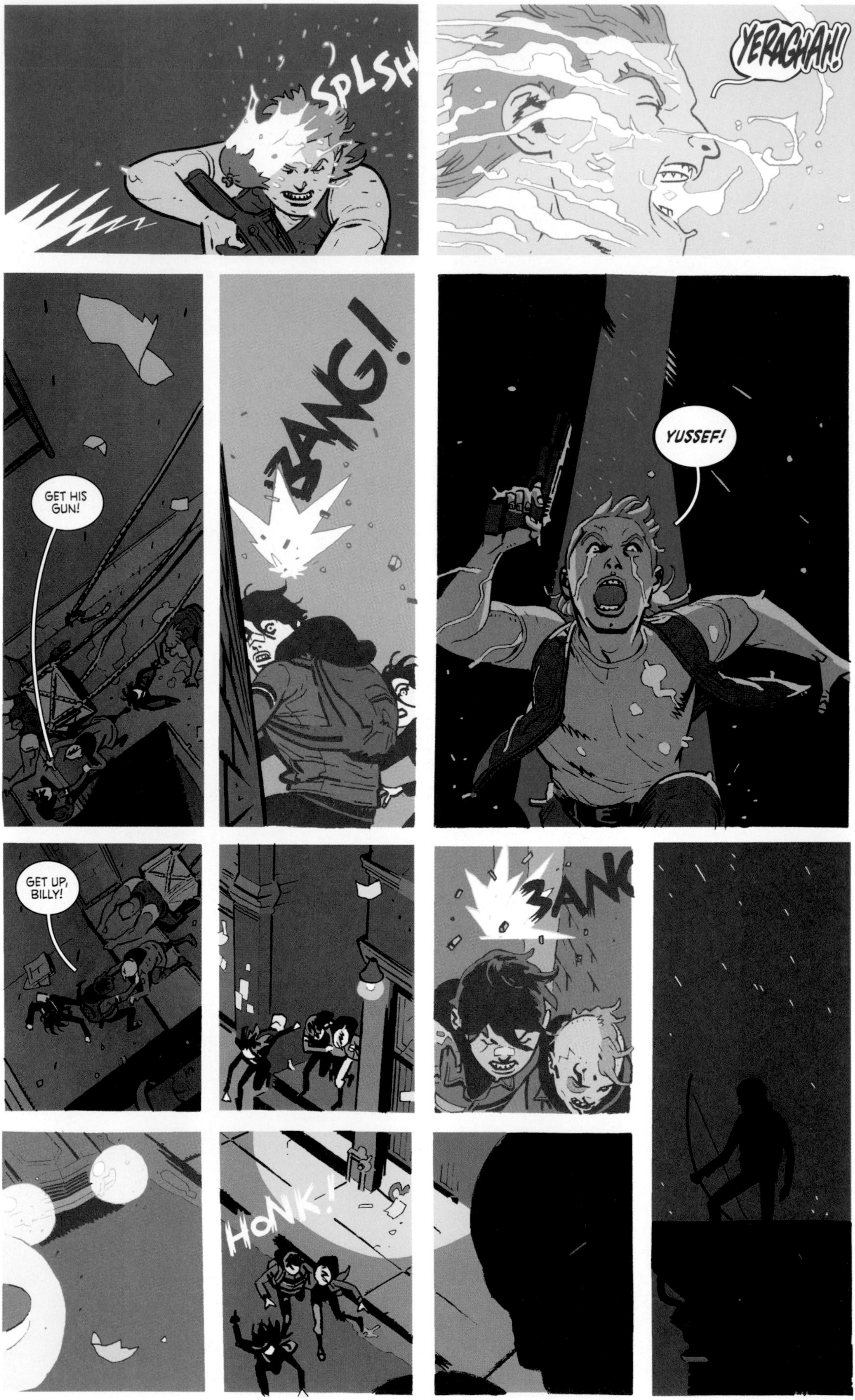
SPLSH
YERAGHAH!
GET HIS GUN!
BANG!
YUSSEF!
GET UP, BILLY!
BANG
HONK!

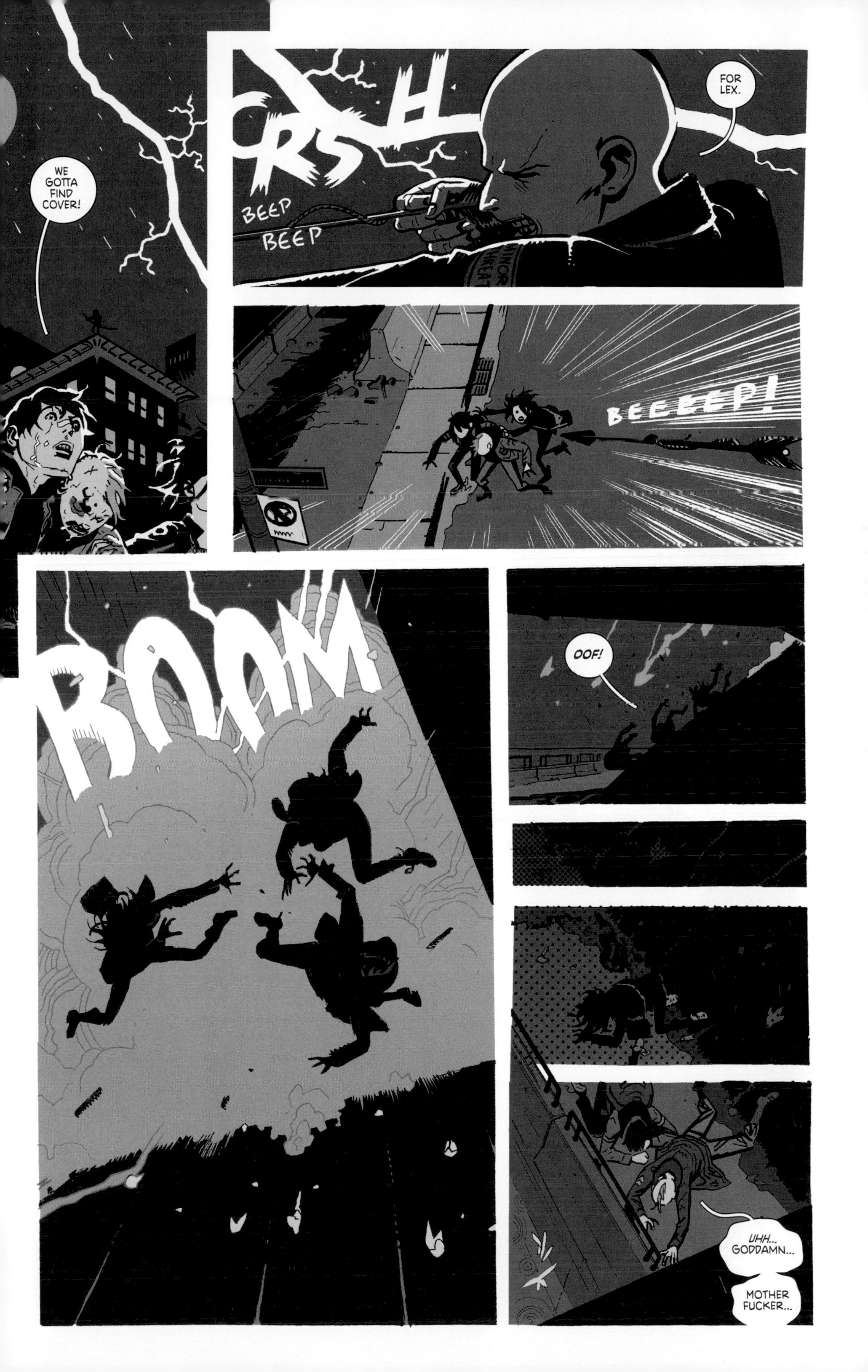
WE GOTTA FIND COVER!
CRSH
BEEP
BEEP
FOR LEX.
BEEEEEP!
BOOM
OOF!
UHH... GODDAMN...
MOTHER FUCKER...

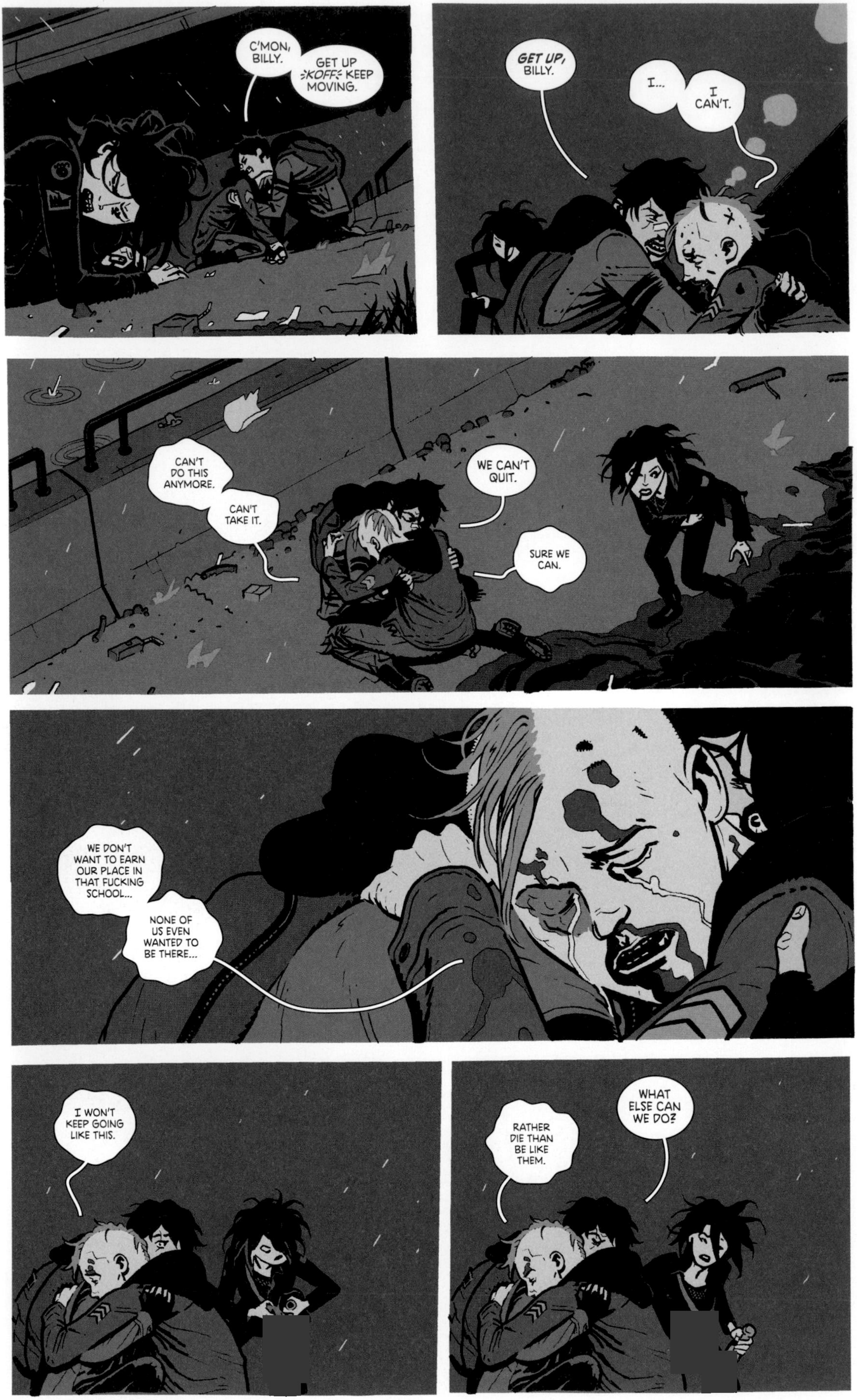
C'MON, BILLY.
GET UP *KOFF* KEEP MOVING.
GET UP, BILLY.
I...
I CAN'T.
CAN'T DO THIS ANYMORE.
CAN'T TAKE IT.
WE CAN'T QUIT.
SURE WE CAN.
WE DON'T WANT TO EARN OUR PLACE IN THAT FUCKING SCHOOL...
NONE OF US EVEN WANTED TO BE THERE...
I WON'T KEEP GOING LIKE THIS.
RATHER DIE THAN BE LIKE THEM.
WHAT ELSE CAN WE DO?

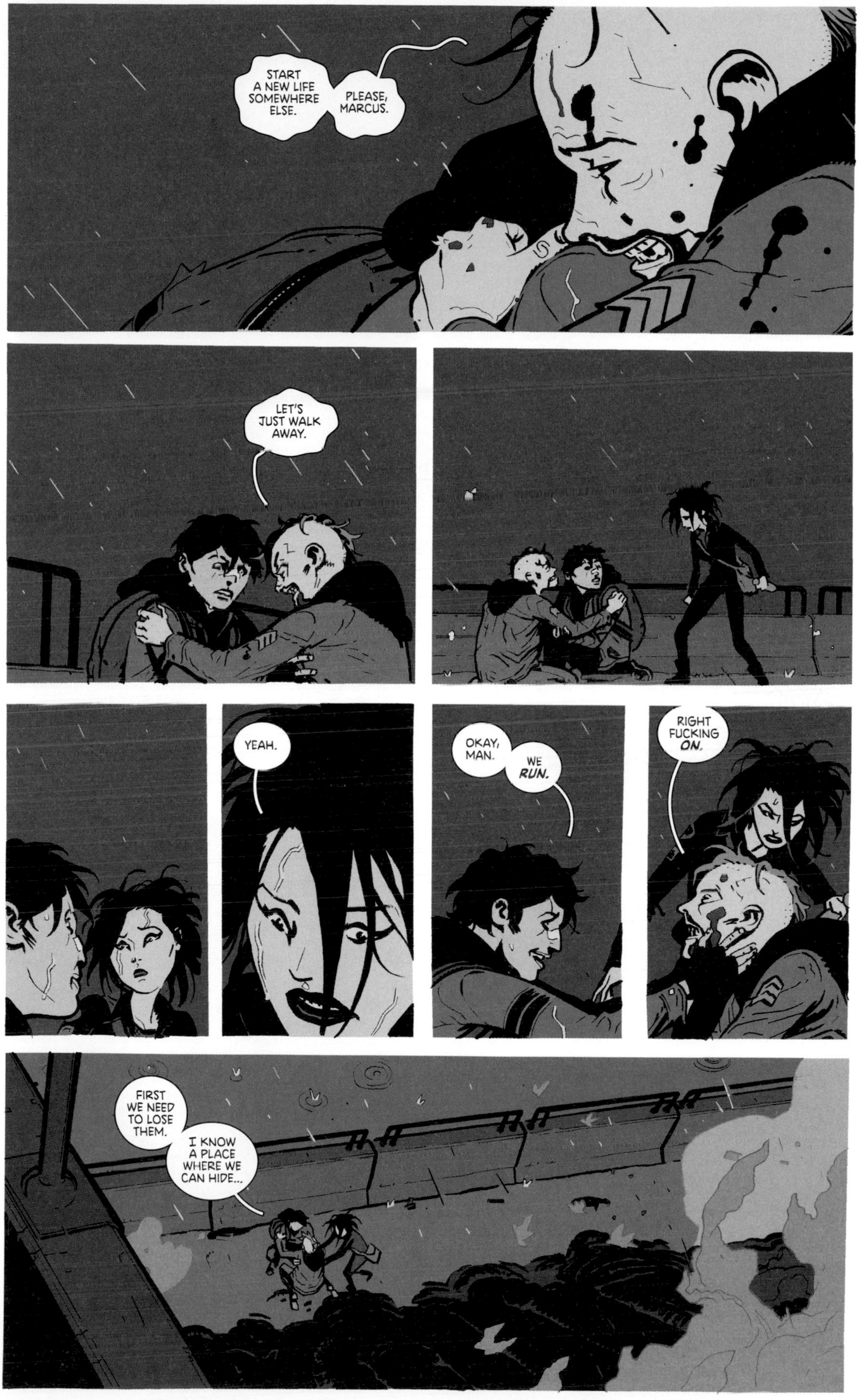
START A NEW LIFE SOMEWHERE ELSE.
PLEASE, MARCUS.
LET'S JUST WALK AWAY.
YEAH.
OKAY, MAN.
WE *RUN.*
RIGHT FUCKING *ON.*
FIRST WE NEED TO LOSE THEM.
I KNOW A PLACE WHERE WE CAN HIDE...

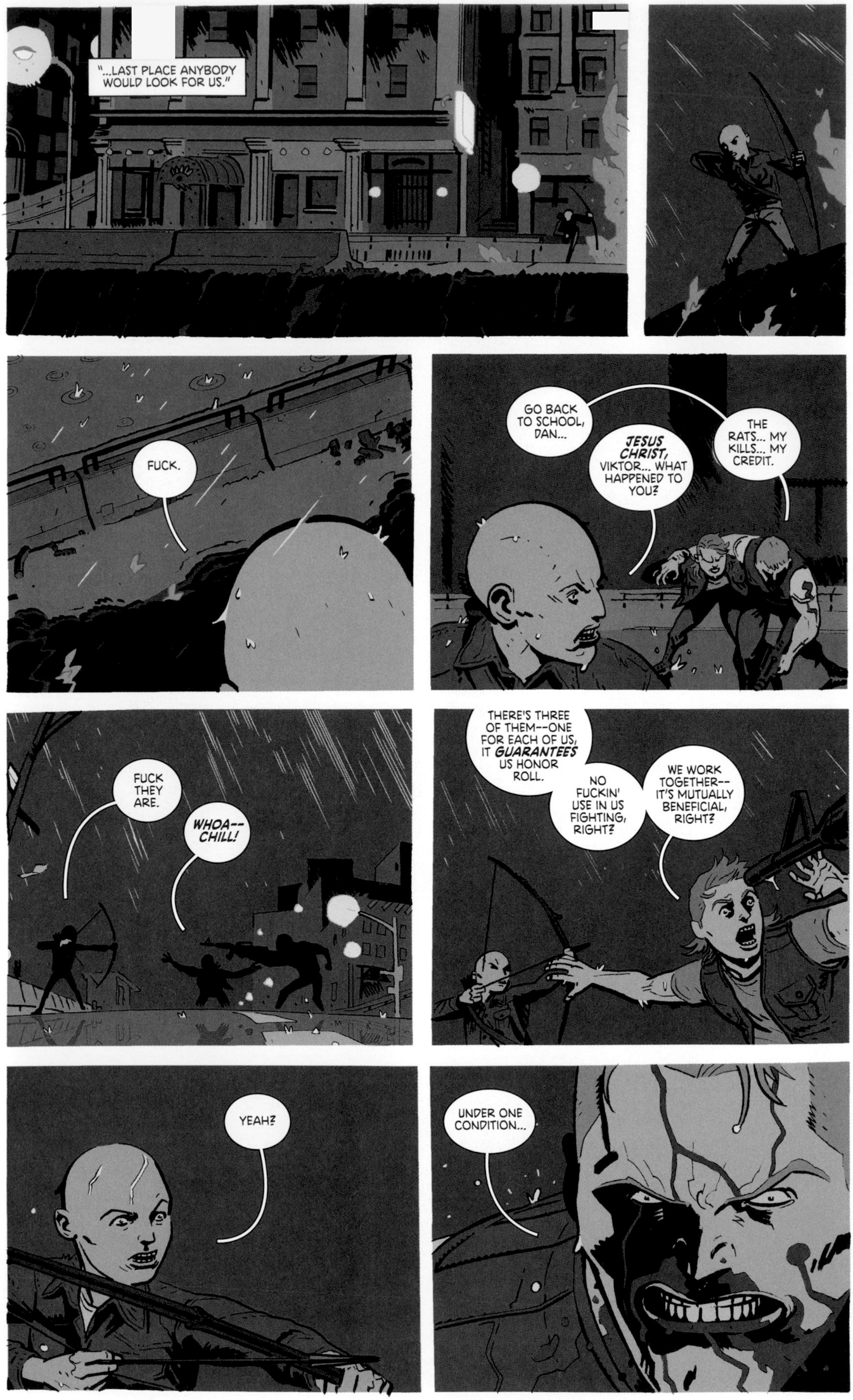
"...LAST PLACE ANYBODY WOULD LOOK FOR US."
FUCK.
GO BACK TO SCHOOL, DAN...
JESUS CHRIST, VIKTOR... WHAT HAPPENED TO YOU?
THE RATS... MY KILLS... MY CREDIT.
FUCK THEY ARE.
WHOA--CHILL!
THERE'S THREE OF THEM--ONE FOR EACH OF US, IT GUARANTEES US HONOR ROLL.
NO FUCKIN' USE IN US FIGHTING, RIGHT?
WE WORK TOGETHER--IT'S MUTUALLY BENEFICIAL, RIGHT?
YEAH?
UNDER ONE CONDITION...

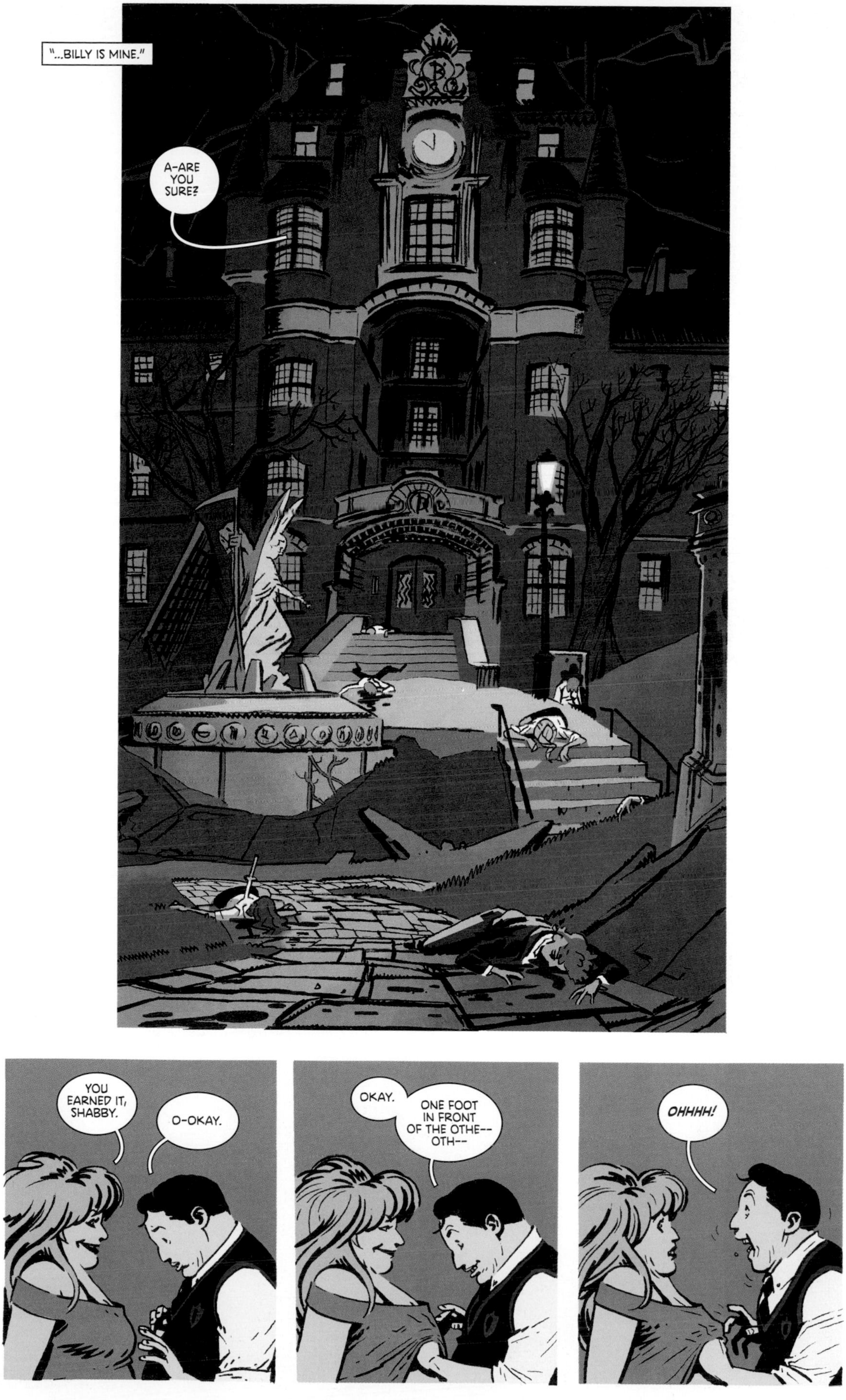
"...BILLY IS MINE."
A-ARE YOU SURE?
YOU EARNED IT, SHABBY.
O-OKAY.
OKAY.
ONE FOOT IN FRONT OF THE OTHE-- OTH--
OHHHH!

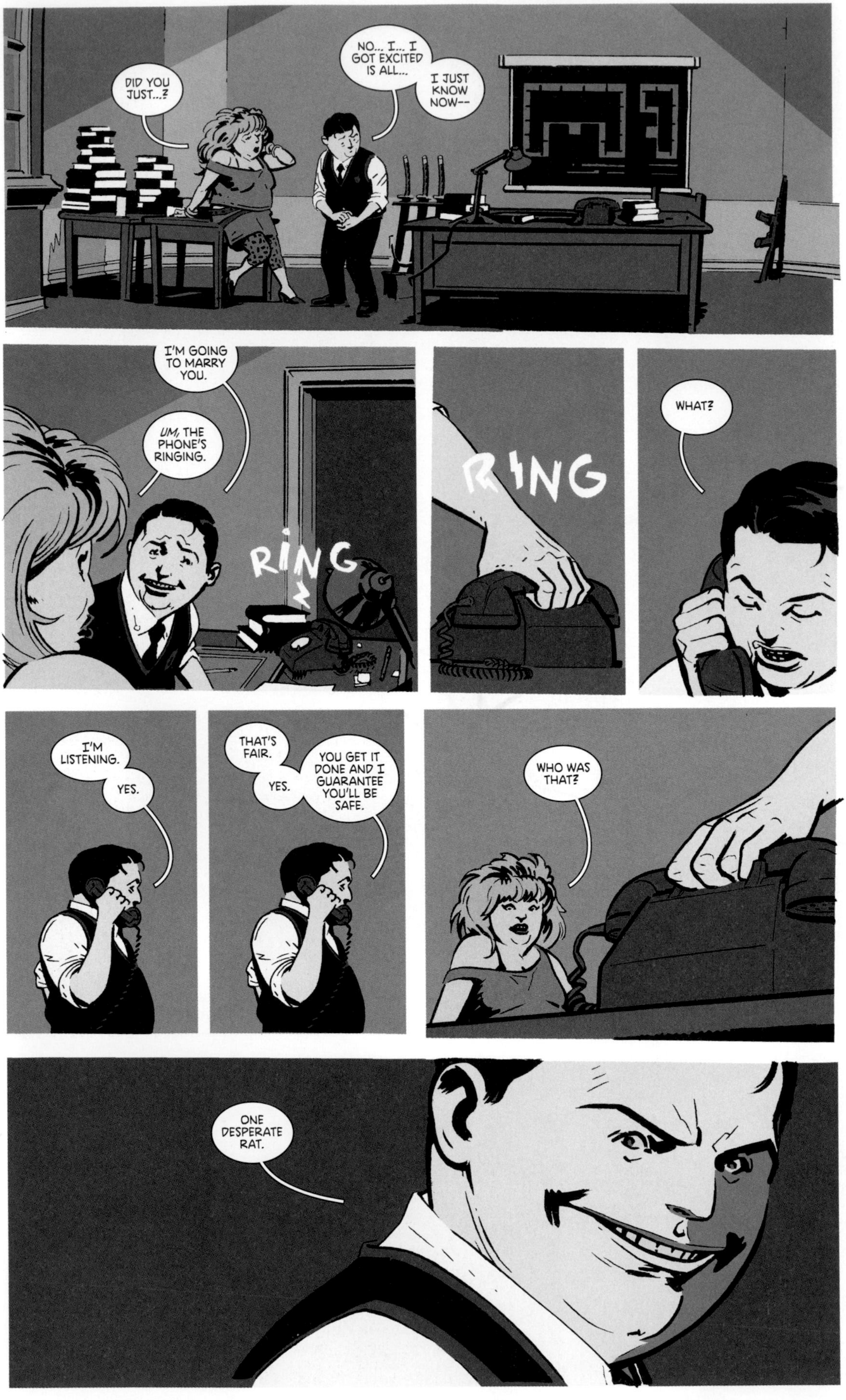
DID YOU JUST...?
NO... I... I GOT EXCITED IS ALL...
I JUST KNOW NOW--
I'M GOING TO MARRY YOU.
UM, THE PHONE'S RINGING.
RING
RING
WHAT?
I'M LISTENING.
YES.
THAT'S FAIR.
YES.
YOU GET IT DONE AND I GUARANTEE YOU'LL BE SAFE.
WHO WAS THAT?
ONE DESPERATE RAT.

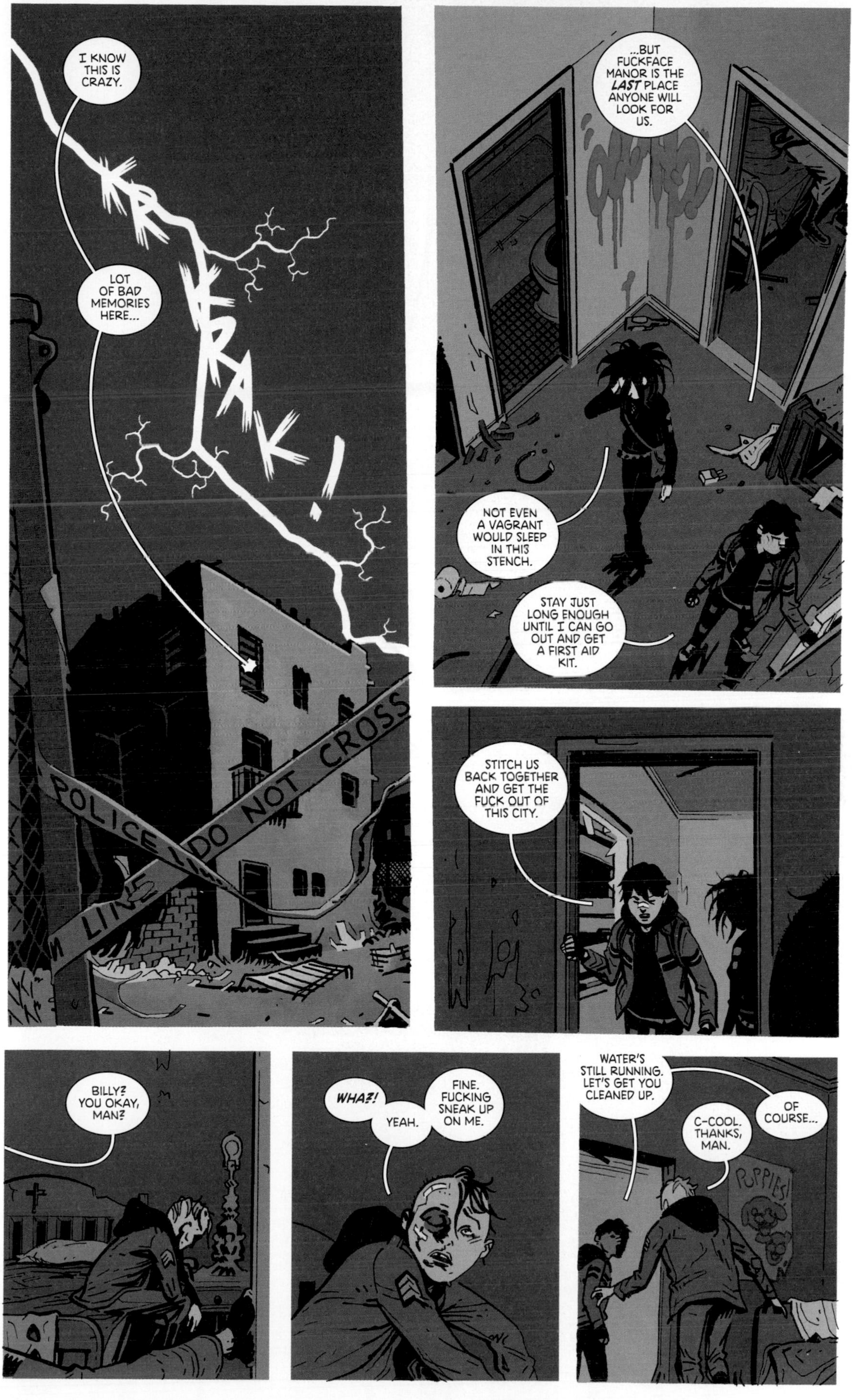
I KNOW THIS IS CRAZY.
KRAKAK!
LOT OF BAD MEMORIES HERE...
POLICE LINE DO NOT CROSS
...BUT FUCKFACE MANOR IS THE *LAST* PLACE ANYONE WILL LOOK FOR US.
NOT EVEN A VAGRANT WOULD SLEEP IN THIS STENCH.
STAY JUST LONG ENOUGH UNTIL I CAN GO OUT AND GET A FIRST AID KIT.
STITCH US BACK TOGETHER AND GET THE FUCK OUT OF THIS CITY.
BILLY? YOU OKAY, MAN?
WHA?!
YEAH.
FINE. FUCKING SNEAK UP ON ME.
WATER'S STILL RUNNING. LET'S GET YOU CLEANED UP.
OF COURSE...
C-COOL. THANKS, MAN.
PUPPIES!

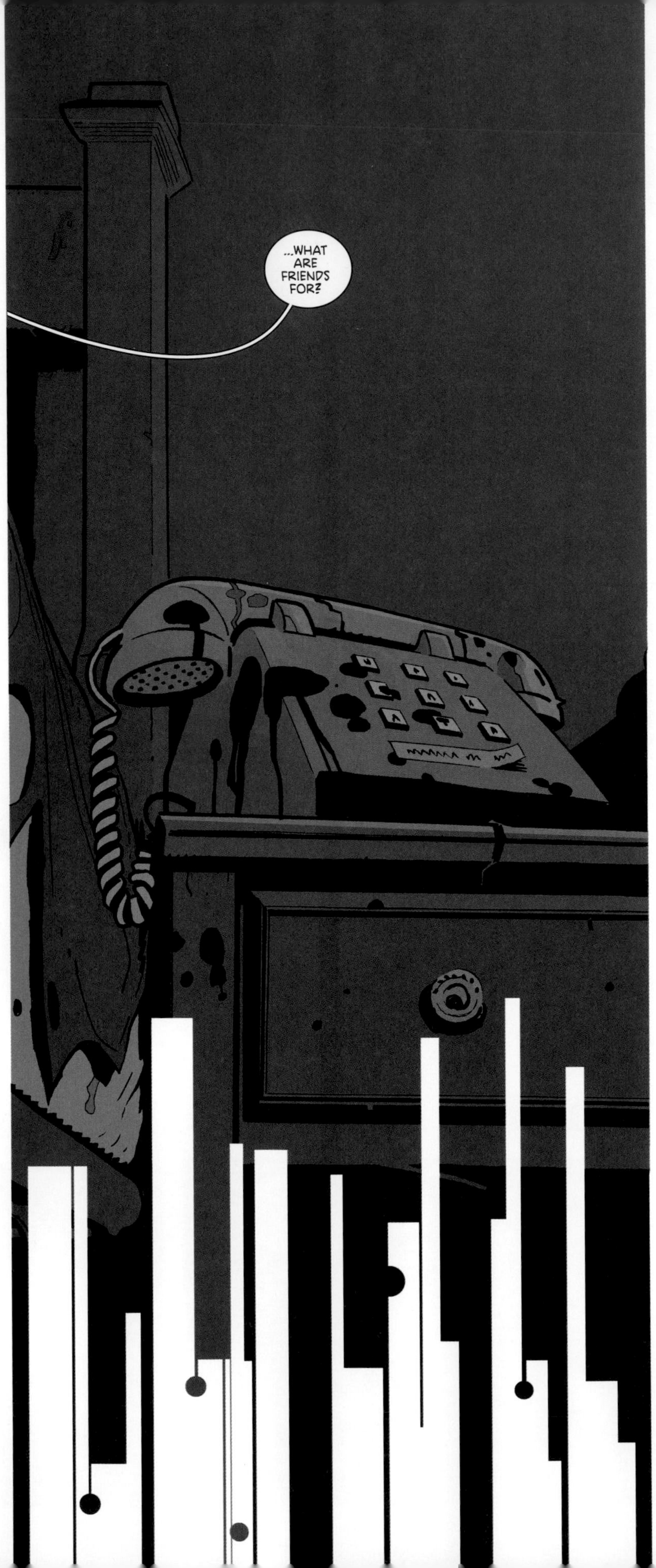
...WHAT ARE FRIENDS FOR?

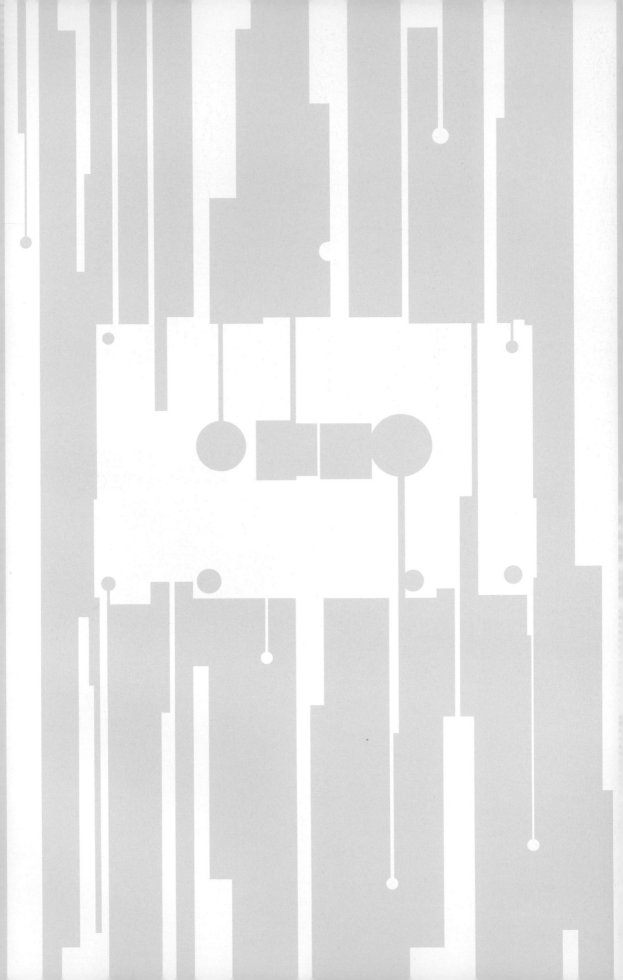

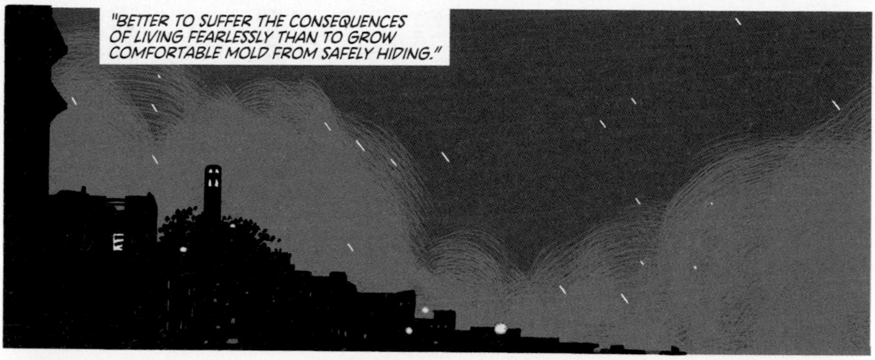
"BETTER TO SUFFER THE CONSEQUENCES OF LIVING FEARLESSLY THAN TO GROW COMFORTABLE MOLD FROM SAFELY HIDING."

THAT WAS MY OPENING IN THIS JOURNAL AT THE BEGINNING OF THE YEAR.

A NUDGE TO TRY AND BE SOMETHING I'M NOT.

THE SORT OF THING A PERSON WRITES TO ADD SOME ROMANCE TO LIVING THROUGH BAD TIMES.

TRUTH IS...

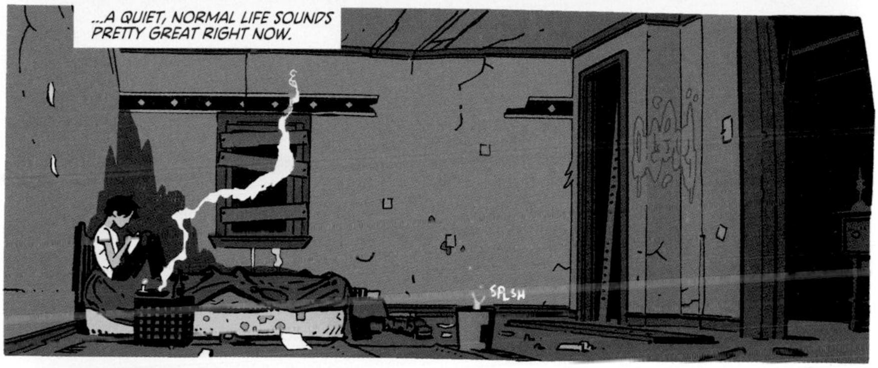
...A QUIET, NORMAL LIFE SOUNDS PRETTY GREAT RIGHT NOW.
SPLSH

LIVING ON THE STREETS IS AWFUL ENOUGH TO MAKE JOINING A SCHOOL FOR ASSASSINS SEEM LIKE A REASONABLE ALTERNA-TIVE.

TELL YOURSELF THAT DECISION WASN'T MADE ENTIRELY OUT OF FEAR

SOME LIES ARE TOO BIG TO SELL YOURSELF.

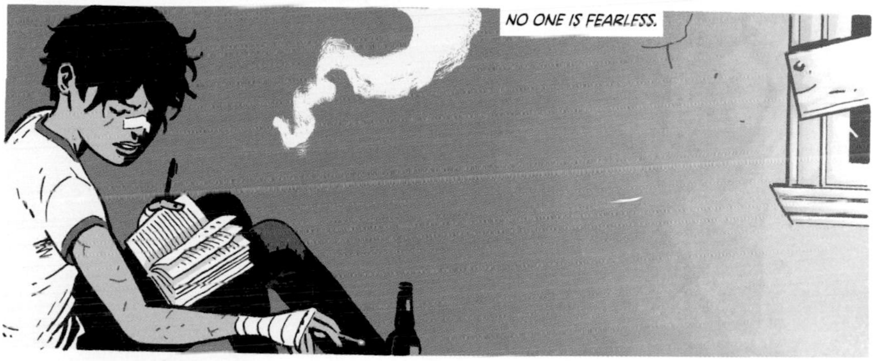
NO ONE IS FEARLESS.

FEAR'S A REASONABLE REACTION TO WHAT'S WAITING OUT THERE.

AN INSTINCT WE DEVELOPED FOR GOOD REASON.

AND I AM AFRAID.

NOT JUST OF THE PEOPLE TRYING TO KILL ME...

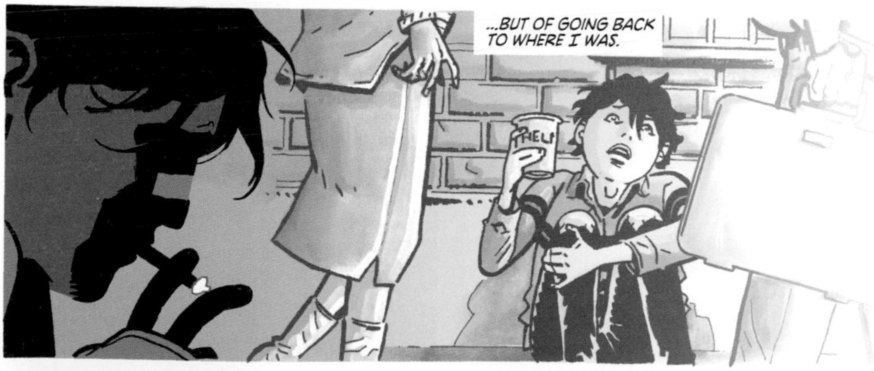
...BUT OF GOING BACK TO WHERE I WAS.
HELP

BECAUSE EVEN IF WE SURVIVE ALL OF THIS, EVEN IF WE DO MAKE IT OUT OF SAN FRANCISCO, I'M RIGHT BACK TO SQUARE ONE.

NO PARENTS.

NO FAMILY.

FACE ON THE FBI'S MOST WANTED LIST FOR A CRIME I DIDN'T COMMIT.

MY YEAR AT KINGS DOMINION HAS BEEN A TORNADO OF BULLSHIT...

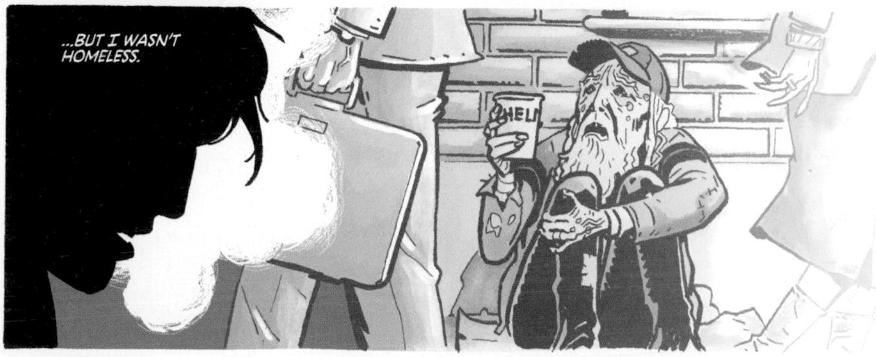
...BUT I WASN'T HOMELESS.
HELP

HOW IS IT THAT THIS NIGHTMARE IS STILL SOMEHOW MORE APPEALING TO ME THAN THAT UNCERTAINTY?

WHAT IS THAT?

FEAR OF A LIFETIME OUT HERE ALONE.

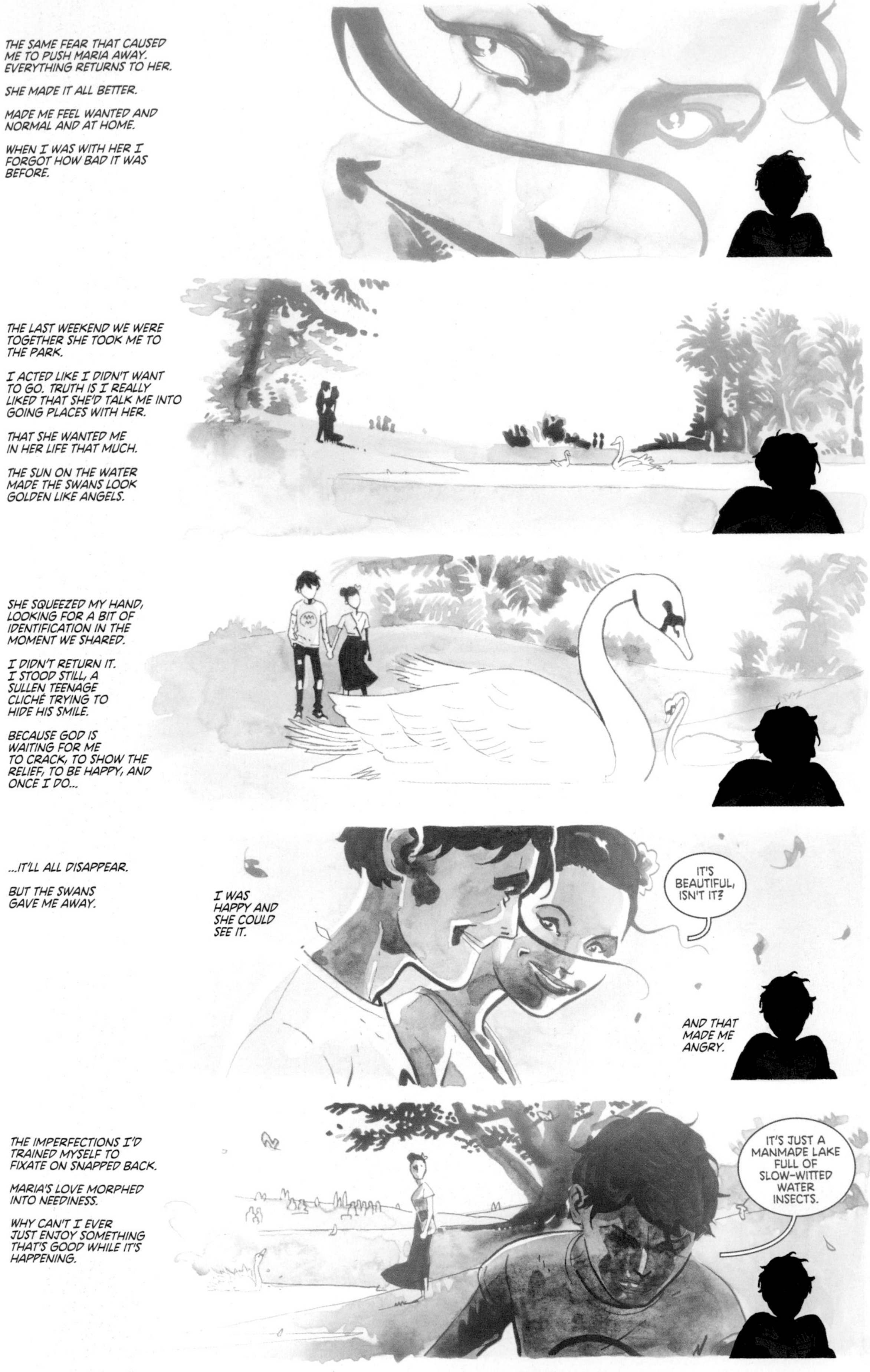
THE SAME FEAR THAT CAUSED ME TO PUSH MARIA AWAY. EVERYTHING RETURNS TO HER.
SHE MADE IT ALL BETTER.
MADE ME FEEL WANTED AND NORMAL AND AT HOME.
WHEN I WAS WITH HER I FORGOT HOW BAD IT WAS BEFORE.
THE LAST WEEKEND WE WERE TOGETHER SHE TOOK ME TO THE PARK.
I ACTED LIKE I DIDN'T WANT TO GO. TRUTH IS I REALLY LIKED THAT SHE'D TALK ME INTO GOING PLACES WITH HER.
THAT SHE WANTED ME IN HER LIFE THAT MUCH.
THE SUN ON THE WATER MADE THE SWANS LOOK GOLDEN LIKE ANGELS.
SHE SQUEEZED MY HAND, LOOKING FOR A BIT OF IDENTIFICATION IN THE MOMENT WE SHARED.
I DIDN'T RETURN IT. I STOOD STILL, A SULLEN TEENAGE CLICHÉ TRYING TO HIDE HIS SMILE.
BECAUSE GOD IS WAITING FOR ME TO CRACK, TO SHOW THE RELIEF, TO BE HAPPY, AND ONCE I DO...
...IT'LL ALL DISAPPEAR.
BUT THE SWANS GAVE ME AWAY.
I WAS HAPPY AND SHE COULD SEE IT.
IT'S BEAUTIFUL, ISN'T IT?
AND THAT MADE ME ANGRY.
THE IMPERFECTIONS I'D TRAINED MYSELF TO FIXATE ON SNAPPED BACK.
MARIA'S LOVE MORPHED INTO NEEDINESS.
WHY CAN'T I EVER JUST ENJOY SOMETHING THAT'S GOOD WHILE IT'S HAPPENING.
IT'S JUST A MANMADE LAKE FULL OF SLOW-WITTED WATER INSECTS.

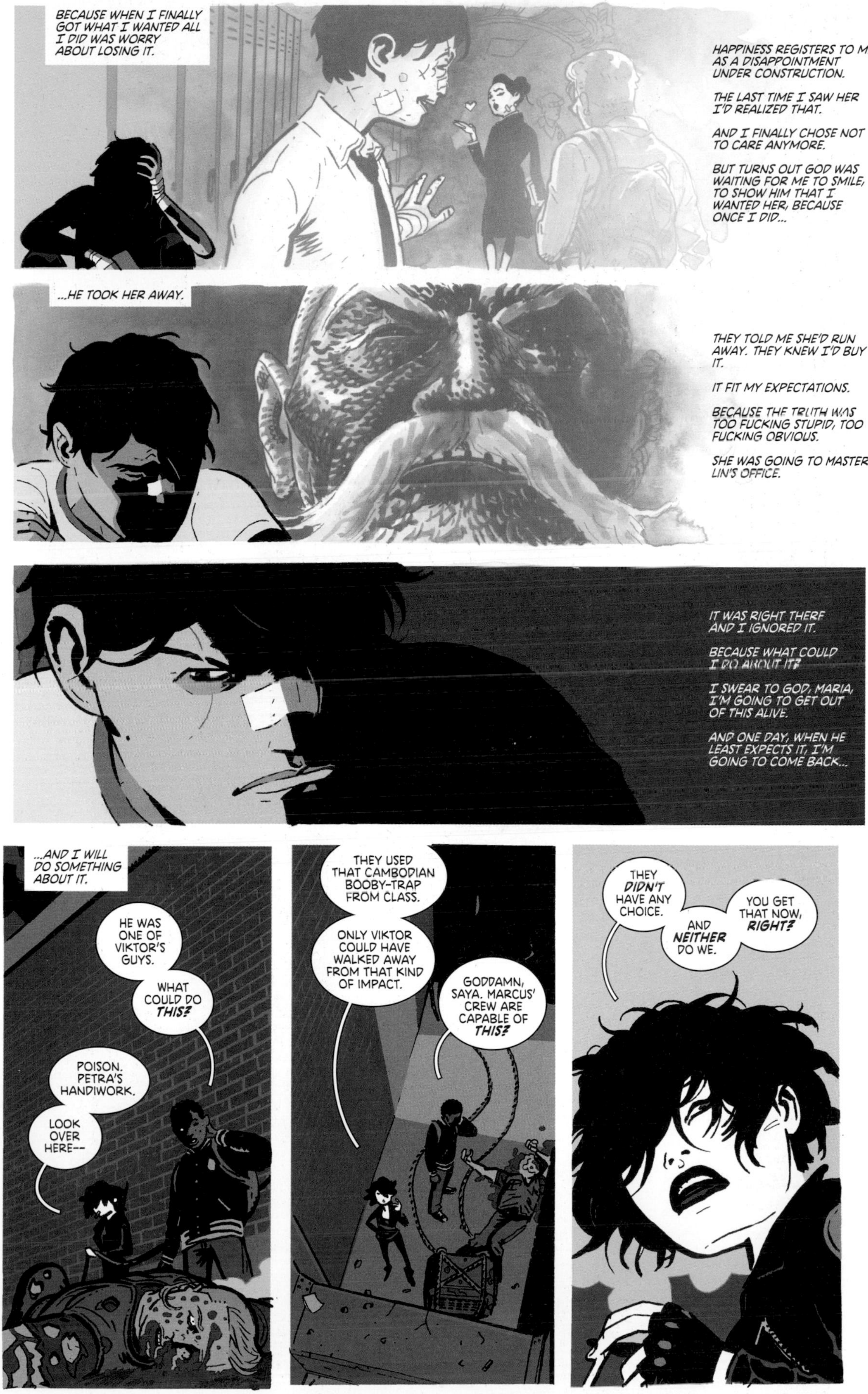
BECAUSE WHEN I FINALLY GOT WHAT I WANTED ALL I DID WAS WORRY ABOUT LOSING IT.
HAPPINESS REGISTERS TO ME AS A DISAPPOINTMENT UNDER CONSTRUCTION.
THE LAST TIME I SAW HER I'D REALIZED THAT.
AND I FINALLY CHOSE NOT TO CARE ANYMORE.
BUT TURNS OUT GOD WAS WAITING FOR ME TO SMILE, TO SHOW HIM THAT I WANTED HER, BECAUSE ONCE I DID...
...HE TOOK HER AWAY.
THEY TOLD ME SHE'D RUN AWAY. THEY KNEW I'D BUY IT.
IT FIT MY EXPECTATIONS.
BECAUSE THE TRUTH WAS TOO FUCKING STUPID, TOO FUCKING OBVIOUS.
SHE WAS GOING TO MASTER LIN'S OFFICE.
IT WAS RIGHT THERE AND I IGNORED IT.
BECAUSE WHAT COULD I DO ABOUT IT?
I SWEAR TO GOD, MARIA, I'M GOING TO GET OUT OF THIS ALIVE.
AND ONE DAY, WHEN HE LEAST EXPECTS IT, I'M GOING TO COME BACK...
...AND I WILL DO SOMETHING ABOUT IT.
HE WAS ONE OF VIKTOR'S GUYS.
WHAT COULD DO THIS?
POISON. PETRA'S HANDIWORK.
LOOK OVER HERE--
THEY USED THAT CAMBODIAN BOOBY-TRAP FROM CLASS.
ONLY VIKTOR COULD HAVE WALKED AWAY FROM THAT KIND OF IMPACT.
GODDAMN, SAYA. MARCUS' CREW ARE CAPABLE OF THIS?
THEY DIDN'T HAVE ANY CHOICE.
AND NEITHER DO WE.
YOU GET THAT NOW, RIGHT?

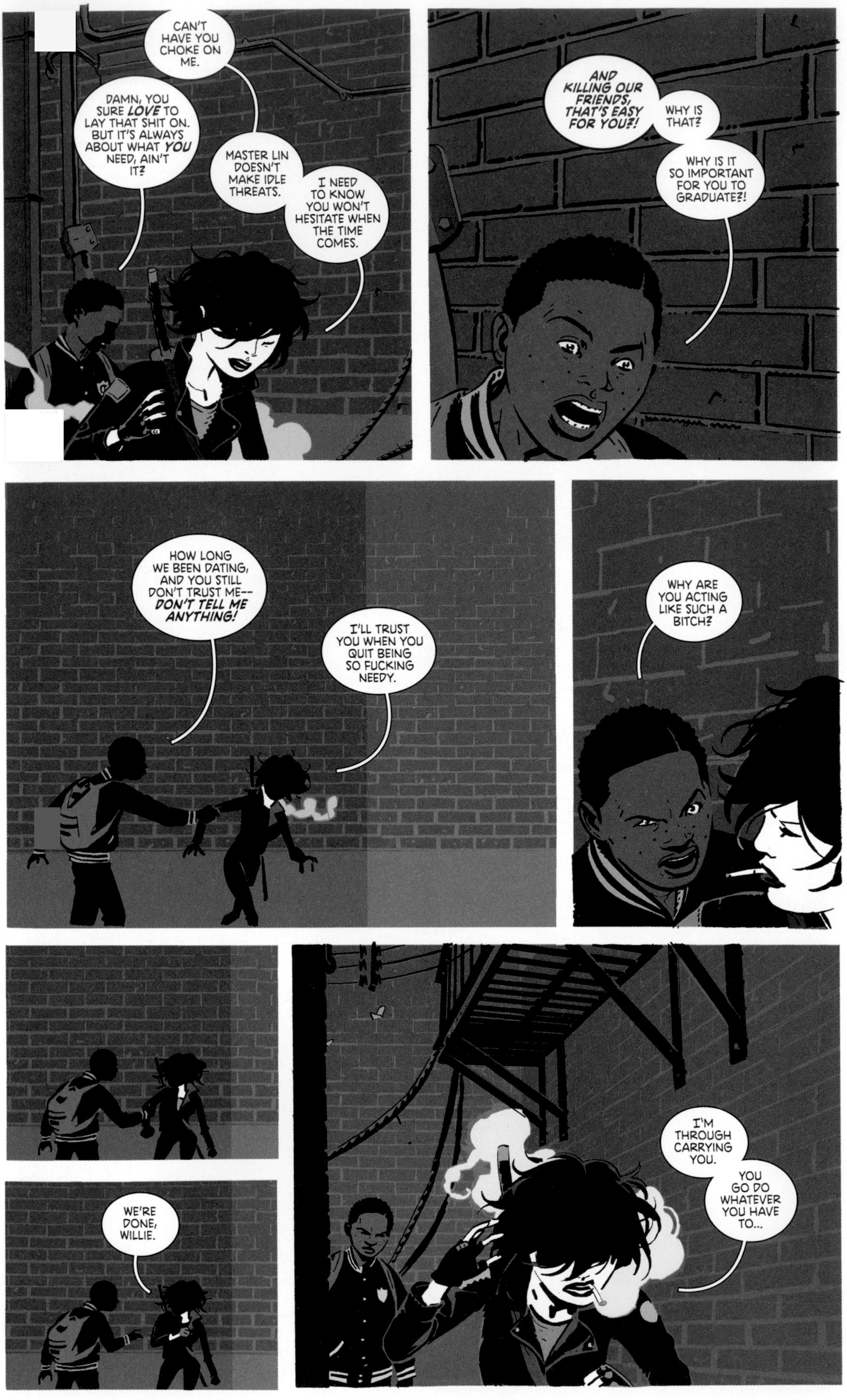

CAN'T HAVE YOU CHOKE ON ME.
DAMN, YOU SURE LOVE TO LAY THAT SHIT ON. BUT IT'S ALWAYS ABOUT WHAT YOU NEED, AIN'T IT?
MASTER LIN DOESN'T MAKE IDLE THREATS.
I NEED TO KNOW YOU WON'T HESITATE WHEN THE TIME COMES.
AND KILLING OUR FRIENDS, THAT'S EASY FOR YOU?!
WHY IS THAT?
WHY IS IT SO IMPORTANT FOR YOU TO GRADUATE?!
HOW LONG WE BEEN DATING, AND YOU STILL DON'T TRUST ME-- DON'T TELL ME ANYTHING!
I'LL TRUST YOU WHEN YOU QUIT BEING SO FUCKING NEEDY.
WHY ARE YOU ACTING LIKE SUCH A BITCH?
WE'RE DONE, WILLIE.
I'M THROUGH CARRYING YOU.
YOU GO DO WHATEVER YOU HAVE TO...

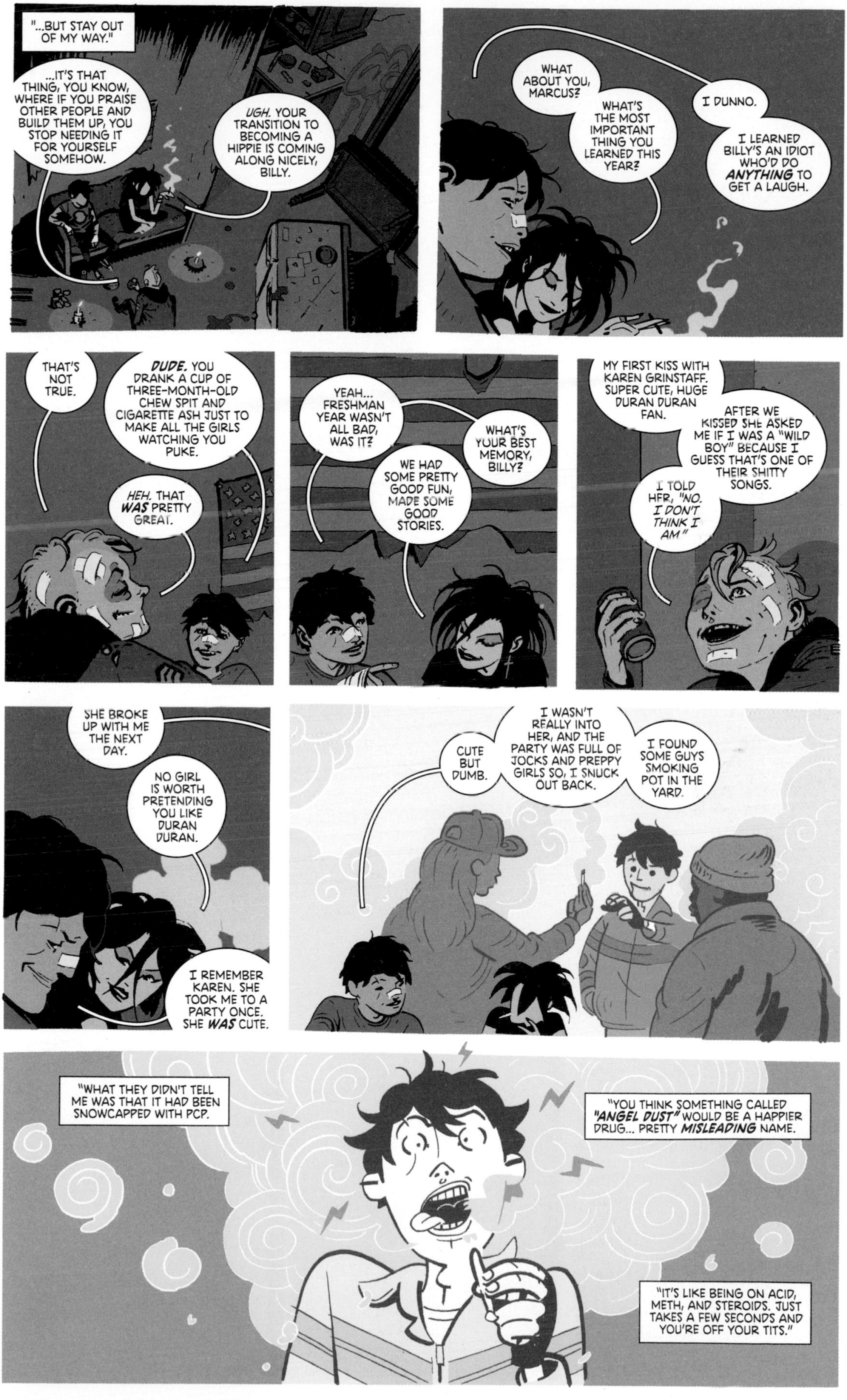
"...BUT STAY OUT OF MY WAY."
...IT'S THAT THING, YOU KNOW, WHERE IF YOU PRAISE OTHER PEOPLE AND BUILD THEM UP, YOU STOP NEEDING IT FOR YOURSELF SOMEHOW.
UGH. YOUR TRANSITION TO BECOMING A HIPPIE IS COMING ALONG NICELY, BILLY.
WHAT ABOUT YOU, MARCUS?
WHAT'S THE MOST IMPORTANT THING YOU LEARNED THIS YEAR?
I DUNNO.
I LEARNED BILLY'S AN IDIOT WHO'D DO ANYTHING TO GET A LAUGH.
THAT'S NOT TRUE.
DUDE. YOU DRANK A CUP OF THREE-MONTH-OLD CHEW SPIT AND CIGARETTE ASH JUST TO MAKE ALL THE GIRLS WATCHING YOU PUKE.
HEH. THAT WAS PRETTY GREAT.
YEAH... FRESHMAN YEAR WASN'T ALL BAD, WAS IT?
WE HAD SOME PRETTY GOOD FUN, MADE SOME GOOD STORIES.
WHAT'S YOUR BEST MEMORY, BILLY?
MY FIRST KISS WITH KAREN GRINSTAFF. SUPER CUTE, HUGE DURAN DURAN FAN.
AFTER WE KISSED SHE ASKED ME IF I WAS A "WILD BOY" BECAUSE I GUESS THAT'S ONE OF THEIR SHITTY SONGS.
I TOLD HER, "NO. I DON'T THINK I AM"
SHE BROKE UP WITH ME THE NEXT DAY.
NO GIRL IS WORTH PRETENDING YOU LIKE DURAN DURAN.
I REMEMBER KAREN. SHE TOOK ME TO A PARTY ONCE. SHE WAS CUTE.
CUTE BUT DUMB.
I WASN'T REALLY INTO HER, AND THE PARTY WAS FULL OF JOCKS AND PREPPY GIRLS SO, I SNUCK OUT BACK.
I FOUND SOME GUYS SMOKING POT IN THE YARD.
"WHAT THEY DIDN'T TELL ME WAS THAT IT HAD BEEN SNOWCAPPED WITH PCP.
"YOU THINK SOMETHING CALLED "ANGEL DUST" WOULD BE A HAPPIER DRUG... PRETTY MISLEADING NAME.
"IT'S LIKE BEING ON ACID, METH, AND STEROIDS. JUST TAKES A FEW SECONDS AND YOU'RE OFF YOUR TITS."

"BY THE TIME I WENT BACK INTO THE PARTY I THOUGHT I WAS MR. ROGERS.

"A WARM-HEARTED CHARACTER BELOVED BY ALL.

"KAREN LOOKED UPSET, BUT I KNEW IT WASN'T BECAUSE I WAS SCREAMING AT HER FRIENDS. IT WAS OBVIOUSLY BECAUSE THE PARTY WAS SO LAME.

"THEY NEEDED ME TO WELCOME THEM TO MY NEIGHBORHOOD.

"THEY NEEDED MORAL INSTRUCTION."

"I'D FOUND A BOX OF RAISINS IN A CABINET IN THE KITCHEN AND RAN AROUND GIVING THEM EACH LITTLE TOMES OF WISDOM. A FEW RACIALLY INSENSITIVE COMMENTS WERE BANDIED ABOUT.

"I TOLD THEM THAT EVERYONE SEES COLOR; IT'S ALL ABOUT THE INTELLECTUAL CHOICE TO NOT JUDGE BASED ON IT.

"WHEN ANYONE TRIED TO GET AWAY FROM ME I THREW RAISINS AT THEM. CHIP FRATSWORTH DIDN'T LOVE THAT AND SO HE PUSHED ME DOWN."

"AFTER A WHILE, THEY FORGOT I WAS THERE. I BECAME AN OUTSIDE OBSERVER TO THIS STRANGE BAND OF ASSHOLES.

"THEY WERE ALL LAUGHING WITH EACH OTHER, LIKE BEST FRIENDS.

"BUT AS SOON AS SOMEONE LEFT THE ROOM THE OTHERS ALL GANGED UP TO TEAR DOWN THE ABSENT 'FRIEND.'"

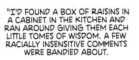

THEY WERE THE KIND OF PEOPLE WHO ONLY KNEW HOW TO BOND BY SHITTING ON SOMEONE WHO WASN'T IN THE ROOM.

IT MADE ME REALLY MISS YOU GUYS. FOR ALL OF OUR FAULTS... WE'RE NOT *THEM.*

YOU WANT ME TO PUT ON SOME ENYA, CAPTAIN SENSITIVE?

SOMETIMES WHEN SOMEONE SEEMS TO GO CRAZY WHAT THEY'RE ACTUALLY DOING IS LETTING EVERYONE SEE WHAT THEY USUALLY HIDE INSIDE.

DRUGS ARE JUST A GOOD EXCUSE TO LET THE TRUE SPAZ COME OUT.

OR AN EXCUSE TO DO SOMETHING YOU ALWAYS WANTED TO.

LAST TIME I DID COKE I TRIED TO FUCK VIKTOR.

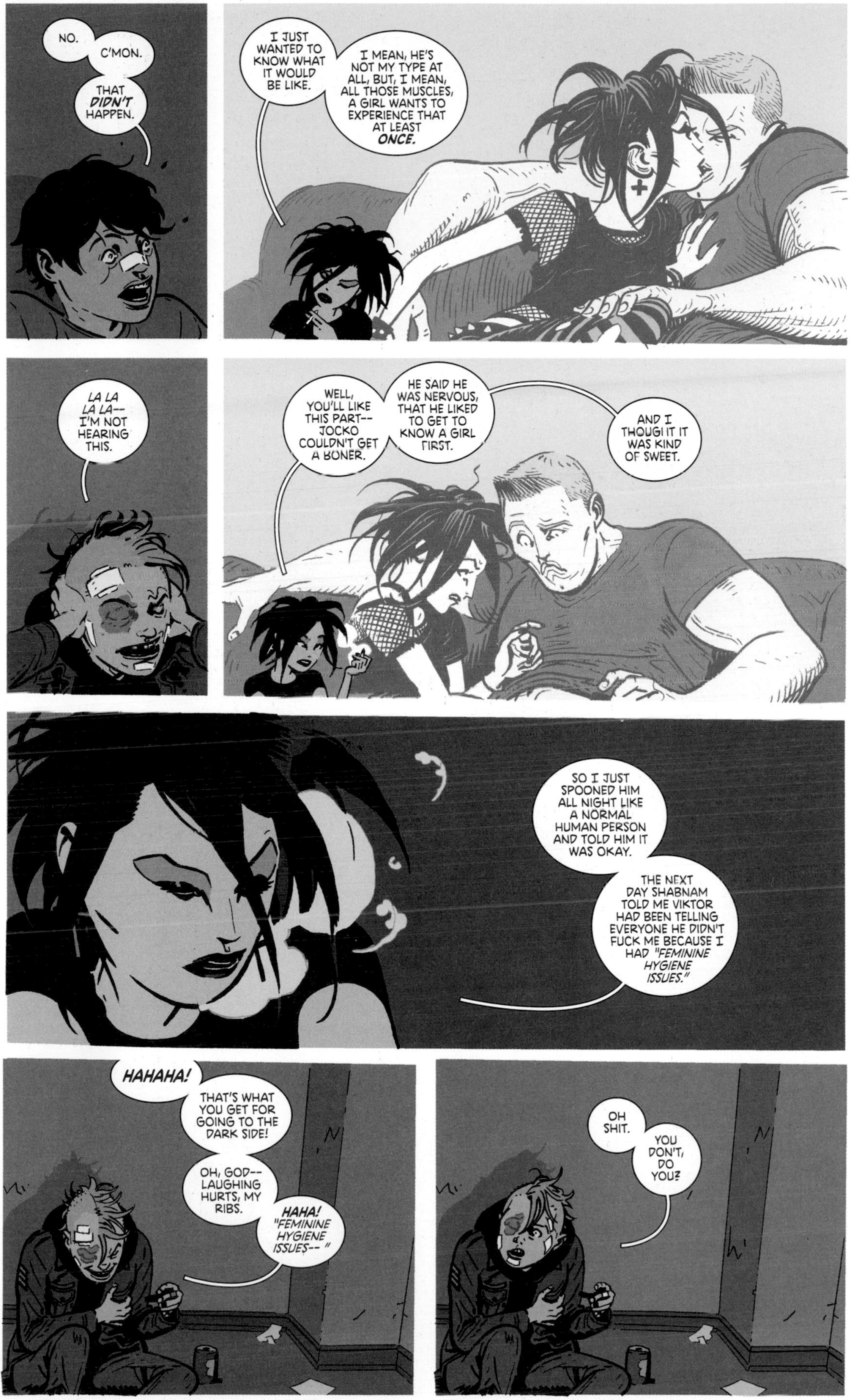

NO.
C'MON.
THAT *DIDN'T* HAPPEN.
I JUST WANTED TO KNOW WHAT IT WOULD BE LIKE.
I MEAN, HE'S NOT MY TYPE AT ALL, BUT, I MEAN, ALL THOSE MUSCLES, A GIRL WANTS TO EXPERIENCE THAT AT LEAST ***ONCE.***
LA LA LA LA-- I'M NOT HEARING THIS.
WELL, YOU'LL LIKE THIS PART-- JOCKO COULDN'T GET A BONER.
HE SAID HE WAS NERVOUS, THAT HE LIKED TO GET TO KNOW A GIRL FIRST.
AND I THOUGHT IT WAS KIND OF SWEET.
SO I JUST SPOONED HIM ALL NIGHT LIKE A NORMAL HUMAN PERSON AND TOLD HIM IT WAS OKAY.
THE NEXT DAY SHABNAM TOLD ME VIKTOR HAD BEEN TELLING EVERYONE HE DIDN'T FUCK ME BECAUSE I HAD *"FEMININE HYGIENE ISSUES."*
HAHAHA!
THAT'S WHAT YOU GET FOR GOING TO THE DARK SIDE!
OH, GOD-- LAUGHING HURTS, MY RIBS.
HAHA! *"FEMININE HYGIENE ISSUES-- "*
OH SHIT.
YOU DON'T, DO YOU?

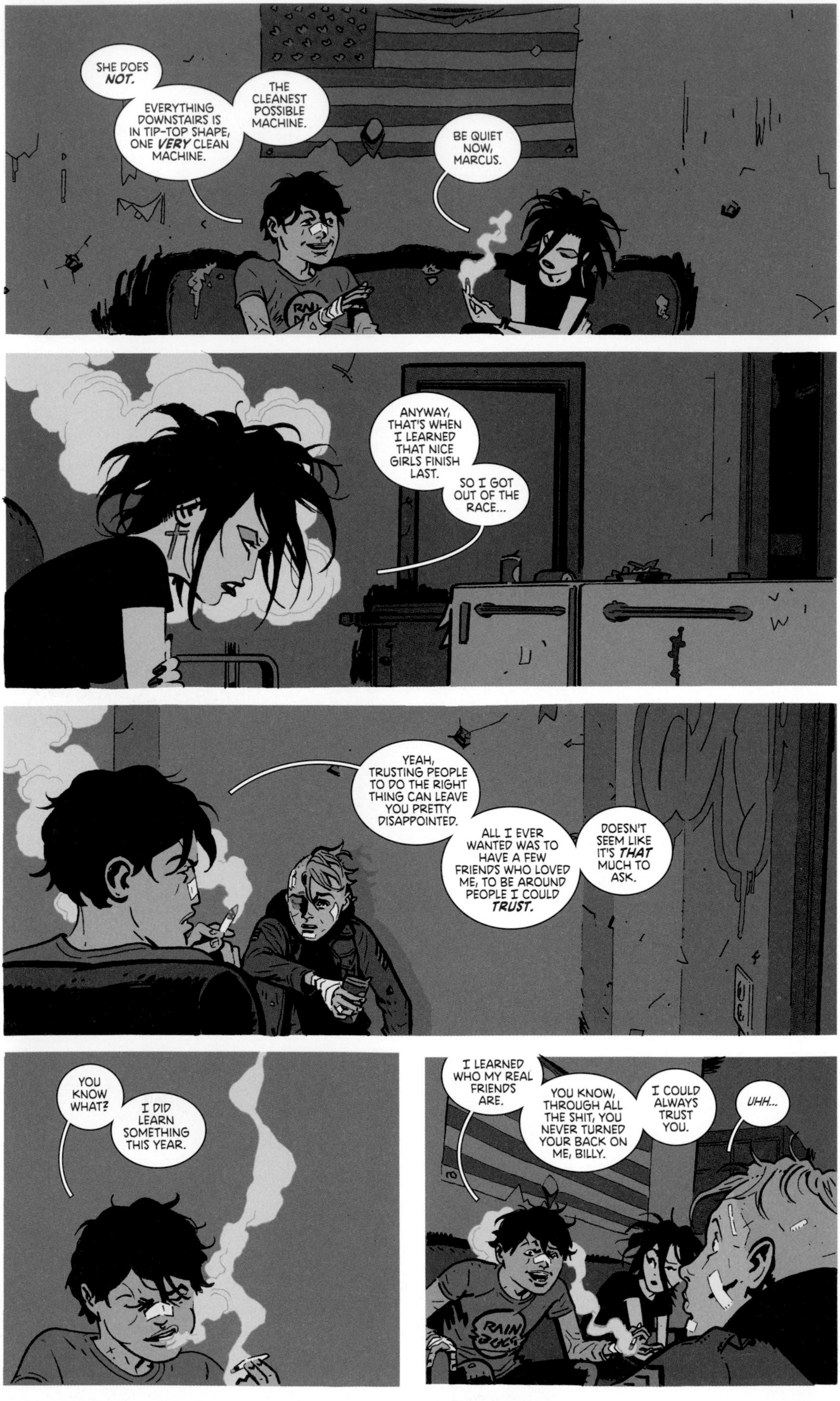
SHE DOES NOT.
EVERYTHING DOWNSTAIRS IS IN TIP-TOP SHAPE, ONE VERY CLEAN MACHINE.
THE CLEANEST POSSIBLE MACHINE.
BE QUIET NOW, MARCUS.
ANYWAY, THAT'S WHEN I LEARNED THAT NICE GIRLS FINISH LAST.
SO I GOT OUT OF THE RACE...
YEAH, TRUSTING PEOPLE TO DO THE RIGHT THING CAN LEAVE YOU PRETTY DISAPPOINTED.
ALL I EVER WANTED WAS TO HAVE A FEW FRIENDS WHO LOVED ME, TO BE AROUND PEOPLE I COULD TRUST.
DOESN'T SEEM LIKE IT'S THAT MUCH TO ASK.
YOU KNOW WHAT?
I DID LEARN SOMETHING THIS YEAR.
I LEARNED WHO MY REAL FRIENDS ARE.
YOU KNOW, THROUGH ALL THE SHIT, YOU NEVER TURNED YOUR BACK ON ME, BILLY.
I COULD ALWAYS TRUST YOU.
UHH...

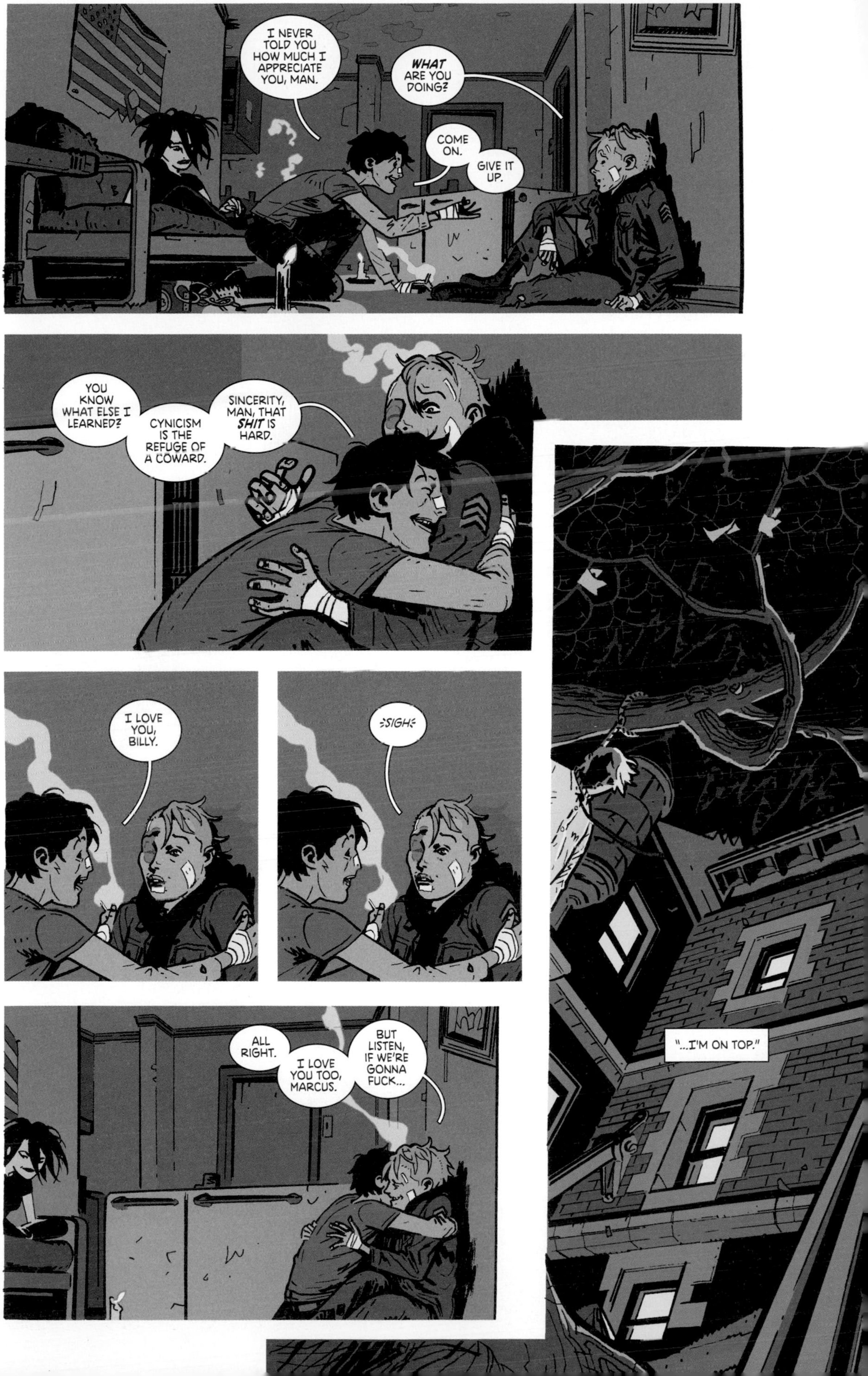
I NEVER TOLD YOU HOW MUCH I APPRECIATE YOU, MAN.
WHAT ARE YOU DOING?
COME ON.
GIVE IT UP.
YOU KNOW WHAT ELSE I LEARNED?
CYNICISM IS THE REFUGE OF A COWARD.
SINCERITY, MAN, THAT SHIT IS HARD.
I LOVE YOU, BILLY.
SIGH
ALL RIGHT.
I LOVE YOU TOO, MARCUS.
BUT LISTEN, IF WE'RE GONNA FUCK...
"...I'M ON TOP."

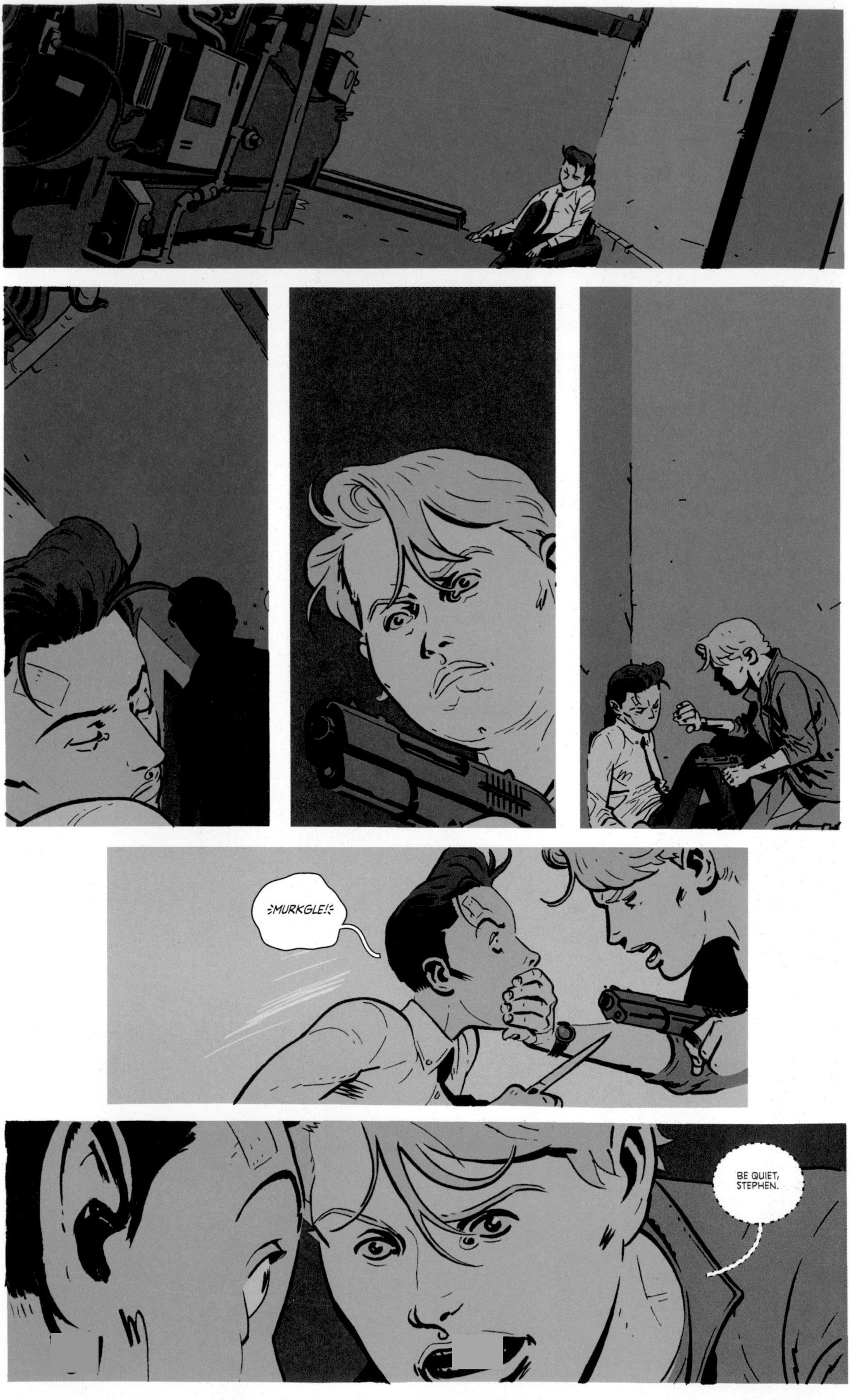

MURKGLE!
BE QUIET, STEPHEN.

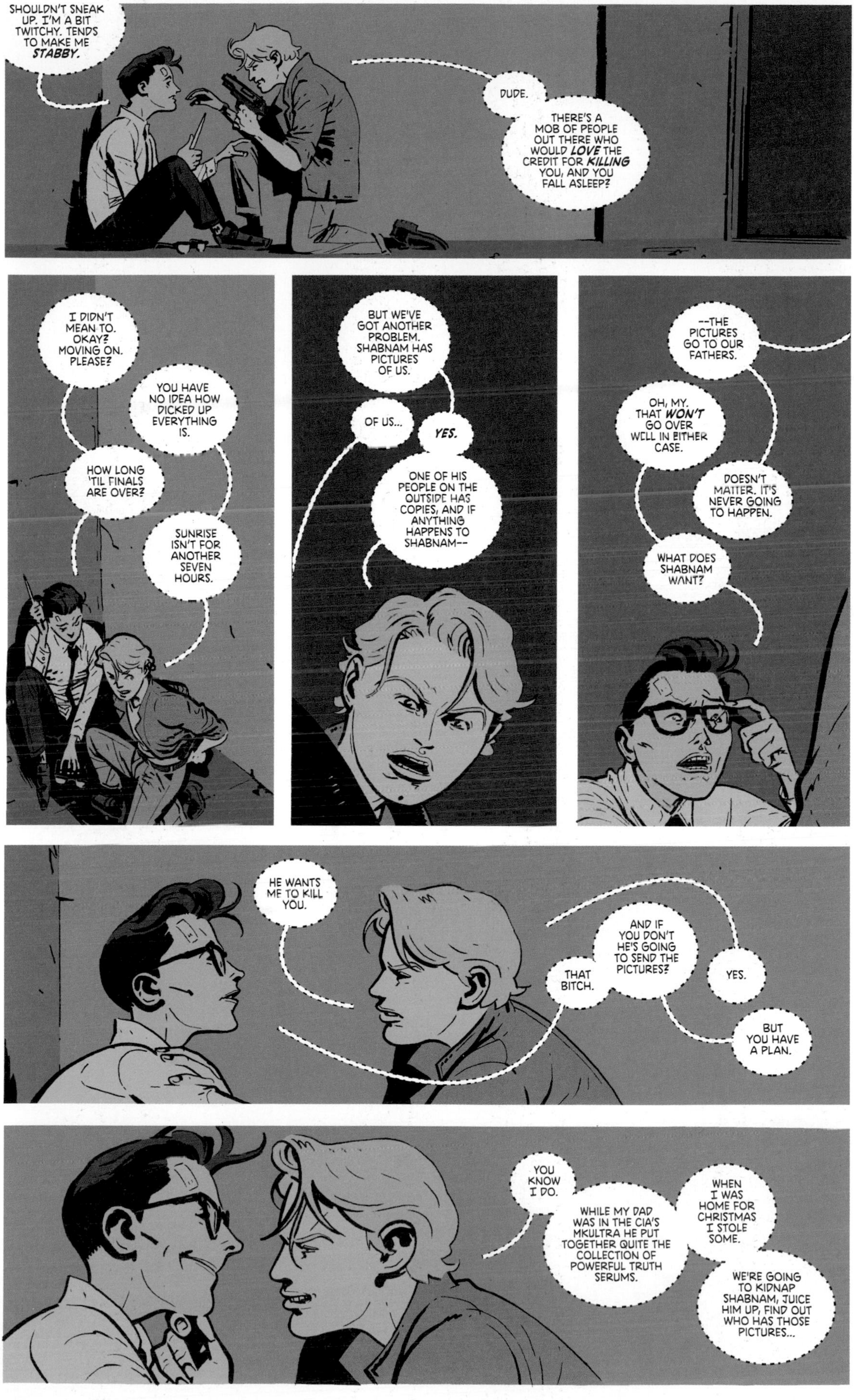
SHOULDN'T SNEAK UP. I'M A BIT TWITCHY. TENDS TO MAKE ME STABBY.
DUDE.
THERE'S A MOB OF PEOPLE OUT THERE WHO WOULD LOVE THE CREDIT FOR KILLING YOU, AND YOU FALL ASLEEP?
I DIDN'T MEAN TO. OKAY? MOVING ON. PLEASE?
YOU HAVE NO IDEA HOW DICKED UP EVERYTHING IS.
HOW LONG 'TIL FINALS ARE OVER?
SUNRISE ISN'T FOR ANOTHER SEVEN HOURS.
BUT WE'VE GOT ANOTHER PROBLEM. SHABNAM HAS PICTURES OF US.
OF US...
YES.
ONE OF HIS PEOPLE ON THE OUTSIDE HAS COPIES, AND IF ANYTHING HAPPENS TO SHABNAM--
--THE PICTURES GO TO OUR FATHERS.
OH, MY. THAT WON'T GO OVER WELL IN EITHER CASE.
DOESN'T MATTER. IT'S NEVER GOING TO HAPPEN.
WHAT DOES SHABNAM WANT?
HE WANTS ME TO KILL YOU.
THAT BITCH.
AND IF YOU DON'T HE'S GOING TO SEND THE PICTURES?
YES.
BUT YOU HAVE A PLAN.
YOU KNOW I DO.
WHILE MY DAD WAS IN THE CIA'S MKULTRA HE PUT TOGETHER QUITE THE COLLECTION OF POWERFUL TRUTH SERUMS.
WHEN I WAS HOME FOR CHRISTMAS I STOLE SOME.
WE'RE GOING TO KIDNAP SHABNAM, JUICE HIM UP, FIND OUT WHO HAS THOSE PICTURES...

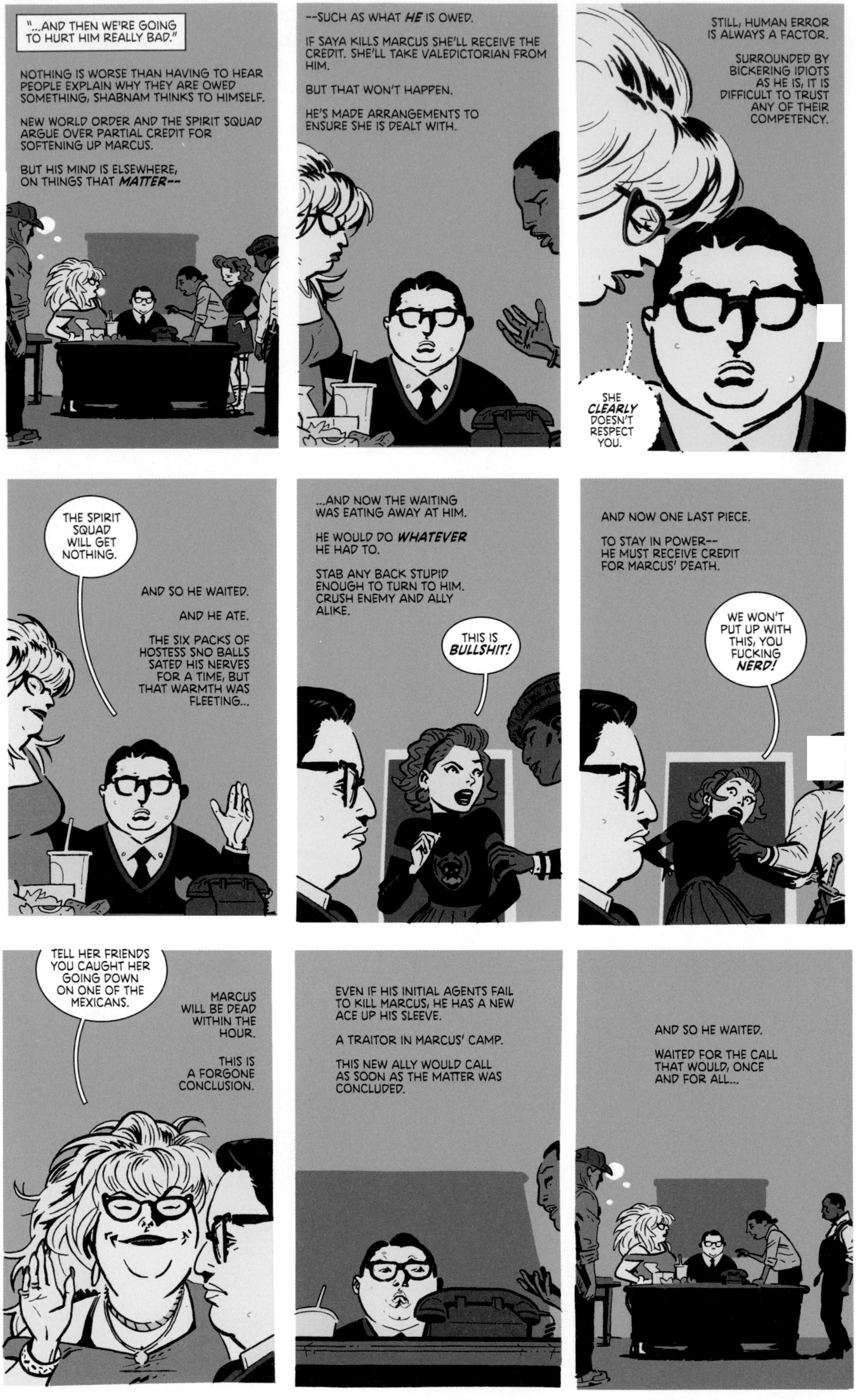
"...AND THEN WE'RE GOING TO HURT HIM REALLY BAD."
NOTHING IS WORSE THAN HAVING TO HEAR PEOPLE EXPLAIN WHY THEY ARE OWED SOMETHING, SHABNAM THINKS TO HIMSELF.
NEW WORLD ORDER AND THE SPIRIT SQUAD ARGUE OVER PARTIAL CREDIT FOR SOFTENING UP MARCUS.
BUT HIS MIND IS ELSEWHERE, ON THINGS THAT MATTER--
--SUCH AS WHAT HE IS OWED.
IF SAYA KILLS MARCUS SHE'LL RECEIVE THE CREDIT. SHE'LL TAKE VALEDICTORIAN FROM HIM.
BUT THAT WON'T HAPPEN.
HE'S MADE ARRANGEMENTS TO ENSURE SHE IS DEALT WITH.
STILL, HUMAN ERROR IS ALWAYS A FACTOR.
SURROUNDED BY BICKERING IDIOTS AS HE IS, IT IS DIFFICULT TO TRUST ANY OF THEIR COMPETENCY.
SHE CLEARLY DOESN'T RESPECT YOU.
THE SPIRIT SQUAD WILL GET NOTHING.
AND SO HE WAITED.
AND HE ATE.
THE SIX PACKS OF HOSTESS SNO BALLS SATED HIS NERVES FOR A TIME, BUT THAT WARMTH WAS FLEETING...
...AND NOW THE WAITING WAS EATING AWAY AT HIM.
HE WOULD DO WHATEVER HE HAD TO.
STAB ANY BACK STUPID ENOUGH TO TURN TO HIM. CRUSH ENEMY AND ALLY ALIKE.
THIS IS BULLSHIT!
AND NOW ONE LAST PIECE.
TO STAY IN POWER-- HE MUST RECEIVE CREDIT FOR MARCUS' DEATH.
WE WON'T PUT UP WITH THIS, YOU FUCKING NERD!
TELL HER FRIENDS YOU CAUGHT HER GOING DOWN ON ONE OF THE MEXICANS.
MARCUS WILL BE DEAD WITHIN THE HOUR.
THIS IS A FORGONE CONCLUSION.
EVEN IF HIS INITIAL AGENTS FAIL TO KILL MARCUS, HE HAS A NEW ACE UP HIS SLEEVE.
A TRAITOR IN MARCUS' CAMP.
THIS NEW ALLY WOULD CALL AS SOON AS THE MATTER WAS CONCLUDED.
AND SO HE WAITED.
WAITED FOR THE CALL THAT WOULD, ONCE AND FOR ALL...

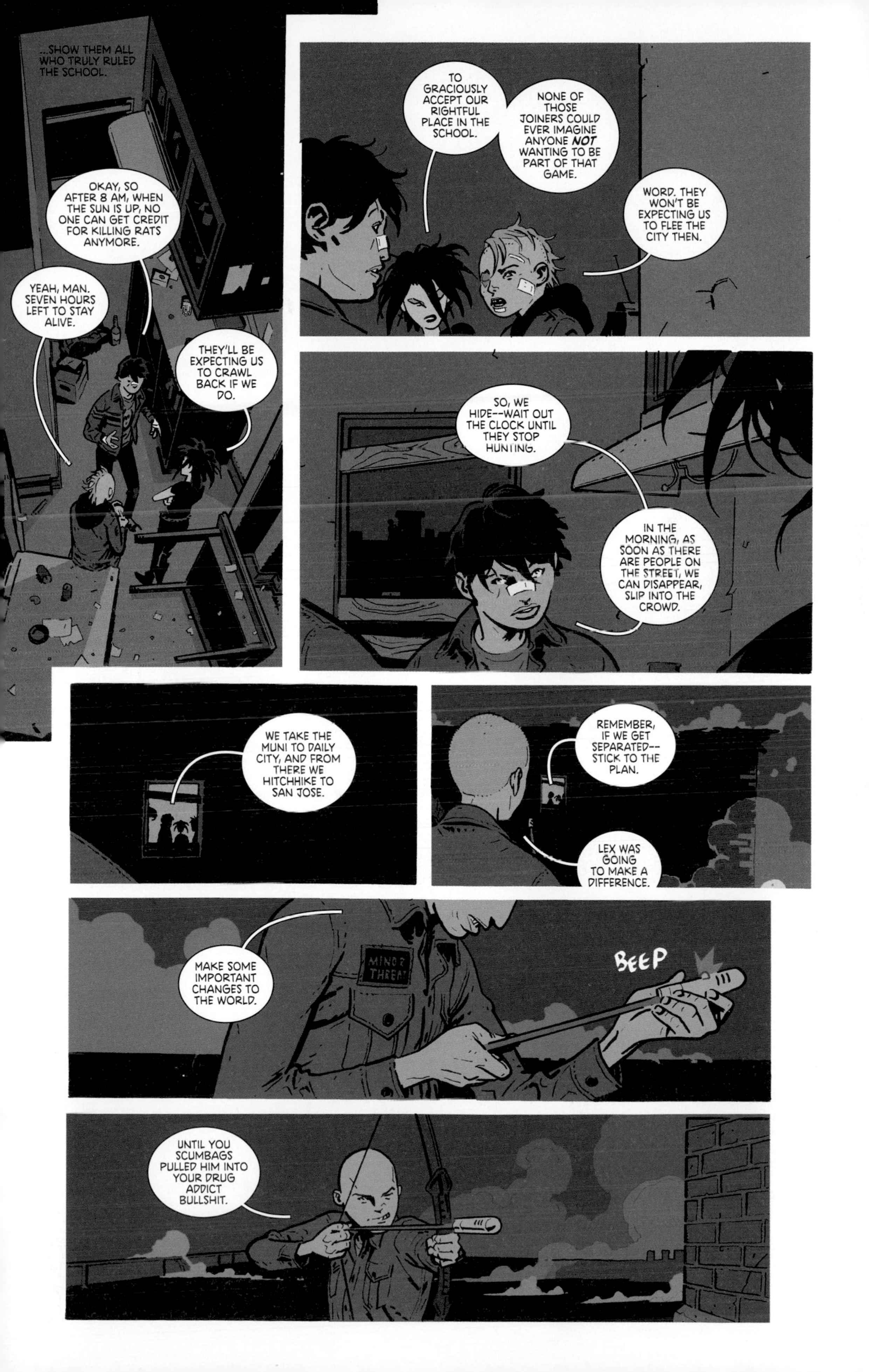
...SHOW THEM ALL WHO TRULY RULED THE SCHOOL.
OKAY, SO AFTER 8 AM, WHEN THE SUN IS UP, NO ONE CAN GET CREDIT FOR KILLING RATS ANYMORE.
YEAH, MAN. SEVEN HOURS LEFT TO STAY ALIVE.
THEY'LL BE EXPECTING US TO CRAWL BACK IF WE DO.
TO GRACIOUSLY ACCEPT OUR RIGHTFUL PLACE IN THE SCHOOL.
NONE OF THOSE JOINERS COULD EVER IMAGINE ANYONE NOT WANTING TO BE PART OF THAT GAME.
WORD. THEY WON'T BE EXPECTING US TO FLEE THE CITY THEN.
SO, WE HIDE--WAIT OUT THE CLOCK UNTIL THEY STOP HUNTING.
IN THE MORNING, AS SOON AS THERE ARE PEOPLE ON THE STREET, WE CAN DISAPPEAR, SLIP INTO THE CROWD.
WE TAKE THE MUNI TO DAILY CITY, AND FROM THERE WE HITCHHIKE TO SAN JOSE.
REMEMBER, IF WE GET SEPARATED--STICK TO THE PLAN.
LEX WAS GOING TO MAKE A DIFFERENCE.
MAKE SOME IMPORTANT CHANGES TO THE WORLD.
MINOR THREAT
BEEP
UNTIL YOU SCUMBAGS PULLED HIM INTO YOUR DRUG ADDICT BULLSHIT.

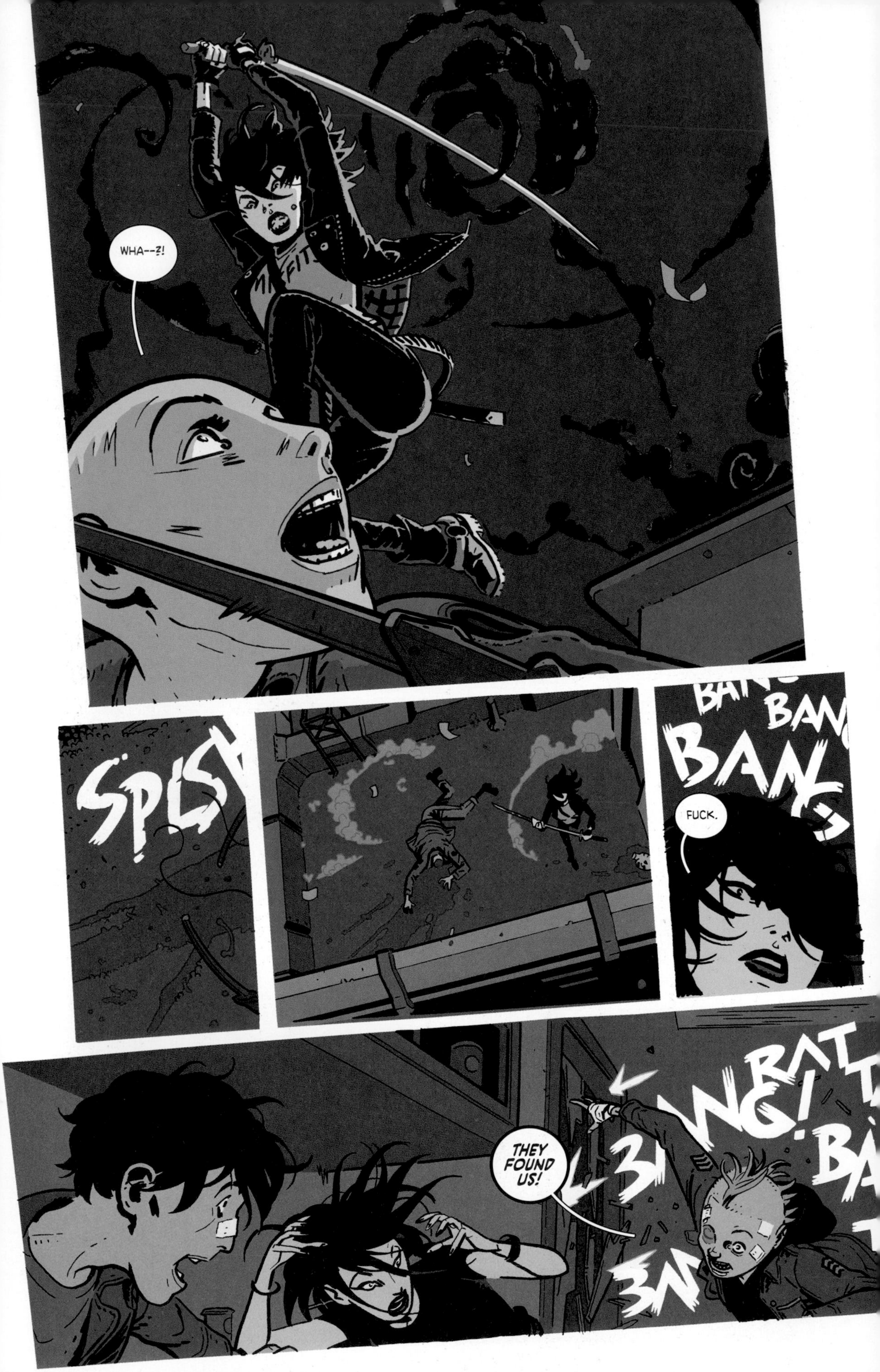

WHA--?!
SPLSH
FUCK.
BANG BANG BANG
THEY FOUND US!

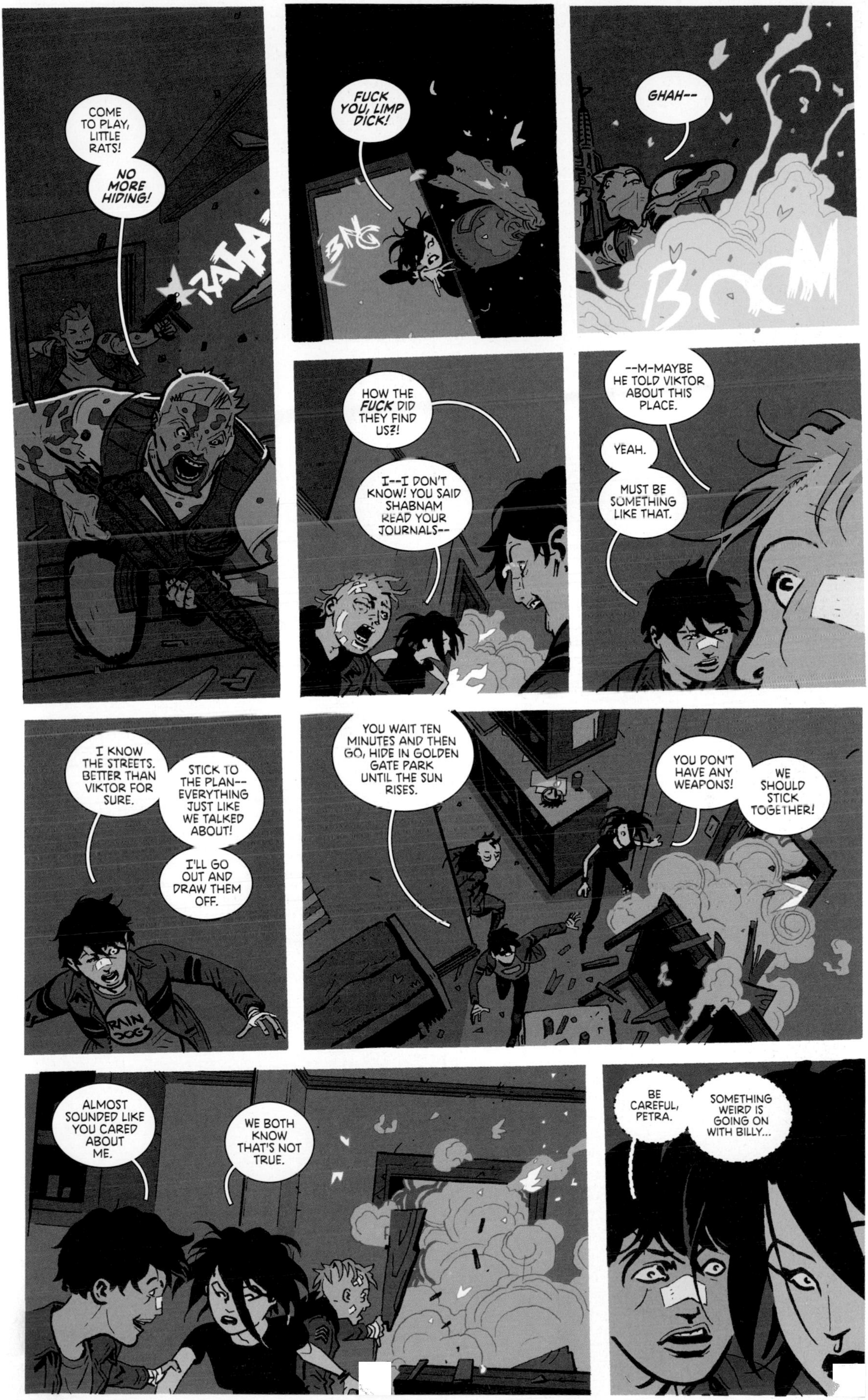
COME TO PLAY, LITTLE RATS!
NO MORE HIDING!
RATAT
FUCK YOU, LIMP DICK!
BANG
GHAH--
BOOM
HOW THE FUCK DID THEY FIND US?!
I--I DON'T KNOW! YOU SAID SHABNAM READ YOUR JOURNALS--
--M-MAYBE HE TOLD VIKTOR ABOUT THIS PLACE.
YEAH.
MUST BE SOMETHING LIKE THAT.
I KNOW THE STREETS. BETTER THAN VIKTOR FOR SURE.
STICK TO THE PLAN-- EVERYTHING JUST LIKE WE TALKED ABOUT!
I'LL GO OUT AND DRAW THEM OFF.
RAIN DOGS
YOU WAIT TEN MINUTES AND THEN GO, HIDE IN GOLDEN GATE PARK UNTIL THE SUN RISES.
YOU DON'T HAVE ANY WEAPONS!
WE SHOULD STICK TOGETHER!
ALMOST SOUNDED LIKE YOU CARED ABOUT ME.
WE BOTH KNOW THAT'S NOT TRUE.
BE CAREFUL, PETRA.
SOMETHING WEIRD IS GOING ON WITH BILLY...

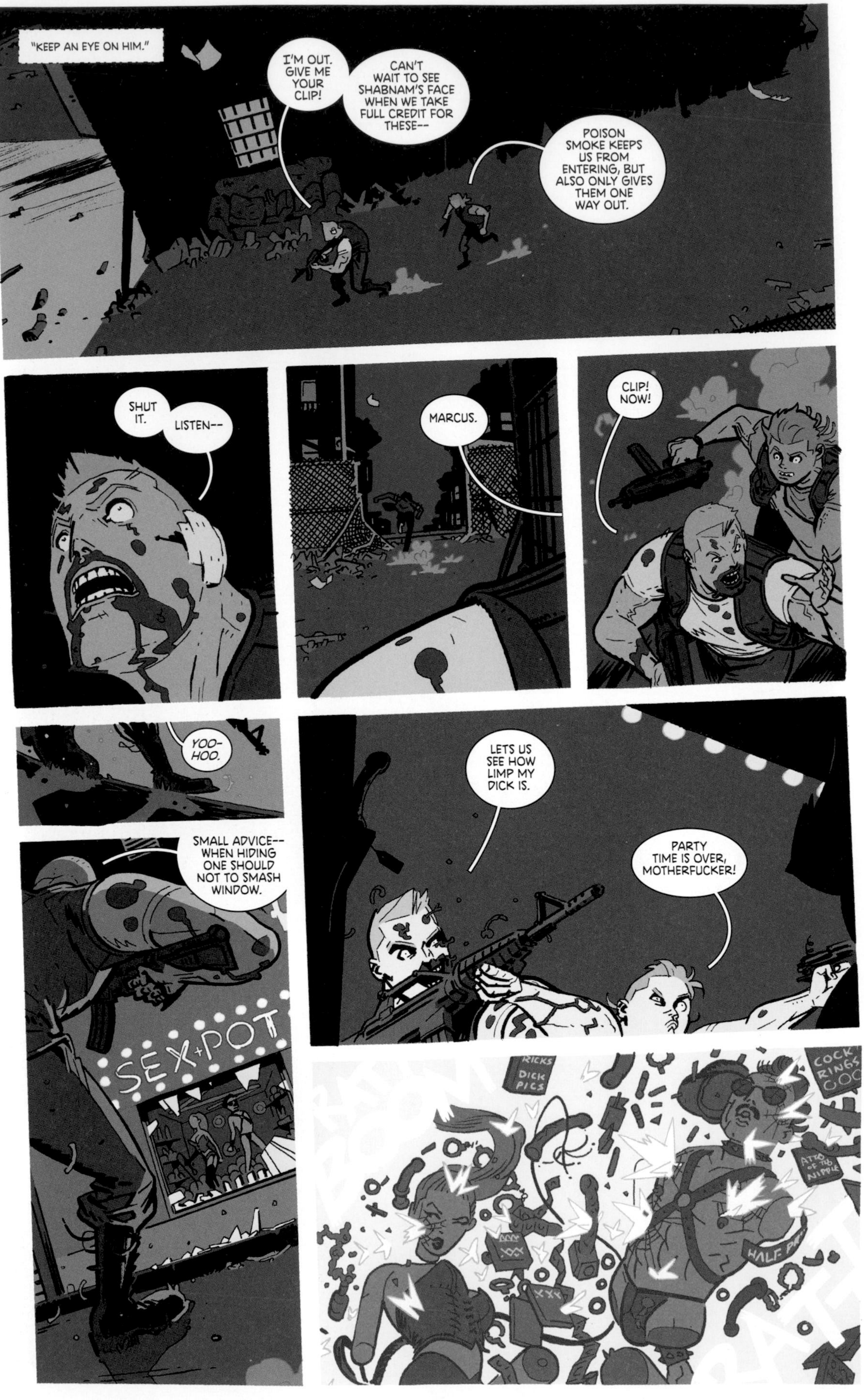
"KEEP AN EYE ON HIM."
I'M OUT. GIVE ME YOUR CLIP!
CAN'T WAIT TO SEE SHABNAM'S FACE WHEN WE TAKE FULL CREDIT FOR THESE--
POISON SMOKE KEEPS US FROM ENTERING, BUT ALSO ONLY GIVES THEM ONE WAY OUT.
SHUT IT.
LISTEN--
MARCUS.
CLIP! NOW!
YOO-HOO.
SMALL ADVICE-- WHEN HIDING ONE SHOULD NOT TO SMASH WINDOW.
SEX+POT
LETS US SEE HOW LIMP MY DICK IS.
PARTY TIME IS OVER, MOTHERFUCKER!
DICK PICS
COCK RINGS

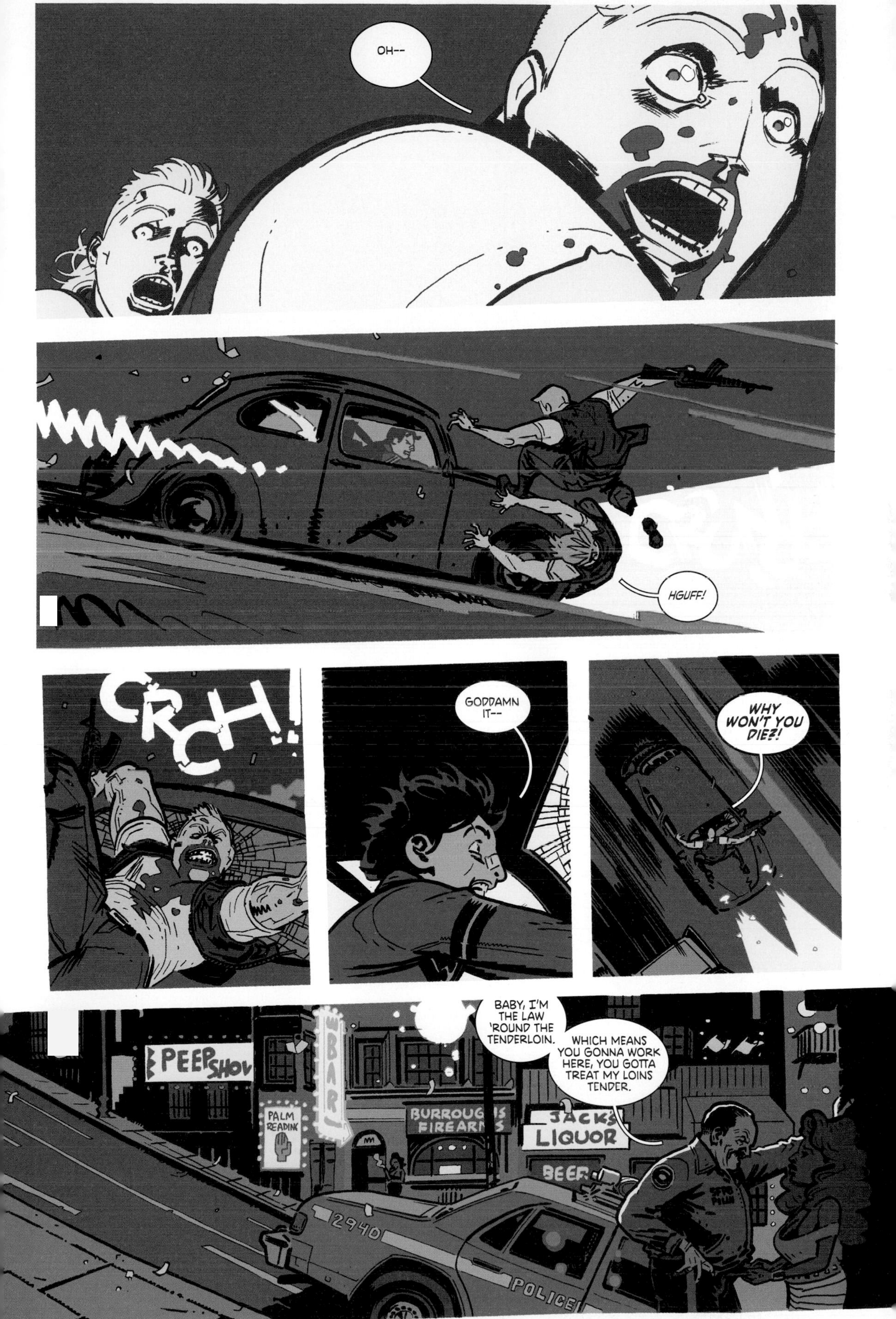
OH--
HGUFF!
CRCH!!
GODDAMN IT--
WHY WON'T YOU DIE?!
BABY, I'M THE LAW 'ROUND THE TENDERLOIN.
WHICH MEANS YOU GONNA WORK HERE, YOU GOTTA TREAT MY LOINS TENDER.
PEEP SHOW
PALM READING
BAR
BURROUGHS FIREARMS
JACK'S LIQUOR
BEER
2940
POLICE

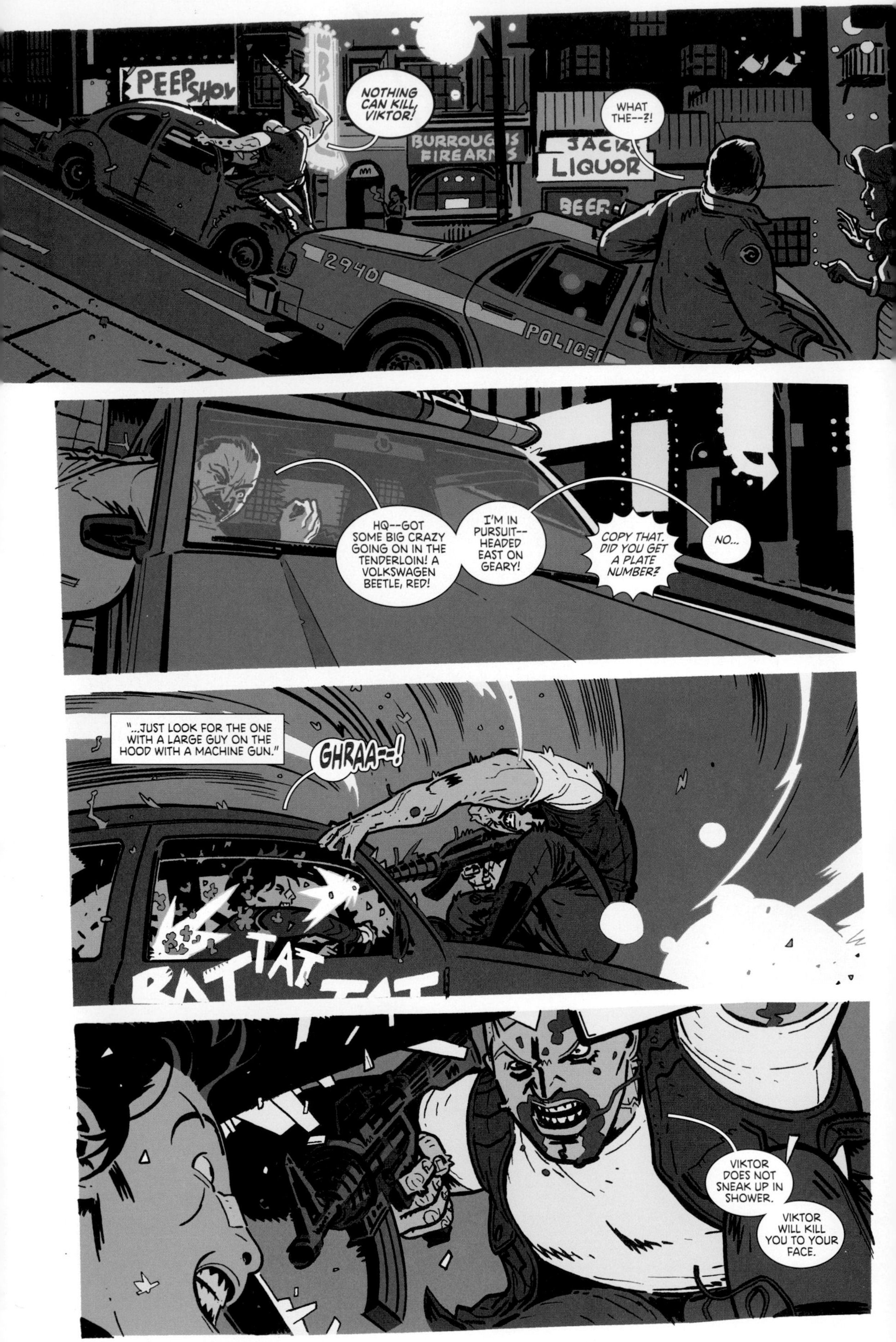
PEEP SHOW
NOTHING CAN KILL VIKTOR!
BURROUGHS FIREARMS
WHAT THE--?!
LIQUOR
BEER
2940
POLICE
HQ--GOT SOME BIG CRAZY GOING ON IN THE TENDERLOIN! A VOLKSWAGEN BEETLE, RED!
I'M IN PURSUIT--HEADED EAST ON GEARY!
COPY THAT. DID YOU GET A PLATE NUMBER?
NO...
"...JUST LOOK FOR THE ONE WITH A LARGE GUY ON THE HOOD WITH A MACHINE GUN."
GHRAA--!
TAT
TAT
VIKTOR DOES NOT SNEAK UP IN SHOWER.
VIKTOR WILL KILL YOU TO YOUR FACE.

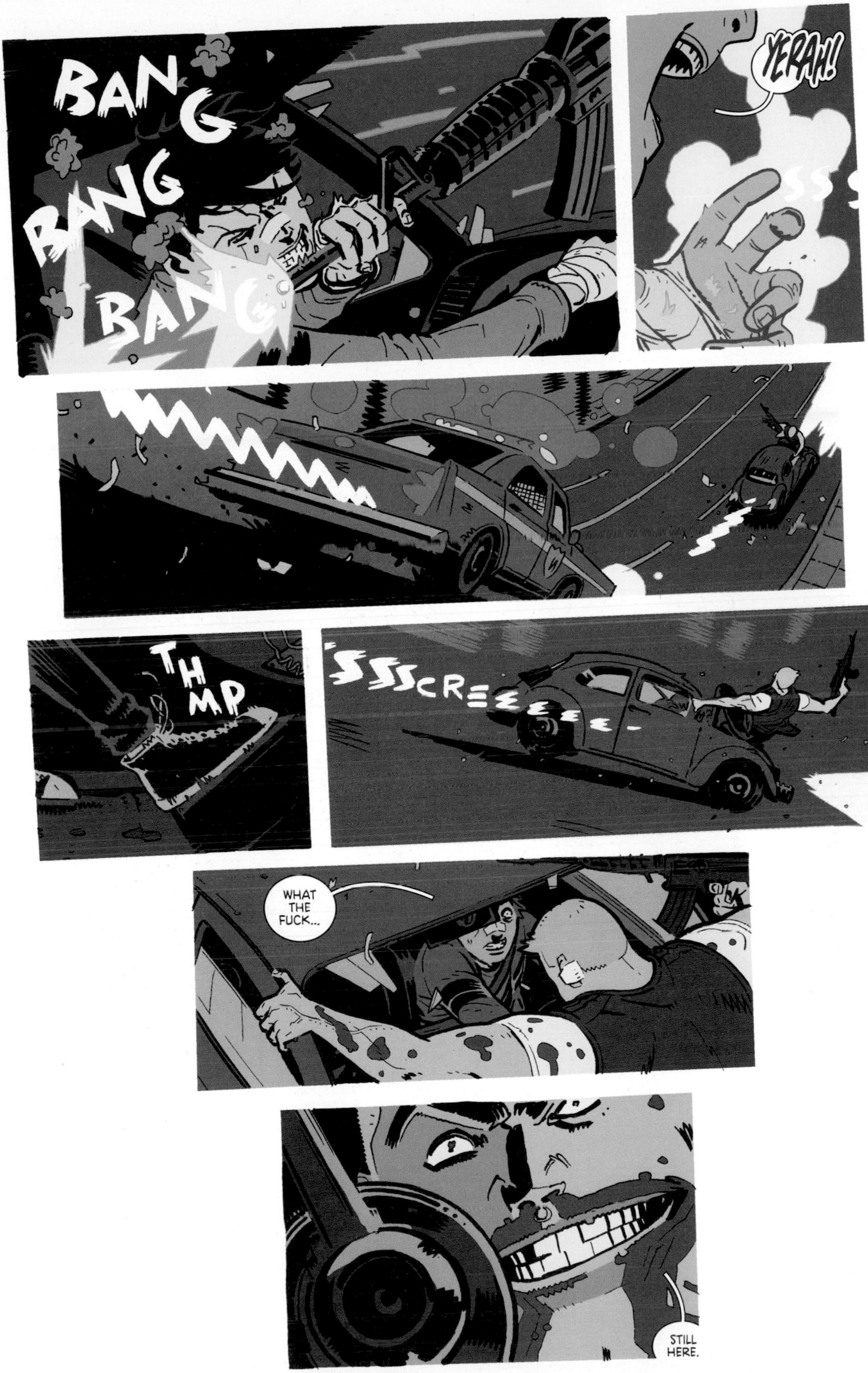
BANG
BANG
BANG
YERAH!
SSS
THMP
SSSCREEEEEEE
WHAT THE FUCK...
STILL HERE.

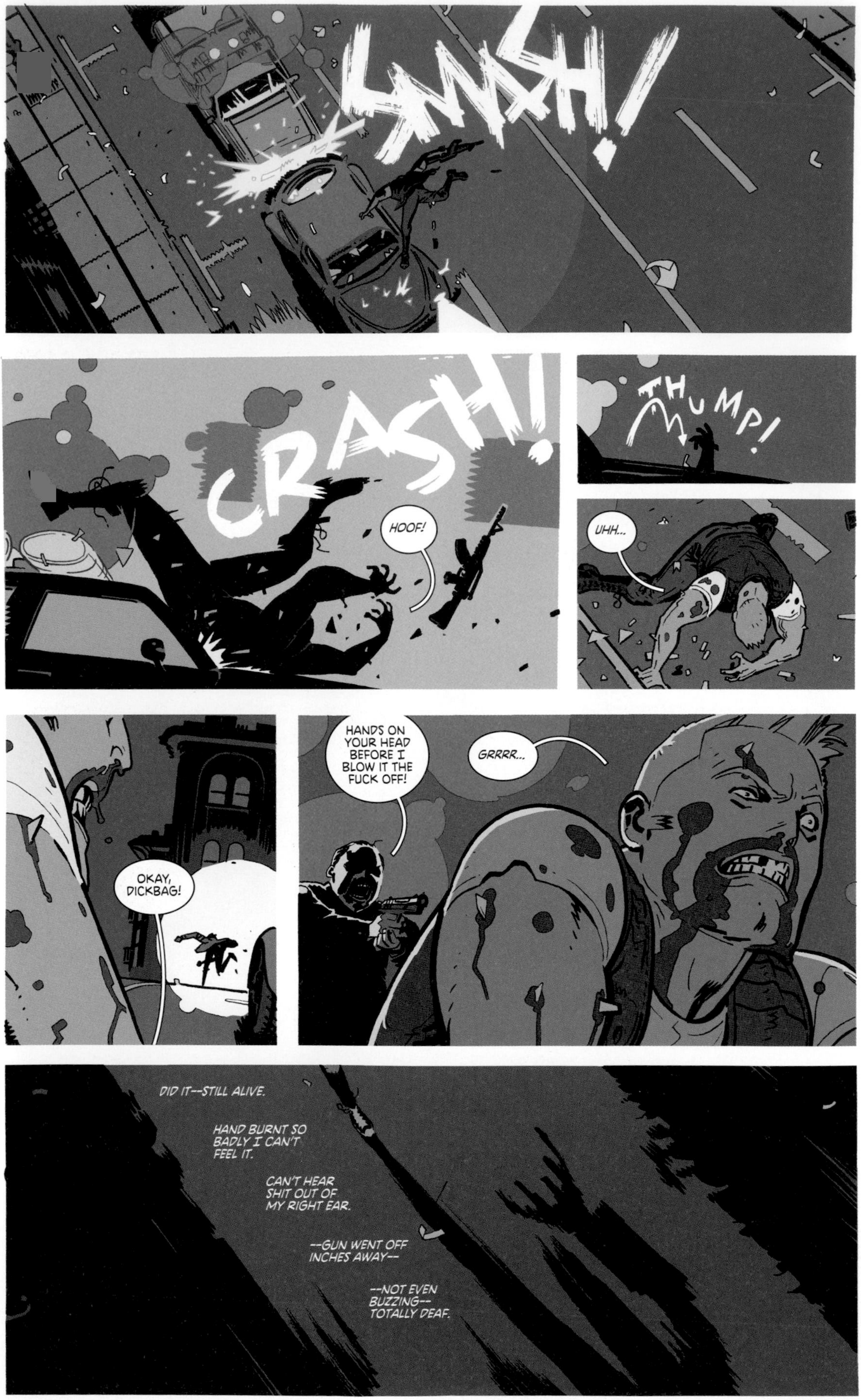
SMASH!
CRASH!
HOOF!
THUMP!
UHH...
OKAY, DICKBAG!
HANDS ON YOUR HEAD BEFORE I BLOW IT THE FUCK OFF!
GRRRR...
DID IT--STILL ALIVE.
HAND BURNT SO BADLY I CAN'T FEEL IT.
CAN'T HEAR SHIT OUT OF MY RIGHT EAR.
--GUN WENT OFF INCHES AWAY--
--NOT EVEN BUZZING-- TOTALLY DEAF.

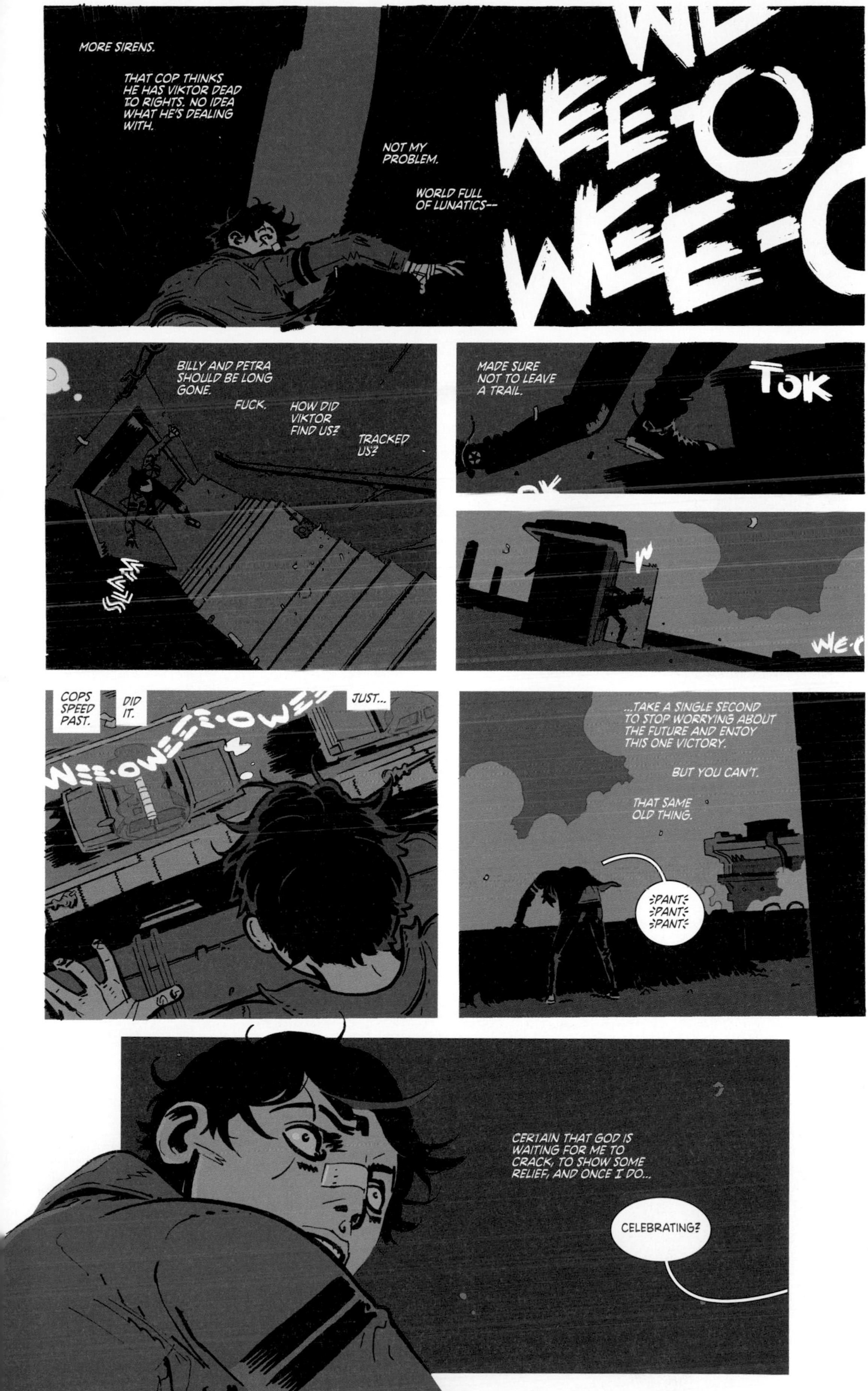
MORE SIRENS.
THAT COP THINKS HE HAS VIKTOR DEAD TO RIGHTS. NO IDEA WHAT HE'S DEALING WITH.
NOT MY PROBLEM.
WORLD FULL OF LUNATICS--
WEE-O
BILLY AND PETRA SHOULD BE LONG GONE.
FUCK.
HOW DID VIKTOR FIND US?
TRACKED US?
SLAM
MADE SURE NOT TO LEAVE A TRAIL.
TOK
COPS SPEED PAST.
DID IT.
JUST...
...TAKE A SINGLE SECOND TO STOP WORRYING ABOUT THE FUTURE AND ENJOY THIS ONE VICTORY.
BUT YOU CAN'T.
THAT SAME OLD THING.
PANT PANT PANT
CERTAIN THAT GOD IS WAITING FOR ME TO CRACK, TO SHOW SOME RELIEF, AND ONCE I DO...
CELEBRATING?

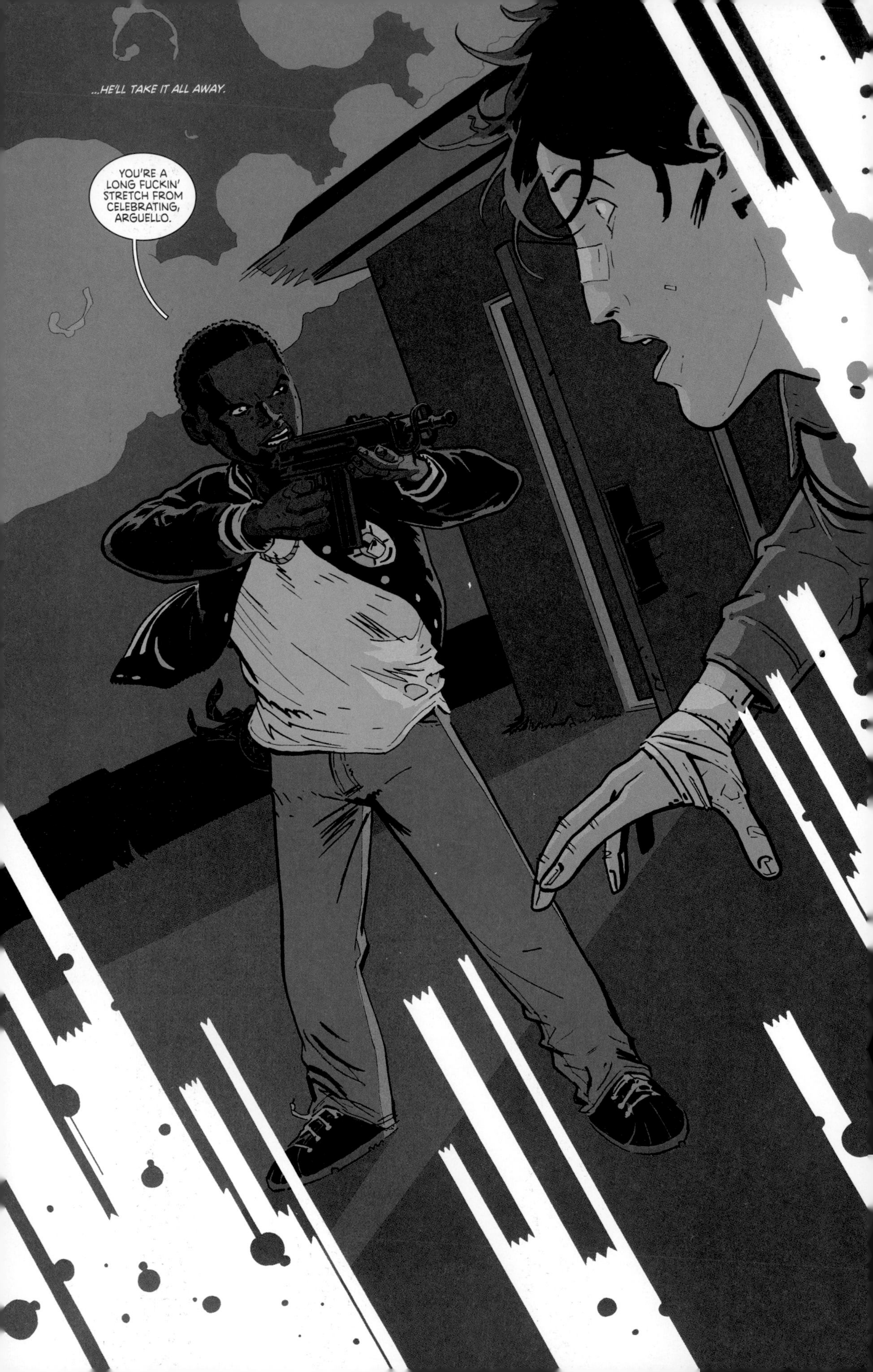
...HE'LL TAKE IT ALL AWAY.
YOU'RE A LONG FUCKIN' STRETCH FROM CELEBRATING, ARGUELLO.

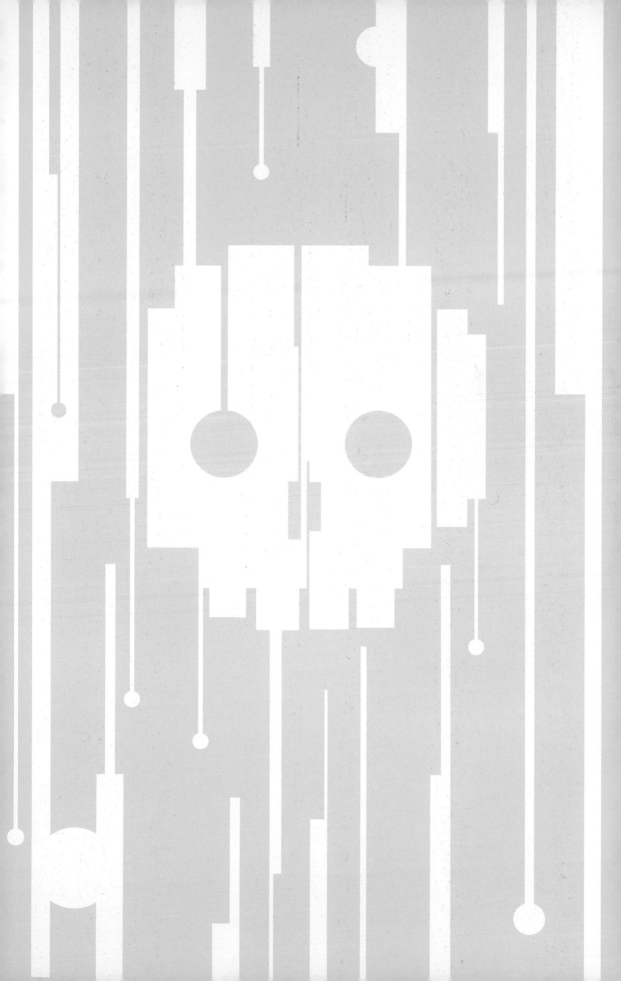

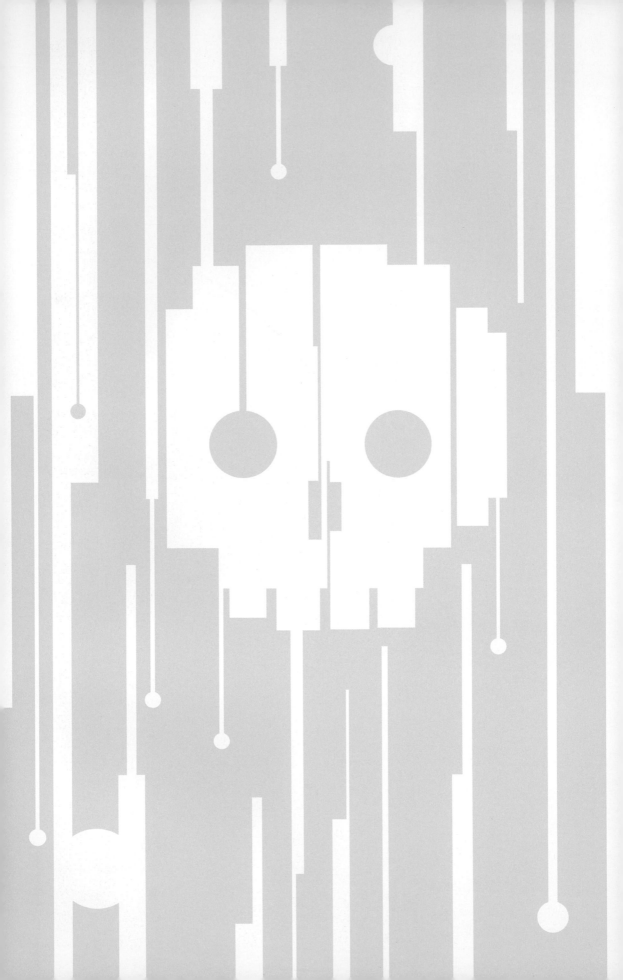

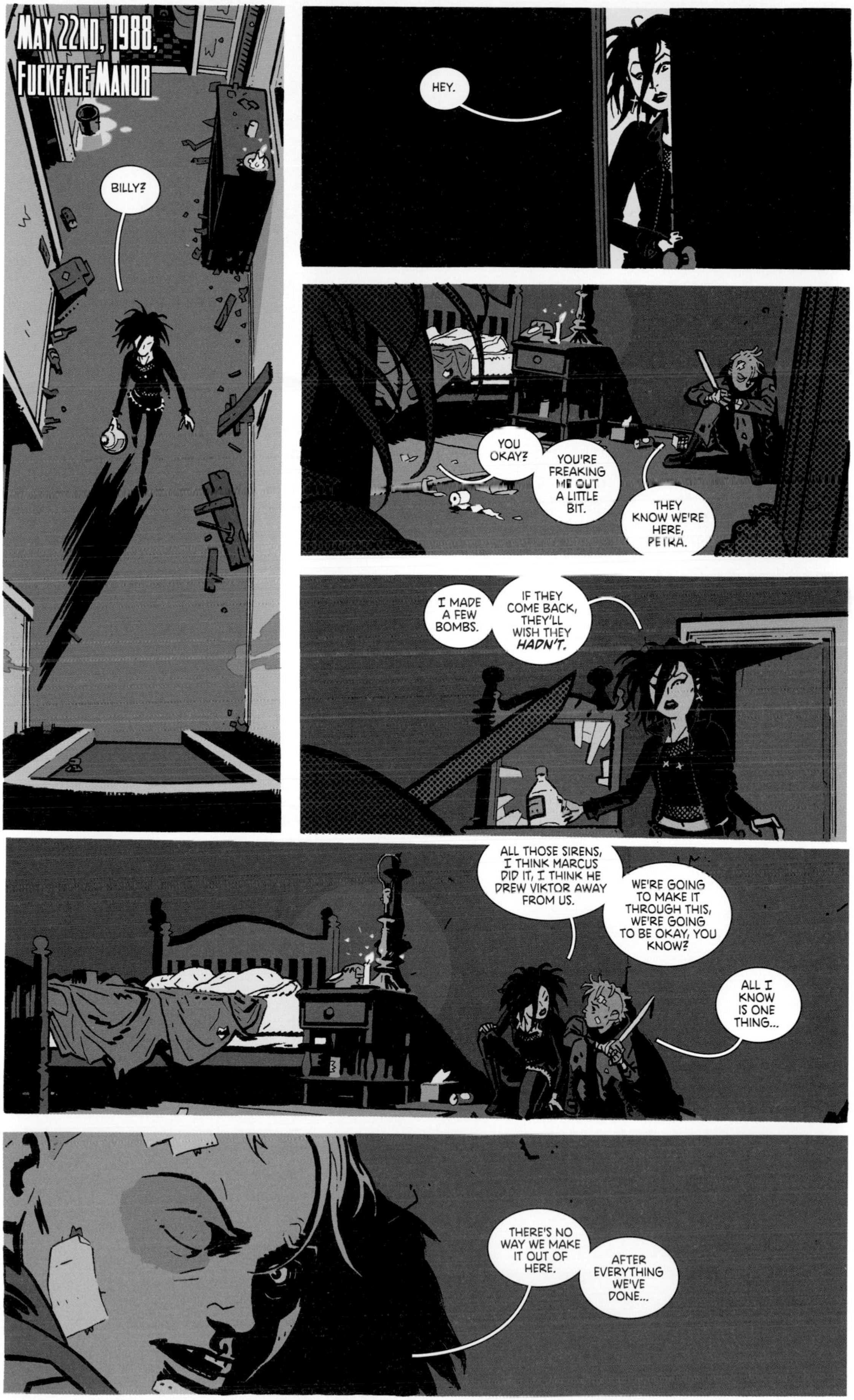
MAY 22ND, 1988, FUCKFACE MANOR
BILLY?
HEY.
YOU OKAY?
YOU'RE FREAKING ME OUT A LITTLE BIT.
THEY KNOW WE'RE HERE, PETRA.
I MADE A FEW BOMBS.
IF THEY COME BACK, THEY'LL WISH THEY *HADN'T.*
ALL THOSE SIRENS, I THINK MARCUS DID IT, I THINK HE DREW VIKTOR AWAY FROM US.
WE'RE GOING TO MAKE IT THROUGH THIS, WE'RE GOING TO BE OKAY, YOU KNOW?
ALL I KNOW IS ONE THING...
THERE'S NO WAY WE MAKE IT OUT OF HERE.
AFTER EVERYTHING WE'VE DONE...

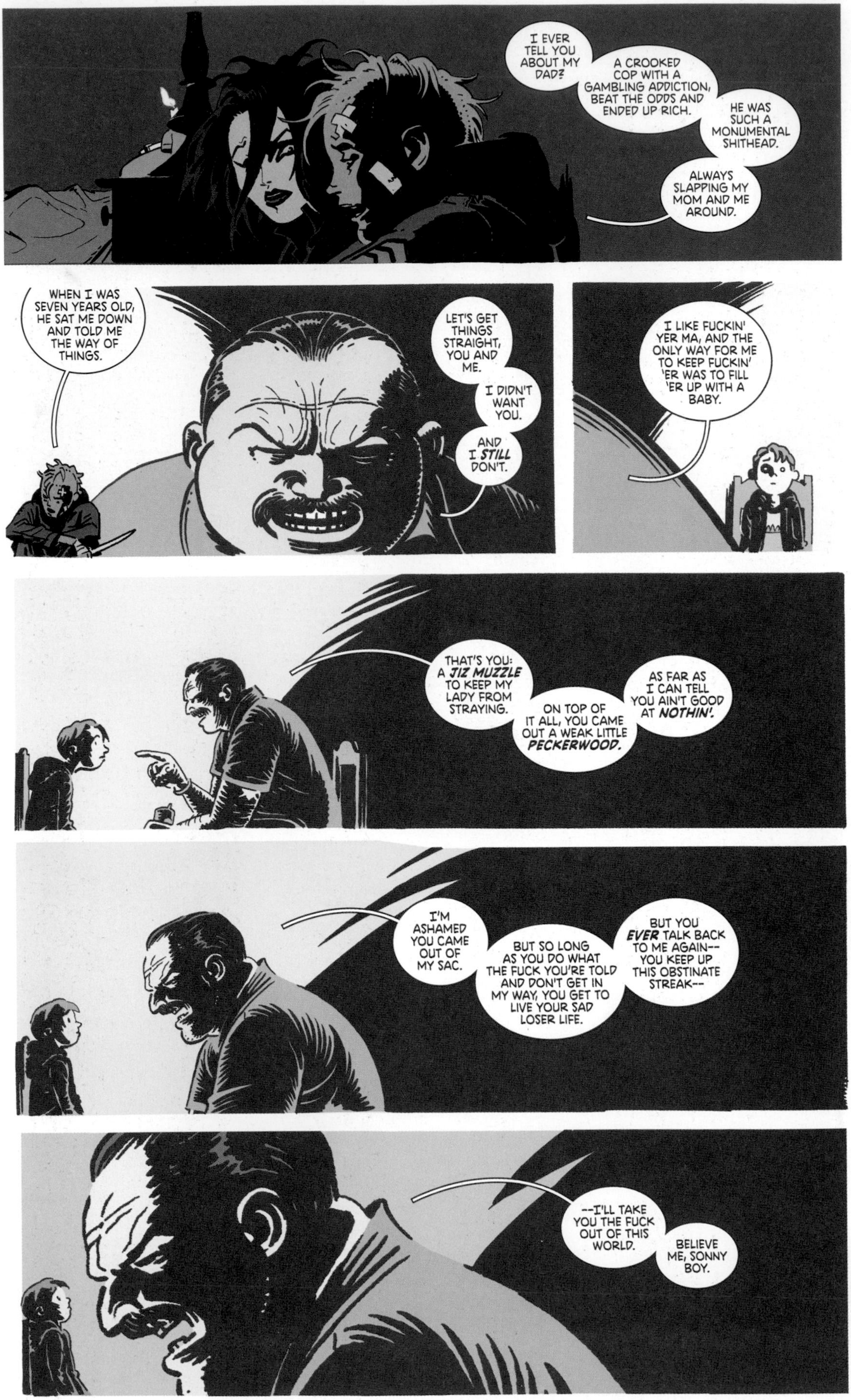
I EVER TELL YOU ABOUT MY DAD?
A CROOKED COP WITH A GAMBLING ADDICTION, BEAT THE ODDS AND ENDED UP RICH.
HE WAS SUCH A MONUMENTAL SHITHEAD.
ALWAYS SLAPPING MY MOM AND ME AROUND.
WHEN I WAS SEVEN YEARS OLD, HE SAT ME DOWN AND TOLD ME THE WAY OF THINGS.
LET'S GET THINGS STRAIGHT, YOU AND ME.
I DIDN'T WANT YOU.
AND I ***STILL*** DON'T.
I LIKE FUCKIN' YER MA, AND THE ONLY WAY FOR ME TO KEEP FUCKIN' 'ER WAS TO FILL 'ER UP WITH A BABY.
THAT'S YOU: A ***JIZ MUZZLE*** TO KEEP MY LADY FROM STRAYING.
ON TOP OF IT ALL, YOU CAME OUT A WEAK LITTLE ***PECKERWOOD.***
AS FAR AS I CAN TELL YOU AIN'T GOOD AT ***NOTHIN'.***
I'M ASHAMED YOU CAME OUT OF MY SAC.
BUT SO LONG AS YOU DO WHAT THE FUCK YOU'RE TOLD AND DON'T GET IN MY WAY, YOU GET TO LIVE YOUR SAD LOSER LIFE.
BUT YOU ***EVER*** TALK BACK TO ME AGAIN-- YOU KEEP UP THIS OBSTINATE STREAK--
--I'LL TAKE YOU THE FUCK OUT OF THIS WORLD.
BELIEVE ME, SONNY BOY.

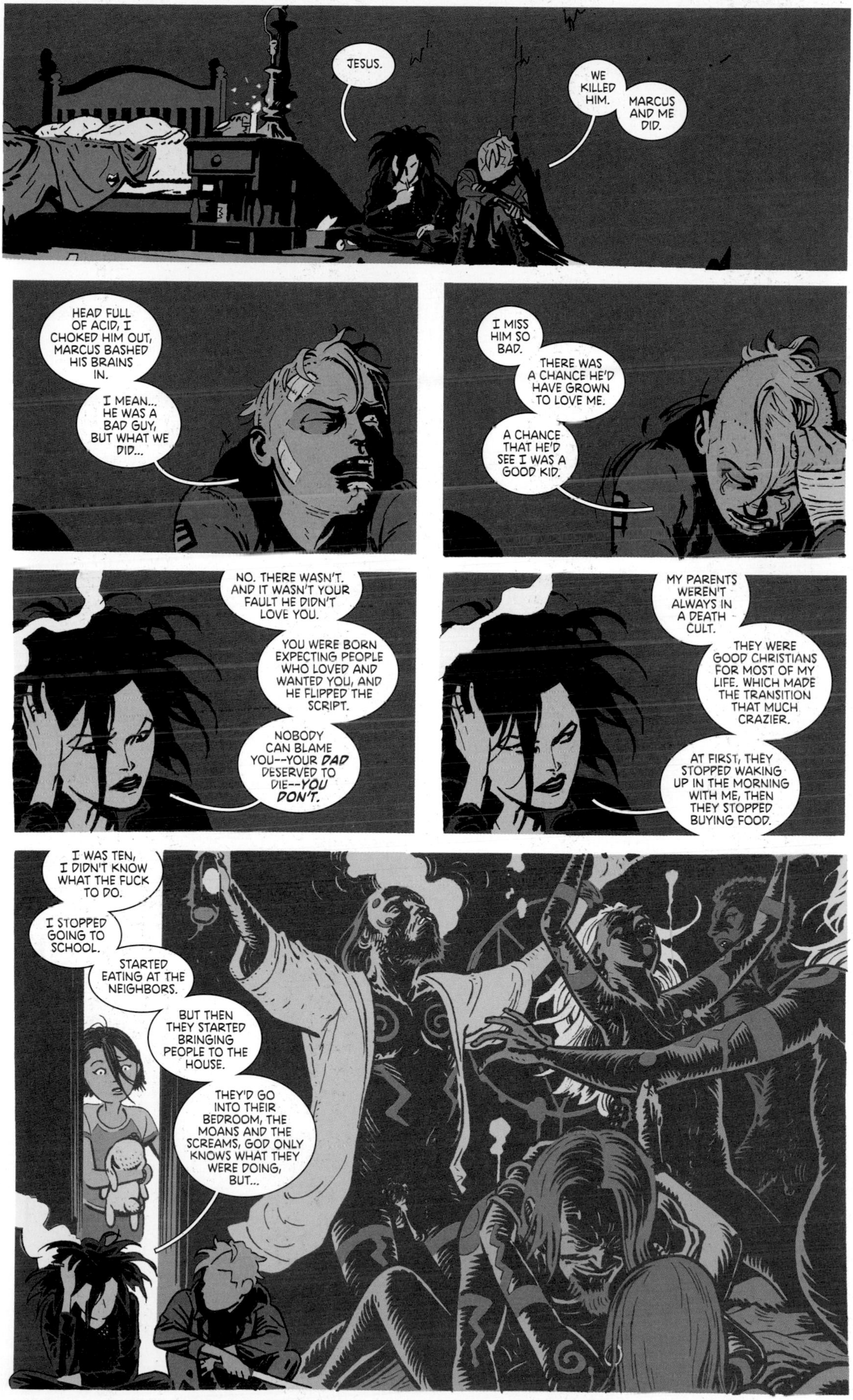
JESUS.
WE KILLED HIM.
MARCUS AND ME DID.
HEAD FULL OF ACID, I CHOKED HIM OUT, MARCUS BASHED HIS BRAINS IN.
I MEAN... HE WAS A BAD GUY, BUT WHAT WE DID...
I MISS HIM SO BAD.
THERE WAS A CHANCE HE'D HAVE GROWN TO LOVE ME.
A CHANCE THAT HE'D SEE I WAS A GOOD KID.
NO. THERE WASN'T. AND IT WASN'T YOUR FAULT HE DIDN'T LOVE YOU.
YOU WERE BORN EXPECTING PEOPLE WHO LOVED AND WANTED YOU, AND HE FLIPPED THE SCRIPT.
NOBODY CAN BLAME YOU--YOUR *DAD* DESERVED TO DIE--*YOU DON'T.*
MY PARENTS WEREN'T ALWAYS IN A DEATH CULT.
THEY WERE GOOD CHRISTIANS FOR MOST OF MY LIFE. WHICH MADE THE TRANSITION THAT MUCH CRAZIER.
AT FIRST, THEY STOPPED WAKING UP IN THE MORNING WITH ME, THEN THEY STOPPED BUYING FOOD.
I WAS TEN, I DIDN'T KNOW WHAT THE FUCK TO DO.
I STOPPED GOING TO SCHOOL.
STARTED EATING AT THE NEIGHBORS.
BUT THEN THEY STARTED BRINGING PEOPLE TO THE HOUSE.
THEY'D GO INTO THEIR BEDROOM, THE MOANS AND THE SCREAMS, GOD ONLY KNOWS WHAT THEY WERE DOING, BUT...

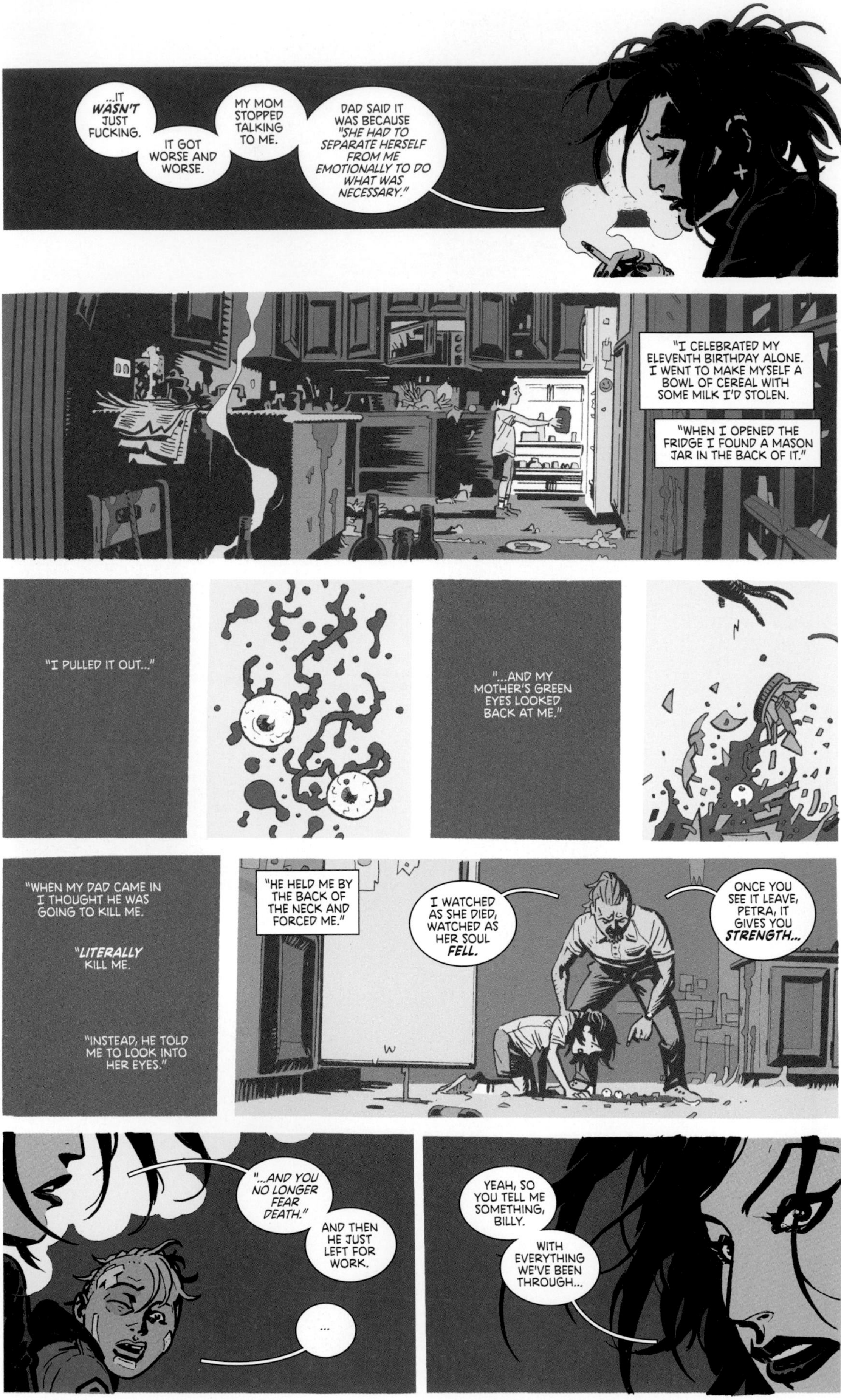
...IT *WASN'T* JUST FUCKING.
IT GOT WORSE AND WORSE.
MY MOM STOPPED TALKING TO ME.
DAD SAID IT WAS BECAUSE *"SHE HAD TO SEPARATE HERSELF FROM ME EMOTIONALLY TO DO WHAT WAS NECESSARY."*
"I CELEBRATED MY ELEVENTH BIRTHDAY ALONE. I WENT TO MAKE MYSELF A BOWL OF CEREAL WITH SOME MILK I'D STOLEN.
"WHEN I OPENED THE FRIDGE I FOUND A MASON JAR IN THE BACK OF IT."
"I PULLED IT OUT..."
"...AND MY MOTHER'S GREEN EYES LOOKED BACK AT ME."
"WHEN MY DAD CAME IN I THOUGHT HE WAS GOING TO KILL ME.
"*LITERALLY* KILL ME.
"INSTEAD, HE TOLD ME TO LOOK INTO HER EYES."
"HE HELD ME BY THE BACK OF THE NECK AND FORCED ME."
I WATCHED AS SHE DIED, WATCHED AS HER SOUL **FELL.**
ONCE YOU SEE IT LEAVE, PETRA, IT GIVES YOU ***STRENGTH...***
"...AND YOU NO LONGER FEAR DEATH."
AND THEN HE JUST LEFT FOR WORK.
...
YEAH, SO YOU TELL ME SOMETHING, BILLY.
WITH EVERYTHING WE'VE BEEN THROUGH...

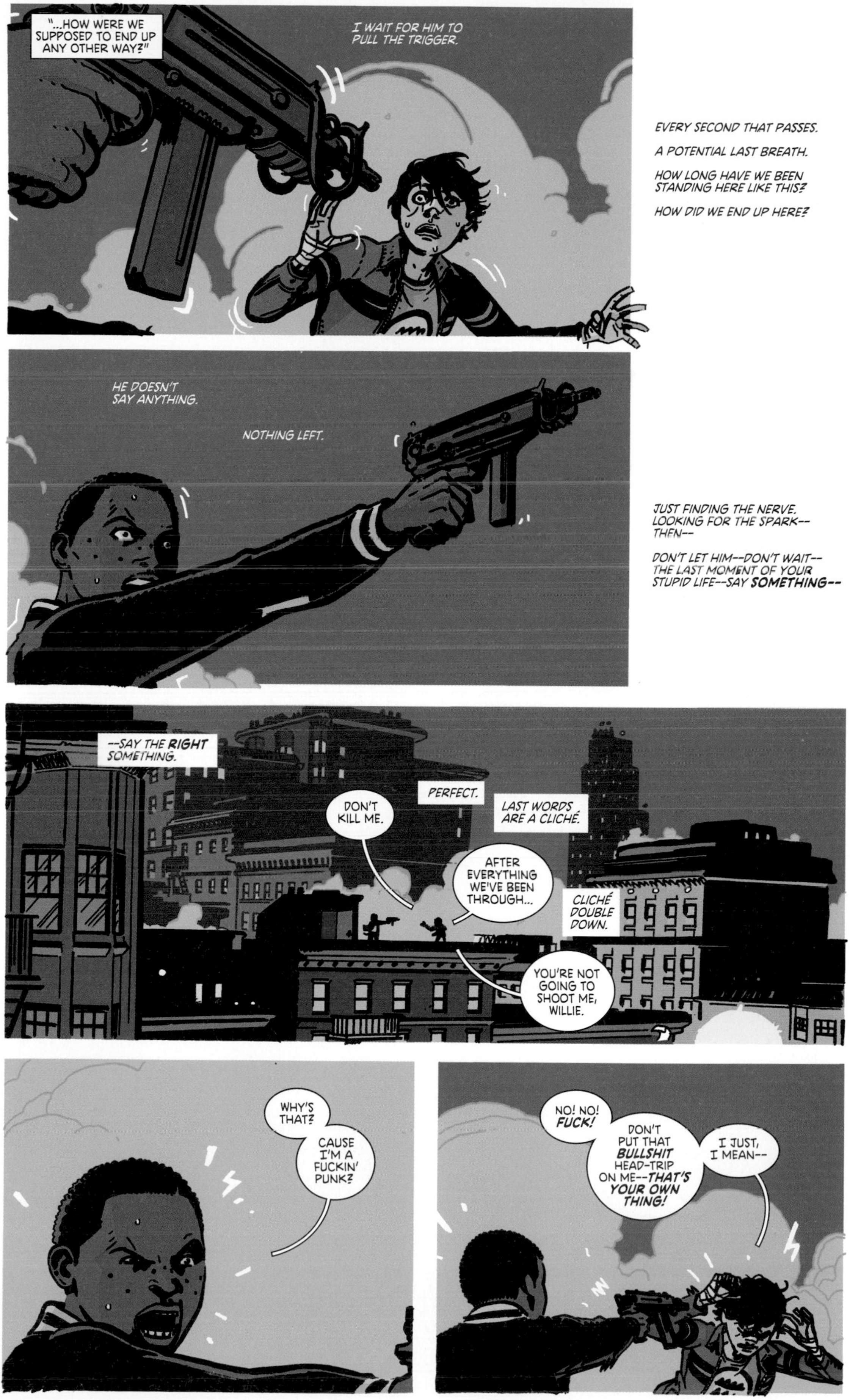
"...HOW WERE WE SUPPOSED TO END UP ANY OTHER WAY?"
I WAIT FOR HIM TO PULL THE TRIGGER.
EVERY SECOND THAT PASSES.
A POTENTIAL LAST BREATH.
HOW LONG HAVE WE BEEN STANDING HERE LIKE THIS?
HOW DID WE END UP HERE?
HE DOESN'T SAY ANYTHING.
NOTHING LEFT.
JUST FINDING THE NERVE. LOOKING FOR THE SPARK-- THEN--
DON'T LET HIM--DON'T WAIT-- THE LAST MOMENT OF YOUR STUPID LIFE--SAY SOMETHING--
--SAY THE RIGHT SOMETHING.
DON'T KILL ME.
PERFECT.
LAST WORDS ARE A CLICHÉ.
AFTER EVERYTHING WE'VE BEEN THROUGH...
CLICHÉ DOUBLE DOWN.
YOU'RE NOT GOING TO SHOOT ME, WILLIE.
WHY'S THAT?
CAUSE I'M A FUCKIN' PUNK?
NO! NO! FUCK!
DON'T PUT THAT BULLSHIT HEAD-TRIP ON ME--THAT'S YOUR OWN THING!
I JUST, I MEAN--

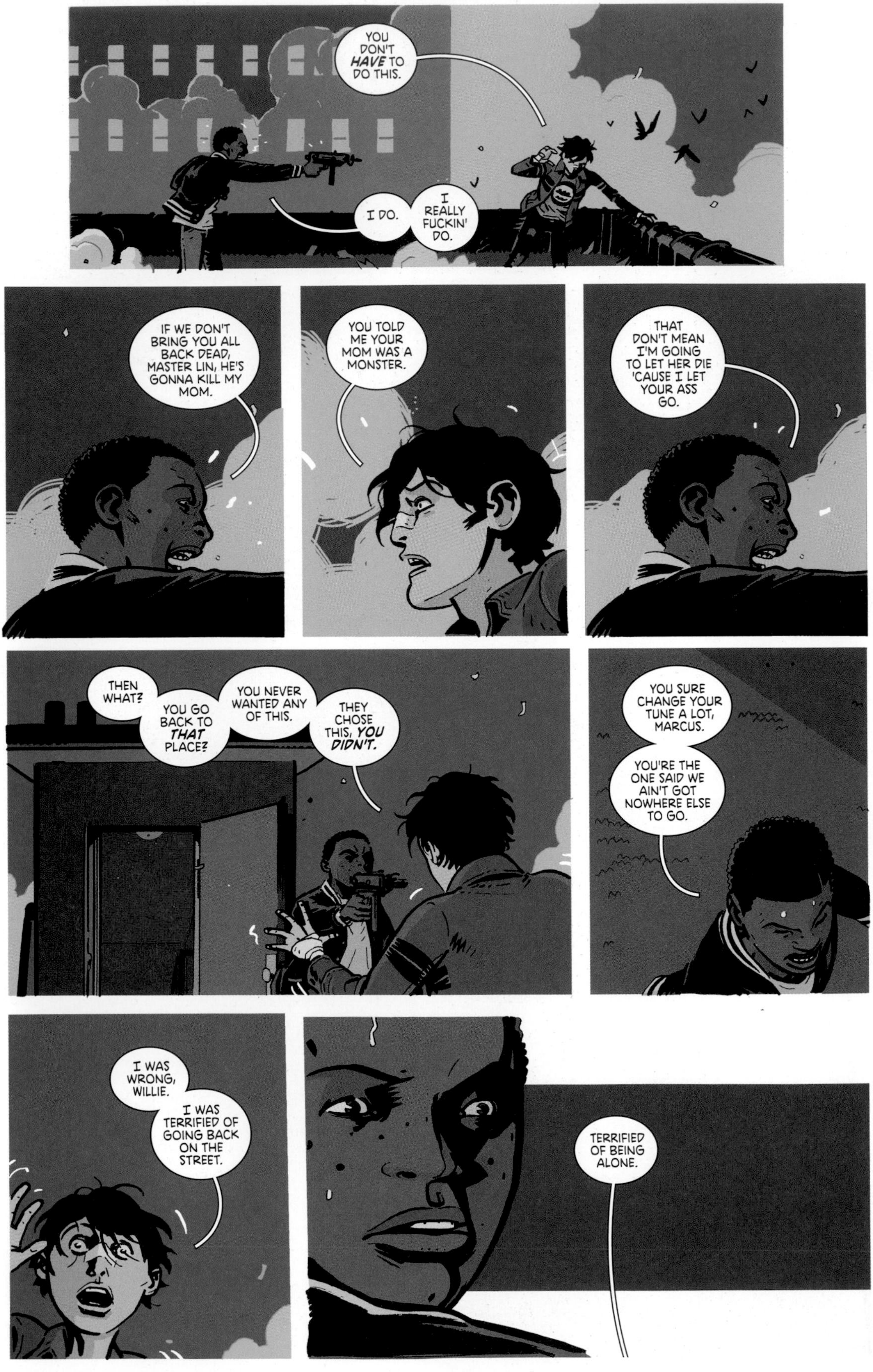
YOU DON'T *HAVE* TO DO THIS.
I DO.
I REALLY FUCKIN' DO.
IF WE DON'T BRING YOU ALL BACK DEAD, MASTER LIN, HE'S GONNA KILL MY MOM.
YOU TOLD ME YOUR MOM WAS A MONSTER.
THAT DON'T MEAN I'M GOING TO LET HER DIE 'CAUSE I LET YOUR ASS GO.
THEN WHAT?
YOU GO BACK TO *THAT* PLACE?
YOU NEVER WANTED ANY OF THIS.
THEY CHOSE THIS, *YOU DIDN'T.*
YOU SURE CHANGE YOUR TUNE A LOT, MARCUS.
YOU'RE THE ONE SAID WE AIN'T GOT NOWHERE ELSE TO GO.
I WAS WRONG, WILLIE.
I WAS TERRIFIED OF GOING BACK ON THE STREET.
TERRIFIED OF BEING ALONE.

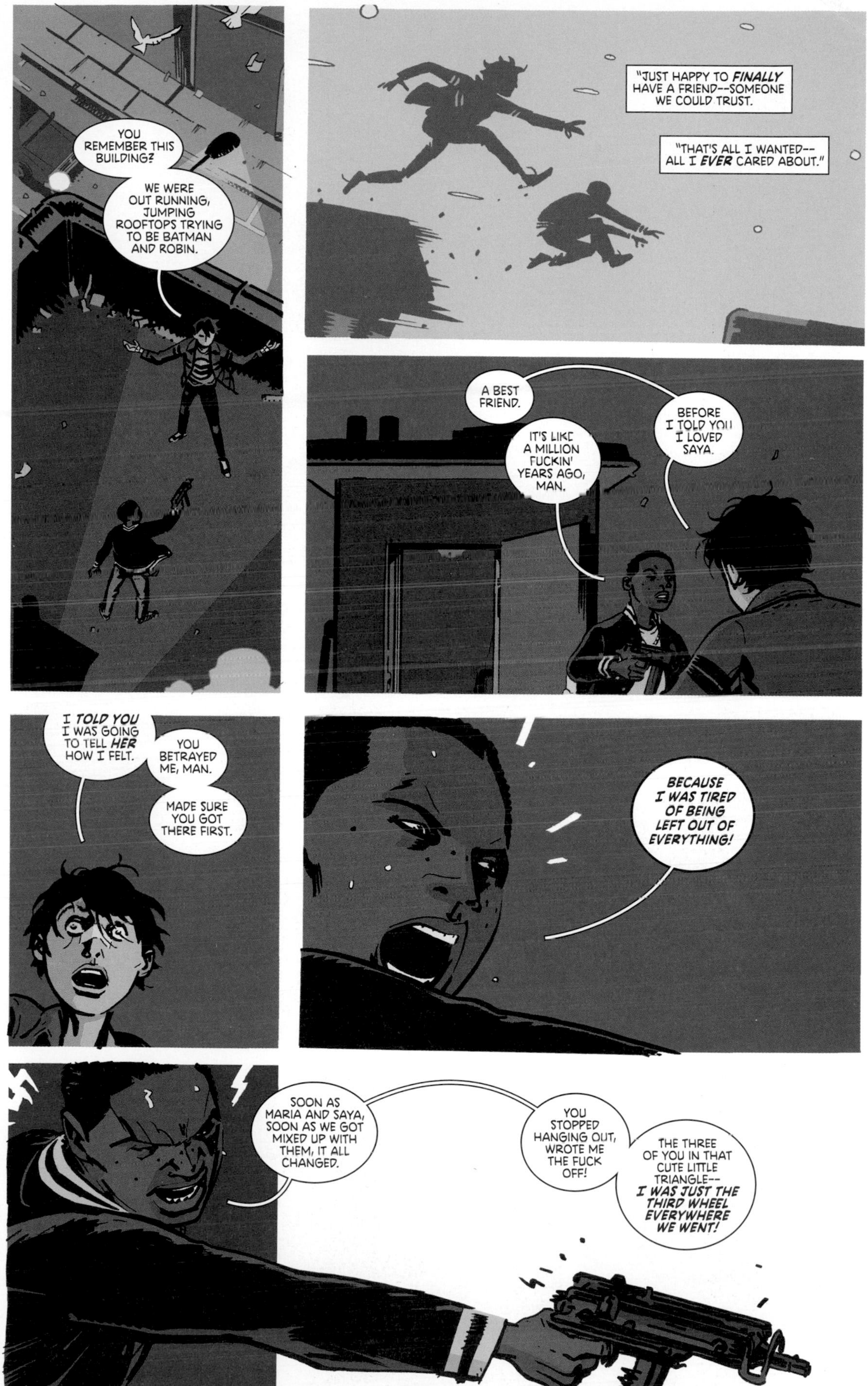
YOU REMEMBER THIS BUILDING?
WE WERE OUT RUNNING, JUMPING ROOFTOPS TRYING TO BE BATMAN AND ROBIN.
"JUST HAPPY TO FINALLY HAVE A FRIEND--SOMEONE WE COULD TRUST.
"THAT'S ALL I WANTED--ALL I EVER CARED ABOUT."
A BEST FRIEND.
IT'S LIKE A MILLION FUCKIN' YEARS AGO, MAN.
BEFORE I TOLD YOU I LOVED SAYA.
I TOLD YOU I WAS GOING TO TELL HER HOW I FELT.
YOU BETRAYED ME, MAN.
MADE SURE YOU GOT THERE FIRST.
BECAUSE I WAS TIRED OF BEING LEFT OUT OF EVERYTHING!
SOON AS MARIA AND SAYA, SOON AS WE GOT MIXED UP WITH THEM, IT ALL CHANGED.
YOU STOPPED HANGING OUT, WROTE ME THE FUCK OFF!
THE THREE OF YOU IN THAT CUTE LITTLE TRIANGLE--I WAS JUST THE THIRD WHEEL EVERYWHERE WE WENT!

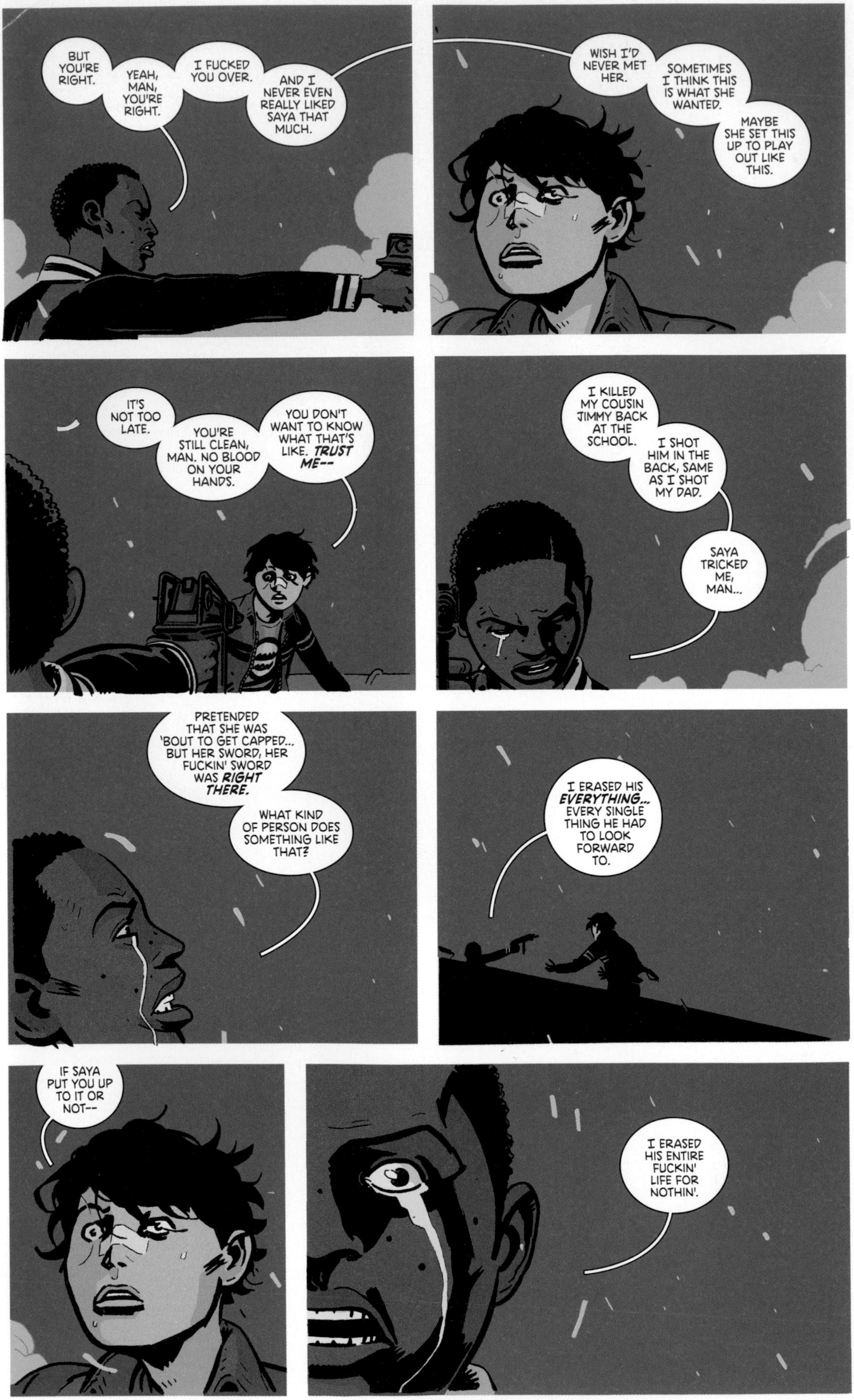
BUT YOU'RE RIGHT.
YEAH, MAN, YOU'RE RIGHT.
I FUCKED YOU OVER.
AND I NEVER EVEN REALLY LIKED SAYA THAT MUCH.
WISH I'D NEVER MET HER.
SOMETIMES I THINK THIS IS WHAT SHE WANTED.
MAYBE SHE SET THIS UP TO PLAY OUT LIKE THIS.
IT'S NOT TOO LATE.
YOU'RE STILL CLEAN, MAN. NO BLOOD ON YOUR HANDS.
YOU DON'T WANT TO KNOW WHAT THAT'S LIKE. TRUST ME--
I KILLED MY COUSIN JIMMY BACK AT THE SCHOOL.
I SHOT HIM IN THE BACK, SAME AS I SHOT MY DAD.
SAYA TRICKED ME, MAN...
PRETENDED THAT SHE WAS 'BOUT TO GET CAPPED... BUT HER SWORD, HER FUCKIN' SWORD WAS RIGHT THERE.
WHAT KIND OF PERSON DOES SOMETHING LIKE THAT?
I ERASED HIS EVERYTHING... EVERY SINGLE THING HE HAD TO LOOK FORWARD TO.
IF SAYA PUT YOU UP TO IT OR NOT--
I ERASED HIS ENTIRE FUCKIN' LIFE FOR NOTHIN'.

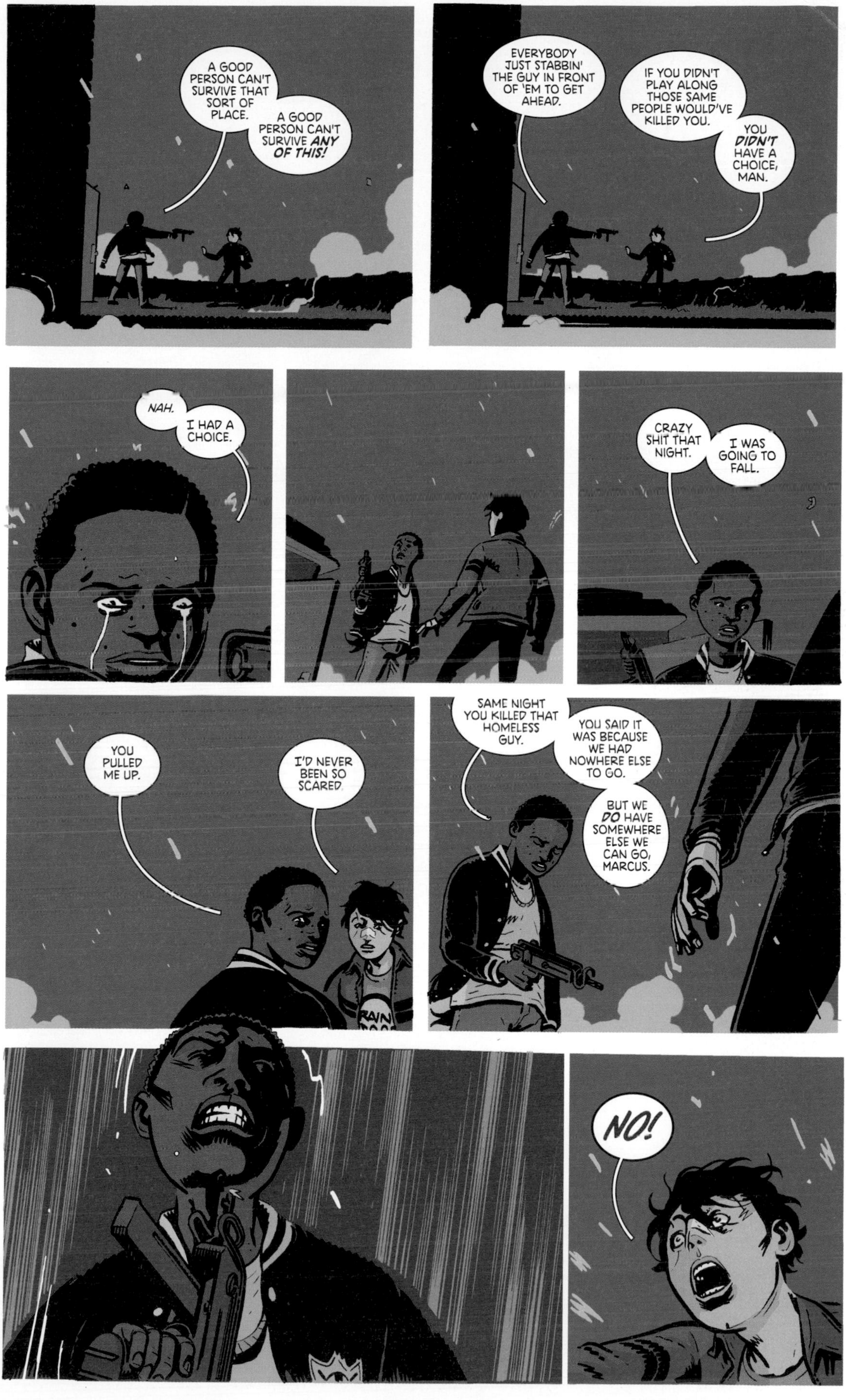
A GOOD PERSON CAN'T SURVIVE THAT SORT OF PLACE.
A GOOD PERSON CAN'T SURVIVE ANY OF THIS!
EVERYBODY JUST STABBIN' THE GUY IN FRONT OF 'EM TO GET AHEAD.
IF YOU DIDN'T PLAY ALONG THOSE SAME PEOPLE WOULD'VE KILLED YOU.
YOU DIDN'T HAVE A CHOICE, MAN.
NAH.
I HAD A CHOICE.
CRAZY SHIT THAT NIGHT.
I WAS GOING TO FALL.
YOU PULLED ME UP.
I'D NEVER BEEN SO SCARED.
SAME NIGHT YOU KILLED THAT HOMELESS GUY.
YOU SAID IT WAS BECAUSE WE HAD NOWHERE ELSE TO GO.
BUT WE DO HAVE SOMEWHERE ELSE WE CAN GO, MARCUS.
NO!

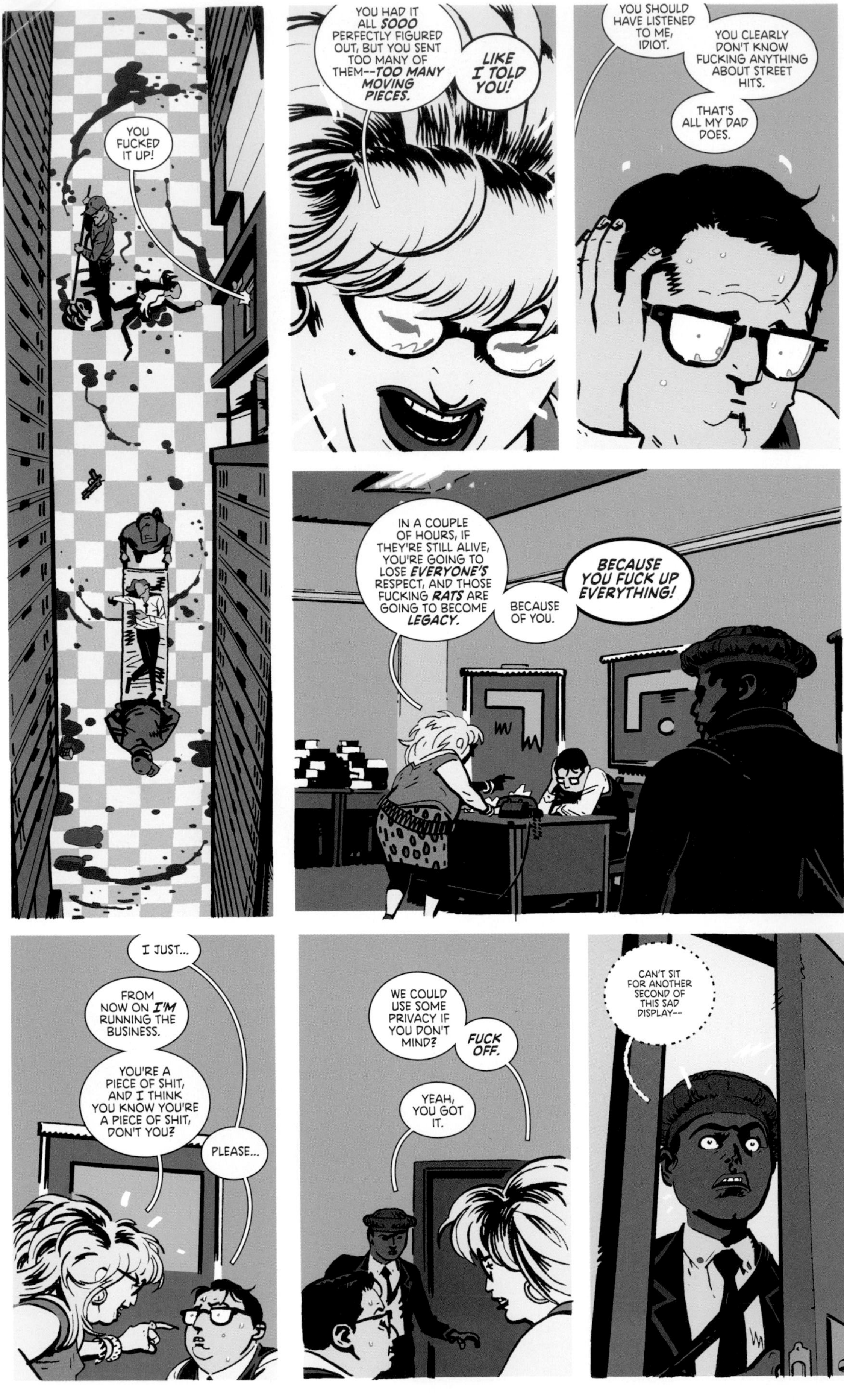
YOU FUCKED IT UP!
YOU HAD IT ALL SOOO PERFECTLY FIGURED OUT, BUT YOU SENT TOO MANY OF THEM--TOO MANY MOVING PIECES.
LIKE I TOLD YOU!
YOU SHOULD HAVE LISTENED TO ME, IDIOT.
YOU CLEARLY DON'T KNOW FUCKING ANYTHING ABOUT STREET HITS.
THAT'S ALL MY DAD DOES.
IN A COUPLE OF HOURS, IF THEY'RE STILL ALIVE, YOU'RE GOING TO LOSE EVERYONE'S RESPECT, AND THOSE FUCKING RATS ARE GOING TO BECOME LEGACY.
BECAUSE OF YOU.
BECAUSE YOU FUCK UP EVERYTHING!
I JUST...
FROM NOW ON I'M RUNNING THE BUSINESS.
YOU'RE A PIECE OF SHIT, AND I THINK YOU KNOW YOU'RE A PIECE OF SHIT, DON'T YOU?
PLEASE...
WE COULD USE SOME PRIVACY IF YOU DON'T MIND?
FUCK OFF.
YEAH, YOU GOT IT.
CAN'T SIT FOR ANOTHER SECOND OF THIS SAD DISPLAY--

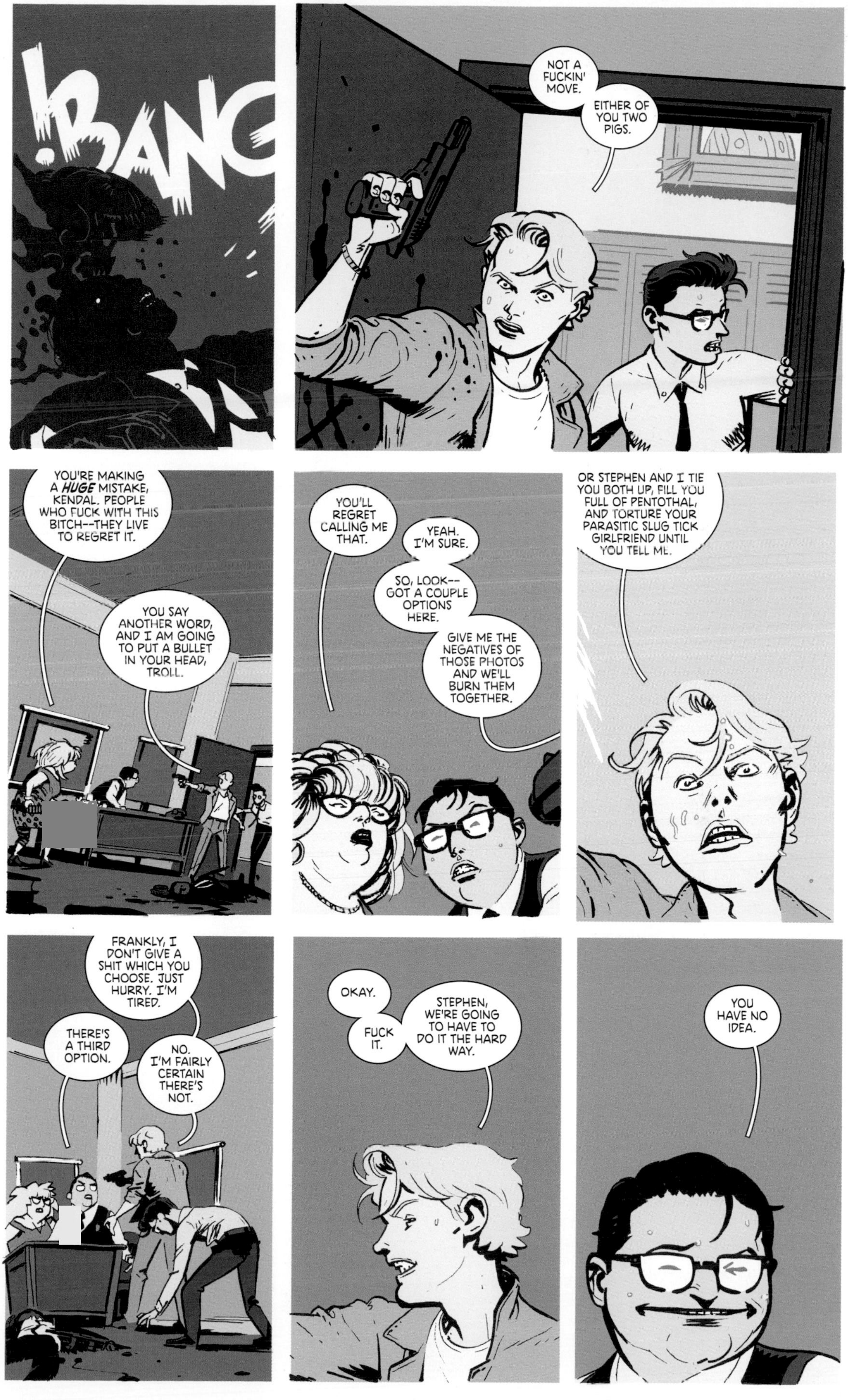
BANG
NOT A FUCKIN' MOVE.
EITHER OF YOU TWO PIGS.
YOU'RE MAKING A *HUGE* MISTAKE, KENDAL. PEOPLE WHO FUCK WITH THIS BITCH--THEY LIVE TO REGRET IT.
YOU SAY ANOTHER WORD, AND I AM GOING TO PUT A BULLET IN YOUR HEAD, TROLL.
YOU'LL REGRET CALLING ME THAT.
YEAH. I'M SURE.
SO, LOOK--GOT A COUPLE OPTIONS HERE.
GIVE ME THE NEGATIVES OF THOSE PHOTOS AND WE'LL BURN THEM TOGETHER.
OR STEPHEN AND I TIE YOU BOTH UP, FILL YOU FULL OF PENTOTHAL, AND TORTURE YOUR PARASITIC SLUG TICK GIRLFRIEND UNTIL YOU TELL ME.
FRANKLY, I DON'T GIVE A SHIT WHICH YOU CHOOSE. JUST HURRY. I'M TIRED.
THERE'S A THIRD OPTION.
NO. I'M FAIRLY CERTAIN THERE'S NOT.
OKAY.
FUCK IT.
STEPHEN, WE'RE GOING TO HAVE TO DO IT THE HARD WAY.
YOU HAVE NO IDEA.

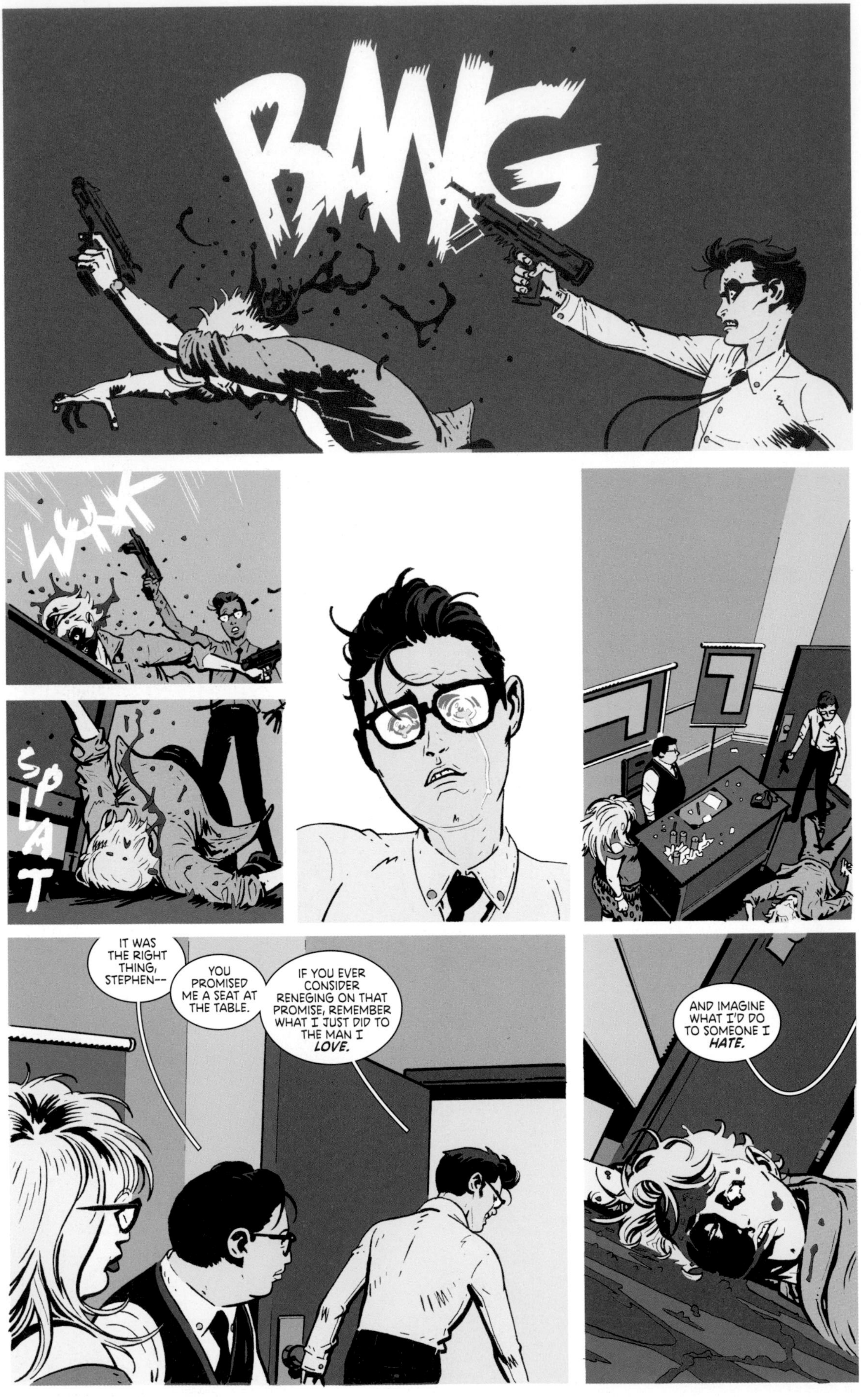
BANG
WHK
SPLAT
IT WAS THE RIGHT THING, STEPHEN--
YOU PROMISED ME A SEAT AT THE TABLE.
IF YOU EVER CONSIDER RENEGING ON THAT PROMISE, REMEMBER WHAT I JUST DID TO THE MAN I *LOVE.*
AND IMAGINE WHAT I'D DO TO SOMEONE I *HATE.*

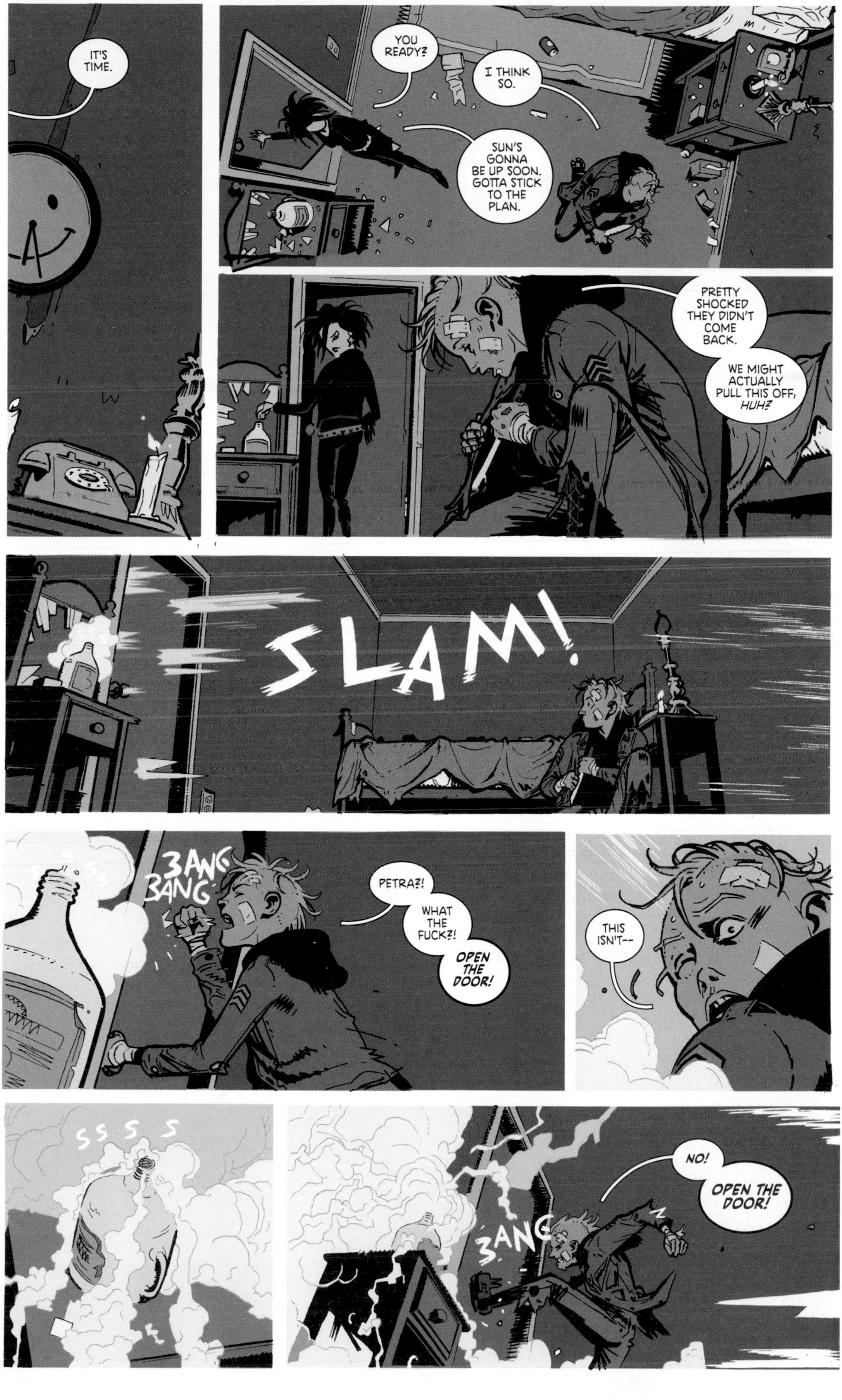
IT'S TIME.
YOU READY?
I THINK SO.
SUN'S GONNA BE UP SOON. GOTTA STICK TO THE PLAN.
PRETTY SHOCKED THEY DIDN'T COME BACK.
WE MIGHT ACTUALLY PULL THIS OFF, *HUH?*
SLAM!
BANG BANG
PETRA?!
WHAT THE FUCK?!
OPEN THE DOOR!
THIS ISN'T--
SSSS
BANG
NO!
OPEN THE DOOR!

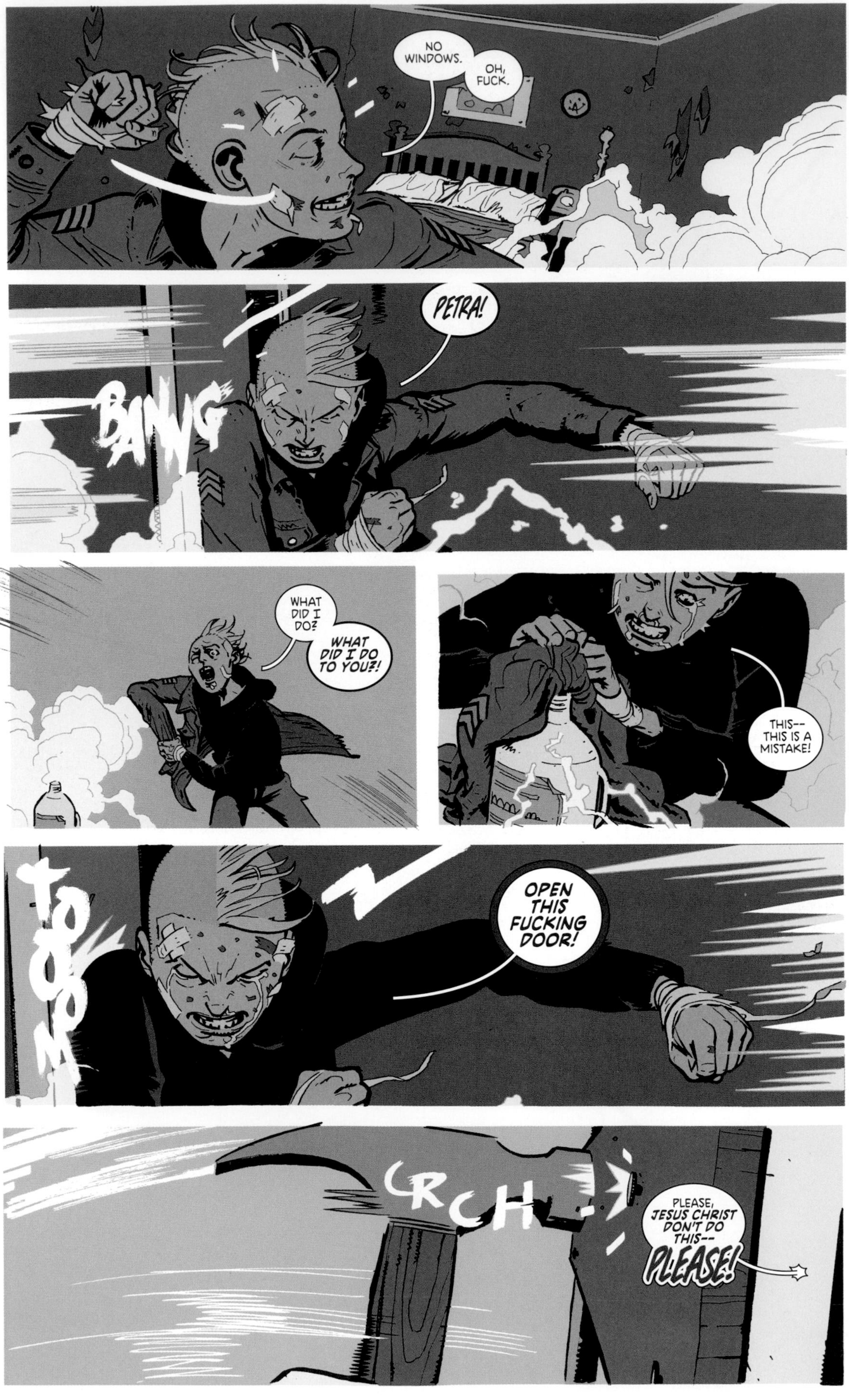
NO WINDOWS.
OH, FUCK.
PETRA!
BANG
WHAT DID I DO?
WHAT DID I DO TO YOU?!
THIS-- THIS IS A MISTAKE!
TOOOM
OPEN THIS FUCKING DOOR!
CRCH
PLEASE, JESUS CHRIST DON'T DO THIS--
PLEASE!

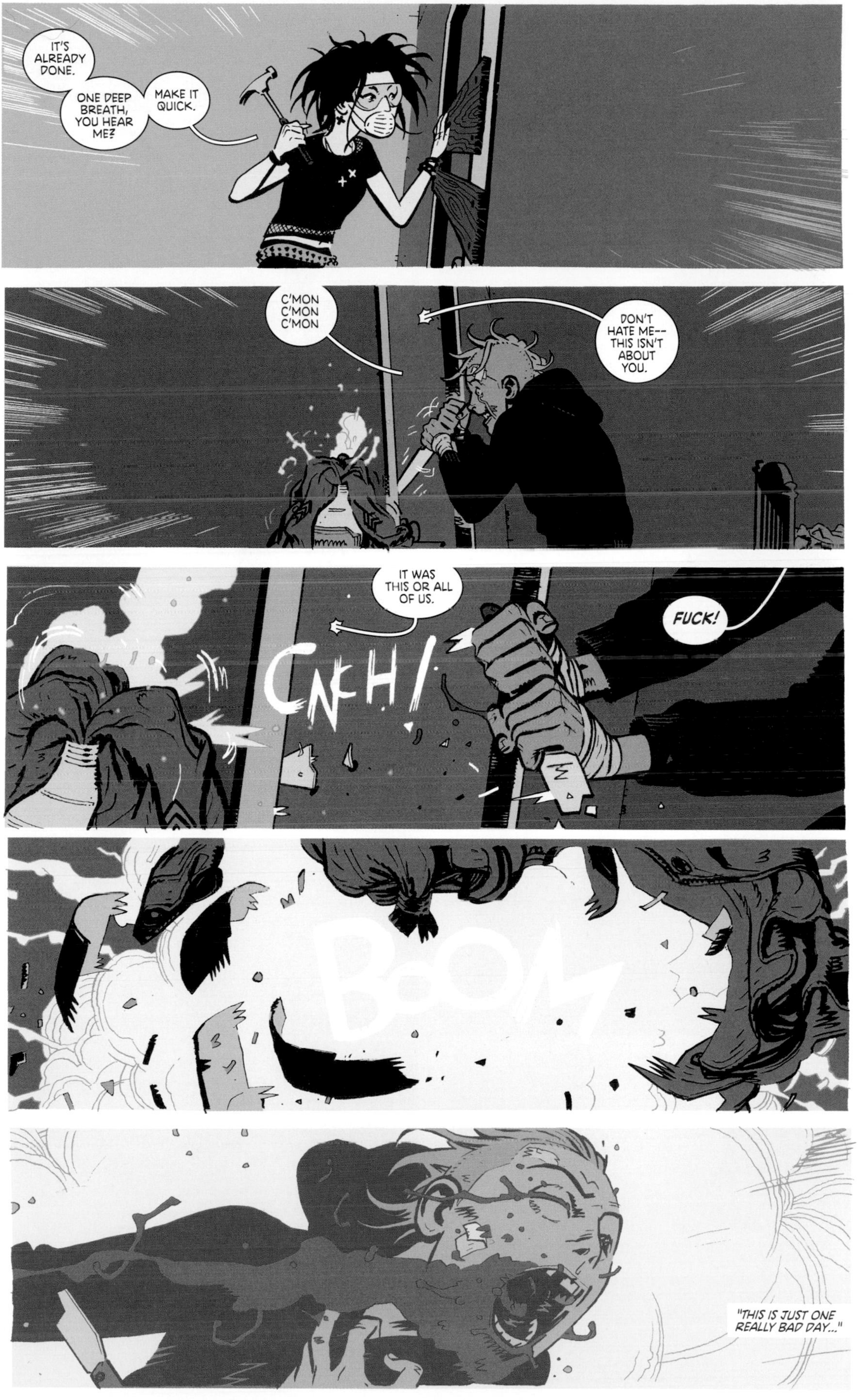
IT'S ALREADY DONE.
ONE DEEP BREATH, YOU HEAR ME?
MAKE IT QUICK.
C'MON C'MON C'MON
DON'T HATE ME-- THIS ISN'T ABOUT YOU.
IT WAS THIS OR ALL OF US.
FUCK!
CNCH!
BOOM
"THIS IS JUST ONE REALLY BAD DAY..."

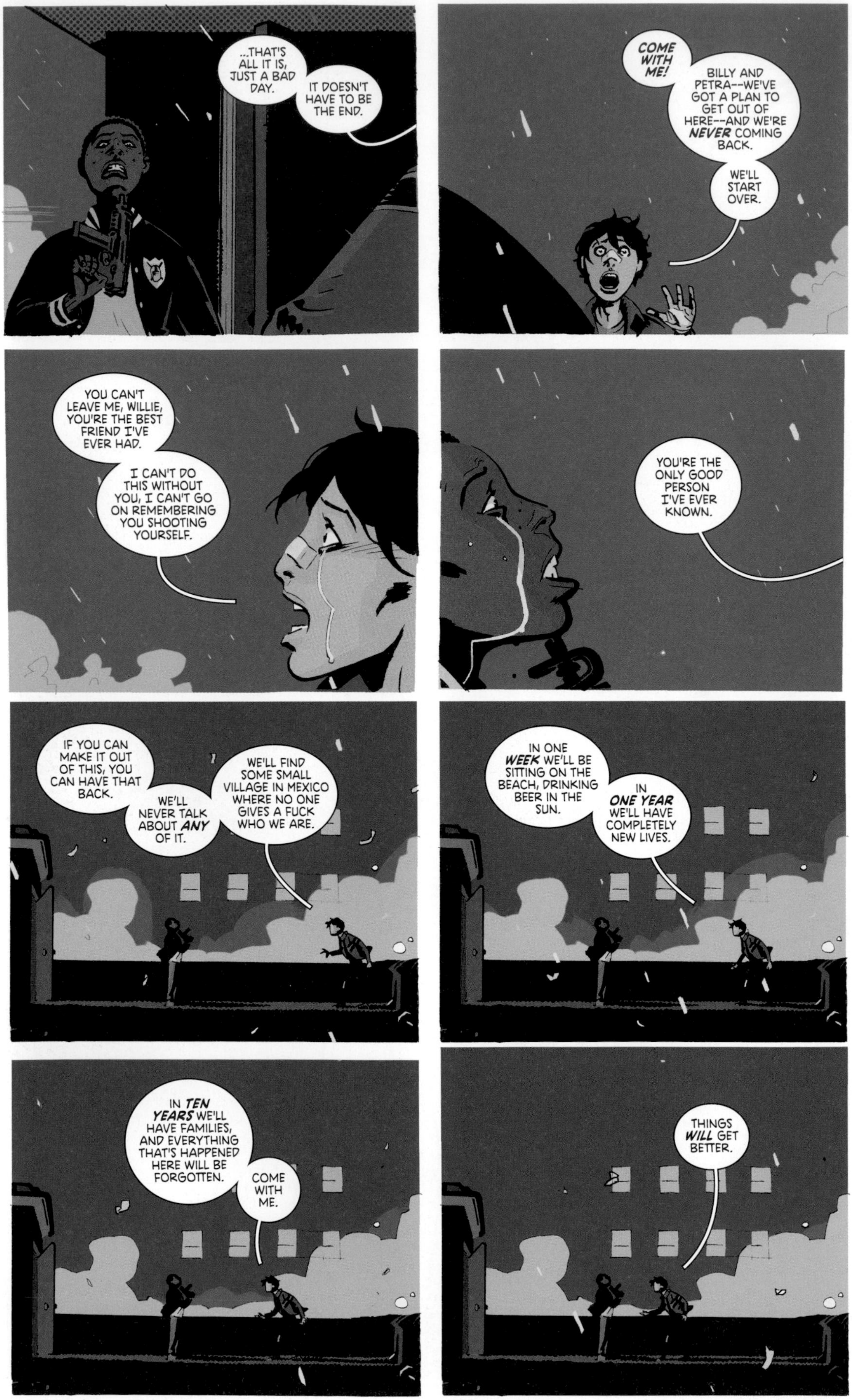
...THAT'S ALL IT IS, JUST A BAD DAY.
IT DOESN'T HAVE TO BE THE END.
COME WITH ME!
BILLY AND PETRA--WE'VE GOT A PLAN TO GET OUT OF HERE--AND WE'RE NEVER COMING BACK.
WE'LL START OVER.
YOU CAN'T LEAVE ME, WILLIE, YOU'RE THE BEST FRIEND I'VE EVER HAD.
I CAN'T DO THIS WITHOUT YOU, I CAN'T GO ON REMEMBERING YOU SHOOTING YOURSELF.
YOU'RE THE ONLY GOOD PERSON I'VE EVER KNOWN.
IF YOU CAN MAKE IT OUT OF THIS, YOU CAN HAVE THAT BACK.
WE'LL NEVER TALK ABOUT ANY OF IT.
WE'LL FIND SOME SMALL VILLAGE IN MEXICO WHERE NO ONE GIVES A FUCK WHO WE ARE.
IN ONE WEEK WE'LL BE SITTING ON THE BEACH, DRINKING BEER IN THE SUN.
IN ONE YEAR WE'LL HAVE COMPLETELY NEW LIVES.
IN TEN YEARS WE'LL HAVE FAMILIES, AND EVERYTHING THAT'S HAPPENED HERE WILL BE FORGOTTEN.
COME WITH ME.
THINGS WILL GET BETTER.

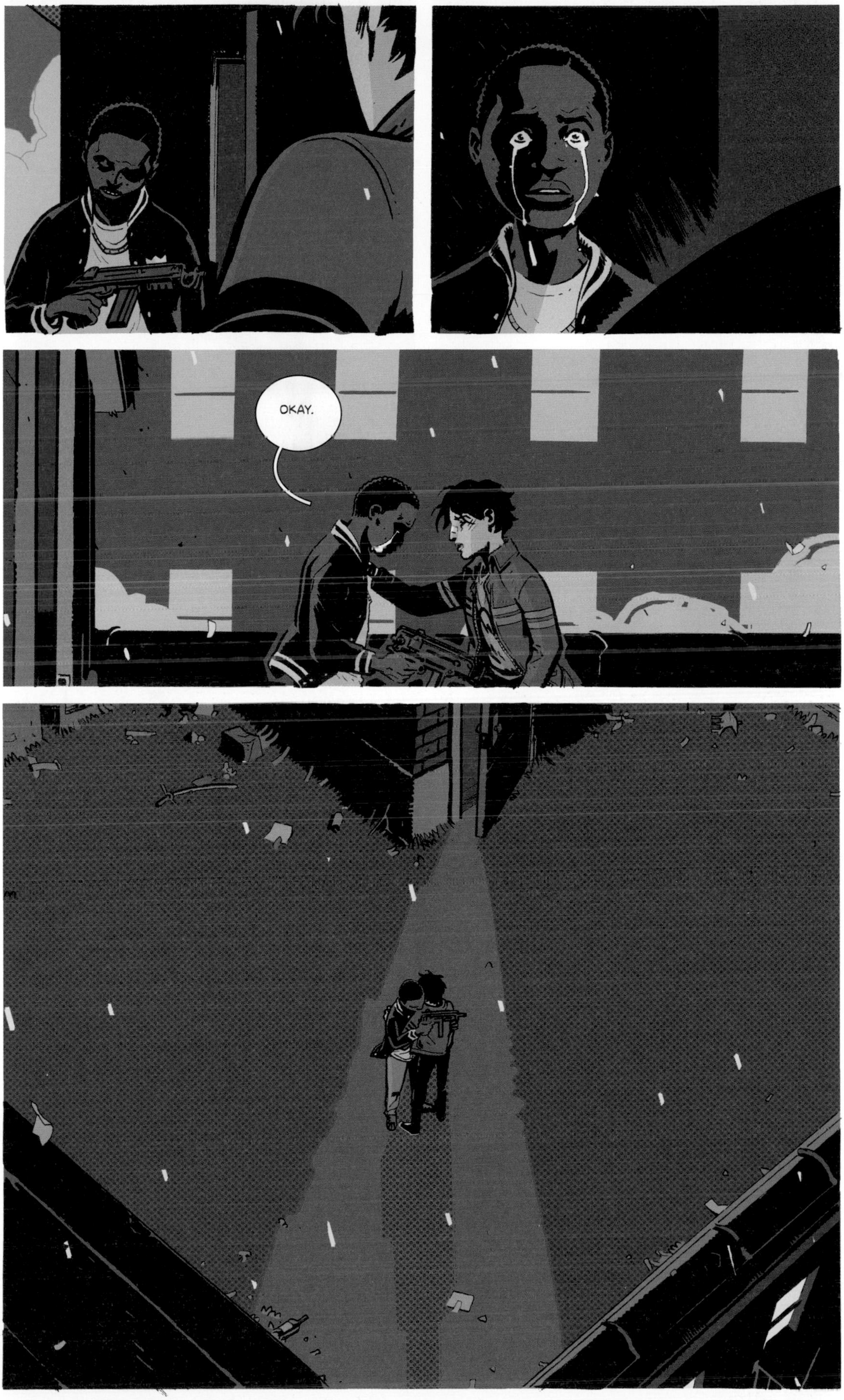
OKAY.

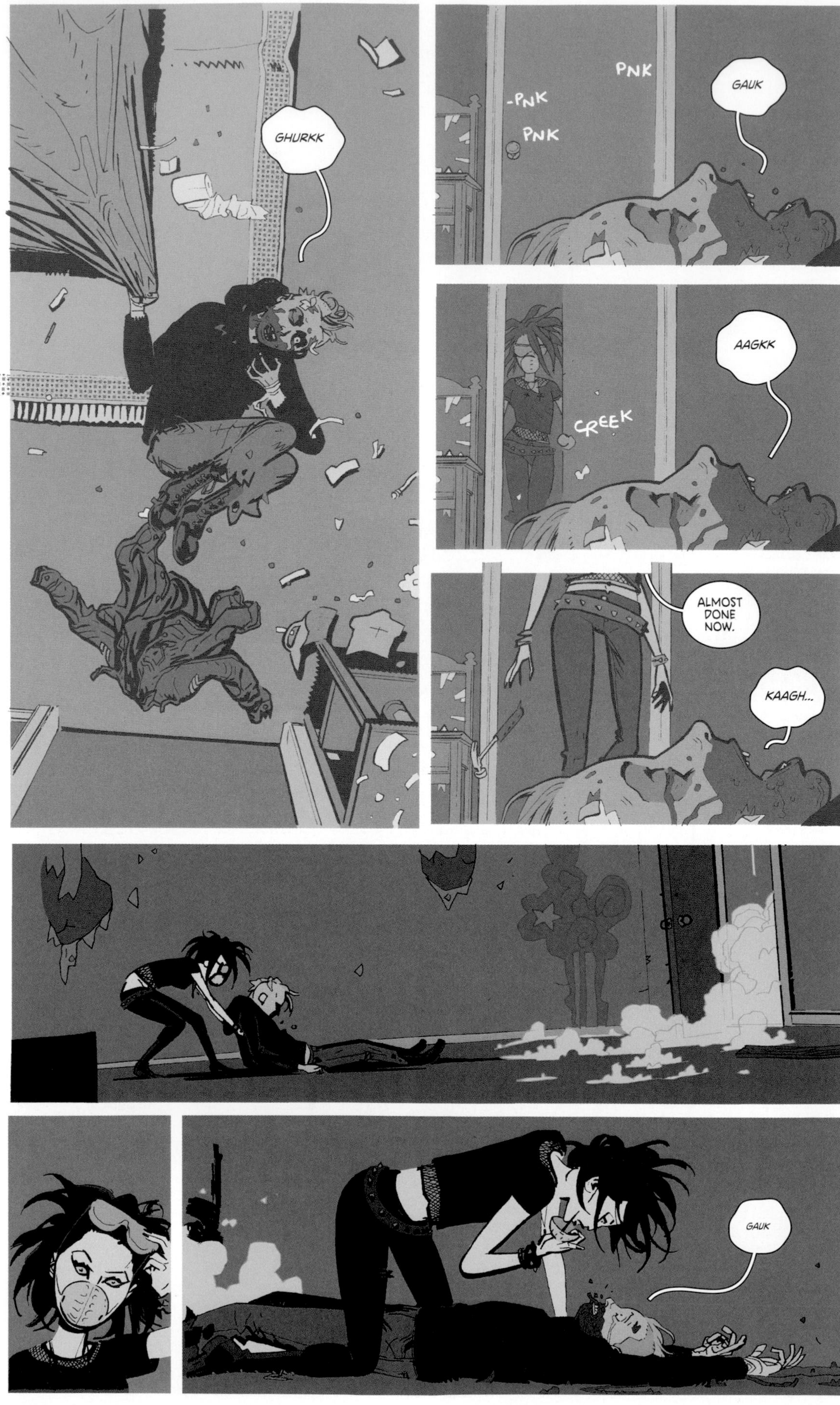
GHURKK
-PNK
PNK
PNK
GAUK
AAGKK
CREEK
ALMOST DONE NOW.
KAAGH...
GAUK

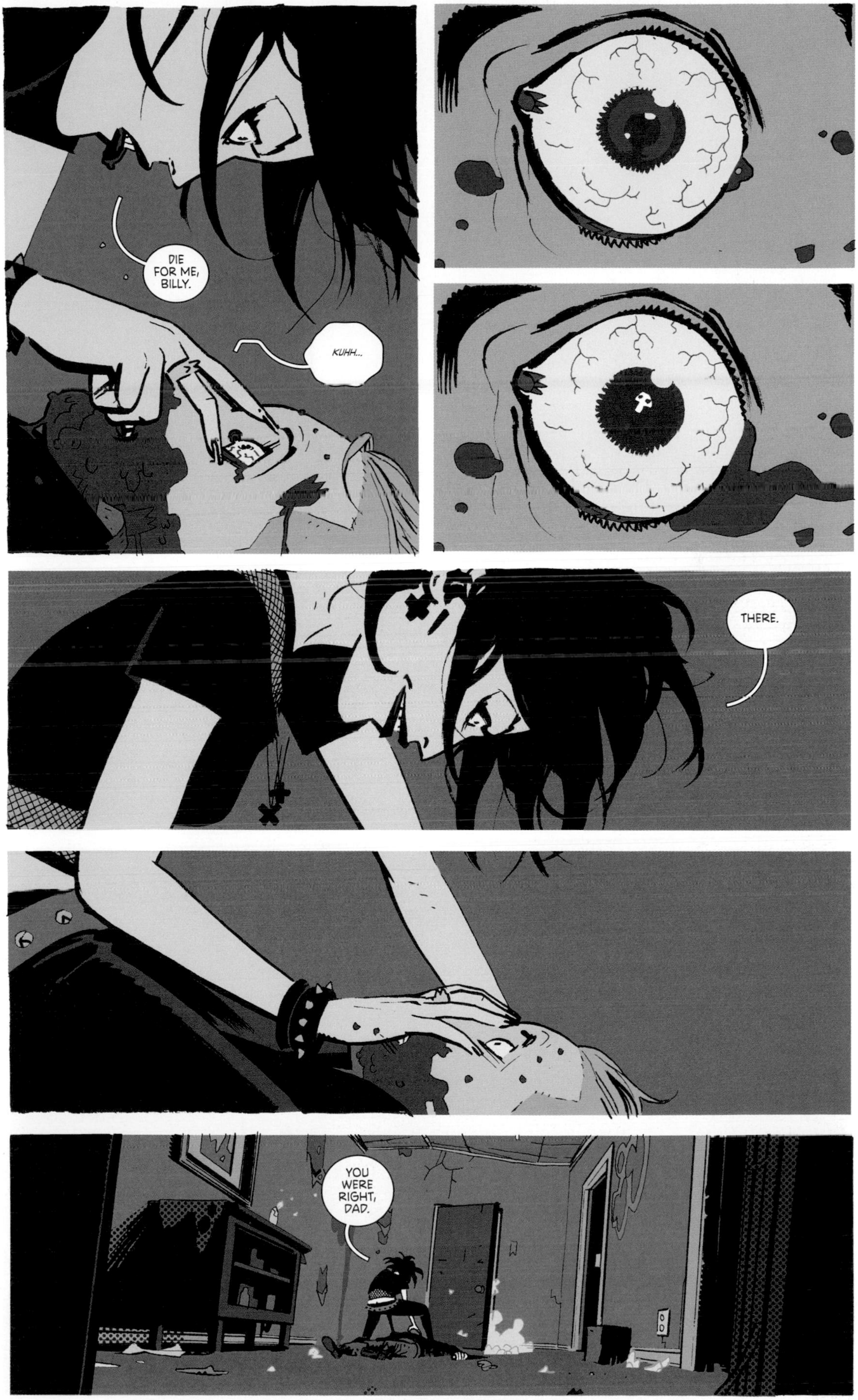
DIE FOR ME, BILLY.
KUHH...
THERE.
YOU WERE RIGHT, DAD.

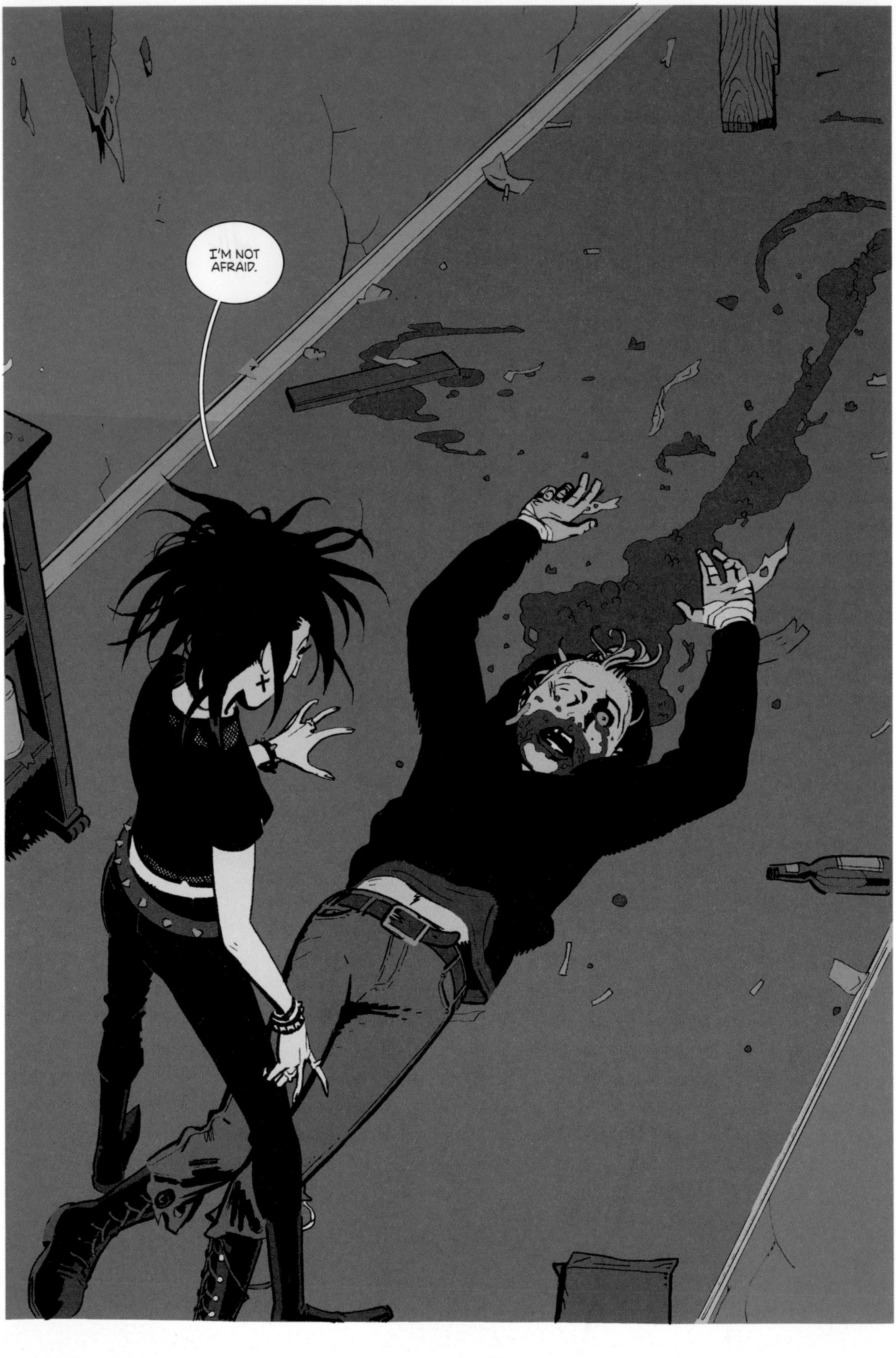
I'M NOT AFRAID.

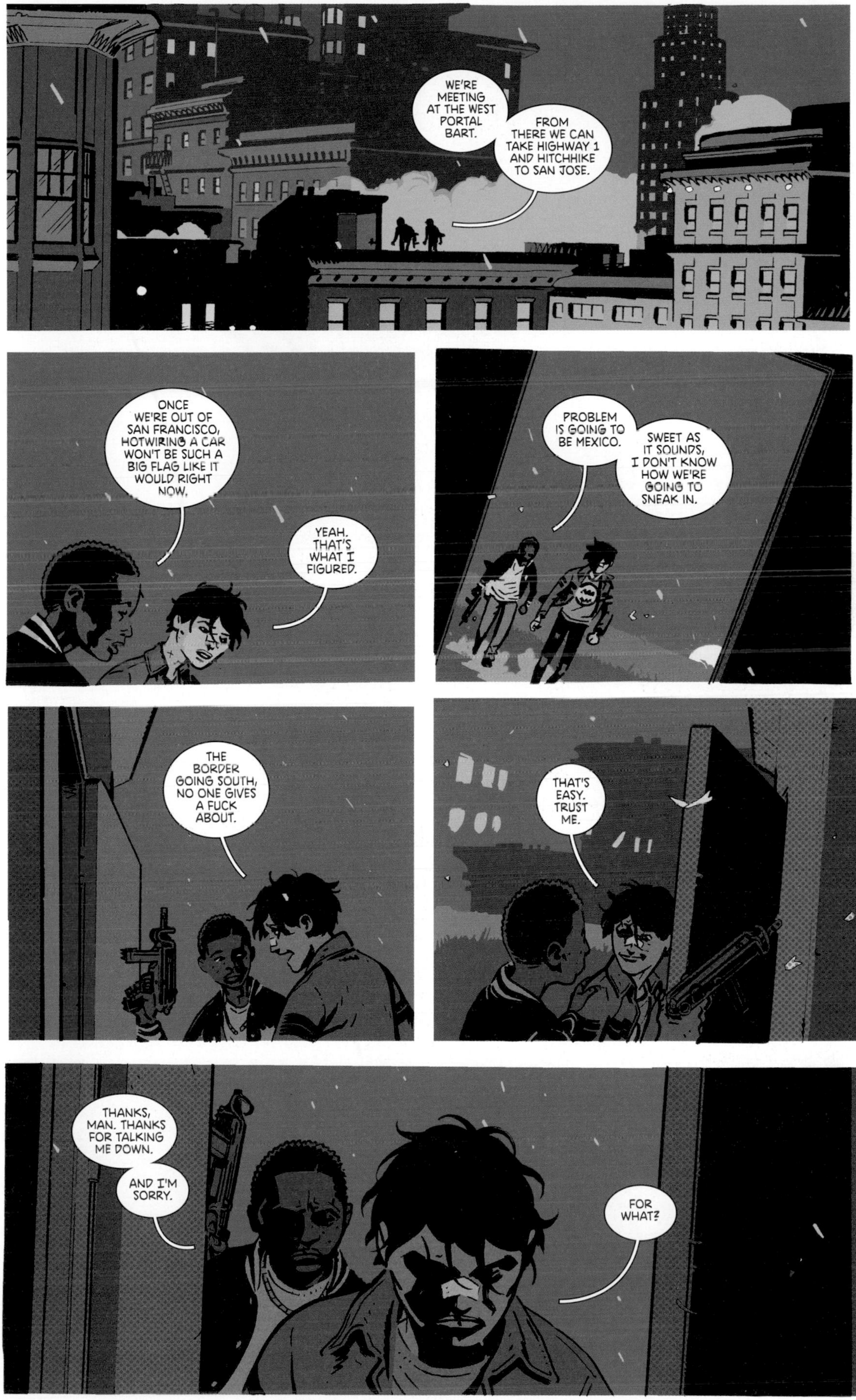
WE'RE MEETING AT THE WEST PORTAL BART.
FROM THERE WE CAN TAKE HIGHWAY 1 AND HITCHHIKE TO SAN JOSE.
ONCE WE'RE OUT OF SAN FRANCISCO, HOTWIRING A CAR WON'T BE SUCH A BIG FLAG LIKE IT WOULD RIGHT NOW.
YEAH. THAT'S WHAT I FIGURED.
PROBLEM IS GOING TO BE MEXICO.
SWEET AS IT SOUNDS, I DON'T KNOW HOW WE'RE GOING TO SNEAK IN.
THE BORDER GOING SOUTH, NO ONE GIVES A FUCK ABOUT.
THAT'S EASY. TRUST ME.
THANKS, MAN. THANKS FOR TALKING ME DOWN.
AND I'M SORRY.
FOR WHAT?

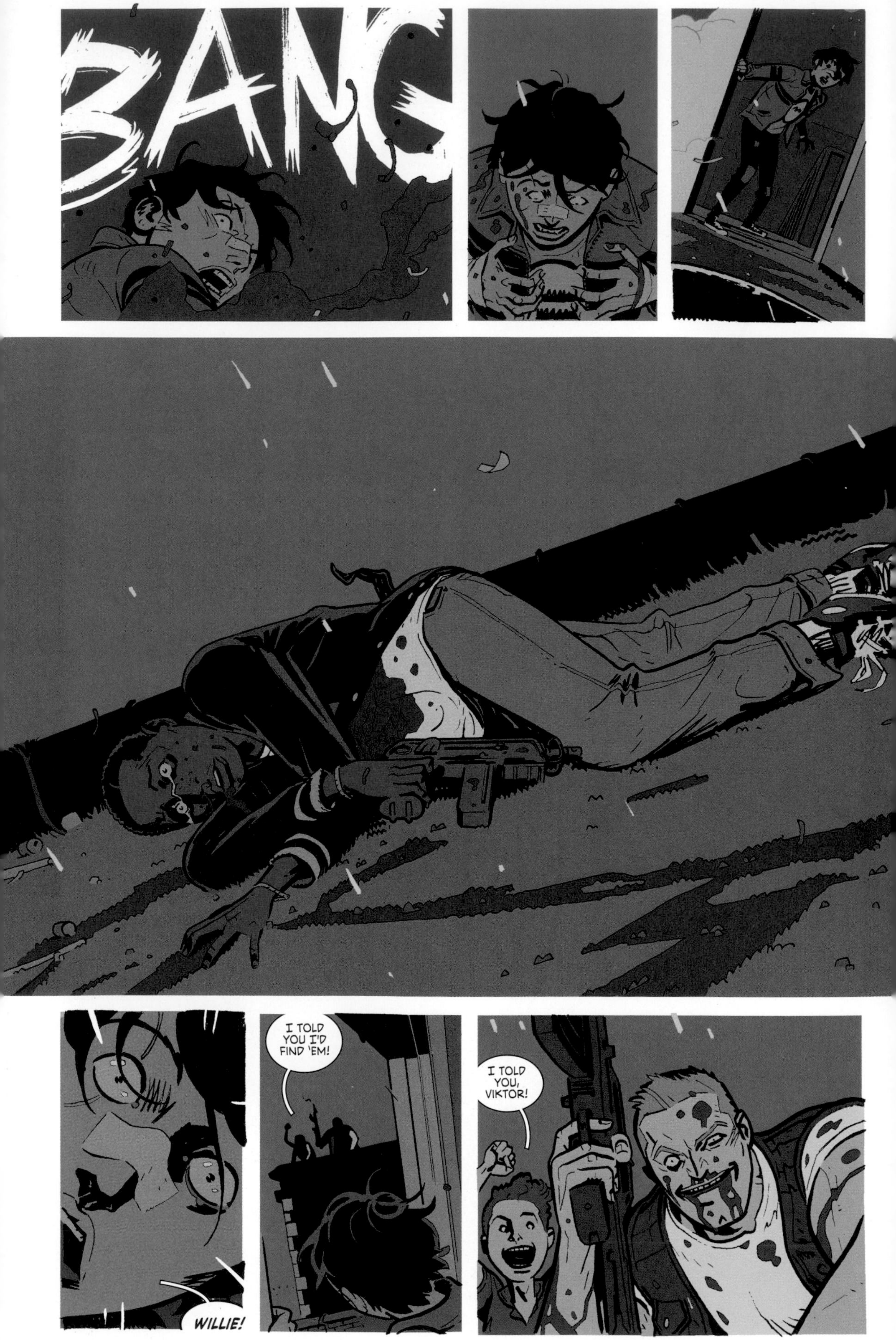
BANG
WILLIE!
I TOLD YOU I'D FIND 'EM!
I TOLD YOU, VIKTOR!

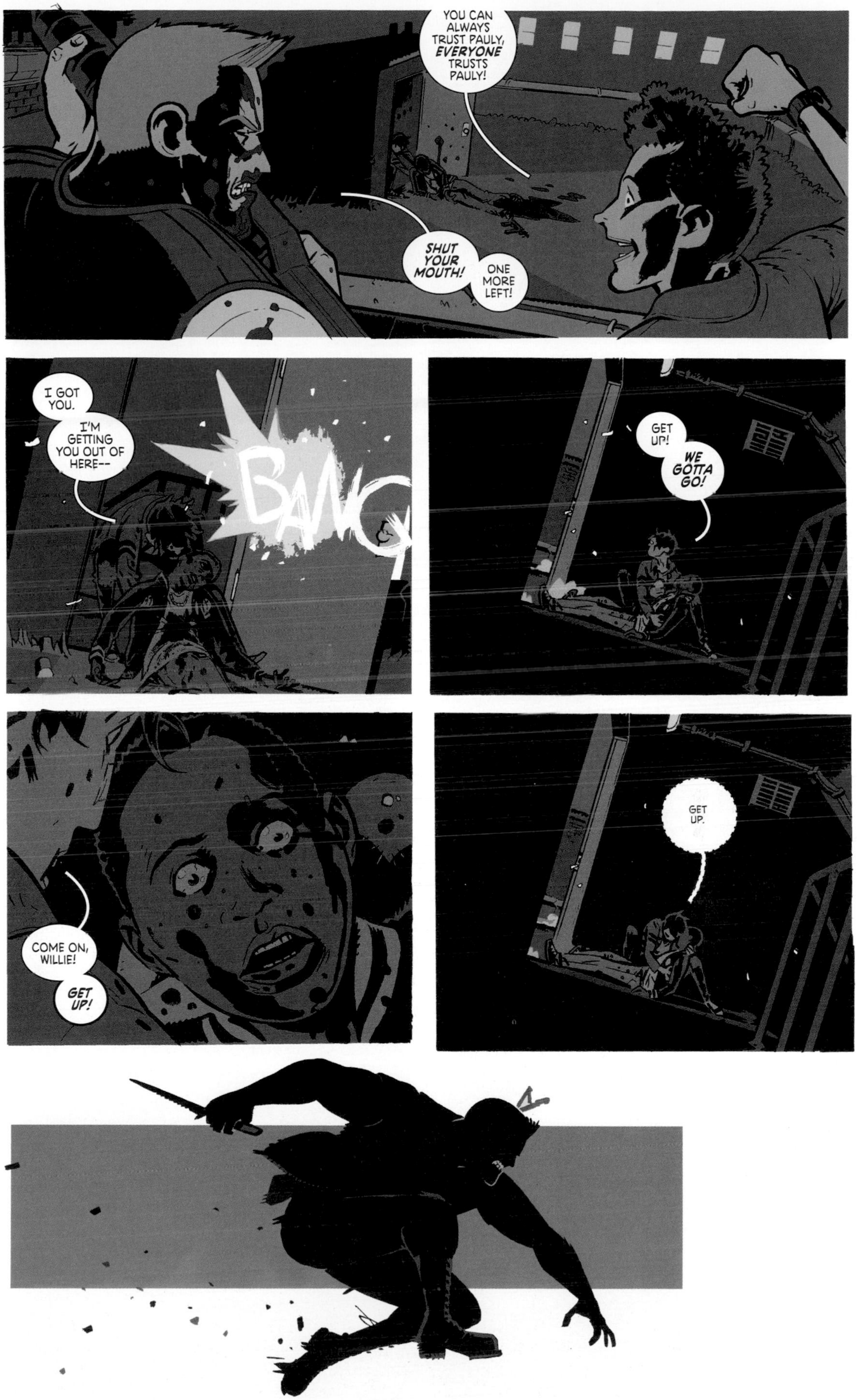
YOU CAN ALWAYS TRUST PAULY, EVERYONE TRUSTS PAULY!
SHUT YOUR MOUTH!
ONE MORE LEFT!
I GOT YOU.
I'M GETTING YOU OUT OF HERE--
BANG
GET UP!
WE GOTTA GO!
COME ON, WILLIE!
GET UP!
GET UP.

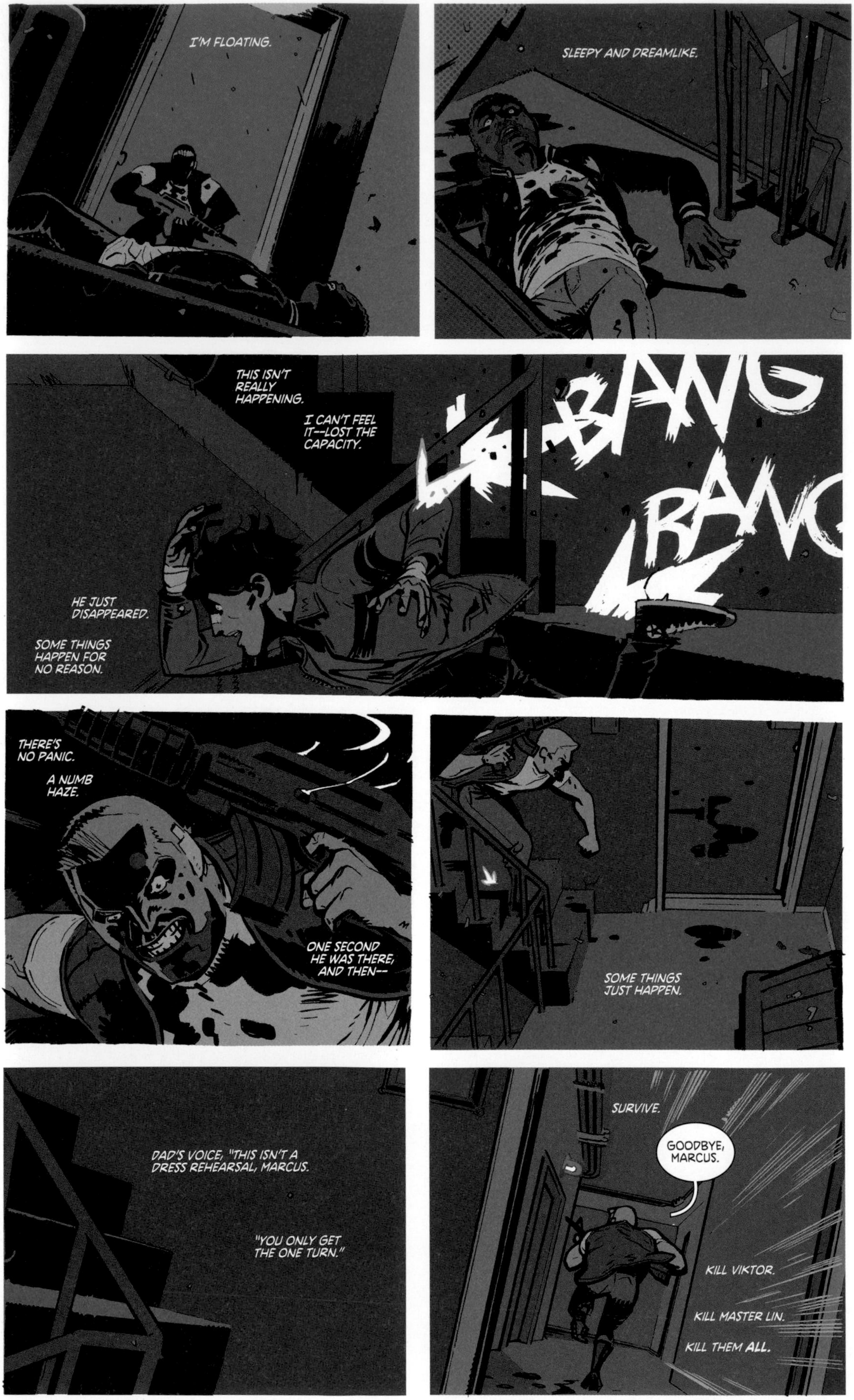

I'M FLOATING.
SLEEPY AND DREAMLIKE.
THIS ISN'T REALLY HAPPENING.
I CAN'T FEEL IT--LOST THE CAPACITY.
BANG
BANG
HE JUST DISAPPEARED.
SOME THINGS HAPPEN FOR NO REASON.
THERE'S NO PANIC.
A NUMB HAZE.
ONE SECOND HE WAS THERE, AND THEN--
SOME THINGS JUST HAPPEN.
DAD'S VOICE, "THIS ISN'T A DRESS REHEARSAL, MARCUS.
"YOU ONLY GET THE ONE TURN."
SURVIVE.
GOODBYE, MARCUS.
KILL VIKTOR.
KILL MASTER LIN.
KILL THEM ALL.

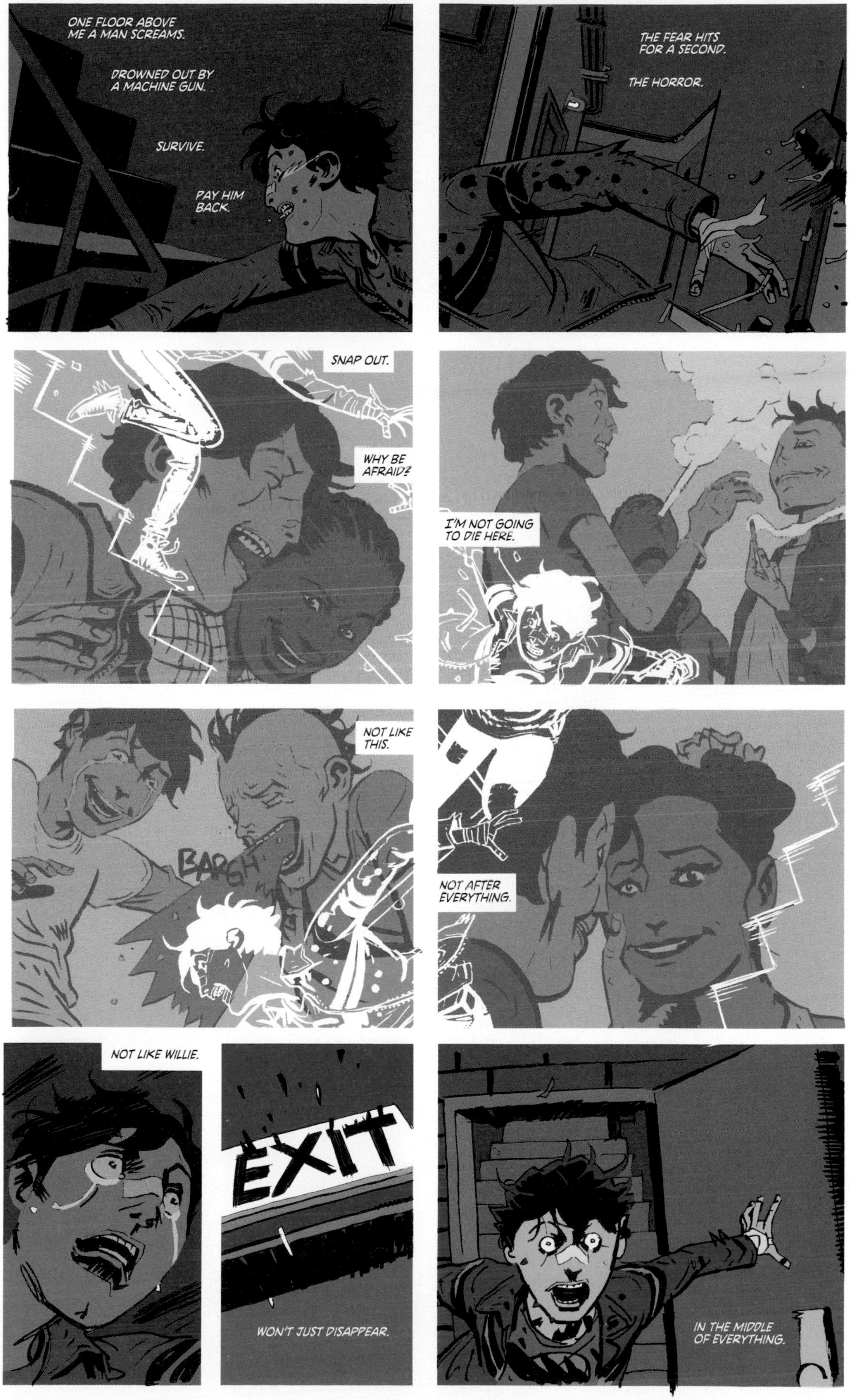
ONE FLOOR ABOVE ME A MAN SCREAMS.
DROWNED OUT BY A MACHINE GUN.
SURVIVE.
PAY HIM BACK.
THE FEAR HITS FOR A SECOND.
THE HORROR.
SNAP OUT.
WHY BE AFRAID?
I'M NOT GOING TO DIE HERE.
NOT LIKE THIS.
BARGH
NOT AFTER EVERYTHING.
NOT LIKE WILLIE.
EXIT
WON'T JUST DISAPPEAR.
IN THE MIDDLE OF EVERYTHING.

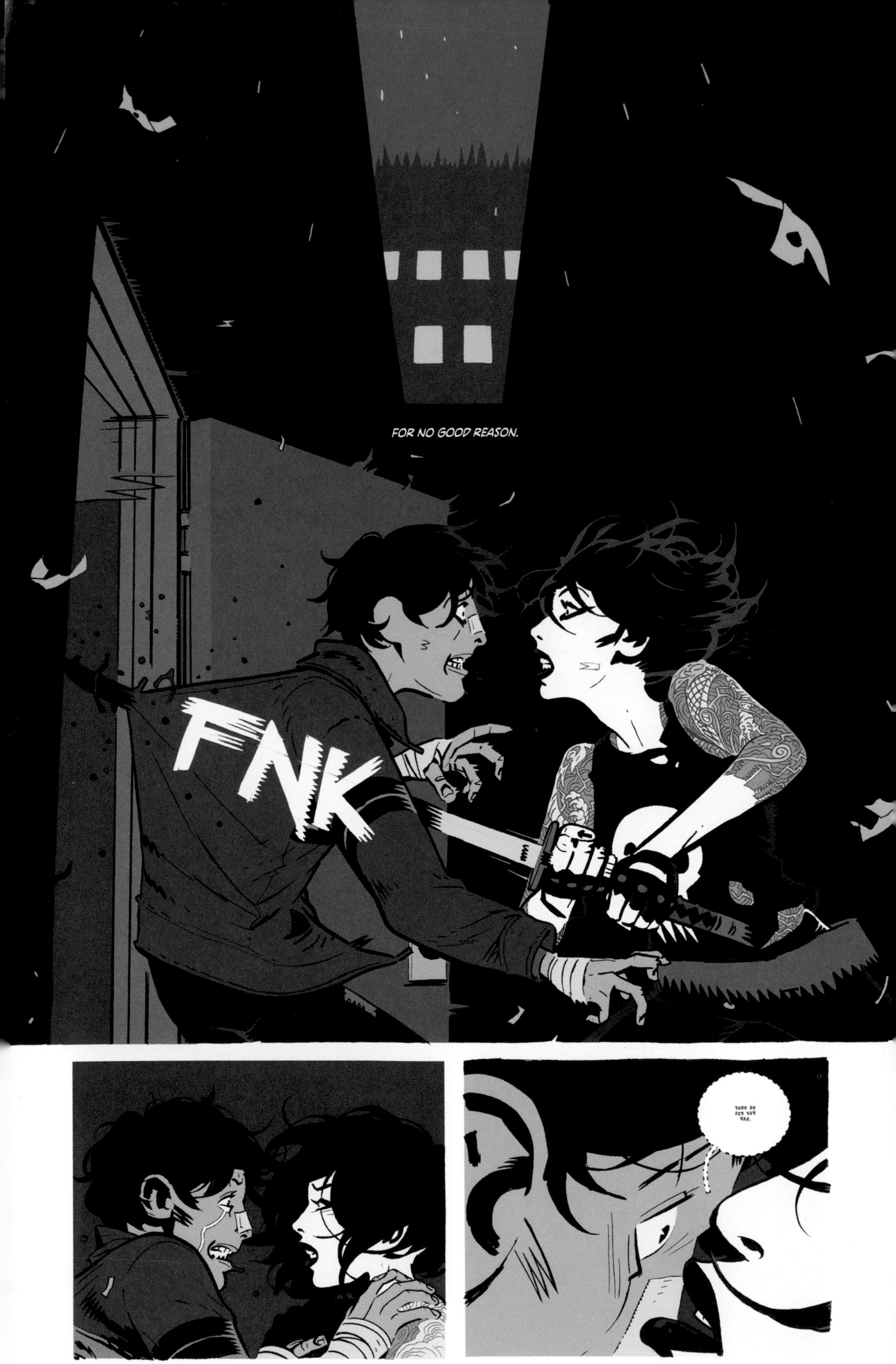
FOR NO GOOD REASON.
FNK

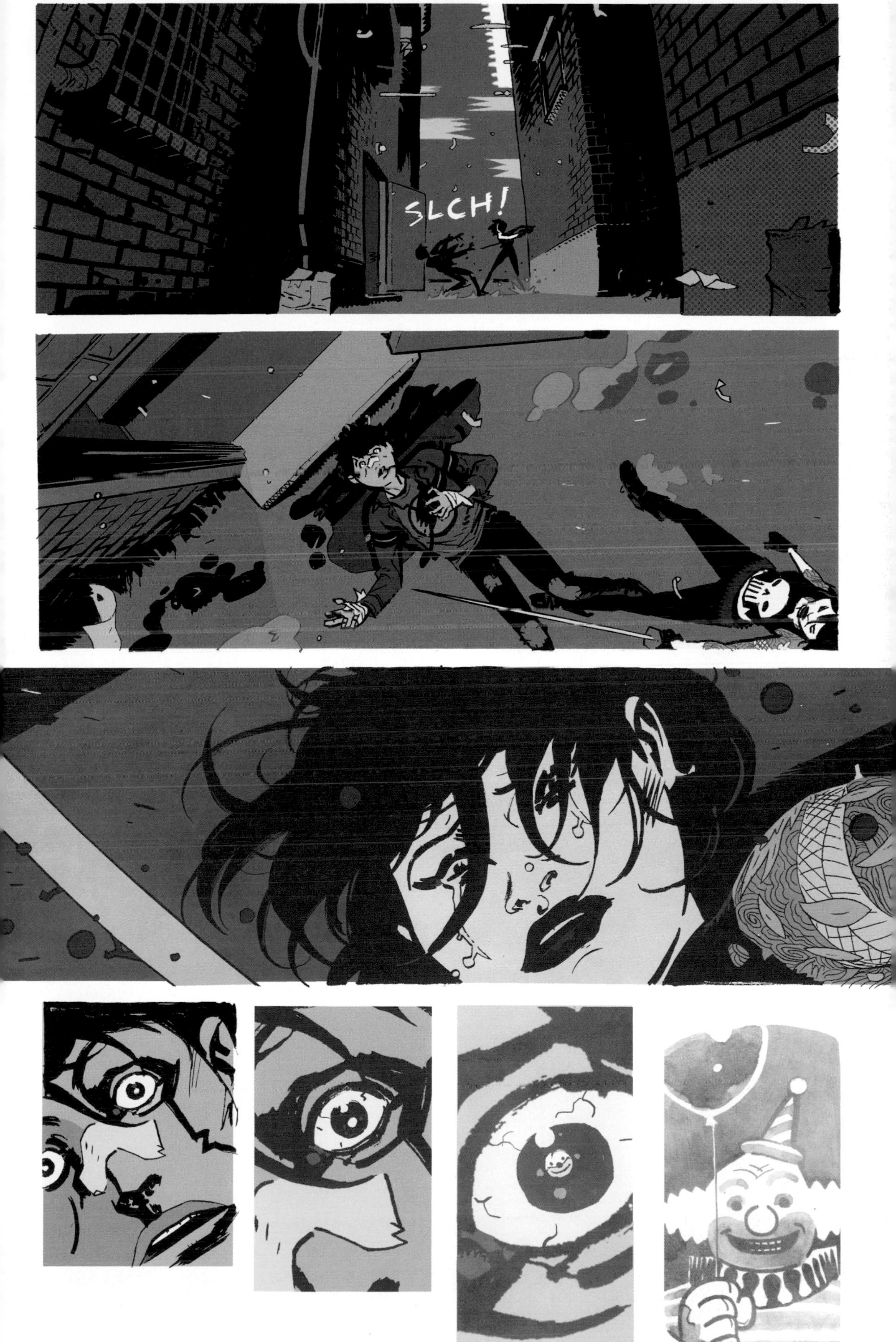
SLCH!

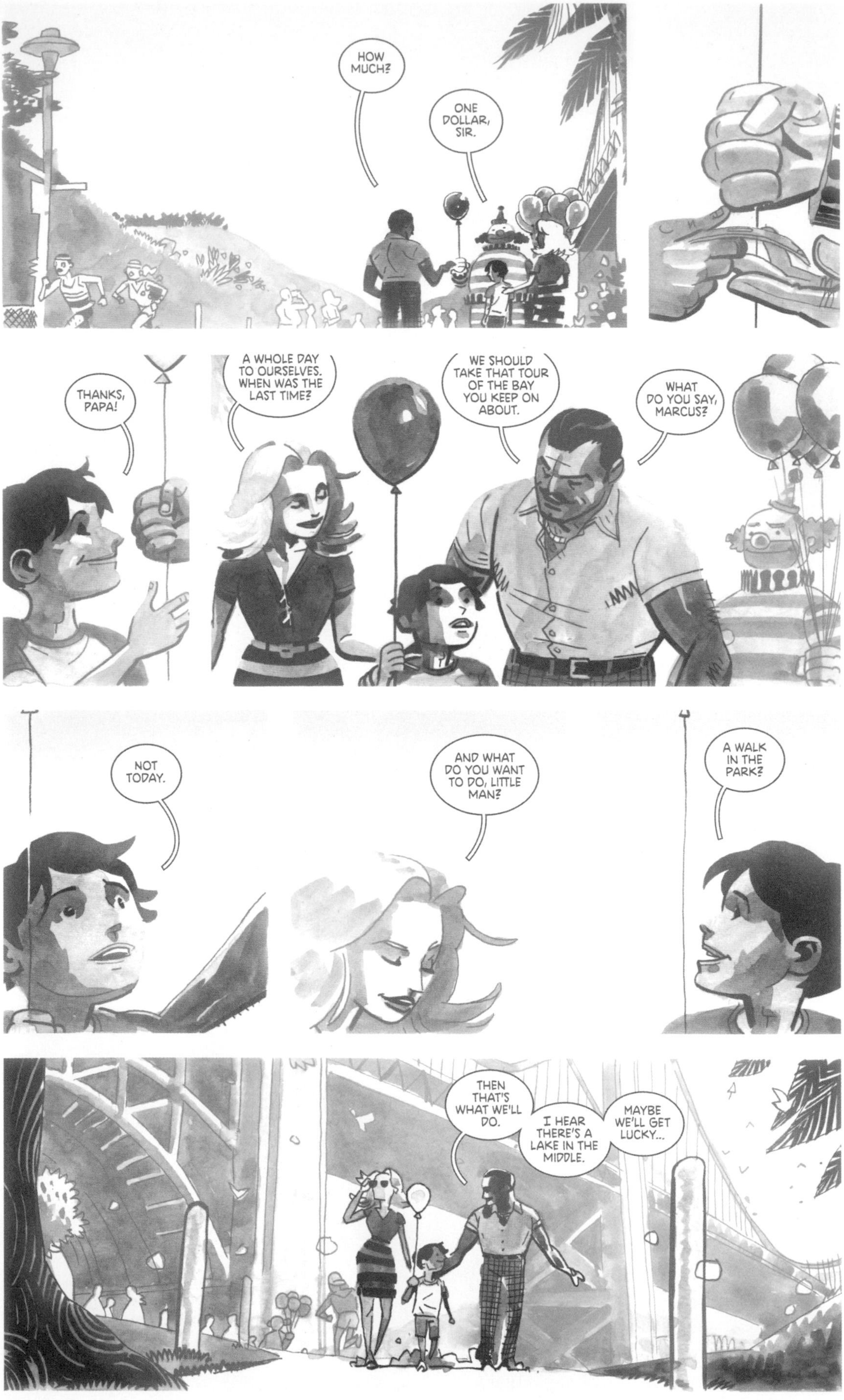
HOW MUCH?
ONE DOLLAR, SIR.
THANKS, PAPA!
A WHOLE DAY TO OURSELVES. WHEN WAS THE LAST TIME?
WE SHOULD TAKE THAT TOUR OF THE BAY YOU KEEP ON ABOUT.
WHAT DO YOU SAY, MARCUS?
NOT TODAY.
AND WHAT DO YOU WANT TO DO, LITTLE MAN?
A WALK IN THE PARK?
THEN THAT'S WHAT WE'LL DO.
I HEAR THERE'S A LAKE IN THE MIDDLE.
MAYBE WE'LL GET LUCKY...

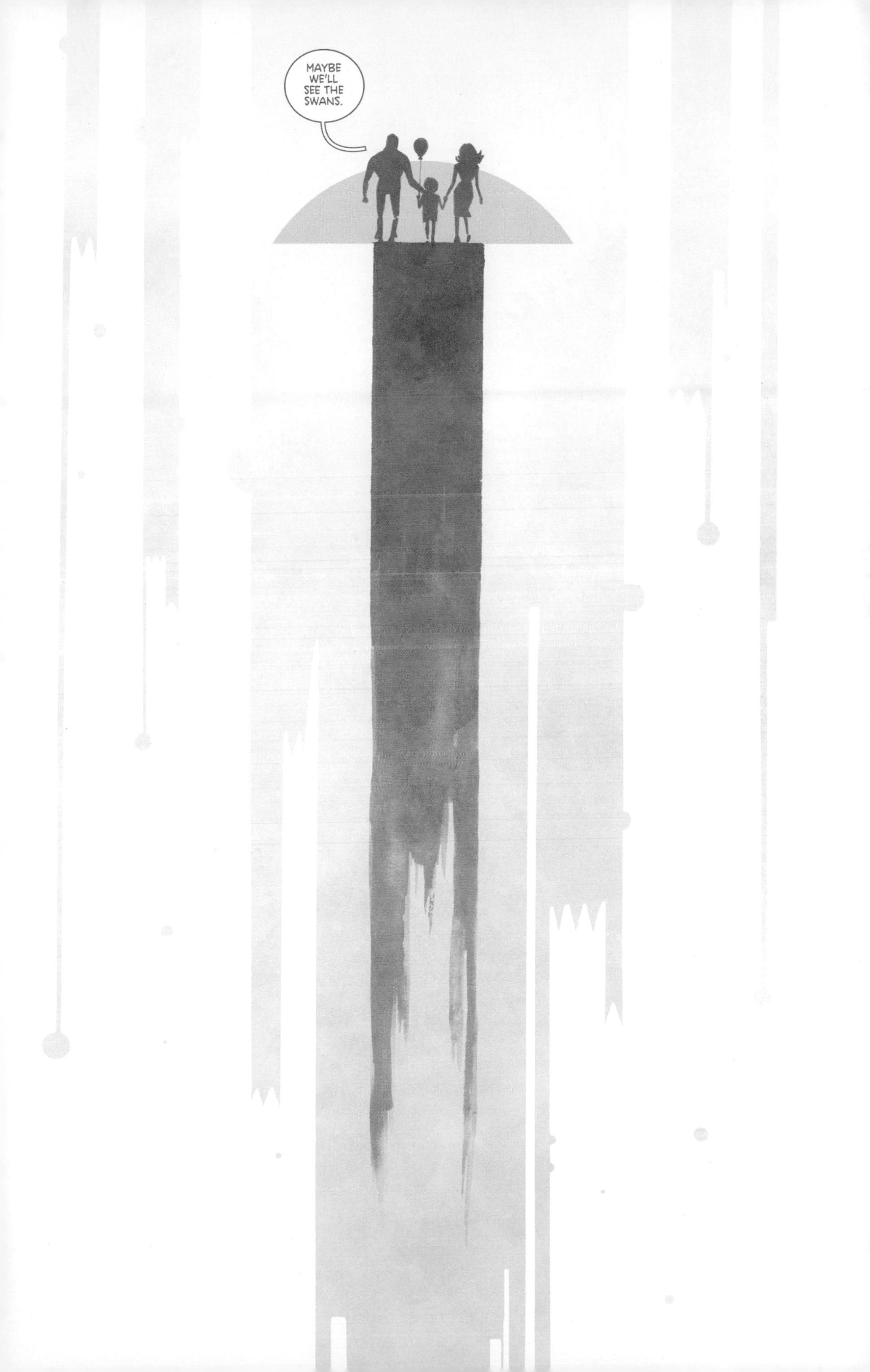
MAYBE WE'LL SEE THE SWANS.

COVER GALLERY

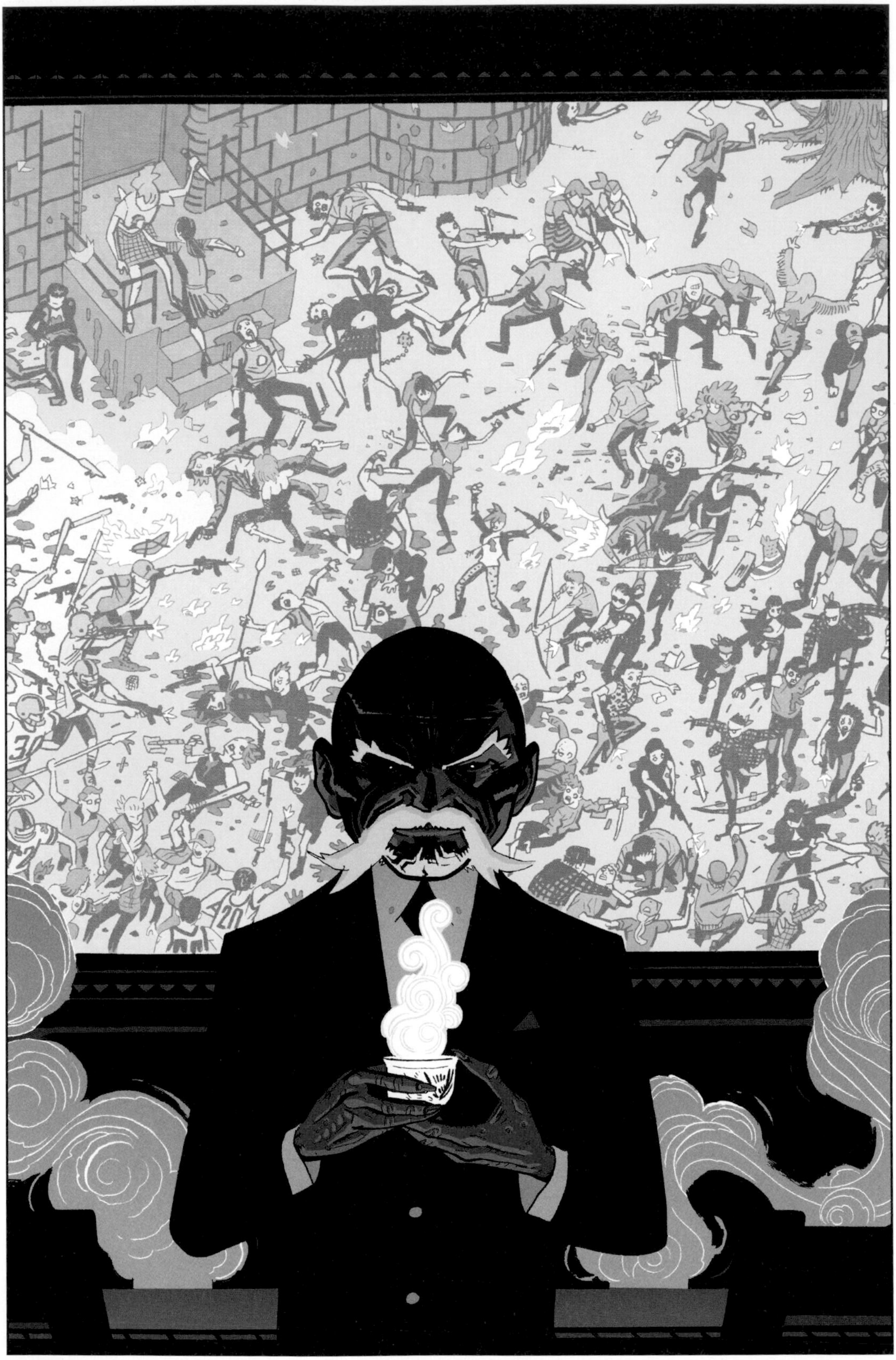

#17 COVER BY **WES CRAIG**

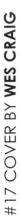

#18 COVER BY **WES CRAIG**

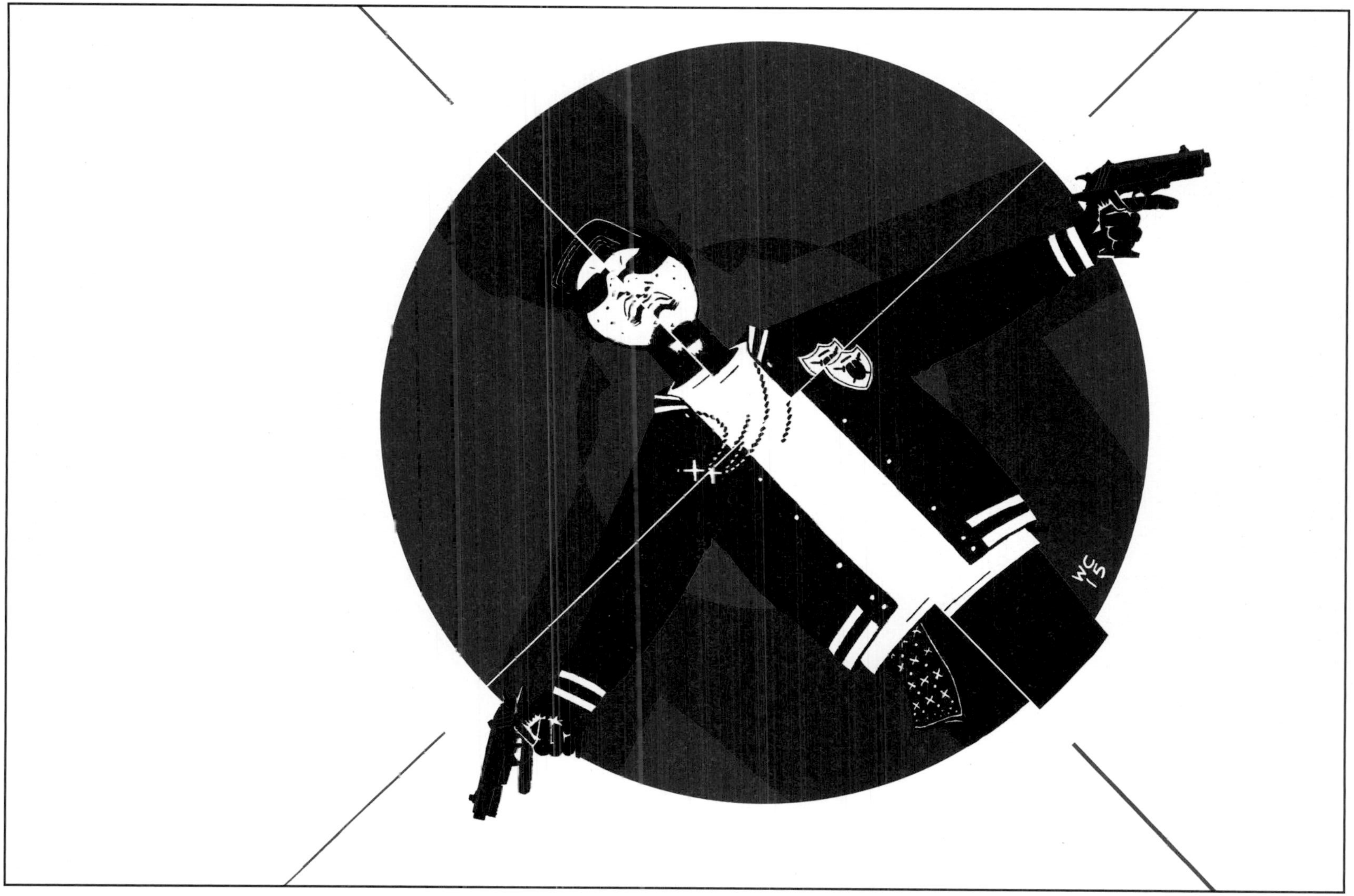
WC 15

#19 COVER BY **WES CRAIG**

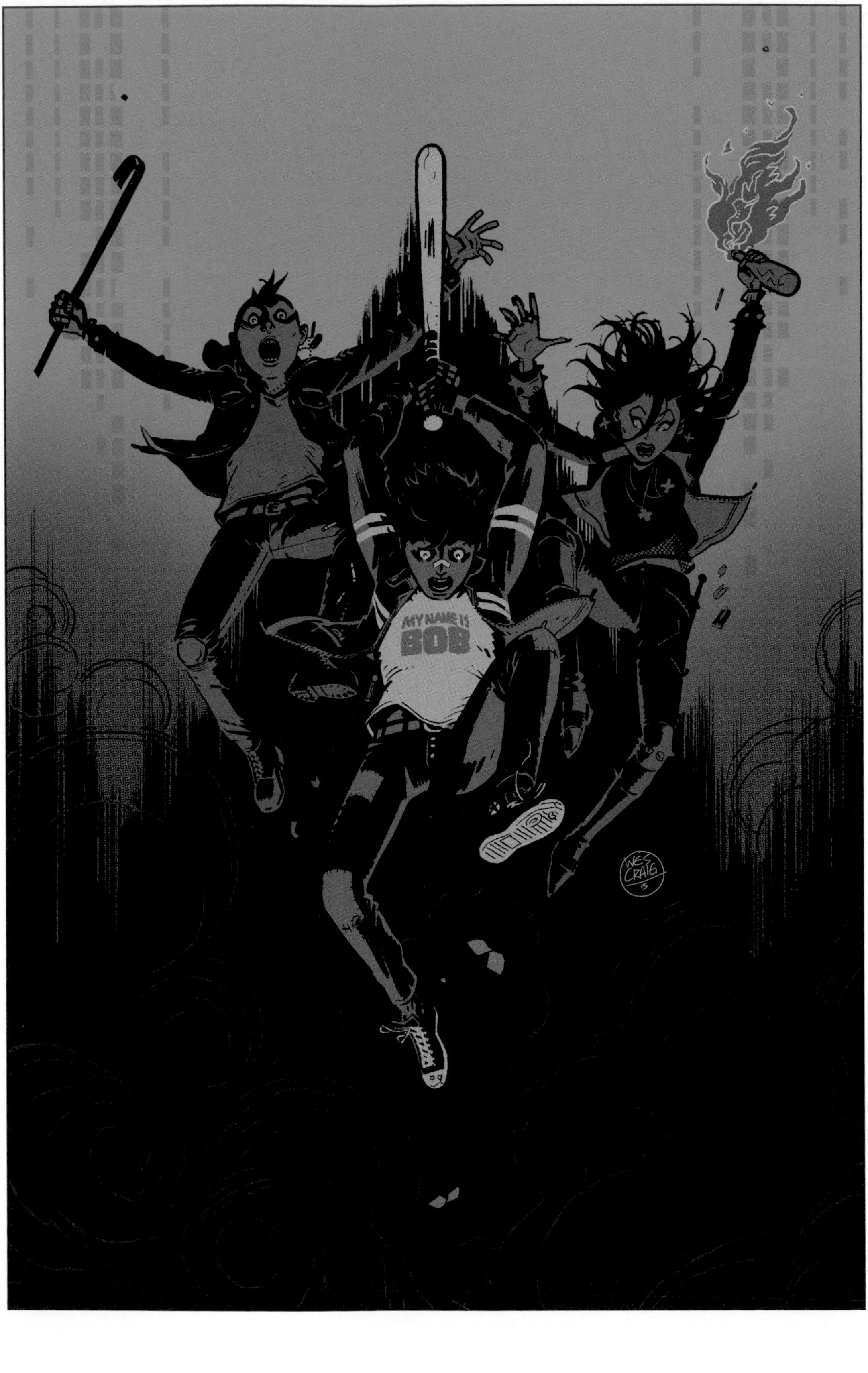
MY NAME IS
BOB
WES CRAIG
'15

#20 COVER BY **WES CRAIG**

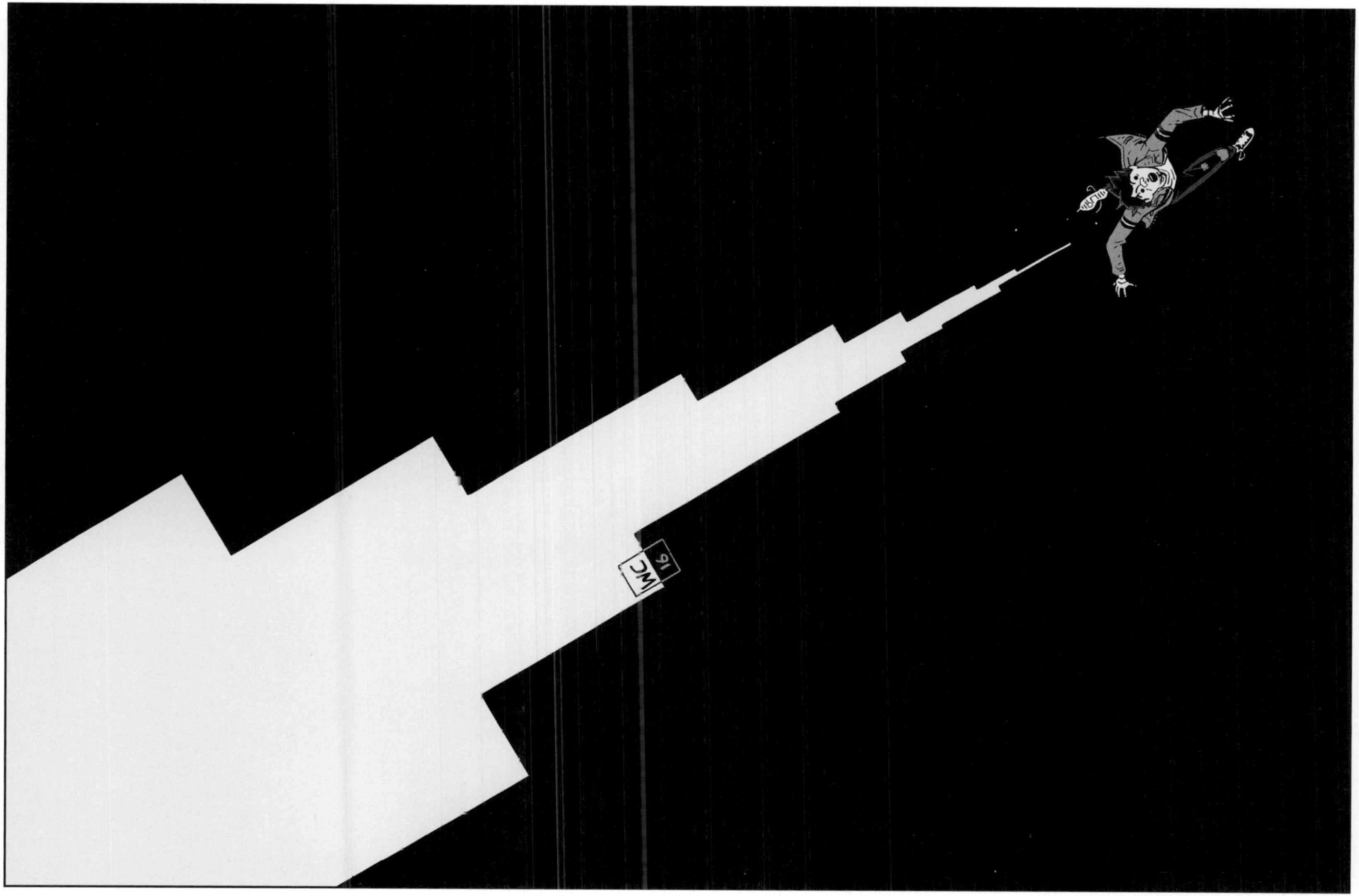
WC
16

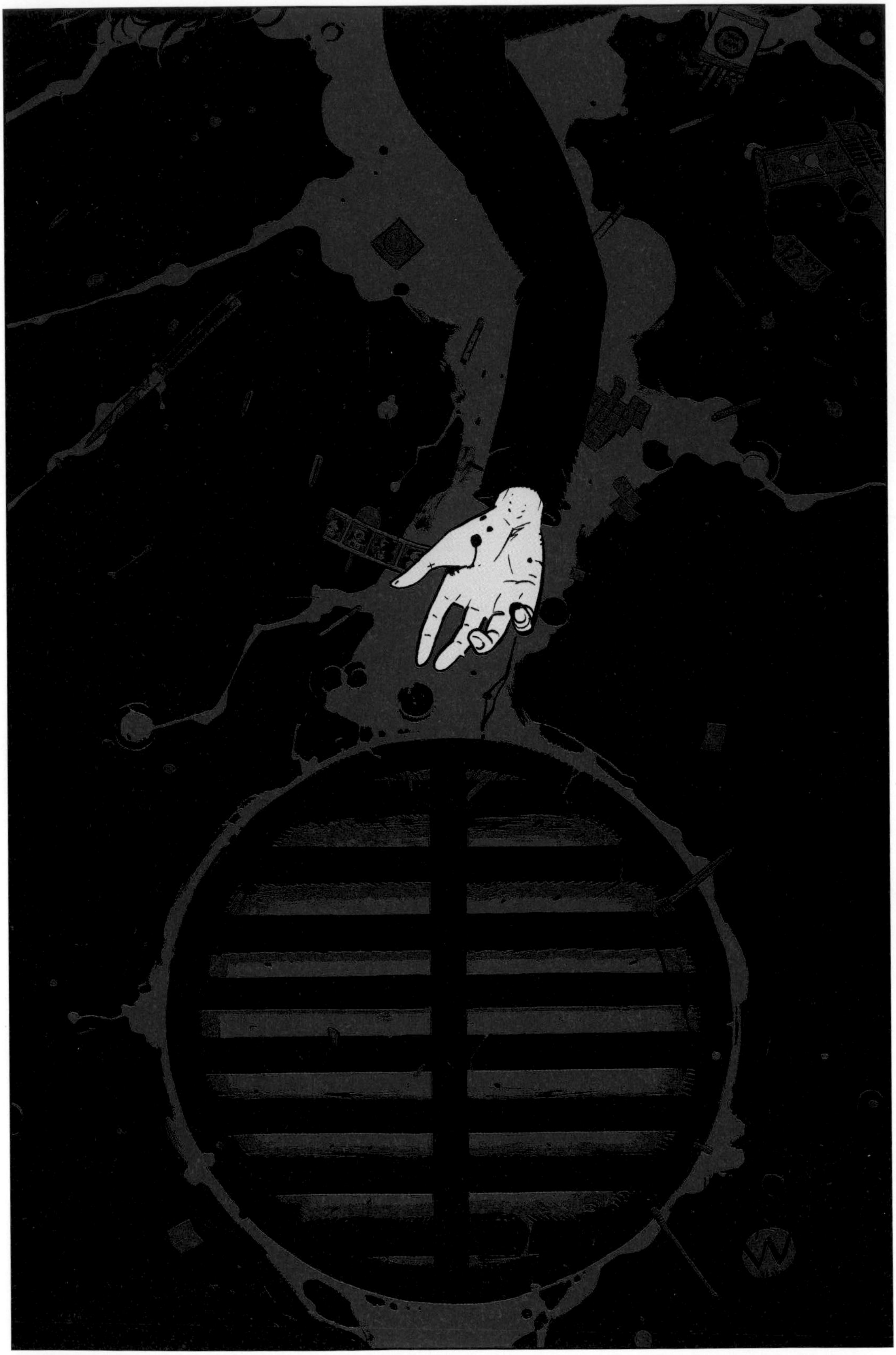

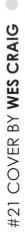

#21 COVER BY **WES CRAIG**

EST
1637
IN VITAM MORTEM

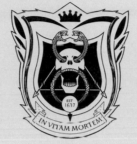

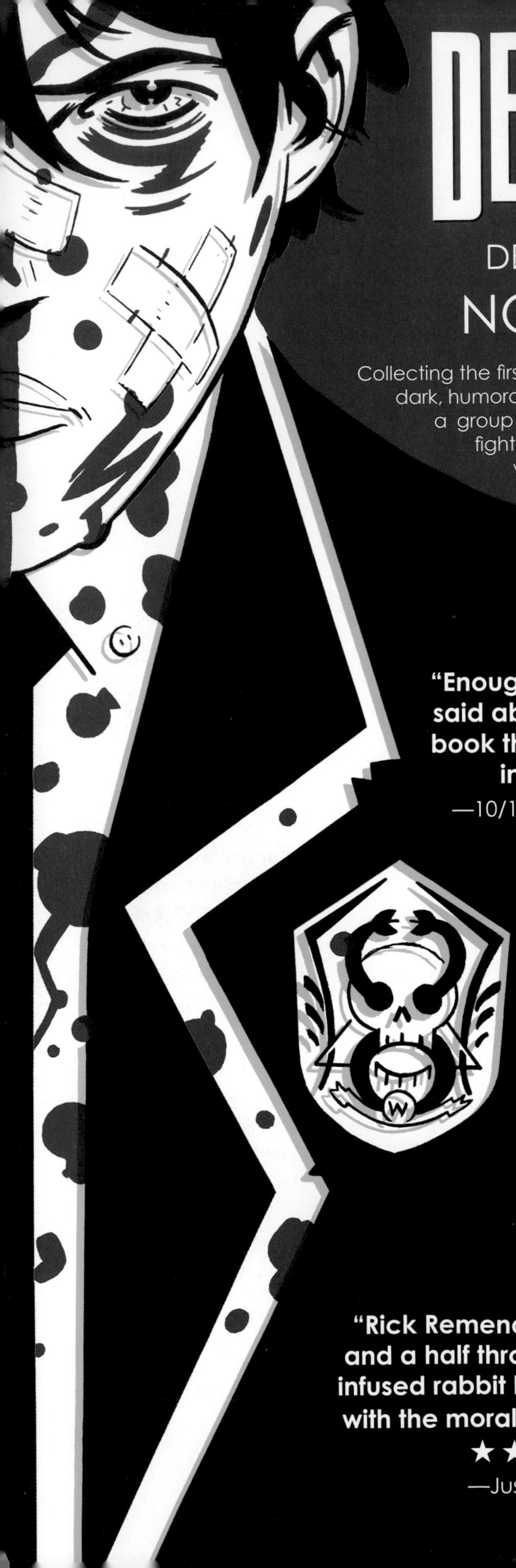

DEADLY CLASS

DELUXE EDITION VOLUME 1

NOISE NOISE NOISE

Collecting the first three arcs of **RICK REMENDER** and **WES CRAIG**'s dark, humorous, and authentic coming-of-age story, following a group of damaged teens in the 1980s underground, fighting a system determined to corrupt them. Loaded with character sketches, concept art, and dozens of other never-before-seen designs.

"Enough good things cannot be said about *DEADLY CLASS*. It's a book that can make people fall in love with comics."

—10/10, Nick Couture, *Comicosity*

"Remender and Craig turn teen angst into thrilling action."

—Oliver Sava, *The A.V. Club*

"*DEADLY CLASS* is one kick ass comic book. Amazing art, lettering, coloring, and story. This is the whole package, folks."

—9.4/10, Benjamin Bailey, *IGN*

"Rick Remender and Wes Craig have a time and a half throwing the reader down the acid infused rabbit hole with Marcus as he grapples with the morality of his current state of affairs."

★★★★★★★★★★

—Justin Partridge, *Newsarama*

RICK REMENDER is the writer/co-creator of comics such as *LOW*, *Fear Agent*, *Tokyo Ghost*, and *Black Science*. For Marvel he has written titles such as *Uncanny Avengers*, *Captain America*, *Uncanny X-Force* and *Venom*. He's written video games such as *Bulletstorm* and *Dead Space*, and worked on films such as *The Iron Giant*, *Anastasia*, and *Titan A.E.* He and his tea-sipping wife, Danni, currently reside in Los Angeles raising two beautiful mischief monkeys.

WES CRAIG is the artist and co-creator of *Deadly Class* with Rick Remender, and the writer-artist of *Blackhand Comics*, published by Image. Working out of Montreal, Quebec, he has been drawing comic books professionally since 2004 on such titles as *Guardians of the Galaxy*, *Batman*, and *The Flash*.

Despite nearly flunking kindergarten for his exclusive use of black crayons, **JORDAN BOYD** has moved on to become an increasingly prolific comic book colorist, and has worked on *Astonishing Ant-Man* and *All-New Wolverine* for Marvel, *Invisible Republic* and *Deadly Class* for Image, *Devolution* at Dynamite, and *Suiciders: Kings of HelL.A.* for DC/Vertigo. He and his wife, kids, dogs, hedgehogs, and fish currently live in Norman, OK.

MARION COUNTY PUBLIC LIBRARY
321 MONROE STREET
FAIRMONT, WV 26554